He's the perfect teacher for
a lesson in desire...

"TEACH ME . . ."

"I require only your expertise in matters of a physical nature."

David's eyes narrowed on hers. "That sounds like an indecent sort of proposition."

"Don't I deserve to know what I should be seeking in a husband before I make the wrong choice? I do not require the whole of the experience. Just enough to properly inform my decision."

Caroline heard him swallow, even over the rush of the ocean. "How much of it?"

"Not *all* of it. But more than kissing." She had already had that from him, and while she was looking forward to repeating the experience, she wanted to know more.

His shoulders tensed beneath the wet fabric of his shirt, and she could see his fists clench and unclench. "You do not know what you are asking of me."

"I do." And she believed, with every fiber of her being, that he was the only man who could accomplish it. "I want this, David."

"You want the experience." He swung around to face her. "It does not have to come from me."

Caroline studied him, frustration shaking her with sharp teeth. "I do not want to ask another man to show me this, David. I want it to be you, precisely because I know my reputation is safe with you." And then, before he could lodge another protest, before he could shove her, once again, into the realm of mere friendship, she stepped forward and kissed him.

By Jennifer McQuiston

SUMMER IS FOR LOVERS
WHAT HAPPENS IN SCOTLAND

ATTENTION: ORGANIZATIONS AND CORPORATIONS
HarperCollins books may be purchased for educational, business,
or sales promotional use. For information, please e-mail the Special
Markets Department at SPsales@harpercollins.com.

JENNIFER McQUISTON

Summer Is for Lovers

AVON

An Imprint of HarperCollinsPublishers

This is a work of fiction. Names, characters, places, and incidents are products of the author's imagination or are used fictitiously and are not to be construed as real. Any resemblance to actual events, locales, organizations, or persons, living or dead, is entirely coincidental.

AVON BOOKS
An Imprint of HarperCollins*Publishers*
10 East 53rd Street
New York, New York 10022-5299

Copyright © 2013 by Jennifer McQuiston
ISBN 978-0-06-223131-4
www.avonromance.com

All rights reserved. No part of this book may be used or reproduced in any manner whatsoever without written permission, except in the case of brief quotations embodied in critical articles and reviews. For information address Avon Books, an Imprint of HarperCollins Publishers.

First Avon Books mass market printing: October 2013

Avon Trademark Reg. U.S. Pat. Off. and in Other Countries, Marca Registrada, Hecho en U.S.A.
HarperCollins® is a registered trademark of HarperCollins Publishers.

Printed in the U.S.A.

10 9 8 7 6 5 4 3 2 1

If you purchased this book without a cover, you should be aware that this book is stolen property. It was reported as "unsold and destroyed" to the publisher, and neither the author nor the publisher has received any payment for this "stripped book."

To *the amazing women who encourage me,*
challenge me, and amuse me every day:
Alyssa Alexander, Tracy Brogan, Kimberly Kincaid,
Sally Kilpatrick, and Romily Bernard.
But especially you, Romily . . . you know why.

Acknowledgments

THIS TIME AROUND, I know so much better who to thank.

To my amazing agent, Kevan Lyon . . . I cannot believe how lucky I am to work with you! Thank you for making everything so easy.

My heartfelt thanks to the team at Avon Books, who have put their all into making me look less like an absent-minded scientist and more like a polished author than I ever dreamed I could be. Thank you to Esi Sogah for the first round of edits on this one, and to Tessa Woodward for taking the reins on this runaway horse. A special thanks to Avon publicist Jessie Edwards, who makes me look oh-so-good and appreciates that I am from Atlanta. Thank you to the always-helpful Dana Trombley, social media soothsayer and giver of excellent advice (such as "you really want to tweet more than once a week"). Thanks to Carrie Feron, who has taken such an active and appreciated interest in my career! And finally, this series of thank-you's would not be complete without a shout of gratitude to Avon's incredible art department . . . especially Tom Egner: I love a man who enjoys the challenge of showing see-through, soaked clothing on a book cover!

As always, thank you to my family for being so vociferously proud of me. Thank you to my husband, John, who reads my books and offers "pointers" in all the wrong places, but who also creates the most amazing book trailers that perfectly capture the spirit of the story. And if you haven't bought my first book, *What Happens in Scotland*, my elementary-school-age daughters will enthusiastically try to sell you one out of the back of our mini-van—and probably charge you double. Just ask their poor teachers.

Summer Is for
Lovers

Prologue

DAVID CAMERON DIDN'T want to die.

It was an important fact, albeit one he may have decided too late.

Instinct pushed his limbs toward shore and his lungs toward the heavens. Unfortunately, Death was proving a greedy bastard and did not want to loosen its hold. He was quite sure he had swallowed more of the Atlantic in the few moments he had been fighting to live than in the entire hour he had been trying to drown.

"Stop fighting the current!"

David blinked through the cold water and whisky haze that enveloped him like a too-tight glove. Despite his heart's lumbering quest for survival, it kicked up a notch when he registered where the voice was coming from.

Someone was swimming toward him.

For a moment he was so stunned he wondered if he had died after all. He had selected this stretch of coast as much for its isolated shoreline as for its turbulent surf. He might be a coward, but he was a coward with some pride. He had not wanted witnesses to his struggle, whichever side of damnation claimed him.

Whoever shouted at him could not be mortal, not tackling the waves as she was, as if they were butter and she was a heated knife. He caught the flash of small hands, one after the other, ordered and relentless. It looked like no swimming stroke he had ever seen.

Mermaids must swim like that, he thought blearily. Only mermaids were beautiful.

And full-grown.

Goddamn it. It was a girl. Where were her parents that she had been permitted to leap into the waves off this violent stretch of coast, just to save his undeserving arse? He was going to have a devil of a time getting himself and a child back to shore.

And the death of another soul on his conscience, even one in need of a proper thrashing, would be his undoing.

"You are going to injure yourself," he growled as she tackled the last set of waves that separated them.

She shifted to tread water, hands fanning out to steady herself amid the choppy waves. "I'm not the one who is drowning." She wasn't even out of breath, blast the chit.

A large wave picked that exact moment to slap against David's head. His neck was slammed sideways, and seawater flooded his mouth. "I am not drowning," he managed to spit out. *Regrettably.*

"If not drowned," she retorted, "you're not far off."

She blurred before him, a bedraggled mess of brown hair and freckles. There was nothing to her sunburned features to suggest a future beauty. Her eyes were green or hazel or something equally mild. They could have belonged to any one of a hundred adolescent girls.

Unfortunately, they belonged to this one. And she was not yet through with him.

"You need to float on your back and let the current carry you out there." She gestured behind him toward the open ocean.

"I prefer to go in that direction." He jerked his head toward shore. "And I dinna need the help of a wee thing who can barely swim herself."

The girl's face colored. "Unless you are trying to kill yourself," she said, her voice arcing high and furious, "I suggest that you stop acting like a clod and *listen* for a moment."

David stilled. Let the merciless waves slam into his body. Wondered if she really understood what he was doing out in the waves.

Prayed that she did not.

"The current on this stretch of beach is too strong to fight," she told him, her pert face pinched with annoyance. "There is a sharp drop-off here, but it levels out again to about waist-deep a little farther out and the current becomes easier to overcome. From there you should be able to walk to shore."

David stared at her a long moment, the ocean churning around them. Her eyes were hazel, he decided. And damned if her explanation didn't make at least a little sense.

After a tension-fraught moment, he let his body go limp, allowing the current to seize him in the opposite direction his mind screamed to go. The girl watched as he was carried to the right spot, then shouted instructions as he got his feet under him.

When he had reached a position about two dozen yards away and his water-clogged boots made grateful purchase with the ocean floor, she pointed toward the beach. "Now try walking for shore!"

David uncoiled his whisky-soaked muscles, preparing to launch himself toward the safety of shore. But whatever remnant of his soul remained jerked his gaze back to the small, brown-haired girl who still bobbed in deep water. Whoever she was, she was his responsibility now, even if he was the last person on earth she should place her trust in.

"You need to come with me, lass." His voice rang hoarse against the distance that separated them. He was resolved to live now. But he would not squander her neck in favor of saving his own wretched hide. "I can't risk coming back to rescue you," he called, hoping she could hear him above the roar of the relentless surf. "And I won't leave you."

As if in answer, the girl smiled impishly. And then she was off and swimming, tackling the current that had just proven too much for his own brute strength.

CAROLINE TOLBERTSON'S FEET found the rocky shoreline a few minutes later. Triumph surged through her, a thumping, twitching sensation that left her breathless. She turned to see the man crawl out a little farther down the shore and collapse in a heap.

She didn't know what she had been thinking, swimming back as she had, but the urge to show this stranger what she was capable of had burned beneath her skin. No one had ever seen her swim except Papa. Certainly not Mama, who had told her just this morning that it was not ladylike for a girl of twelve years to swim in front of others.

Or half so well.

But it felt natural to be embraced by waves and buoyed by salt. Far more natural than it had felt this morning, sitting still for an endless hour to have her hair put up.

Oh. Her hair. And her clothes, for that matter. Reality snagged on the splinters of those thoughts. She had been gathering shells on the beach when she spied the man struggling, and had leaped in without kicking off her boots or even untying her apron. What to tell Mama when she stumbled into the foyer, her frock soaking wet? She fell into the water?

Yes, that was much preferred to diving in. Falling in was a much more ladylike thing to happen to someone.

She trotted toward the man who had put her in this predicament. He was crouched on his knees, retching with a violence that made her stomach twist in sympathy. Who was he, and how had he come to be here? Except for her father, who had shared the secrets of this cove with Caroline and her sister, she had never seen another soul here. Brighton was an hour's walk to the west, and the only inhabitants of this stretch of coast were the swallows that dipped and chattered in the white chalk cliffs, tending nests in the furrows wrought by wind and rain.

It occurred to her, now that the gentleman was safe, that she might not be. Well, if it came to it, she knew which parts could drop a man and leave him writhing in pain. Her father had made sure she knew how to protect herself.

The man in question staggered to his feet. He was tall, taller even than Papa had been. But despite his height and the very adult golden stubble on his face, his face had a boyish quality to it, as if he were just a few years past twenty. His damp hair fell in curls that showed every intention of lightening to gold when dry. The parts of his eyes that weren't rubbed red from his dip in the ocean were the sort of enviable blue that brought to mind a clear, sunny day.

Now that he had escaped the surf, she could see he was wearing a red military jacket, which had somehow retained its stiff formality despite its thorough soaking. She was used to such sights in town. The nearby Preston Barracks lodged cavalry and infantrymen alike, and the officers sometimes came to Brighton on leave.

But she wasn't used to seeing one of those officers thrashing about in the water, much less tossing up the contents of his stomach on the shore.

He dragged an apologetic arm across his mouth. "You are quite the swimmer, lass." His words seemed thick and slurred, even accounting for his obvious brogue.

"You, sir, are not." She began to wring out her skirts, realizing with dismay that there were bits of seaweed clinging to the hem.

"What is your name?" His voice rumbled down at her, and she peered the long way up it took to meet his eyes. She should not be speaking with this man, much less diving into the ocean save him. But what was the harm, now that the worst of it was done?

She smoothed a hand over her wet apron. "Caroline Tolbertson."

"Miss or lady?"

"Miss." She knew could not claim the title of lady, even if her mother was determined to fashion her as one.

"Well, Miss Caroline, I am Second Lieutenant David Cameron, and you have just saved my life." A reluctant dimple flashed across his face, and it occurred to Caroline that this was very much the sort of young man her older sister, Penelope, was always swooning over. She loved her sister dearly, but she would never be such a ninny.

Any boy she swooned over—and she suspected she was not going to be much of a swooner—would have to be a *much* better swimmer than Lieutenant Cameron.

"Where did you learn to swim like that?" he asked. "I've never seen the like."

Caroline paused, considering how to answer. Swimming and honesty did not often go hand-in-hand in her world. "My father taught me," she answered, her throat tight. Saying it out loud made her loss seem far too real.

Worse, it reminded her how things had changed in the four months since her father's death. Papa had founded the town's first newspaper, the *Brighton Gazette*, but most of the family savings had been invested in the venture. Since his passing from a sudden fever, some of the furniture had been sold, and almost all of the servants let go. They had not even been able to afford new mourning clothes, settling instead for dying their dresses black in great pots in the kitchen.

"Papa died over the winter," she whispered. It had been terrible, seeing her father's lungs labor for breath and his eyes shuttered with pain. He had hung on for two days, no more. Not long enough to say a proper good-bye, but long enough to extract a promise that came close to paralyzing her now. *Take care of your mother and sister, Caroline.* A father's dying words, an assurance too easily delivered.

But how could she take care of her family when he had left them so little money?

"He always said I could do anything I put my mind to," she added, as much to her soaked, scuffed boots as to the young man watching her.

"Your father must have thought you very special to encourage such thinking, and to teach you so well," he said after a long moment.

She looked up, surprised. The lieutenant was the first adult who had taken the time to listen to her since her father's death. Mama had been too consumed by grief, shuttering the windows and turning away visitors who might come to pay their respects. "Well," she said, pleased her bedraggled soldier had not laughed at her. "You are lucky he did or else I suspect you'd be kissing the bottom by now."

One side of his mouth quirked up. "Do you always speak your mind?"

"No." Caroline fought the urge to squirm as he lifted a brow in disbelief. "Well, sometimes," she admitted, trying not to chatter and failing. "Mama declares it 'my lamentable habit.' Although, as far as habits go. I don't think it's such a bad one. Not like biting one's nails, or fidgeting in church. My sister, Penelope, does all those things. Although Penelope doesn't fidget as much as I do." She paused for breath and for the first time caught the distinct scent of whisky on the breeze.

A terrible thought occurred to her. "Are . . . are you *drunk*?"

His mouth settled into a firm line. "Not drunk enough."

The words settled into the gaps of her understanding like sand between paving stones. No wonder he had almost drowned, and no wonder he was retching like a man who had eaten too many green apples. It occurred to her, then, that the only adult who had ever praised her swimming abilities, aside from Papa, was a drunkard who very likely didn't know his knee from his elbow.

Idiot. It was a word she was not permitted to say in polite company, especially to an adult. Pity it was so fitting. A smart man would never have tackled the current off this particular stretch of beach.

Caroline hugged her arms across the front of her wet apron. "You should not swim under the effect of spirits," she told him. "And Papa taught me you should not swim alone."

He inclined his head and gave her a quick look up and down. "Then I am lucky indeed you were here to save me. I suppose the gentlemanly thing would be to escort you home and offer an explanation to your family for your bedraggled appearance."

Caroline looked down at her dark, wet frock. Lieutenant Cameron was going to tell her mother. Dread seeped beneath her wet skin, chilling her far more than the cold temperature of the channel.

She knew it. She should have let him drown.

"But I won't, you see."

Caroline's gaze jerked upward. "Because you're not a gentleman?"

"Aye, there's that, lass." He gave her an odd look. "You'd best avoid my sort in the future, I think. But no, there's another good reason you and I should keep this a secret and never let anyone know what happened here. I've just been saved by a girl who swims far better than me. My reputation would never live it down."

Relief flooded Caroline's limbs. She nodded, all too happy to agree to his terms, all too eager to believe his explanation. Keeping quiet would mean *her* reputation would stay safe too.

Perhaps he wasn't such an idiot after all.

"I won't tell," she promised, crossing her heart with a damp, earnest finger.

And she didn't. Hours later, after he had disappeared down the footpath that led back to Brighton, after she had been lectured by Mama and teased by Penelope, Caroline kept the details of their meeting, and how she had come to be soaked through to the skin, locked up tight.

And as she drifted off to sleep, she decided if she ever *did* become the sort of silly girl who swooned over boys, Second Lieutenant David Cameron was maybe—just maybe—the sort of young man who might be worth the effort.

Chapter 1

CAROLINE TOLBERTSON KNEW she would never forget her first kiss . . . even though she desperately wanted to.

It wasn't the mechanical part of the act that bothered her. One almost expected some discomfort in a first kiss: a bump of noses, a clash of teeth. Technique could be learned and practiced, and she had mastered far more difficult tasks in her twenty-three years. No, the execution of the kiss was not the problem. It was the aftermath she couldn't tolerate.

And that aftermath was heading straight for her.

Caroline froze, distracted not by the sound of seagulls or the chatter of nearby strollers along the Marine Parade, but by the perforating sound of Brandon Dermott's laughter. And just like that, the kiss she had tried so hard to forget came flooding back in all its inglorious detail.

The awkward parting of lips. The amused frown on Mr. Dermott's face. And the next day, the cupped hands and whispers among the vacationers down from London.

"It was like kissing a boy," Dermott had told them all. Not the kind of notoriety a girl wished for.

Especially a girl like Caroline.

Panic twisted its knife as Dermott made straight for her. The breeze off the ocean held not even a prayer of cooling the sweat pricking beneath her arms. A member of the summer set who arrived in Brighton every June, Dermott dressed the part. Today he sported a check-patterned waistcoat and a four-in-hand necktie that proclaimed him as one of those fashionable young men with more money than good sense. His smile stretched to catch the sun's rays and dazzle unsuspecting girls with its brilliance.

And as usual, this prime specimen of the species carried with him a simpering, primping young lady dressed in summer white. Caroline didn't recognize the girl, but she recognized the sort. Mr. Dermott's companion was an absolute vision of ladylike decorum, her properly gloved right hand holding a yellow parasol aloft, her left resting on the man's arm.

"Good afternoon, Caroline," Dermott drawled as they pulled within striking distance. His gaze traveled upward the inch or so it took for his eyes to meet hers. "You look robust today."

Caroline searched her memory. Had she given the man leave to use her first name? Or had he merely presumed it his right following the circumstances of their unfortunate last encounter? "Mr. Dermott," she managed between clenched teeth.

He smiled down at his petite partner as if she was a hothouse flower, ripe for picking. "Miss Baxter, may I present Miss Caroline Tolbertson. Miss Julianne Baxter is the daughter of Viscount Avery, and is visiting from London."

Caroline eyed the pretty young woman. Bile pricked the back of her throat. Why should it bother her whom Dermott walked with? She didn't even like the man.

But for heaven's sake. It had been only two weeks since he had kissed her, quite uninvited, at the end of the Chain Pier.

She had not known at first why he had kissed her. He was handsome and popular, while she was the girl whose chest resembled nothing so much as a board. It was only later she had heard the rumors of the wager that lay behind her humiliation, most likely orchestrated by Mr. Dermott for no purpose other than to relieve his own boredom.

She knew why *she* had done it, despite the fact that kissing a man who had not declared his intentions was a poor idea. She wished she could claim her lapse in judgment had been for a defensible reason. But Caroline had not kissed him for any logical purpose, such as the fact that his family was wealthy enough to own a summer home in Brighton and a town house in London's fashionable Belgravia district. No, she had done it for a much more regrettable reason.

She had been curious.

The idea of her first kiss had occupied a place in her dreams ever since she was twelve years old and had first imagined growing up to kiss a fair-haired, half-drowned soldier. A text her sister, Penelope, had discovered among their father's musty collection of books proved shockingly explicit regarding things of a physical nature, but lacked all mention of emotion and feeling. And so, having reached the age of three-and-twenty without garnering so much as a wink from a member of the opposite gender, much less a kiss, Caroline had been ill-inclined to look her gift horse . . . er . . . *male* in the mouth.

She would not make that mistake again. She had no thought—or desire—to repeat the failed experiment.

Caroline studied Mr. Dermott's companion, sorting out where she stood in the unfolding feminine hierarchy. Somewhere beneath the tiny girl's three-inch heel, she would imagine. The new chit looked fresh and rich and dreadfully pretty. The few curls visible near the edge of her bonnet were a fetching red. Miss Baxter was possessed of the sort of delicate pallor and want of height that were the hallmark of a London beauty. Beside her, Caroline felt close to a broad-shouldered simian, dragging her knuckles across the sun-weathered walkway.

After all, *she* wasn't dressed in fresh summer white, and while she was quite sure she owned a parasol, she was hard-pressed to say what color it was. She was wearing an old cotton dress that was several inches too short, having dressed for a far more practical purpose than strolling Brighton's Marine Parade.

"Are you here for the summer too?" Miss Baxter asked, brushing one of those copper-colored curls from her cheek.

"I live in Brighton." For some reason the girl's imperious tone set Caroline's teeth on edge.

"Oh, I do so enjoy meeting locals." Miss Baxter cocked her head and examined Caroline as if she was a rare species of lizard.

A dozen insults flashed to mind, but Caroline wrestled each one into submission. She should walk on, leave Mr. Dermott to his gossip and his pretty companion to her sunstroke, and seek out the solace of her private beach. But then her tongue got away from her.

Much as it had during that humiliating kissing business.

"My family lives here year-round," Caroline said. "And Mr. Dermott's family comes nearly every summer. But I find myself curious I have not seen you in Brighton before, Miss Baxter. What brings you down from London?"

And where was the chit's chaperone? Caroline herself often skirted this necessary bit of propriety, but her family had only a single maid-of-all-things, and the dear woman couldn't be expected to traipse all over Brighton following Caroline and her sister around. But Caroline couldn't think of the last time she had seen a well-bred young lady, especially the daughter of a viscount, walking on the beach without a maid or relation in tow.

Unperturbed by the directness of the question, Miss

Baxter giggled. "Why, the social possibilities, of course. My father is delayed a few days, but he has permitted me to come down ahead of him. Lord and Lady Beecham are already here, with their son, Mr. Harold Duffington. And the Traversteins arrived last night." She smiled, as if Caroline should not only know who those people were, but be agog at the thought of meeting them. "It promises to be the London Season, all over again. There will be parties every night, and dancing until dawn."

An unsteady beat of panic bloomed in Caroline's chest. "But . . . *why*?" was all she could think to say.

It couldn't be true. This was Brighton, the seaside town where she had lived her entire life. The fashionable season, if indeed Brighton could even be said to have one, was in February, when Londoners sought a milder climate and relief from the coal-dust air of a London winter. Summer attracted a different crowd, people who preferred spa treatments and long walks over ballrooms. In fact, the most exciting thing that happened here in the summer was watching the sun set over the spires of the Royal Pavilion.

Miss Baxter leaned in, her pale, pretty nose twitching in excitement. "Well, you mustn't tell anyone you heard it from me, of course, but I have it on excellent authority the royal family is rumored to be planning a visit this summer."

The explanation did little to erase the confusion knocking about in Caroline's thoughts. "But . . . I thought the queen preferred Brighton during the winter months."

Miss Baxter shook her head, as if Caroline was an absolute recluse to not have already heard the gossip. "That was *last* year. You may trust my word on this, Miss Tolbertson."

"Indeed." Mr. Dermott grinned down on his partner as if she possessed a rare, world-changing talent. "Miss Baxter is quite an authority on the latest gossip from London."

Caroline must have squeaked, or hiccupped, or something equally unladylike, because Miss Baxter leveled an assessing stare in her direction. There was no telling what sound she had made to pull the girl's sudden, sharp-eyed notice.

And she *had* been known to snort on occasion.

But the only noise Caroline could discern at the moment was the pounding in her ears. It was frightening enough to imagine a summer spent dodging a London socialite whose worth was measured by how well she repeated others' failings. But if the queen's purported residence this summer shifted from rumor to fact, Brighton would descend into an entire month of celebratory fervor. And that meant summer, the season Caroline lived for, the only time of year when the ocean warmed to tolerable and she could venture into the water without fear of pneumonia, would become a thing of nightmares instead of pleasure.

"There is an informal dinner at Miss Baxter's house tonight, and there be will parlor games after." Mr. Dermott broke through her swirling thoughts. "It promises to be jolly good fun. You should come."

"Of course," Miss Baxter added, a smile blooming on her pretty face. "We would be honored to have you."

I'll just bet you would. Caroline had a pretty clear idea of her role in the promised parlor games, should she have the brass to show her face at Miss Baxter's dinner. "I believe I am otherwise engaged," she said. "Dinner with my family."

Miss Baxter blinked. Then two bright spots of color appeared high on her cheeks, and Caroline realized her mistake. She had just rejected an invitation from the daughter of a viscount, and for no reason other than a quiet family dinner.

"Well, Miss Baxter will send an invitation around to your house, in case you change your mind," Mr. Dermott gleefully interjected, as if he had chummed the water and discovered the situation offered a bit of good sport. "You should bring your charming sister too. How old is she now, twenty-nine? Thirty?"

"Twenty-five," muttered Caroline.

"Oh. And still unmarried. Shame, really. Although, with her stammer, is anyone surprised? Well, perhaps luck will turn for both of you this summer." He laughed.

Miss Baxter, to her credit, did not laugh. But then, why would she? She had just been snubbed by a nobody, and her cheeks were still flushed with the sort of bright, florid color that came from either stiff indignation or indigestion.

Not that the girl appeared to permit much food pass through her mouth. She looked as if a stiff gust of wind would punch a hole clean through her.

As if bored by the course of the conversation, or else fearful of that threatened gust of wind, Miss Baxter squeezed her companion's arm. "You promised to show me the famous Chain Pier, Mr. Dermott," she reminded him.

"And I would not want to be remiss in a promise made to such charming companion." Dermott tossed Caroline a last, suspicious smile over his shoulder. "I look forward to becoming reacquainted tonight, Caroline."

And then they were off, a pair of fashionably dressed predators poised to rip her quiet summer from its hinges and leave her, vulnerable and exposed, to their swirl of gossip and mean-spirited fun. As the pair faded into the crowd, Caroline permitted her shoulders to relax an infinitesimal degree. *Reacquainted.* As if the man hadn't already become acquainted with her lips, and then spread the tale far and wide.

She glanced toward the row of white chalk cliffs that beckoned in the far distance. The unpleasant interlude had cost her a quarter hour, but surely it would be several hours before Miss Baxter was able to pen an invitation, if indeed she even meant to.

Desperate for the peace a walk would bring, her feet automatically began to move toward the one place in the world where she could escape. As she walked, she fumed. Hadn't she considered whether Mr. Dermott might be the tiniest bit unsound when he had first expressed interest in her? She no longer had to wonder.

The man was deranged if he thought she was going to make an appearance tonight.

Chapter 2

DAVID CAMERON STOPPED dead in his tracks and let memory knife him in the gut.

One moment he had been walking that ever-changing line between land and ocean, focused on the act of *not* remembering. It had taken him an hour to hike to this isolated bit of coast, and much of that walk had tested his athleticism, with sharp rocks and narrow footholds where the ocean encroached on the white chalk cliffs. He had not recalled navigating such a grueling footpath eleven years ago, but he had barely been walking at the time, and his thoughts had been focused on things more difficult than the landscape.

The next moment he spied a woman, emerging from a break in the cliff walls a hundred feet away, and those denied memories split open and threatened to swallow him whole.

He squinted, sure his eyes were deceiving him. But the prickling awareness that set up beneath his skin at the sight of her only intensified with each passing second. This was no mere memory, conjured to life by an active imagination. Their only prior meeting had been a chance encounter more than a decade earlier, but there was no denying his Brighton mermaid still haunted the same section of beach he had narrowly escaped with his life.

And apparently his savior, whom he had more than once suspected of being nothing more than a drunken mirage, had been real.

He moved toward her, pulled by memory, prodded by manners. He discerned the exact moment she recognized him. Her limbs arrested, as if she were suspended in time and place, and her mouth opened in surprise.

"Miss Tolbertson, isn't it?" he asked as he drew up in front of her, because under the peculiar circumstances, what else could he say?

Her mouth seemed to work around the words she wanted to say. "You remember my name, Lieutenant?"

Her words settled in the space between his ears, the voice more mature than he recalled. Time had a way of taking a memory and turning it into a still miniature in one's head, to be tucked away and brought out on special occasions. When he thought of her at all, it was always as the child who had pulled his sorry arse from the surf.

This was not that child.

Oh, she had the same freckles and dark hair, although this time those tresses were dry and pulled back from her face in a ruthless knot. She possessed the same sharp nose, the same flat chest. Christ, she had on near the same girlish frock, some plain thing that came down only to her calves and looked to have seen one too many summers.

But she was far taller now. Lanky, he would have called her, had she been a horse he was contemplating at auction. Her shoulders seemed ill-contained by her clothing, and strained against the seams of her dress. Her expression was different too. The girl he remembered—although, admittedly, it was a memory distorted by grief and a Highland malt—had been extraordinary. Full of life, leaking emotion.

The woman seemed better contained.

"A man retains certain facts regarding near-death experiences," he admitted ruefully. "The name of his rescuer tends to be one of them." He looked down at her, and realized he did not have to look very far. Her nose came nigh up to his chin, a singular experience when one considered he was six-foot-two in stocking feet. "And it's no longer Lieutenant. I sold my commission last year. Please, call me David."

Her eyes widened. "I don't think . . . I mean . . . I do not *know* you."

"You've known me for eleven years. You rescued me from this very spot, when I should have drowned. Formality seems a little pointless, under the circumstances."

She drew in a deep, audible breath, and then her mouth found a smile that reached her eyes. He recalled now too how he had to search his mind to identify whether her eyes were green or brown or somewhere in between.

"Then you must call me Caroline." She sent a furtive look in two directions before her gaze came back to rest on him. "It is not as if there is anyone to hear our frightful lack of propriety anyway." She assessed him in a broad, hazel sweep. "I confess, you have taken me a bit by surprise. No one else visits this stretch of beach."

David had not known what to expect on returning here today. An epiphany, perhaps. A dark memory of the boy he had once been, and a sharp reminder of the man he must be. But he had not expected her.

"I am not surprised, given the calmer waters and wider beaches of Brighton. It is a bruising walk." He glanced down to the high hem of her skirts and the sturdy half boots that graced her feet. She had dressed properly for the walk, it seemed. He was wearing shoes better suited for a casual stroll along Brighton's Marine Parade, and a vicious blister had taken up residence on his right heel.

"Why did you never return?" she asked, her voice lower and huskier than the one in his memory.

His gaze pulled back to her face. After the events of that fateful day, he had returned to nearby Preston where his infantry unit had been stationed. He had been close enough to have come back any time he had wanted.

But he *hadn't* wanted. The less he thought of Brighton, and the fewer visual triggers he forced on himself, the easier it had been to go on during those early, guilt-ridden years. "I live elsewhere. This is my first visit back since that day."

"Oh." Her wrinkled forehead softened. "I suppose that explains why I never saw you again."

"Do you live in Brighton?" Though her accent was more educated than the dialect he had picked up from the few local fishermen he had encountered in town, it seemed too much of a coincidence to see her twice in two visits if she did not.

"Yes, on the east side. Our house sits right on the ocean." As if prompted by the question, her eyes pulled toward the crashing surf. He followed her gaze and caught the diamond flash of waves peaking before boiling over into gray. The tide was coming in, and it was a fearsome sight. The high cliff walls surrounding them formed an inlet that seemed to force the water into a constricted space, intensifying the effect.

Had the waves been this rough that day when she had swum out to save him? He couldn't remember. But the thought of such danger, heaped on a child's shoulders by his own stupidity, chilled him thoroughly.

"I wouldn't want to keep you." Her voice broke through his thoughts. She motioned toward the footpath down which she had just come. "Not if you have a schedule to keep."

She seemed anxious to be rid of him. He wondered if she felt a need to hurry him along, in case he was considering another ill-advised swim off this section of treacherous, rocky coast.

Truly, there wasn't enough whisky in the world.

"I am not expected elsewhere at the moment. I am staying at the Bedford with my mother, but she has eschewed my company for the afternoon."

In point of fact, his mother had tossed him out of the room they had taken at the grand hotel, insisting she was fine, snapping at him when he tried to plump her pillow or read to her out loud from the novel she kept on the table by her bed. He might have been plagued by troublesome memories in the three days since their arrival, but his mother seemed better, at least. The physician's prognosis a month ago had not been favorable, but already her lungs sounded clearer. Perhaps there really *was* something to the restorative power of Brighton's seawater cures.

Two weeks ago, when his mother had first suggested this trip, he had argued against her wish for a recuperative holiday here. He felt no desire to return to the town of Brighton and the nightmares he sensed would await him there. But he had not been able to refuse his mother when she had told him her heart was set on Brighton. Not when she had been so ill for so long.

And not when she had implied it might be her last request.

"You are here for the summer then?" Caroline asked, oblivious to the maudlin direction of his thoughts.

"Two weeks," he answered. Ten more days. It was a bloody long time, all things considered. "We shall return to Scotland near the start of August."

"Oh. Still, it is longer bit of time than many take. The new rail system even permits Londoners to come for the day, if they want. Can you imagine? London to Brighton and back again, in only a few hours." She smiled, stretching a remarkable constellation of freckles far and wide. "Last year they came in droves every Saturday, to soil the beaches and overrun the sewers and trample over every blade of sea grass they could find. We have begun to earn the moniker London-by-the-Sea, I'm afraid. I hope you won't be disappointed here."

A grin worked its way into residence on his face. She was the same, but different too. She no longer chattered on with quite the same fervor as she had as a child, but she still chattered. He was fascinated by the changes time had wrought, both in her appearance and in her demeanor. Although he would have expected the opposite reaction, given the circumstances of their history, her voice drew him from his self-flagellating thoughts and diverted him from painful memories.

Suddenly his remaining ten days' penance in Brighton no longer seemed so long, or so threatening. He offered her the full force of his smile. "I have not been disappointed in the least. And while Brighton's popularity among Londoners is a diverting topic, I would prefer to talk about you."

CAROLINE DREW A deep breath, wondering why her stomach skittered so at the sight of one man's straight, white teeth.

David Cameron was not quite as handsome as she remembered. Although his shoulders were every bit as broad as they had been eleven years ago, today they were covered in a brown woolen sack coat instead of an eye-catching military uniform. He was not wearing a hat, and his straw-colored curls mocked the shimmering spun gold of her memory. His face had lengthened into the hard planes of adulthood, framed by tiny lines etched by sun and experience, there at the corners of his blue eyes.

Handsome, to be sure, but not *that* handsome.

And for heaven's sake, a younger and every bit as attractive specimen—Mr. Dermott, to be precise—had smiled at her not an hour before, and the sight had caused nothing but an urge to rake her nails across his face.

Of course, David Cameron was the man she had fallen a little bit in love with before she was old enough to know better. The man she had imagined kissing when she had, in fact, been kissing Mr. Dermott.

When she had first caught sight of him, framed by sea grass along the eastern edge of the white cliff walls, she felt as if she had been slammed against the rocks that broke the waves into fragmented pieces, a dozen yards or so from shore. She couldn't believe he had appeared after eleven long years. It was astonishing, really, as was the fact that he was speaking to her as if she was a lady and as if he was enjoying the conversation.

But despite his kind teasing, she was going to do anything it took to prevent the conversation from turning to her.

"You mentioned Scotland?" She wet her lips, wishing she didn't feel so nervous. "Although your brogue is not so strong as my memory."

He grimaced. "Ah, I treated you to my brogue during our last meeting, did I?" He leaned in, one conspirator to another, and she felt his nearness as acutely as if he had pressed himself against her. "I'm from a town to the north, called Moraig. And I'll share a little-known secret. My accent tends to come out when I have had too much to drink."

She pursed her lips around a smile. "Well, that explains it. You smelled like a distillery the last time we met." She took an exaggerated, in-drawn sniff. "Not today, however."

In point of fact, he smelled . . . interesting. Like salt and ocean and, ever so faintly, laundered cotton that had been heated by exertion. In contrast, Mr. Dermott, who was the only other male in recent memory she had taken the opportunity to sniff, had smelled of Watson's hair pomade, and his mouth had tasted too much of the tankard of ale he had purchased from a vendor on the pier.

She wondered, for a heart-stopping moment, what David Cameron's mouth would taste like. Her cheeks heated at the audacity of such an inappropriate thought, and she cast about for a diversion. "Why does your mother not wish for your company today?"

He sighed, and she could pick apart the different tones of worry and exasperation that formed the sound. "She has been ill, and the doctor prescribed a rest cure. I brought her to Brighton with every expectation of serving as a doting son. But since our arrival, she seems to harbor other opinions for how I would spend my time."

Caroline smiled. "Long walks to undiscovered beaches?"

He laughed, a spontaneous burst of mirth that the wind snatched up and tossed against the cliff walls. "No, nothing so pleasurable. The baroness harbors aspirations of a social agenda that eclipses anything to be had in my hometown of Moraig. I don't understand the fuss. I am only a second son."

Caroline was startled enough to take a half step back. She had not known of his status, that day eleven years ago. She had seen his military uniform and presumed him a common soldier, but by Brighton standards, he was borderline royalty. "Well, the son of a baron attracts some notice, especially in a town like Brighton."

"A Scottish barony is not the same thing as an English barony." David waved a modest hand. "Really, it is more that my father owns a small estate. There are those who would dispute whether he even rates the title of peer."

Caroline blinked. She supposed that made sense. Although it still stood to reason that if Mr. Cameron moved in the circles she suspected, he was not just out of her social sphere.

He was *in* Mr. Dermott's.

"I brought my mother here to heal," David continued, "but it seems her constitution is less dire than the pressing matter of her youngest son's lack of marriage prospects. She has already accepted not one, but *two* invitations on my behalf."

Caroline shuddered. "Sounds lovely."

"Truly?" He sounded surprised.

"No." She shook her head. "I confess I would rather play shuttlecock. And shuttlecock is a game I despise."

That had him laughing again. "If not shuttlecock, what then? We've established you don't mind a bit of impropriety. Do you still swim, mermaid?" he teased.

And just like that, the desire to direct the conversation away from her eccentricities circled full round to take her by the throat. He might not have heard the rumors about her recent ill-considered kiss, but he had once seen her swim. Even if it had occurred eleven years ago, even if it was something they had both sworn to silence, that kind of secret was dangerous to a girl like Caroline, who already hovered on the outer fringes of society.

And while she was not sure she wanted to be accepted by the summer set, Mama expected her to act like a lady, even if she couldn't actually claim such a title.

"No." Caroline squirmed against guilt. In Brighton—indeed, in Britain—a lady did not swim. She might stroll along the shore, as long as she remained bundled to her chin in sweltering layers of wool and lace. She might partake of a seawater treatment in one of the ridiculous wheeled bathing houses that ensured privacy and propriety. If she were very brave, or very desperate for a "cure," she might even don a flannel bathing costume and venture out to take a medicinal dip in open water before scrambling back to the safety of those wooden walls.

But a lady did not *swim*. Not if she wished to be considered a lady.

"You don't swim here?" he asked, looking perplexed. "Or at all?"

For a moment she contemplated changing her answer, telling him the truth. But how to explain that, despite her knowledge of Society's expectations, Caroline's soul—

nay, her *sanity*—cried out for something different? The ocean might pull and push her. It might occasionally threaten to kill her.

But it did not degrade her.

She felt *whole* amid the waves, in a way she never did among the crowd.

And so she swam in secret. Furtively, like one of the silver-finned fishes that darted among the rocks, escaping the larger toothed fish that sought to consume it whole.

"Ladies do not swim," she told him, weakly to her own ears.

His brow lifted. "You used to swim very well. You had an unusual stroke, if I recall, but it was quite effective. "

The warm day and the uncomfortable bent to the conversation made the perspiration break out along her forehead in what she had to presume was a most indelicate sheen. The swim she had come for, the swim that was now out of reach, would have helped restore her to rights. But the reality of her circumstances stopped the words from lifting off her tongue.

David Cameron seemed to like her. Why would she destroy that with a bit of uncalled-for honesty?

"You were drunk that day," she pointed out. "You probably don't remember things very clearly. And I was never very experienced. I doubt I could manage much more than a bit of uncoordinated splashing now."

He nodded, as if her lie made all the sense in the world, when it didn't even make sense to her. And just like that, the idea of telling the truth shriveled into something unrecognizable.

He believed her. It was a pity too. The heat of the day was pooling, damp and ominous, in the space between her breasts.

Well, the space where her breasts *should* be.

"I never told anyone, you know," she murmured.

"That you used to swim?"

"That you could not. I never told anyone about that day, not even my sister, Penelope."

He inclined his head, a physical acknowledgment of the courtesy she had shown. "That is a long time to keep a promise. I would not have faulted you if circumstances had compelled you to share such a secret."

"I think someone's word is the most important part of his character," she told him. "A promise is something you must keep."

His mouth flattened into a thin line. "An admirable sentiment. I wish I could claim to keep my promises half so well."

For a moment, fear knocked the base of her spine. "You mean you told someone about me?"

He shook his head. "No. I was referring to another promise I made once. A long time ago."

When he made no move to explain further, Caroline wiped her damp palms on her skirt. The sun mocked the awkward silence. It was always this way, next to the white chalk cliffs, an unexpected blast of blinding color and energy. As a result of this peculiar convergence of sun and wind, she was tanned in places a proper lady should not be, just from her daily swim. She could feel her nose burning now.

It occurred to her, in a flash of annoyance, that Miss Baxter's yellow parasol would come in very handy in a place like this.

Oh. Miss Baxter. The invitation for the dinner party.

She had been so shaken by the excitement of seeing David Cameron—indeed, by the thrill of revisiting the past—she had forgotten about the unfortunate state of her future.

"I must go," she said in a rush, already turning toward the footpath. If Miss Baxter had actually sent the threatened invitation, her mother would be searching for her in every corner of the house. "Mama will expect me home for tea."

"Will I see you here tomorrow?" David called after her, breaking the silence that had engulfed him since his last peculiar statement.

Caroline hesitated. While his unexpected appearance had stirred her hopes, it had also interrupted today's opportunity to swim. As long as she could remember she had come to this hidden cove with her father, first to collect shells, and then, in the years before he had died, to learn to swim. And despite this man's easy smile, despite the fact he had already seen this beach, she did not want to share it with anyone else.

Not even David Cameron.

"I don't come here every day," she hedged. "But you can call on me in town, if you prefer, and we can walk on the Marine Parade, or along the Steine. My house is the large Georgian with red shutters, the first one you encounter on the footpath back."

He grinned, whatever melancholy that had gripped him tucked away for another time. "I shall do that."

For a maddening moment, a moment she could not regret, but which she wished she could control, her stomach churned its agreement. Did he mean to court her, then? Eleven years of yearning, secret dreams stretching from childish fancy to adult curiosity, rose up in hope. No one, not even Mr. Dermott, had ever called on her at home before.

And then he ruined it. Took her swelling hope in his hands and pressed it flat, as if her dreams were a whimsical castle made of sand and he was the inevitable tide.

"After all," he said, as if the matter of Caroline Tolbertson receiving a gentleman caller was not an astonishing thing. "If I am going to resist my mother's harried matchmaking efforts this summer, I suspect I am going to need a good friend in Brighton to make it through unscathed."

Chapter 3

CAROLINE ARRIVED HOME just in time to see a uniformed messenger step off her front porch.

The sight sent her pitching over the last stretch of shoreline in a panic. Her lungs protested as she pushed herself into a full-bore sprint.

Why, oh why, couldn't the afternoon's conversation with David Cameron have concluded about five minutes earlier? She could not regret their meeting, or even the loss of her precious swimming time. She was still overwhelmed by the unexpected direction of her afternoon. All the way home, her thoughts had skipped ten paces ahead of her feet. But if the pleasure of conversing with her childhood obsession had ended five minutes earlier, she would not be catching the backside of the courier who had with certainty just delivered Miss Baxter's invitation.

And more importantly, she would not be left with the bitter declaration of friendship echoing in her ears, from the mouth of the man who had shaped every womanly thought she had ever entertained.

She took the weathered wooden front steps two at a time, hurtling past the porch railing with its peeling paint, tripping over her exuberant shell collection that grew larger every summer. She flung open the door and skidded to a halt across the parquet floor, fingers itching to snatch up whatever had just been delivered and escort it to the rubbish heap.

Her sister, Penelope, was standing in the foyer. A letter lay open in her hand, and excitement widened her eyes. "Oh Caroline, you'll never g-guess!" She waved the piece of paper. "We have been invited to a d-d-dinner party tonight."

Caroline's stomach turned over. She had thought to keep the dreadful thing out of her mother's hands. She had not considered what greater calamity it would be for the invitation to fall into her sister's.

"It's mine, Pen." She shook her head. "And I did not plan to accept."

"But it was addressed t-t-to me too. I would not have opened it otherwise."

For a moment, her sister's words rattled around Caroline's head. And then she realized she had been outmaneuvered. Miss Baxter must have realized that the only way to ensure Caroline appeared at the sacrificial altar was to extend the invitation to her sister.

"Pen, it isn't what you think."

"I think I should wear my pink striped taffeta with the flounced hemline. I've always felt that color complemented my complexion."

"You always look lovely." And it was true. Penelope, with her fair hair and kind—if overserious—blue eyes, had a quiet beauty about her. Not that any of the summer set had ever taken the time to see it.

"Oh, say you'll go," Penelope pleaded. "You know Mama won't let us go unless we serve as each other's chaperone."

Bess, the family's maid-of-all-work, emerged from the depths of the house like a well-timed wish, bearing a tea service and clucking to herself. When she caught sight of Caroline standing in the foyer, she heaved a relieved sigh. "Lord, child, there you are. Wasn't sure how I was going to explain your absence again. You know you promised your mama you would try to be on time today."

Caroline cringed at Bess's well-meaning words. The kindly, stooped servant had been with them for ages, and was as much a household fixture as afternoon tea. "I told her I would *try*, Bess. But sometimes I . . . er . . . get a little lost on my walks."

"Hrmph." The servant's snort was all too audible over the clatter of porcelain. "Distracted is more like it." She headed down the hallway balancing the overfilled tray, the smell of fresh baked scones wafting behind her.

"Do not tell Mama," Caroline pleaded as she and Penelope followed Bess into the parlor. She received no definite answer from her sister, but she did attract the notice of their mother, who was already seated on the threadbare blue settee.

Mrs. Tolbertson's gaze swept her Caroline's windswept hair, and her mouth tightened like a drawstring. "Tell me what? And heavens, child, your hair is an absolute fright. Why you insist on taking a long walk every afternoon is beyond me."

"I enjoy my walks." Caroline reached up a hand try to smooth the humidity-snarled wisps at her temples. Her mother had never understood Caroline's desire to walk about.

Then again, her mother rarely left the house.

As per usual, Mama was dressed today in a high-necked black bombazine gown, though it was nigh on sweltering in the house. Her blond hair, which was showing just the beginning streaks of gray, was still as perfectly curled this afternoon as it had been at breakfast. She might head a family who had not been able to afford a London Season for either daughter, but she nonetheless insisted on appearances, even if there was no one to see her but family.

And in the area of appearances, Caroline was usually a disappointment.

"Did either of you happen to see today's *Gazette*?" Penelope asked as she removed the day's wrinkled newspaper and a small mountain of books from her favorite chair. "Someone should speak with the editorial d-department. It was an absolute d-d-disgrace, full of grammatical errors and lacking any direction. Papa would have never permitted such shoddy editing when he was alive."

Their mother's lips thinned into the usual line that accompanied any mention of Penelope's interest in anything bookish. "I hardly think that is an appropriate topic for afternoon tea," she reprimanded. "Home should be an oasis of tranquillity, not a nest of critical thinking. It upsets the digestion, dear. Why, in London, my mother would never have permitted such a topic of conversation during tea."

Determined to avoid being drawn into the agony of reminiscing about Mama's London upbringing, Caroline leaned forward. "I heard a bit of news today. The royal family might take up residence this summer." The memory of Miss Baxter's soliloquy on the virtues of dancing until dawn sent an indelicate shudder across her spine. "If it goes the way it did when the queen visited this February, I imagine Brighton will be quite overrun."

"It d-does seem as if there are more visitors down from London than usual." Penelope cleared her throat. "I imagine there will be a great many parties to celebrate."

Irritation twisted beneath Caroline's skin at her sister's obvious intent. "Pen . . ." she warned, low under her breath. "I do not want to go."

"Go where?" Mrs. Tolbertson glanced up from the task of pouring the tea. "Whatever are you talking about?"

"Er . . . go to visit the new modiste on East Street," Caroline improvised. She picked up her cup and took a tentative sip, stretching for time to think. "Madame Beauclerc. I believe she's French."

"French?" Their mother's blue eyes widened in surprise. "Why, when I first moved here from London after marrying your father, there were still fish nets being laid out every day on the Steine. It is hard to believe Brighton now has a French modiste." Her gaze settled on the old dress Caroline still wore. "I confess I am surprised to hear you noticed such a thing, dear. As I always say, a well-dressed lady stands a far better chance of making a good match than a woman dressed like . . . well, someone from *Brighton*."

The old familiar pattern of anger and guilt set up its dependable beat inside Caroline's skull. She had been born in Brighton, as had Penelope. Mama might have been raised in London, and once upon a time been presented at court, but she had chosen their father, and in doing so had chosen this town. What was so wrong with Brighton?

Or, for that matter, with her?

"I think we should procure the services of the new modiste, Mama," Pen said. "We could have new dr-dresses made for this summer."

Their mother shook her head. "You already have three dresses apiece. Now that Caroline has finally stopped growing, it would be wasteful to spend money on new clothing when you have a wardrobe in hand."

"I am not suggesting replacing our wardrobe," Penelope clarified. "B-but maybe a formal gown or two appropriate for parties."

Their mother's brows formed a deep furrow between her eyes. "You know money is dear, Penelope. I hadn't wanted to say anything, but . . ." She sighed. "The truth of the matter is we have less than a hundred pounds remaining in our savings. I am afraid it will only stretch so far."

Caroline cringed to hear their financial situation explained in such bald terms. They had lived off Mama's small inheritance for so long, it sometimes seemed as if it might stretch on forever. Of course, that was a childish fancy. She had known their finances were tight, but this was the first time in memory her mother had put an actual figure on the amount they had left.

She squirmed in her chair, reminded anew that she was not keeping the promise she had made to her father. Oh, she watched out for Pen, and tried to obey Mama when she could. But in the matter of ensuring their financial security, she had done little to fulfill the promise she had made her father.

"P-perhaps just one gown?" Pen asked wistfully. "Mayhap we could even sew it ourselves."

"I am afraid that spending what little we have left on dresses for parties you will not be invited to would be a dreadful mistake." Their mother sighed.

Penelope placed her cup and saucer on the little table at her elbow as precisely as if they were live ammunition. She drew the invitation out of her pocket, avoiding Caroline's glare. "But that is just it, you see. We received an invitation for a d-dinner party tonight. From Miss Julianne Baxter."

Their mother picked up her quizzing glass from the chain around her neck to give the proffered note a thorough perusal. She turned it over to examine the seal.

"And if we make a g-good impression tonight," Penelope added, "additional invitations might follow."

Their mother's finger smoothed over the broken red wax imprint. "Miss Baxter is the Viscount Avery's daughter?"

"Yes," Caroline replied. "Do you know the family?"

"I knew Lord Avery, once upon a time. I had read that his wife passed, about a year ago. They must be out of mourning then." Mama's eyes narrowed in thought. "It was kind of Miss Baxter to include you, although it is odd that the invitation only arrived today."

Yes, it was odd, Caroline wanted to scream. And telling. They were an afterthought. They were not being invited to enjoy the entertainment, they *were* the entertainment.

"If the peerage imagines the royal family will be in residence here, it stands to reason that many Londoners will choose to come to Brighton this summer," their mother mused. "I must say, our current financial circumstances would be much ameliorated by a good match for one of you."

Caroline suppressed a groan. This was rapidly devolving into a situation so much worse than a single humiliating dinner party.

"You know I have always regretted not being able to afford to give you a come-out in London. But if the Season comes to *us* . . ." Their mother tapped the invitation on her outstretched palm, her forehead creased in thought.

"There will likely b-be a score of eligible young men there tonight," Penelope added, a bit too helpfully.

Their mother rose in a flutter of black skirts and rosewater essence. "You are quite right Penelope. It is already past four o'clock, the invitation says dinner is at seven, and we don't have much time. Caroline, for pity's sake, you don't have time to wash your hair, but you *must* brush it properly for once. And you'll have to make do with your current selection of dresses for tonight, but I am inclined to agree that a ball gown apiece might be a wise investment this summer."

"Mama, will you come with us?" Penelope asked.

Caroline couldn't fault her sister for trying to draw her mother out of her shell, but they both already knew the answer to Pen's hopeful question. Her mother lived a reclusive existence, at best. She had been this way ever since Papa's death, although the oft-repeated stories of her time in London painted a gayer picture of her life before.

Their mother's eyes widened in alarm. "Oh no, dear. Lord Avery . . . well, I am sure his daughter does not mean to invite me." She rubbed a telltale hand against one temple, a sure sign of an impending headache. "I am feeling a little off, truth be told. And the invitation suggests this is a young persons' party. You are both of an age and capable of serving as each other's chaperones. And after all, we are in Brighton, not London. The rules are more relaxed."

And then she was gone in a swirl of dark skirts, translucent excitement trailing in her wake. Perhaps she was recalling the single Season she had enjoyed before marrying their father and moving to Brighton, or dreaming of happier days before Papa died and left them in genteel poverty. Or perhaps she was hoping that this, finally, was going to be the key that unlocked her daughters' futures.

Whichever it was, Caroline didn't have the heart to tell her it was a farce.

Penelope picked up her cup and saucer and offered Caroline an apologetic smile. "I am s-s-sorry, truly I am, but I've never attended a dinner party before."

Caroline responded with a terse nod. She didn't blame her sister. She didn't blame her mother. She didn't even blame Miss Baxter, although she really, really wanted to.

No, she blamed Mr. Dermott. This was really well played of him. It was as if the scheming man could see inside her head to her most hidden vulnerabilities, and knew just how to capitalize on the knowledge.

It had been taken out of her hands, and so she would go. She would brush her tangled hair and put on a false smile. She would endure the whispers and try to protect her sister from the sorts of veiled barbs and hidden insults she herself had grown used to over the past two weeks.

But whatever else she did, she would not enjoy it.

BY THE TIME he had made his way back up the rocky coastline and sighted the line of houses and hotels lining Brighton's Marine Parade, David was ready for nothing more stimulating than a quiet evening and a hearty dinner. Instead, his mother pounced as soon as he walked through the door to their lavish Bedford Hotel suite.

"Where have you been?" She set aside a tray of un-touched food and dismissed her ladies' maid with a nod. "You are filthy," she told him. Her face pinched with worry beneath her halo of gray hair. "And *late*."

David kissed his mother dutifully on her presented cheek, the skin threadbare beneath his lips. He could not object to her characterization of his cleanliness. His collar was damp with sweat and humidity, and the relentless wind along the chalk cliff route had left his exposed skin pelted by grit and coarse sand.

But surely "late" was a matter of debate. It was six o'clock, with the sun still high in the sky.

He sank down into the wingback chair beside her bed and rested a tired foot across his knee. "I took a long walk this afternoon. Per your orders, if you recall."

His mother leaned back into a mountain of embroi-dered pillows, which, like those on his own vast bed in the adjoining suite, seemed to change in shape and color every hour or so. The Bedford was renowned for its exemplary service and luxurious rooms. To David's eye, that noto-riety seemed to be expended mostly on the production, cleaning, and changing of bed linens. These were not the sort of lodgings he would have chosen for himself.

Hell, these were not the sort of lodgings he could have afforded for himself.

But as his father had made the arrangements and was footing the bill, he did not begrudge his mother a few lux-uries, not if they brought her comfort.

"Brighton scarcely strikes me as the sort of town that can absorb six hours of a man's time with nothing more stimulating than a stroll," she observed. "Did you meet anyone of note on this walk?"

David suppressed a frown. Yes, he had met someone of note. And no, he was not going to reveal her identity to his mother. She would immediately begin reconnoiter-ing the poor Tolbertson family, including sussing out their ancestral history, the amount of the girl's dowry, and quite possibly her shoe size.

Which was probably something monstrous, given the girl's height.

"I engaged in quiet contemplation," he said, unwilling to throw Caroline into his mother's matchmaking hands.

"Well, I hope you at least contemplated meeting an eligible young woman." His mother pretended to frown at him but could not hide the hopeful smile that threatened.

David grimaced at the blatant reference to his mother's desire to see him married. Seeking to change the subject, he glanced over the untouched filet and wilted mound of watercress that sat on the tray by his mother's side. The doctor had prescribed a blood-building diet, but it could not work if she did not eat. "You had a tray sent up? I had thought we were taking dinner together tonight."

"Have you forgotten you are attending the dinner party organized by the Viscount Avery's daughter? You have less than an hour to wash, dress, make yourself presentable, and convey yourself there." Her voice rose in pitch, her concern now directed to the matter of his future punctuality, rather than the question of his past whereabouts.

Uneasiness sent his spine rigid. His mother's insistence on such things was beginning to grate. "I do not want to leave you when you are not feeling well," he protested. "Is your appetite off again?"

"The only thing 'off' is my worry that I shall leave this world without grandchildren."

David leaned forward, tenting his fingers. "You have grandchildren," he replied dryly. "Three, last I counted." Thank God his older brother had not shirked his duty in providing a future succession.

"I want *your* grandchildren," she lamented. "*You* are the son who takes after me in coloring and temperament. I want a pretty, blond-haired granddaughter before I die, and as your brother seems to produce only male issue, I must resort to whatever means necessary."

David sighed. "You are not on your deathbed, Mother." At least, he prayed she wasn't.

A blue-veined hand fluttered at the hollow of her neck. "Are you *trying* to put me there? I declare, you give me palpitations every time we have this discussion." She lifted a brow that, despite her oft-lamented fragility, was anything but delicate. "David. You are a grown man, a decorated military hero, a respected Moraig citizen. Yet you are still living under our roof. Isn't it time you at least *thought* about starting a family?"

David's foot slid off its perch and hit the floor in a hard thump. He didn't enjoy living with his parents. What self-respecting man would?

But he was a second son, lacking fortune and title. A past military career was not a path to solvency, and the investments he had funded with the sale of his commission had yet to pay out. Serving as Moraig's magistrate was a good solution to dispel the boredom that had initially threatened to drive him insane after ten years of busy army life, but the position did not come with a stipend.

Marrying a young woman with a decent dowry would be the obvious solution for most in his position. But there was a good reason he was still unmarried, and an even better reason why he would remain so.

He wondered, not for the first time, how much his mother knew of his past. Moraig was a small town, and rumors had a way of finding a solid foothold there. Ten hard years in an infantry unit and countless acts of sacrifice for queen and country had dulled some of his pain, but not his determination never to marry. He had not courted a girl in eleven years, not since he had destroyed the life of the only girl he had ever loved. He might not be a man of honor, but he had enough decency left to understand he did not deserve a second shot at it.

That wasn't to say he hadn't bedded plenty of women, women who understood his personal limits and welcomed him anyway. The army's camp followers had warm beds, open arms, and few expectations. The serving girls in Moraig had a way of falling over themselves to bring his first pint and whatever else he might be interested in sampling. Plenty of women had stirred his lust, but the transient comfort they offered was as much as he permitted himself. He didn't deserve more, and so he didn't seek it.

Not the sort of thing one told his mother.

"And you *will* attend this dinner," his mother continued, "because I accepted the invitation in your name. Your reputation as a man of his word requires it."

David leaned back and contemplated his response. He had not come to Brighton to attend parties or flirt with eligible young ladies or, God forbid, find a wife. He had come to improve the delicate balance of his mother's health and to spend as much time with her as possible, in case the doctors in Moraig were correct in their dire prognosis.

But he had also come to make her happy, and that expectation now poked at him with the persistence of a sharpened stick. He sighed in resignation. A wise soldier, after all, knew when to retreat. He took up her hand and squeezed it, taking care of her fragile bones. "Just tonight, then."

"And the Traversteins' ball on Friday. I've already returned your acceptance, David. It would be rude to change your mind now."

He sighed. "All right, Mother. But I did not come to Brighton to find a wife, so please, do not accept any more invitations without first consulting me. Agreed?"

His mother offered him a long-suffering smile and patted the top of his hand with her free palm. "Of course, dear." Her eyes narrowed. "You know, Viscount Avery's daughter, Miss Baxter, is as yet unmarried. I met her at the bathhouse yesterday. A lovely redhead, the picture of decorum. Will you at least promise me you will seek her out tonight?"

"I will try," he said wearily, rising from his chair. "But only to make you happy."

She called after him as he made for the door to his own adjoining suite, "It would make me happier if you put at least a little effort into finding a woman who sparked your interest, dear."

David shut the door before he said something regrettable. His mother's final words, and the silence of his own room, inexplicably turned his thoughts toward Caroline Tolbertson. *She* had sparked his interest today, but not in the way his mother intended. Rarely had he permitted himself to get close enough to a woman to engage in more than a furtive coupling. But his reaction to Caroline had been different. There was little about their exchange on the beach that chased his thoughts in a carnal direction. She should have been nothing more than a reminder of that day eleven years ago, vivid and regrettable and something best avoided.

But perversely, she made him feel safe. Comfortable, as if she shared and understood his past and forgave him for it.

He intuitively knew she didn't, of course. She had been a child, and could not have understood the dark forces that had brought him out among the waves that day.

But no one else knew about that desperate piece of his past. Not his best friend, Patrick Channing, who lived in Moraig and was always ready to lend a willing ear. Not his former best friend, James MacKenzie, who had still not forgiven him for the few pieces he did know.

As he began the necessary process of shaving, David realized that Caroline Tolbertson alone knew something of what he had faced that day. And as grateful as he was to have come across her this afternoon, he found himself looking forward even more to seeing her again tomorrow.

But first he had to get through tonight.

Chapter 4

DAVID'S ARRIVAL SPARKED no small degree of fluttering and preening among the colorful, vulture-eyed females attending Miss Baxter's dinner party. He almost turned around at the door, but at the last minute his military training kicked in and steadied his nerves.

Stepping into the parlor, he could immediately see this was no small party, intended for intimate conversation and stealthy flirtations. This was a full-on social assault, with twenty or more young people in an array of dizzying colors.

And there were no appropriate chaperones to be seen.

Within five minutes, David deduced this was closer to the sort of parties he had attended with his friends during his four years at Cambridge, lacking only the fraternal spirit and a few well-paid whores. Necklines appeared to have no southern boundaries in Brighton's warm climate, and without proper chaperones on the premises, the degree of cleavage on display had reached lewd proportions. Clouds of perfume floated above the room like a floral stranglehold, fragrant weapons dueling for supremacy.

If the new crop of girls looking for husbands looked and smelled like this, was it any wonder they were all so prone to hysteria? The entire thing made him feel drab, inelegant, and about a decade too old.

But then he spied Caroline Tolbertson, hovering at the edge of the crowded parlor, and his distaste for the evening his mother had forced on him settled into something more tolerable.

She was impossible to miss, standing a half foot above most of the other young ladies. She wore an uninspired navy gown that looked to have been fashioned for a woman either incapable of—or uninterested in—displaying herself to full advantage. Her hair was up again, pulled ruthlessly away from her face, but in his mind's eye he could see it as had been eleven years ago, wavy brown tendrils whipping in the ocean breeze.

In a sea of frivolity and artfully placed curls, she stood out like a lighthouse beacon. Only he was pulled toward, not away from, her rocky shores.

Despite his mother's strict instructions to seek out Lord Avery's beautiful and available daughter, he found himself drifting in the direction of *this* young lady, who was neither Miss Baxter nor beautiful. Without logical explanation, the idea of conversing with the sure-to-be-delightful Miss Baxter paled in comparison to the idea of speaking with the sure-to-say-something-interesting Miss Caroline Tolbertson.

And so he approached her, taking the long way around, ducking and swerving around a clattering flock of girls. He could tell he had surprised his quarry, because she gasped as he leaned over to whisper in her ear, "Wishing for a game of shuttlecock?"

Any other girl would have flushed, he was sure. And she might have, though it was difficult to gauge beneath the unfashionable golden glow of her skin.

But her most discernible reaction was that her body went rigid. She scanned the room before her eyes slid back to his. "I had not realized *this* was the invitation you referred to so cryptically this afternoon, Mr. Cameron," she said, her voice a low and unmistakable warning. "I hope you plan to be circumspect about any prior acquaintance."

He opened his mouth to reassure her that he had no intention of revealing anything of their history, but then a servant rang the bell for dinner, and the crowd began to organize itself.

"Have you any idea how we will be seated tonight?" he asked, turning in a confused circle. *Confound it.* He should not have arrived so late.

"By precedence, I am sure. Which places us on opposite ends of the table, Mr. Cameron." She took the arm of a blond woman in a pink dress and began to make her way to the back of the line.

David almost started after her. But then a delicate hand touched his shoulder and he turned to look down upon an angelic vision in white.

She was five-foot-nothing. Had a headful of cascading red curls, which gave off glossy little sparks under the overhead chandelier. Eyes of a color one didn't have to fumble for: unapologetically green. The lovely Miss Baxter, he presumed, if his mother's description of the girl was accurate.

"Mr. Cameron." She smiled. "We are seated together at dinner."

CAROLINE HAD NAÏVELY imagined David Cameron was different from the rest of the summer crowd. He had flirted with her this afternoon, she was sure of it. That business about shuttlecock, and those quick, easy smiles.

But here he sat, in the middle of the crush—nay, at the head of the table. To his right, Miss Baxter was chattering away like a locomotive on a track to nowhere good. It would be only a matter of time before David either heard the whispers regarding Caroline's ill-fated kiss, or started more on his own. He wouldn't even have to do it purposefully. A casual mention of their history, an innocent slip of the tongue, would be more than enough. David's dinner

companion was a self-admitted gossip, and would probably like nothing better than to propagate such a titillating
bit of rumor.

And that, Caroline knew, would be the end of any hope
she held to attract a suitor.

Her mother's pronouncement about the state of their
finances had dogged her all through the evening. Mama
was right, even if it pained her to admit it. A good match
would solve their problems. In some ways, she had been
acting selfishly, depending on Mama's meager savings to
see them through. She had always known this path was
expected of her. She had just not anticipated her feet to be
put to the fire quite so soon.

Then again, she was already three-and-twenty. Surely
that fire was starting to go out.

But between herself and Penelope, she wasn't sure who
was *less* likely to marry. She was the too-tall Tolbertson
sister who kissed like a boy, and Penelope was the shy
spinster whose thoughts got tangled on her tongue.

It was a wonder the men weren't beating down their
door.

Dinner was interminable, a fact worsened by her acute
awareness of the man seated at the far end of the table.
Minute by minute, she watched David Cameron fall under
the spell of the enchanting Miss Baxter. Honestly, how had
a girl with such coloring escaped the freckles that plagued
Caroline's own skin? David laughed often, bending his
blond curls toward his partner's red ones, and Caroline
could not help but wonder if the humor was at her expense.

Oh, but he looked handsome tonight, very nearly the
image of the man her dreams had built him up to be. Tonight his strong jaw showed to prime advantage working
the overcooked bit of beef. The sun had turned him golden
on his afternoon walk, making him appear as some tanned
Grecian god, dropped from Mount Olympus.

Or some such poppycock.

As the endless meal dragged on, she was quite sure she had never wanted to see the back side of a dessert, or an evening, so desperately. But then they were through, and eight bottles of the absent Lord Avery's best wine had fallen to the wolves, and Mr. Dermott was calling for the start of the promised parlor games.

And Caroline realized she had never wanted to return to an ill-prepared pudding so much in her life.

She seated herself on a settee facing Penelope, at the far edge of the crowded parlor. Nothing of note had happened so far during the evening, beyond the fact that Penelope had struck up a conversation with a red-haired young man who spoke with animated interest on the subject of the new process of developing photogenic drawings. Most importantly, Mr. Dermott had not approached her. Miss Baxter had greeted her arrival with a tentative smile. The beef sitting precariously in her stomach had not insisted on making a return appearance.

But these small miracles did not keep her from looking for danger, uncertain of when it would come but so sure of the attack she couldn't breathe.

Of course, her difficulty breathing might have also been influenced by the cheroot someone had lit, just behind her. Several young men were passing it around.

"What is that odor?" Penelope paused in her conversation with the young photographer to sniff the air.

Caroline followed her sister's line of sight, her nose wrinkled in distaste. "The cheroot?" She might be an uncultured girl from Brighton, but their mother had instructed them in social niceties. Even she understood that women were not supposed to be subjected to such indignities. That was the entire purpose of men and women separating for a time after dinner.

This crowd, however, seemed uninterested in following such conventions.

"It has a peculiar fragrance," Penelope mused.

"That's because it is cannabis, not tobacco." The red-haired man with whom Penelope had just been conversing reached out to take his turn at the end of the cheroot as it was offered to him. He inhaled, making a great show of his skill at holding the smoke in his lungs before exhaling it through his nostrils. He pulled it out and glanced at it with a critical slant to his brow. "Christ, what a waste. Hashish is best when eaten."

Caroline was as shocked by the idea as by the man's appalling language. Cannabis was . . . was . . . well, "forbidden" was the word that came to mind. Laudanum was the only medicinal drug permitted in the Tolbertson home, and that was reserved for matters of extreme need.

Such as her mother's threatened headaches.

"I've read it is supposed to b-be less hallucinogenic when inhaled." Penelope watched in fascination as the gentleman took another pull at the end of the lit cheroot. "It is supposed to induce more of a state of relaxation than torpor."

Caroline choked, as much on surprise as on the cloying smoke. Who *was* this curious creature masquerading as her bookish sister? Right when the cheroot was poised to sail on by, Penelope reached out her hand and lifted it to her own lips.

"Pen, no!" Caroline gasped. They were already on the fringe of social acceptance. What was her sister thinking?

Undeterred, Penelope inhaled, and then her whole body convulsed on a jagged sputter.

Caroline leaped to her sister's side and clapped her on the back, unable to sort out whether her panic was due to the party's forbidden offerings, the lack of any apparent chaperone over the age of forty, or her sister's uncharted daring. She was quite sure this was not the sort of dinner party her mother had imagined them attending.

The gentleman who had given Penelope the cheroot scrambled backward, whether from shock at seeing one sister attack another, or to give her more room to maneu-ver, she could not be sure. As Penelope's coughs grew more strangled, Caroline whacked harder, right between her sister's hunched shoulder blades. The motion sent Penelope sprawling onto the carpet in a puddle of pink striped fabric, and the group of young men who had started the proceedings into peals of laughter.

"She's a strong one."

"What did you expect, with those shoulders?"

"Not much to look at, is she?"

Caroline froze under the weight of those anonymous snatches of conversation. Thankfully, they were directed toward her, not her sputtering, cheroot-trying sister. She had felt the rumbles all evening, the undercurrent of whispers that told her Mr. Dermott's comments had left their mark.

But Penelope, thank goodness, did not appear to be their prime target.

David Cameron materialized from the depths of the party to lift her still-coughing sister back to sitting. "It is meant to be inhaled gently," he told her, a half smile etched on his handsome face.

"Or not at all," Caroline added, her heart thumping against her ribs. At first she thought it was her body's re-action to the man's proximity, or to her worry he might have overheard the ill-spirited comments about her lack of femininity.

But then she realized the feeling was not occurring in an even rhythm.

Was . . . was a drum being played somewhere in the house? Yes, it was. And another reveler was belting out an ill-kempt time on a piano, singing like a sparrow whose feathers were being plucked out, one at a time. She felt as if she might be hallucinating, and she had not even taken a turn at the end of that cheroot.

"Oh my." Penelope pulled a stunted version of the che-root from her mouth. "I think I sw-swallowed some of it."

At that very moment, Miss Baxter materialized in a rush of heated white silk, glaring at the young men who were still snorting with laughter and making a great show of lighting another cheroot. Dread seeped beneath Caroline's skin. Miss Baxter lived to spread gossip. Thrived on it, in fact. This was *not* the person she wanted around Pen at the moment.

And yet, this wasn't exactly the composed young woman Caroline had seen earlier in the night. At this moment, Miss Baxter looked dreadful, in a pretty-girl-from-London sort of way. Her copper curls had started to frizz, no doubt because several of the partygoers had flung open the terrace doors to let in the humid night air, and her face was flushed a most unbecoming shade of red. Caroline was struck with the uncharitable thought that, at times, being beautiful had its drawbacks.

Such as the stark contrast when one did not look one's best.

Miss Baxter plucked the glowing cheroot from the young man's fingers and deposited it in an empty wine-glass someone had left too close to the edge of side table. "There will be no smoking inside the house, gentlemen. My father does not permit it."

"Your father isn't here in Brighton," one of them had the gall to say.

Which, Caroline considered with new understanding, explained both the dinner's descent into debauchery and Miss Baxter's earlier lack of chaperone on the beach. A hesitant vein of respect stirred in her breast. She hadn't imagined a well-bred girl from London could possess such daring. And Caroline could respect a rebellious skirting of propriety, even if her own choices didn't involve parties that threatened a house fire.

Miss Baxter morphed into a red-haired paragon of virtue, pointing an angry finger toward the open terrace doors. "Nevertheless, please take yourselves outside to the terrace, if you must indulge in such a disgusting habit."

"It's just a little cheroot," one of them protested, waving a fresh one about for his friend to light from another smoking tip.

Miss Baxter snatched it from his hand, any pretense at polite discourse gone. "And please remove your feet from the furniture!" she snapped. "We are renting the house for the summer. My father will be very upset if he arrives on Saturday to find the place in shambles!"

Caroline was shocked to see the gleam of perspiration on the girl's face. Somehow, she summoned the good spirit to feel sorry for the chit. But Miss Baxter had organized this party, apparently without her father's knowledge, and left the mechanics of the evening's entertainment up to Mr. Dermott. What on earth did she expect?

As the raucous group of young men made a great show of trooping outside, Miss Baxter put a gloved hand to her temple and groaned, "Heavens, what was I thinking. And that *noise*. Where is it coming from? There are far too many people here, and I—" The sound of shattering glass filled the room. "The china!" she gasped, whirling toward the dining room.

As Miss Baxter's heels clicked a furious retreat on the tile floor, Caroline risked a glance at her sister. "Are you set to rights, Pen?" she asked, concern for her sister superseding any concern she felt for herself or the curious Miss Baxter.

"Y-yes," hiccupped Penelope, arranging her skirts on the settee with a limp hand. A smile had bloomed across her sister's face. "It didn't work. I had wondered if c-cannabis might help my stammer. B-but still, this is ever so much fun."

Caroline blinked. "Fun" was not the word Caroline would have reached for.

Of course, she had not swallowed the end of a cannabis cheroot.

She spared a glance for David, who had settled himself in the space next to her. His large frame hovered an inch away, and it occurred to her that despite their long history, despite a good number of formative years imagining his touch, she had never so much as felt contact with the man's gloved hand. This was the closest she had ever been to him.

And all she could think was how much she wished she wasn't here.

She sat there, rigid, thinking the evening couldn't get any worse. And then Mr. Dermott staggered into the room and clapped his hands.

"It's time for Shadow Buff!" he declared, swaying under the effects of the one bottle of wine he had consumed, all on his own.

And suddenly, "worse" was no longer a figment of her imagination.

Chapter 5

Λ SHEET—OR WAS IT the tablecloth?—was thrown up between two tall potted palms. Someone fetched a pair of oil lamps.

"Oh, this is *not* what I agreed to." Miss Baxter stomped back in, her heels angry punctuation marks. "I told him *charades*. Shadow Buff is much too . . . too . . ." She waved a shard of a broken dish her right hand. "Suggestive."

Beside David, Caroline Tolbertson leaped to her feet as if discharged from a revolver. "It is time for us to take our leave," she announced, tugging on her sister's arm.

But the elder Miss Tolbertson had been replaced by a giggling lump of flesh in pink silk. "I want to st-stay." She laughed. "Shadow Buff sounds delightful."

David rose and put a steadying hand on Caroline's shoulder as she renewed her grip on her sister's arm. Surprisingly strong muscles flexed beneath his fingers, a glaring contrast to the smooth slide of silken fabric. She was wrestling her limp sister off the settee now.

"You can't return her home like this," he told her in a low warning tone, prying her fingers from her sister's reluctant arm.

She whirled on him, her forehead almost colliding with his chin. "What do you know of it?"

"I have a Cambridge education," he said mildly. "I've

attended more than one dinner party where cannabis was the main course."

Her mouth worked itself into an outraged circle as she turned her anger on him. "I suppose you think this is acceptable?"

David fought back a smile. No, he did not approve. What magistrate would? The professional side of him disapproved of the evening's descent into debauchery, especially with such mixed company. But cannabis, while enjoying a dark reputation, was not illicit. Furthermore, Brighton was not within his jurisdiction.

And anything that brought a flush to this girl's tanned cheeks was something worth needling her over.

"It has been a long time since I indulged in these sorts of childish games. But as long as no one is injured," he reasoned, "there is little harm in staying the course."

Caroline gestured toward her sister, who had reseated herself and was now listening to the young man who had given her the cheroot with rapt attention. "No harm? This is my sister." She kept her eyes trained on the pair, as if to make sure the innocuous exchange did not descend into wantonness. "My kind, sensible, proper sister! Penelope scarcely had a glass of wine during dinner, but now she's . . . she's . . ."

David crossed his arms, amusement feathering the edges of his sympathy. "Enjoying herself?"

"I hardly think her public intoxication tonight is going to be something she enjoys tomorrow, Mr. Cameron," she snapped, her gaze swinging back to him with lethal precision.

Ah, finally. There she was. David had wondered if the passionate girl of his memory still existed beneath the buttoned-up version of the woman she had become. In this moment, she appeared very close to the spirited creature he remembered from eleven years ago, battling to save someone who neither deserved—nor appreciated—the effort.

"If you try to take your sister home in this condition, she is very likely to collapse halfway there, or twist her ankle," he reasoned, pulling Caroline back down onto the settee with gentle but determined fingers. "Best to let the effects wear off here, where there are those who would help. An hour should suffice. I will not let anything happen to her." *To either of you*, he added silently.

As if on cue, Mr. Dermott, a London dandy who seemed to fashion himself ringmaster of this circus, leaped onto a chair at the front of a room and motioned for everyone to find a seat. David was forced to squeeze closer to Caroline on the settee as two more people claimed territory on the piece of furniture that had been fashioned, at most, for two.

She hovered on the edge of the seat, fingers curling into the upholstery, close enough to taste but holding herself so aloof she might as well have been a mile distant. "I cannot stay here," she whispered.

David raised a brow. He had once seen this girl take on the hellacious current off a rocky coast, just to save his fool arse. It seemed incongruous she would be afraid of a simple parlor game.

Dermott lifted a finger to his lips and pantomimed a great need for quiet. The smell of smoke and perfume replaced the noise as the loudest thing in the room.

"The rules," Dermott announced, "are simple. The women shall pose behind the screen, and the men shall guess their identity based on the shadow they cast. The object for the men is to match their guess with the correct young lady." He grinned. "The object of the ladies, of course, is to make it as difficult as possible for the men to know who they are."

The crowd made their approval known by a stamping of feet and a few shrill whistles. "What is the reward?" called out one drunken soul.

"Nay, what is the forfeit?" shouted another.

"The reward and the forfeit are one in the same." A smile stretched the corners of Dermott's mouth. He scanned the crowd and his gaze came to rest on Caroline Tolbertson. "A kiss."

David could have sworn he heard a groan, low in Caroline's throat.

As the crowd erupted in approval once more, Dermott lifted his hands and waved them for silence. "The reward for the gentleman who guesses correctly, and in turn, the forfeit for the lady who fails to avoid detection, shall be a kiss lasting two minutes." His grin stretched higher, and he paused for dramatic effect. "Outside on the terrace."

Still standing beside them, Miss Baxter gasped. She waved the bit of ruined china clutched in her hand for attention. "Mr. Dermott, I am not sure—"

"Our hostess is our first volunteer!" pronounced Dermott, clapping his hands in mock appreciation.

Miss Baxter narrowed her eyes, and for a moment David thought she might refuse, as any sensible girl would. But apparently Miss Baxter was not entirely sensible, because at the exuberant urging of the other guests, and the stone-faced assurance from Mr. Dermott than if she played the game well she didn't have to kiss anyone, she squared her shoulders and made her way behind the impromptu screen.

"Now we need five other ladies," Dermott called out, searching the crowd.

"I volunteer!" The elder Miss Tolbertson lurched to her feet, one hand waving in the air.

"Pen!" The strangled objection came from the woman to his right, loud enough for Dermott to hear too.

"Oh, I say!" he crowed. "We have *both* the Misses Tolbertson participating tonight!"

A general chorus of approval and a few snickers pierced the crowd. David leaned over and heard Caroline's ragged intake of breath. "Did you mean to volunteer?"

She raised a set of stricken eyes, and swallowed. "I mean to be sick."

David risked a glance toward her sister, who was clambering over a few people who had been forced to sit on the floor, not even realizing her ankles were being displayed to all and sundry. "Perhaps you ought to go with her," he advised. "She may need assistance. And . . . er . . . a reminder for decorum."

Caroline's eyes widened. And then she was on her feet and being pulled behind the screen.

Dermott conjured a quorum of other young ladies to participate, and the game was on. The women were given ten minutes to develop their strategies. There was a great deal of whispering and giggling from behind the screen. The room was plunged into darkness as several young men set about extinguishing the other lights in the room.

An expectant hush fell over the room as the oil lamps behind the screen were turned up. The shapes of the volunteers materialized on the white screen.

He had to admit, the ladies had given it some effort. Several of the women appeared to have rearranged their hair, making it difficult to sort out identifies from that measure alone. Whichever one was the petite Miss Baxter had apparently found a stool to stand on, because none appeared shorter than the majority of the group.

But that only emphasized the identity of the sixth young lady, whose height was indisputable. She stood still, arms wrapped around her middle, a tall shadow of acute discomfort.

The elder Miss Tolbertson fell to the crowd's speculation first. Her name was guessed by the young man who had given her the cheroot earlier. How he had known was anyone's guess.

Of course, her shadow *was* waving her arms about and giggling quite madly.

The elder Miss Tolbertson emerged forthwith, and then

she and the red-haired gentleman slipped out onto the terrace for their allotted two minutes. The game paused for the forfeit, and only after they had stumbled back inside to the approving shouts of the crowd did the proceedings, well, proceed.

He expected someone to shout out Caroline's name with immediacy, as her identity alone was the most obvious, but instead, as each man took his turn at guessing the identities of the ladies behind the screen, it became clear they were hell-bent on identifying anyone but her.

And then it was David's turn, and there were only two women left who had not been identified: Miss Baxter, and Caroline. He drew a breath, recognizing, somehow, the ill spirit that permeated the room. He supposed the smarter thing would be to choose Miss Baxter. After all, she was the woman his mother had pushed him here to meet, and it would be no hardship to spend two minutes on a darkened terrace with such an attractive girl.

But then his hand gestured to the taller image on the screen. "Miss Caroline Tolbertson," he announced. The crowd roared, as if he was the butt of a jolly good joke.

She stepped around the edge of the screen looking as if she might be ill, which was not the sort of reaction one wanted when contemplating kissing another person on a dark terrace.

"Good luck, Cameron."

"Beware that one!"

And while he was contemplating the oddity—or more correctly, the idiocy—of those statements, they were pushed by eager hands out the open terrace doors.

Chapter 6

THE SOUND OF laughter trailed them as Caroline stumbled into the grateful darkness. The revelry of the crowd receded as the doors were closed on them, but it did not lessen the sting of their comments.

"How much time again?" she asked, drawing in deep breaths of salt-tinged air. Overhead the stars laughed down at her, winking their amusement at her predicament. In the distance she could hear the soothing sound of waves meeting shoreline. She closed her eyes and focused on that. Usually the sound of the ocean brought her peace.

Tonight it came closer to mocking her.

"Two minutes." He sounded as resigned as she did.

What a pair they made. At this moment, shuttlecock would have seemed the most welcome diversion imaginable.

"What should we do?" She gave a self-conscious laugh and risked a backward glance. He was standing beside her, staring up at the stars. Her eyes followed the moon-shadowed line of his jaw and the corded muscles that disappeared into the depths of his collar. *At least it is David Cameron, and not one of the other men.*

Although that didn't seem quite right. Wouldn't it be better for it to be someone whose opinion didn't matter?

"We could try that kiss." His voice came at her as a low rumble, sending tremors up her spine.

Her eyes flew wide, unable to believe he had suggested it, desperate for a way to dissuade him. "Why would you want to kiss me?"

He shifted to face her, and one side of his mouth quirked upward. "Why not, lass? It is expected, after all."

Her heart beat a mad new rhythm in her chest. His Scottish accent was strong tonight, no doubt brought on by whatever portion of the eight bottles of Madeira had made it into his glass. She recalled how fascinated she had been by that lopsided grin and pulse-fluttering brogue eleven years ago, a girl of twelve who did not yet understand the mechanics of the unfortunate infatuation that would push her into womanhood.

She understood now, though. She only wished she didn't.

"Do you *want* to kiss me?" she whispered, astonished and miserable and hopeful, all at once. He had spent the majority of the evening thick with the summer crowd. Was it possible he had not heard of the infamous kiss and resulting rumors that plagued her?

"Well, I dinna give much thought to it when I called your name out," he admitted. "I suppose you could say I can't think of a specific objection to a kiss. Do you want to kiss me?"

"No." *Liar.* She wanted it desperately. Although surely their two minutes were almost up. And surely this was just a dream from which she would be yanked by the dawn soon enough.

"You seem awfully certain of your answer." He sounded irritated. "A rejection so swift surely demands an explanation."

Her first reaction was to roll into a ball and keep her secrets curled up tight. She could not imagine confessing her long-standing obsession to the man who had inspired it, or admit that, despite a lamentable first attempt at kissing, she was considering giving it another go if she could do it with him. But would that be fair to him? After all, he would learn soon enough why kissing her was an ill-advised thing if he continued to insist she pay the forfeit.

"I wouldn't recommend it," she warned him, honestly this time. "I've been told I'm a terrible kisser."

He regarded her a long, stomach-churning moment, and then he began to remove his gloves, one lazy finger at a time. "According to whom?" he pressed.

"Does it really matter?" She sighed, closing her eyes in mortification. "It's the sort of reputation one earns, not the sort one is born with."

His chuckle hit her then, high across the gut. It rumbled across the shadowed space of the terrace and the blissful anonymity of her closed lids. "Did I mention I serve as the local magistrate in my town of Moraig?" he said, his voice growing ever deeper, his brogue more distinct. Firm hands framed her face, deliciously bare fingers testing the contours of her cheeks. Thumb pads brushed over her eye-lids like the slightest of feathers. She felt the gentlest of pressure, guiding her to him.

"No," she managed to somehow choke out, her eyes still clenched tight.

"It means I'm an excellent judge of the truth, especially in difficult cases."

She had the fleeting sensation of a smooth-shaven cheek before his lips, warm and dry, moved over hers. She drew in an experimental breath, willing her knotted muscles to relax.

Everything about this kiss felt different, starting with the man who was pressing his lips against hers. This time there was no uncomfortable bumping of noses. It was as if he had learned the shape of her with his fingers and known exactly how to tilt her face so they met in harmony.

This time, there was no thrust of tongue down her throat either. No groping hands. No ale-scented breath. No . . . no . . . no . . .

No hint of similarity to her previous experience with the thing.

And so Caroline leaned in, and tried to decide if this kissing business warranted a second chance.

SHE WASN'T A very good kisser.

David had a sense of lithe muscles and graceful contours, agreeable things that had his treacherous body paying attention in remarkably short order. But she was a little too eager, as if she sensed better possibilities below the surface of the almost chaste kiss he offered. She seemed uncoordinated, unsure of her body and how to move it, or where her hands went in relation to her lips.

He broke the tension between their mouths and, guided by her untutored gasp, pressed his lips to other offered places. The indented hollow of her throat. The shadowed space behind her ear. Most women tasted of floral cologne, or sometimes wood smoke in these secret places, depending on whether he sought his evening's entertainment with a comely widow or a willing camp follower. In contrast, the woman in his arms tasted of salt. It distracted him, that tart, unexpected taste. The oddity of discovering such a sharp flavor here, on a moonlit terrace, amid such a raucous, inebriated, *perfumed* crowd, tugged at the seams of his consciousness.

It didn't fit. *She* didn't fit.

And no matter the taste or feel of her, Caroline Tolbertson just wasn't the sort of woman he usually enjoyed kissing. She was far too young. Far too innocent. And not nearly as well-endowed as the nameless, faceless women he usually took to bed.

Not that he had any intention of taking Caroline anywhere but back inside.

Still, she showed promise. Therein lay the problem. Though his reaction to her was not that heated rush he preferred in a partner, she reminded him, both in her eagerness and in her inexperience, of someone else who once *had* made him feel that way. Someone he had loved and then destroyed through his selfish choices.

And that was what made David push her gently away.

"Did . . . did I do it wrong?" Her words tapped against his conscience. It wasn't *wrong*, per se. It just wasn't . . . right.

If he had to analyze his physical response to the kiss he had just shared, it was a gentle warming from the outside in, not the breathless, sinking sensation he usually attributed to sexual attraction. Caroline stirred a mild interest, tinged with respect.

And regret. There was some of that tangled in his emotions. This was a woman he could hurt, so easily. He had spent most of his adult life ensuring enough distance between himself and anything or anyone breakable, that he didn't quite know what to do. She felt like live powder in his palms, while he was flintlock and frizzen.

He offered her a self-deprecating chuckle meant to soothe any wounded feelings his abruptness had caused. "It is just—"

A spear of light interrupted his explanation as the terrace doors were wrenched open. Someone had relit the candles in the parlor, and David blinked against the offending brightness.

Caroline stood every bit as frozen by the sharp light of discovery. She was staring at him. Or more correctly, she was staring at his mouth, her eyes wide.

The moment shifted, twisting from something pleasant and poignant to something terrible. A cry escaped her lips, so low as to be almost inaudible. Those ever-changing hazel eyes narrowed, and then she gave a hard shove against his chest, a push powerful enough to send him stumbling backward on the flagstone tiles.

"Caroline, wait—"

But it was too late. She marched inside, her head held

high, the crowd of curious onlookers parting before her like some great biblical sea. She grabbed her sister by the arm, and this time was successful in hauling the girl to her feet. David stumbled inside, determined to speak with her, desperate to know why she was so upset. But she brushed past him, the open terrace doors providing the easiest escape possible.

He came to realize the room was engulfed in silence. Finally, someone cleared his throat. "How did it go then, Cameron?"

David fixed the inquirer with a stern glare. "A gentleman does not kiss and tell."

Mr. Dermott snorted with laughter, a harsh, mean-spirited sound. "Oh come on, it's just a bit of good sport. We all want to know. Was it like kissing a boy for you too? Took a bloody impressive wager to get *me* to kiss her, I can tell you."

The snickers he had detected earlier from the crowd returned, growing in volume and meaning. Clarity descended, swift and unfortunate. Young men were infamous for such wagers. During his years at Cambridge, he had been little different, having once wagered—and lost—an entire month's allowance on the outcome of a race between two very uncooperative snails. He had no idea why young men did such things. Perhaps it was because their brains were not yet fully formed.

Or because their cocks unfortunately were.

No matter the reason, men of a certain age were undeniable idiots. They hurt people for no reason other than their own sport or their own selfish, shortsighted needs.

He ought to know.

In that moment, David understood who among this crowd had convinced Caroline of her inadequacy. And he was tempted to reach his hand down Dermott's throat, just for the privilege of ripping out his vocal cords.

The man was an utter fool. While David might not have

felt attraction for Caroline, at least not in the strictest sense of the word, she had definitely felt feminine during those scant moments in his arms, both in the softness of her lips and the breathy sighs that had escaped her. And no matter his limited corporeal reaction to the two-minute interlude on the terrace, no matter his resolve to not become involved, his emotional response to the crowd's taunts was undeniable. He wanted to protect Caroline from the likes of all the Brandon Dermotts in the world.

And he knew of only one way to turn the tide of speculation.

He raised a brow, sweeping the crowd with a lingering gaze. Dermott and his followers were like inexperienced pups, panting their exuberance and wagging their tails when they had no true notion of how to please a woman. David might be lacking any capacity for true love, but he had brought plenty of women to completion since he had been their same regrettable age. He almost felt a little sorry for the female faction here tonight, with only young men like Mr. Dermott to show them how it was done.

"It was not in the least like kissing a boy," he said lazily, letting his mouth curve upward. "And I assure you, ladies, if Mr. Dermott carries that interpretation of Miss Tolbertson's kissing skills, he surely hasn't kissed enough women."

Chapter 7

I̶T WASN'T ENOUGH for Caroline to retreat, stumbling through Brighton's dark streets, dragging Penelope behind her. She needed space. She needed escape.

She needed the swim that had been denied her some hours before.

Mama was already asleep, taken to bed by her headache some hours earlier. Bess had waited up, but Caroline sent the yawning servant off with apologies for keeping her so many hours past her usual bedtime. She ensured Pen had at least stepped out of her dress and found her mattress before her sister fell asleep.

And then Caroline let herself out the front door.

A full moon lay over the ocean, guiding her feet faster than she would have thought possible. She had never done such a foolhardy thing before. Surely it was a poor idea to trot in slippered feet along the treacherous footpath, guided by nothing more than a midnight moon. Surely she flirted with calamity to swim at a time of night when the more frightening varieties of sea life patrolled shallow waters.

But her memory of the night's humiliation suffocated her good sense and honed her internal compass. This was not a night for sane arguments, or careful considerations.

David Cameron, the man she had dreamed of for eleven long years, had kissed her.

Her cheeks heated, and refused to be placated by the evening breeze. Yes, he had kissed her. Expertly, with the skill of a man who knew what he was about. And then he had laughed at her. Well, he wasn't the first man to kiss her and display such a reaction.

But God help her, he was going to be the last.

She stuffed her self-doubts into the same dark corner where she kept her other secrets. They sat below the surface of her skin, clamoring for attention. By the time Caroline reached her swimming cove, those secrets were starting to chafe. She had never fit in among the popular crowd, not even when she tried very, very hard to hide her oddities. The only person who had ever come close to accepting—indeed, encouraging—her had been her father.

Her mother was convinced of the need to reform her, and they remained locked in frequent combat over things like her wardrobe. Her regrettable height. Her too-brown skin, and her insistence on traipsing about Brighton without a chaperone. Her mother only meant to help, she knew.

But Mama couldn't help Caroline with this. The die had been cast, opinions formed. The parlor game tonight showed Caroline where she stood among Brighton's seasonal crowd. Any opportunity she might have once had at finding a respectable match with a gentleman from the summer set was gone.

The only surprise of the evening was that she had survived most of the dinner party in relative obscurity before cresting the peak of mortification.

The moon shadows stretched out all around her as Caroline peeled off her dress and underskirts. Her corset came next. She pulled the pins from her hair with frantic fingers and welcomed the mantle of security as her heavy tresses fell across her shoulders.

The humid air settled over her bare skin like a sigh of relief, dampening her shift and easing her mood. The scents of marine life and moisture combined in an aromatic symphony, and it was a song she knew well. No other section of beach smelled as this one did. The indented cove and the steep cliff walls caught the scents off the ocean and held them fast.

She lifted her face to the chalk cliffs, the usual chatter of the swallows silenced by night. By daylight, she knew every crevice, every occupied nest above her. She had spent hours lying on a nearby rock, waiting for her hair to dry, staring up at the cliff face. But at night the contours of the place seemed different. The stark white geologic formations, peculiar to this part of Britain's coast, were almost iridescent in the moonlight. She felt as if she were standing in a magnificent spotlight, and the ocean was her stage. The evening's comedic failure receded as she took a step forward. The surf churned about her ankles, a parody of polite applause.

She had long since stopped trying to analyze why she was so drawn to the water, even to her own ruin. Perhaps it was her father's legacy, an inheritance as indelible as the color of his hair. Or perhaps, through his own example, he had imprinted her with the things he loved. She could remember his obsession with the ocean as surely as she could still recall the smell of his pipe tobacco. Swimming was her most significant connection to her father, the last personal thing he had shared with her before he died. She cherished the memory, even though too often she felt plagued by the unwanted eccentricity.

Tonight she was grateful for his gift.

She pushed farther into the surf, until her hands skimmed the roiling water. The tide was nearly at its lowest point. Following the turmoil of the afternoon's high spring tide, the water was calm tonight, and the pebbles along the ocean floor shifted to accommodate her progress. She gave a gasp of surprise as she stepped on something that wriggled away beneath her feet, but it wasn't nearly enough to dissuade her. She was used to the risks of the ocean, be they dangerous eddies, stinging jellyfish, or sharp rocks. And so she drew a breath, filled her lungs, and let her body pitch forward into the waves.

She welcomed the rush of cool water over her head, filling her ears. The sound of the ocean was like a soothing balm, muffling the din of the night's humiliation and the shriek of her internal voices. She glided effortlessly, knowing that the world below the surface was far calmer than the one that awaited her atop.

But as always, her body eventually demanded air.

She surfaced to noise of a different sort. An angry shout in a familiar voice.

"You stupid girl!" Tension snapped at her from the shoreline. The calm she had been seeking deserted her, chased by the anger in the voice.

She had come here to reflect on the indignity of the night. *Alone*. But David Cameron, the man who had caused that indignity, stood two dozen yards away on the shoreline, bristling in the moonlight. She didn't know much about men, but if she had to hazard a guess from the sound of his voice, this one was very, very angry.

And she was all but naked.

Caroline sank down in water that regrettably came up no higher than her hips. The full moon was unbearably bright, and there was no doubt that David would be able to see every lack of curve beneath the soaked fabric, should he come close enough and be inclined to look.

The overhead moon illuminated his progress along the shore. It was too dark to see every detail, but the whispered shadows of night only made her look harder. He paced, the rigid slant of his shoulders speaking louder than words.

"Are you trying to get yourself killed?" he demanded, raising his voice to reach her over the sound of the ocean.

Anger began to edge out her initial panic. This was *her* hidden cove. *Her* chance to swim. He didn't belong here, no matter how the sight of him, touched with moonlight and rage, sent her stomach tumbling. He had no business coming here, chastising her.

Tempting her.

He took a step toward her. She took a complementary lurch back.

"Any idiot knows you shouldn't swim alone," he shouted. "I recall you even telling me that once, although you clearly don't heed your own advice." He ran his hands through his hair in a tension-filled swipe. "Christ, Caroline, do you know how frightened I was when I saw you go under and not immediately come up?"

That gave her pause. He might have laughed at her after the kiss on the terrace, but he wasn't laughing now.

"How did you know where to find me?" she demanded. "Did you follow me?"

His anger was palpable, thickening the air between them. "I took a guess." His moonlit silhouette shrugged out of his evening coat. "An accurate one, it seems. I suspected as much after the kiss."

Her gasp was indignant this time. How dare he bring the kiss into this . . . this . . . well, whatever *this* was. "I don't recall inviting you to take that liberty," she shouted back at him, striving to reach him over the sound of the water. "In fact, I recall warning you against it. So if you didn't enjoy it . . ."

"I could tell from the way you tasted." He retreated several steps to toss the coat onto a large rock that rose up, dark and menacing, behind him. *Her* rock, she thought, a bit uncharitably. "You tasted of salt, but not of perspiration. I couldn't figure it out at first. But now it all makes sense." He headed back toward her, and then she saw him strip off his waistcoat and toss it onto the shore. "Perfect. Bloody. Sense."

She took a quick step backward through the water, shocked to hear in such indelicate terms how she had tasted. Somewhere nearby, the ocean floor dropped away and plunged to several feet or more over her head. She was paying far more attention to the man on the shore than to the water, and that was a sure guarantee for disaster.

And yet, she couldn't look away. Her eyes followed the arc of his shirt as it joined his waistcoat's insouciance on the shingle beach. "What are you doing?" Her voice sounded faint to her own ears.

His shoes were kicked off without ceremony, and then his trousers followed suit.

Surely he wouldn't. Surely he *couldn't.*

He entered the water and began to close the distance between them in great, gasping strides. As he advanced on her, his shape became clearer, more distinct. Caroline's earlier restrained panic began to jerk on its rope at the sight of so much of David Cameron's exposed skin. And yet it was impossible to keep her eyes averted from the sight.

Her thoughts were flying, fast and furious, scattering to the wind and then coming back to coalesce on him. This was no childish dream, to be stored away and cherished in girlish naïveté as the years passed by. David Cameron was no longer a young man in a soaked military uniform. He was a hard, angry male, and he was clothed in so little it might as well have been nothing. Far from providing adequate cover, the night's strong moon made his skin glow like polished granite. The ribbed slant of his abdomen drew her eye in a southerly direction before the ridge of muscle dipped into smallclothes she feared might soon turn as translucent as her own shift.

Though it was shallow where she stood, he dove into the last stretch of waves and finished the meager distance between them with an enviably constructed breaststroke. She stared at him, her mouth agape, as moonlight and water sluiced off his powerful arms. How could this be the same man who had once almost drowned on this stretch of beach?

"This isn't proper," she gasped as he came within arm's reach. "I . . . I am not clothed, David."

"We have already established you aren't the sort of woman who cares overmuch about propriety. You wouldn't be here risking your foolish neck, forcing me to take a midnight swim, otherwise."

"I thought you *couldn't* swim," she protested.

He seized her around the waist and jerked her close. "I never said I couldn't swim. I just can't swim as well as you, mermaid."

She could feel his pulse thumping in the grip of his fingers, there against her waist. "Then again," he went on, his mouth lowering to her ear. "I don't believe I've ever met another soul who could." The last words were growled onto her neck, fanning out in tendrils of unwelcome warmth.

Dimly she realized he was pulling her closer to shore. The feel of his hot hands through her woefully insufficient shift broke the fragile hold she had on her panic. She dug her protesting feet into the ocean floor, rocks and sand scattering beneath her desperate toes. "It is none of your concern," she panted.

He reacted by flexing his fingers into her protesting skin, as if to prevent her from bolting into the waves. "*You* are my concern, though I wish to God you weren't. So tell me, Miss Tolbertson. Why do you come here, alone, risking your life on a lark? And just as important, why in the deuces are you pretending to be someone you aren't?"

Chapter 8

DAVID WAS SO angry he could have shaken her till her teeth rattled.

It wasn't only the hour-long walk he had just endured for the second time today, or the fact that she had left him thinking far too much about a kiss that should not have meant anything. He was angry that his suspicions about her had been correct. How could she be so reckless? He had danced with the intelligence sparking behind those kaleidoscope eyes. It boggled the mind, then, that she had thrown herself into this dangerous current.

Although, now that he was here, he had to acknowledge the water lapping around them seemed less intense than his memory predicted. In fact, compared to the churning surf he had glimpsed here just this afternoon, the ocean seemed about as dangerous at this moment as a half-filled hip bath.

As if in agreement with his unspoken thoughts, she struggled against him, her shoulders pummeling his chest. He was struck by her lissome strength and, by contrast, the softness of her water-slick skin.

How could he have missed it?

She had a swimmer's build, all broad shoulders and narrow waist. He had thought her lanky when he had first seen her this morning, as if during some crucial years she had grown too fast and eaten too little. But now he readjusted that thinking.

She hadn't grown into her body, her body had grown into *her*. She kept her form hidden behind the most god-awful frocks, but if you looked closely enough—or wrapped your arms around her—it was impossible to miss. What Dermott had intimated at the dinner party, that she was a girl with masculine leanings, was nothing close to the truth. She had her secrets, but Mr. Dermott had not hit upon them.

And David was a fool to have not seen it before.

"Let me go!" she gasped, rewarding his conjecture with a sharp elbow to the ribs. "I promise I am perfectly safe."

His spleen protested the onslaught, but his grip remained firm. "You'll forgive me if I lack a certain trust, given that not eight hours ago you assured me that ladies don't swim."

"Ladies don't!" She spat the words with vehemence, her lean body writhing against the prison of his arms. "And I didn't claim to be a lady. But a proper gentleman would not handle me in such a fashion, lady or no."

He lowered his head and brought his lips flush against her ear. "If you recall, lass, I once told you I wasn't a gentleman either."

He felt her shocked intake of air, and his grip loosened. Nothing like reminding himself of his shortcomings to bring the matter home. If memory served, he had also once told her she should avoid men like him. And yet, where were they?

Stripped to their underclothes, drenched in seawater, grappling under a midnight moon.

He had spent the last eleven years avoiding the sort of entanglements that might lead him to become involved in an innocent young woman's life. And he had just leaped into a raging ocean to save Caroline Tolbertson.

Even if it wasn't actually raging tonight. And even if she appeared in no need of his proffered aid.

She took advantage of his slackening arms to twist herself 'round to face him, bringing her hands up to push against his chest. "I am in no danger, David."

"I saw the surf this afternoon. You cannot convince me this is a safe place to swim."

She drew a deep breath. "At high tide, there is some danger here, I will readily admit. The inlet and the cliff walls make the current very strong at times. But not now. It is heading toward low tide, and there is a full moon at that."

One of his arms fell away, but the other proved stubborn. It was enjoying being wrapped around Caroline, ensuring the ability to jerk her to safety in the event of a rogue wave.

Or strangle her should the situation call for it.

"You clearly swim here at other times as well," he said, unwilling to relinquish his anger or his hold on her. "Do not deny it, you were planning on swimming this afternoon, and the tide was up higher then." He dared her to contradict him. This was a girl who took unnecessary risks, of that he had no doubt.

She wrenched from his weakened grasp and gathered herself warily, a few feet away. "Yes," she admitted, still breathing hard. "I come here to swim. It is not as dangerous as you think, if you know and respect the current and the changing tides. I cannot swim at Brighton's beaches, and so I come here. Where no one can see me."

His anger refused to loosen its teeth. "That is ridiculous. Women swim in Brighton all the time. They construct bathing machines for the express purpose of swimming. In gentle surf. With people nearby to save you if you find yourself in trouble."

"That is not swimming, David. That is torture. Think, for one moment, what it would be like to be denied the one thing you love." Her words slashed at his heart in places that were supposed to be dead, places he was quite sure he had burned and buried eleven years ago. "This is the only place I can swim in open ocean," she added, her voice cracking with emotion. "As fast as I dare, for as long as I want. With no one to judge me."

David let his gaze snag on her damnable, ever-changing eyes and full, quivering lips, even though it was folly to be looking at her in this way, in this moment. He could understand something of what she was saying, but it did not deflect the worry that simmered in his gut at the thought of her swimming here, alone, risking her life. He, of all people, knew what it felt like to be out in this stretch of ocean when it had its claws in you.

Under his intense scrutiny, her arms crept up out of the water to cover her chest. The motion drew his eye, and for the first time his gaze settled on her shift, instead of her face.

Her very wet shift.

Much as he had when he had kissed her on the terrace, David felt the stirrings of an ill-timed interest, uncertain and hard and regrettable. She awakened something in him other than lust, although if he stopped to consider it, there was a bit of that surging to the surface too.

Damn it. He had thrown himself into the ocean to rescue her, not gawk at her.

Irrespective of his better sense, his gaze fell lower, to where her shift was plastered against her skin. Between the waves, when the water receded, he could see the outline of her thighs. It was dark, but not so dark he couldn't see . . . well . . . everything. She looked far too lovely, with the water lapping about her hips and the moonlight reflecting off the rivulets of water that coursed along her bare skin. Her legs were covered by water, and her arms were busy protecting the upper half of her body that seemed to worry her so much. She didn't even realize that left her middle parts free for scrutiny.

And that was when he realized that while she might be willowy, there was nothing at all boyish in the gentle swell of her hips, or the womanly shadow that hovered at the seam of her legs.

"Please, don't look at me like that." Her words clipped his expanding thoughts as efficiently as a pair of sharp shears.

David swallowed, aiming his eyes back toward the safer direction of shore. He knew he should apologize, but he could not find the words to beg her pardon when all he wanted to do was look again. "You should have told me this afternoon." His voice came out hoarse. He tried to focus on the nearby shoreline, on the waves that pushed against his body, instead of the direction his mind and his eyes wanted to wander. "I would not have judged you."

He heard a gentle sloshing that indicated she moved closer to him, apparently deciding he was trustworthy after all. "You judged me just now, presuming I couldn't take care of myself, or know my own limits." Her words were accusing, but her tone had gentled.

Guilt nudged at him. "I am sorry," he said. "Clearly, I was wrong."

And deranged. Otherwise, he would be taking his leave from the water, and tossing her the gown he had spied on shore, and demanding she button it up and not take it off in his presence ever gain.

He kept his line of vision anchored beyond her, to the gray cliff shadows that rose along the shore. Through sheer force of will, his stirrings started to settle. After all, she was not the sort of woman he was usually attracted to. And his gaze was no longer directed at that lust-provoking shadow at the junction of her legs.

And the water was damnably cold.

After a moment's silence, he heard the soft, welcome sound of her laughter. "Not that I don't appreciate the effort, and not that you don't appear to have a capable—if overtutored—swimming style, but did you really think you could have saved me had I needed it?"

He risked a look at her then. His eyes settled on her lips, which were curving upward. The gesture remolded her features into something passably pretty. The last residue of anger drained away at the evidence of her amusement, and his own lips pursed around a smile. "Overtutored? I reached you, didn't I?"

"That was hardly a challenge, given we are standing in no more than waist-deep water." Her eyes narrowed, though her lips never faltered from their delicious upward curve. And then she dove into the waves.

She swam away so fast David didn't even have time to blink. Beyond the heart-wrenching plunge he had seen her take a few minutes ago, he hadn't seen her swim since that day eleven years ago, and then he had been something like two dozen sheets to the wind. He watched her a moment, analyzing her movements. She didn't have the serious, perfect form she had just teased him about. Truth be told, she splashed a great deal as her hands cut into the water.

But Christ almighty, she moved like lightning.

Caroline's unusual swimming stroke, with alternating hands and feet working like shears, gave her an efficiency of motion the likes of which he had never seen. He was no slothful swimmer himself. In addition to ensuring his sons could fire a revolver with enviable accuracy, and pass, if not excel, during their required four years at Cambridge, David's father had impressed upon him and his older brother the necessity of a powerful, well-formed breaststroke.

But David was used to swimming in the fresh water of Loch Moraig, not open ocean. Even though the low tide was not particularly difficult to navigate, he floundered as he followed her. His arms' synchronized motion kept getting tangled in the choppy, irregular waves that bounced off nearby rocks.

But she did not slow down in the slightest.

And David could do nothing but chase her.

CAROLINE TOOK PITY on him just as she reached the rocky foothold of the sandbar.

She waited there, trying to settle her stomach. This was the ocean, the one place in the world where she felt comfortable. But tonight she felt as if fleas were jumping under her skin.

If only he didn't look so masculine. His shoulders showed evidence of his years in the army, sinew and muscle, flexing in purpose. She had seen more than her fair share of men in shirtsleeves while growing up along Brighton's beaches, but David Cameron looked nothing like Mr. Dermott and the other dandies who came down from London each summer and shed their coats as the temperature rose. In fact, she suspected that, if stripped down and compared to the nearly naked man swimming toward her, Dermott would look very much like the boy he had accused *her* of being.

She greeted David with a spontaneous splash of water, right to his face. "Not a laudable effort," she teased.

He grinned, white teeth flashing in moonlight. "You'll never get saved properly if you keep outswimming your rescuer," he told her, shaking the water from his eyes.

And then he was ducking beneath the black water and grabbing her ankle and jerking her under. She came up sputtering and spewing and choked with laugher. The enjoyment of that moment threatened to submerge her as thoroughly as David had just done.

She was swimming, for the first time since her father's death, with someone else. Someone who wasn't judging her. Someone who made her laugh.

Someone who made her *want*.

Before she could give voice to those emotions, before she could even sort out the delicious skitter of her stomach, he looped an arm around her shoulders and began to haul her back to shore.

She couldn't breathe. Not because his arm was too constricting, but because her lungs went rigid with surprise and repressed longing. She could have stayed that way forever, caught in his grip, even if it was purely for demonstration purposes. But all too soon the ocean floor met her feet, and then her posterior as he tossed her into the shallows.

He flung himself down next to her, loose-limbed and comfortable in the surf lapping along the shore. In contrast, Caroline felt as if she was waging a silent battle to pretend she was far less affected than she actually was.

"Did I answer the challenge well enough, mermaid?" He chuckled.

"I'll admit that wasn't a poor showing, for someone who only recently learned how to swim." She peeked at him from beneath her lashes.

"That was a commendable showing, my friend." He looked terribly pleased with himself, as if he rescued not-drowning girls every day. "And I'll have you know I've been swimming since I was a child."

His admission was unexpected. So was his easy reference to her as a "friend." Her heart withered, just a little. She understood what David felt for her. He considered her a friend, nothing more.

But for heaven's sake. Did he have to point it out quite so often?

Rather than dwell on the irritation his declaration brought, she sorted through her memories of that day when he had almost drowned. She had always presumed he had floundered because he hadn't known how to swim, and that his folly had been magnified by the false bravado that often came at the bottom of a bottle. But with this new bit of information, she was unable to reorder the pieces into something approaching logic.

He shoved his way through her thoughts, nudging her with one bare shoulder. "You once told me your father taught you to swim. Where did he learn such an unusual style?"

Caroline pulled her mind from the physical and emotional conundrum David Cameron presented. "I believe he learned from an American who spent several years in Brighton. Apparently, the man had learned from the Natives in his own country. I realize it doesn't look quite the thing, but . . ."

"It matters not what it looks like," he interrupted. His moon-touched expression grew serious. "You should share your skill, Caroline. Show someone. Teach someone. Why, employing a stroke like that, I don't doubt someone could swim all the way across the channel."

She shook her head. As if she could ever be so brave. "The men in Brighton already consider me enough of an oddity without adding swimming to the mix."

"Do not berate your skills," he told her quietly. "I find much to be impressed with in you."

She gave a self-conscious laugh. His words had her hand skimming the length of her side, though she had spent much of the evening disinviting his visual scrutiny. "Impressed? Look at me, David. I'm taller than Mr. Dermott, for heaven's sake. My hands are better built to handle a plow than manage a formal place setting. Tonight's dinner party was a rarity in my world. My mother hoped it might lead to additional invitations, and look how I mucked it up."

His gaze turned piercing. "Why do you want to be in thick with that juvenile crowd, anyway? You did not strike me as enjoying their company overmuch. Surely you don't want to marry one of them?"

The man was far too astute. She couldn't see the color of his eyes in the dim light, but she could imagine the stab of blue, there in her own eyes. "My father did not plan well for the possibility of his death. Papa asked me to take care of Mama and Penelope before he died, and there can be no other way to make good on that promise. Marrying someone from the summer set would mean my family never had to worry about money again."

"But to be bound to a man who may not deserve your trust, who might harm you in fact, all for a little financial security . . . would it really be worth the risk?"

Caroline's eye fell on David's clenched jaw. He spoke of marital vows as if he had given it a good deal of thought and found nothing worth considering. He described a marriage dredged in chains. What of love and affection?

"And why *you*?" he railed. "Why not your sister?"

Caroline shook her head. "You heard Penelope's stammer tonight. It does not matter to the popular crowd whether she might have a kind disposition, or a vivid imagination. As much as it pains me, I can admit that I need to be the one to marry well. For my own future and my sister's well-being."

"Your sister struck me as a capable enough conversationalist during my limited interactions with her this evening."

Caroline sighed. "She had enough wine tonight that her stammer was hardly noticeable. But come morning, she will be stumbling over her words again. I wouldn't trade Penelope for anything in the world, but she has had as much, if not more, difficulty securing a good match as I. Therein lies my problem. I am my family's best hope, but scarcely anyone will speak to me, much less offer for me. Mr. Dermott has made sure of that."

A beat of silence ensued. "Mr. Dermott doesn't strike me as a young man worthy of your notice. Why do you let yourself feel so uncomfortable around him?"

The shore beneath her refused to swallow her up. "I . . . I let him kiss me. Just once, but it was enough. He was the one who told me I was a poor kisser. Only he didn't just

tell me. He told everyone. And then suggested there were
reasons for it beyond inexperience." She shook her head.
Her sigh sounded long-suffering, even to her own ears.
"The summer crowd seized onto it as an explanation for
what they already considered my eccentric nature."

David was silent a long, measured moment. Her heart
filled the space with an increasing rhythm. His voice,
when it came, curled around her insecurities and threatened to strangle her. "So I was only your second kiss?"

"Yes." She whispered her response. "My second *failed*
kiss."

He shifted, his body moving the small pebbles beneath
her. "Why do you count the kiss we shared as a failure?"

She risked a look at him. "You pushed me away. You
laughed at me."

He shook his head, his lips a grim line in the moonlight. "You misread my response, Caroline. You reminded
me of someone. It made me . . . uncomfortable. And as that
is a memory I have no wish to revisit, it seemed safer to
impose some distance. But rest assured, I was not laughing at you. Far from it."

She didn't know what to say to that. And so she said
nothing at all, just turned his words over in her head and
let them thicken in her chest.

"Besides," he went on, "that was not even a proper
kiss."

She laughed, a choked, lamentable sound. "I assure
you, it seemed more than proper enough to me. Lips met.
Amusement ensued. I shall not be repeating the experience."

"I hardly think that sort of decision will hold you in
good stead when you are trying to find a husband. And if
you are going to make an informed decision on the matter,
you should at least have all the facts."

"I have all the facts I need." She turned back to stare
at the moon hanging on the horizon. She felt miserable at

how wrong a turn this conversation had taken. She had been far more comfortable when they had been talking about swimming.

Then again, swimming was something at which she excelled.

"Perhaps Mr. Dermott is correct," she breathed. "Perhaps there *is* something unnatural about me."

His shoulder made contact with hers again. This time it stayed, pressed flush against hers. Her skin fairly sang from the contact with this man. She felt the heat radiating off him, sliding beneath her skin and warming the blood in her veins.

"Put that coxcomb Dermott in a box for now and lock him up tight. Do you feel an attraction for men in general? Or to a particular gentleman who has caught your fancy?"

Dear God, she could not be having this conversation. Not tonight.

Not with him.

Her eyes stayed anchored on the luminous moon and its orange halo. She wrapped her lips tight around the words that would be a certain declaration of her feelings for him. The cautious nod she summoned felt as if she were being shaken to her core.

"Then look at me, lass."

She turned her head toward him. His eyes glittered in the scant light, but they might as well have been illuminated by torchlight. She could not look away.

"You deserve to know what sort of a man—and what type of a kiss—you should be looking for," he said. "So let's give this another go."

And before she knew it, before she had time to even draw a breath, his lips were on hers.

Chapter 9

HE SURGED AGAINST her mouth like an incoming tide, determined and powerful and impossible to stem. She stilled, sure she couldn't survive another round of this humiliation, sure she would rather die than admit to herself—again—that she wanted David Cameron far more than he wanted her.

He offers this tutelage to a friend, she reminded herself. *Nothing more.*

But her body refused to believe her thoughts.

He tasted of the same saltwater that marked her own lips. It lent a degree of familiarity, of rightness, to the intimacy he demanded. His hands came up to tangle in her wet hair, pulling her closer still. She could feel the persistence of his fingers, tight against her scalp.

The book she had read—the one Penelope kept hidden beneath her bed—gave very little information on kissing. She had little to rely upon except her limited past experience. On the terrace earlier, David had touched her gingerly, as if she might shatter if he pressed too hard or too fast. This time he kissed her as if he *wanted* to, not as if he owed her a polite favor. He was far less gentle now, insisting on her participation, dictating the terms of her acquiescence.

"You can kiss me back," he murmured against her startled, open mouth. "Like this." His hands shifted to tilt her chin just so, and his tongue moved inside her mouth. She met his offering with a tentative touch of her own tongue.

Shattering became a very real possibility.

Thank God they were sitting in cool, shallow water, because she was sure her knees would have buckled and pitched her headfirst onto the ground had she been standing.

"Good, lass." He breathed the praise into her mouth, and her heart glowed bright in response. "You're a quick study."

Dimly she realized her hands had crept up to grip his bare arms. She curled her fingers against him, wishing her spinning head was clearer. She had never touched a bare-chested man before. Not to put too fine a point on it, she had never *seen* a bare-chested man before. She wanted to savor the vitality of him, explore by touch the rough rasp of hair that seemed to cover so much of him.

But it was impossible to capture such thoughts properly. The sensation spiraling inside her left her grasping at memories that whirled away almost as soon as she made them.

The mortification she had been clutching during the first tentative seconds of the kiss slipped away, lost to the flood of emotions his touch unleashed. She gasped his name, and was rewarded by the sweep of his tongue down the sensitive column of her neck.

His hold on her head loosened as his attentions shifted lower. He lingered along her neck, his teeth nipping at the thin skin there. "Wait for that. Wait for a husband who kisses with a mind to bring you pleasure." His words were breathed against the curve of her collarbone, and were followed by the press of his tongue there. "He should not stop until you are squirming with need."

If he was looking to prove some demented point, he was performing admirably, because Caroline was indeed squirming. She had never felt this way. Had not imagined it, even in her most heated of dreams. She had imagined a kiss bringing only a simple, sweet happiness, such as could be found in a good iced dessert, or in the opening of an unexpected gift.

This feeling was not sweet. It was certainly not simple. It was closer in both form and function to one of the wild storms that sometimes ravaged the coast in summer and left all matter of flotsam littering the shoreline. She was tossed by it, broken into pieces, pushed under. She couldn't breathe.

She couldn't stop.

She gasped as David's tongue found the damp edge of her chemise. She dug her nails into the skin of his arms and welcomed the warmth of his mouth as he traced the scalloped border of lace. The realization that men found pleasure kissing women in places other than lips was only just eclipsed by the simultaneous discovery that she enjoyed being kissed elsewhere too.

And then her mind skipped several spaces ahead. This was heading nowhere good.

What was she doing? What was she *thinking*?

She sucked in a breath, stunned by a painful clarity that intruded on the moment and demanded closer scrutiny. This interlude might be more pleasurable than her first two kisses, but it was also far more dangerous. David Cameron was not a marriageable sort of gentleman, by his own admission. He had expressed a distrust—indeed, an intense dislike—of the institution of marriage and everything that came with it.

And yet, wasn't a kiss supposed to be an exploration of compatibility for just such an inevitability? Wasn't it, if she was lucky and the man was a gentleman, supposed to be only a prelude to a betrothal?

She didn't know. But her heart, naïve and eager as it was, told her it was *not* supposed to be just a desperate melding of tongues or a carnal fusion of breath or a gnawing ache inside her.

It was supposed to mean *more* than just the moment.

She kicked away from him then, found her feet and stumbled further ashore. She heard David scramble up after her in a clatter of rocks, heard him call out her name. She ignored him, trying to bundle the heavy mass of hair up into a knot against her neck as she lunged for her discarded clothing. Better to leave now, before something happened between them that spelled her ruin.

At that moment, a light appeared. It bobbed around the copse of high grass that bordered the footpath's entrance to the cove. Her heart, which had been laboring to put some space between her body and the man who made it want so much more, hitched in the complete opposite direction.

"Oh, I say, this is a nice beach." Dermott's voice rang out behind the bright flare of a lantern. The light swung in an erratic circle, as if he was inspecting the place. "Why haven't we come here before?"

"It's a bloody hour's walk" came a slurred male voice she didn't recognize. "And we aren't usually drunk enough to attempt it."

"Does that mean you aren't going to help finish off the bottle I brought?" came a third voice she thought might belong to the red-haired man with whom Penelope had spent much of the evening conversing.

"'Course not. There's always room for another drink, you sodden fool."

In an instant, David was beside her, sheltering her with his enormous, bristling presence. Her pulse rate kicked higher. She didn't know whether to grab his hand for safety, or to strike him for putting her in this untenable situation.

Dear God, they could not be seen together. That would be an entirely different sort of ruin from the physical one she had just feared. As if in agreement, he pushed her toward the boulder where he had flung his jacket earlier. She fumbled her way toward it. The danger of discovery felt as tangible as the pressure of his fingers on the small of her back.

The glow from Dermott's tilting lantern swung around at that instant and caught David in an indistinct sweep of light. She froze behind him, cornered like a small, hunted animal.

And then she was diving for the safety of the rock, all thoughts of kisses and regret overcome by the single, all-consuming urge to hide.

"SAY, IT'S CAMERON and some chap!"

David straightened and raised a hand, determined to draw their attention away from Caroline. Dermott came closer and held the lantern high, peering up at David's face.

Thank God. If Dermott had directed the light a little to the left, he would have caught sight of Caroline's hand snatching his jacket off the edge of the rock. A little lower, and he would have caught an equally suspicious eyeful. After all, David's body was only just beginning to recede to a respectable degree.

"You look like you've taken a dip," Dermott said. He appeared drunk, although not so drunk that he had either forgotten—or forgiven—the insult David had lobbed at him earlier. "Is the swimming here good, then?"

David struggled with dueling urges. On one hand, he was sorely tempted to correct the man who seemed determined to be the village idiot. The beautifully responsive woman who had been in his arms only moments ago was no "chap." He had a flagging cockstand to prove it.

On the other hand, Dermott's presumption that Caroline had been just another inebriated gentleman, out for a midnight swim, was a misperception worth encouraging.

"It's not bad swimming tonight," he admitted, the

memory of his playful romp with Caroline simmering in the back of his head. "Of course, I wouldn't recommend it unless you are a good swimmer. The current here is devilishly strong."

"I took first in a swimming competition during one of my terms at Oxford." Dermott came even closer, swinging the damned lantern and casting dizzying shadows far and wide. The smell of whisky-soaked breath assaulted David's nose as the man sneered, "And I won Brighton's annual race last year. Perhaps we should have a little race ourselves, here tonight."

David sought a different diversion, one that wouldn't take a drunken dandy out into the water. "Perhaps we should have a little drink, instead." He prayed Caroline had the good sense to stay hidden through the negotiations. Her appearance right now might result in the sort of churlish behavior from Dermott that David would have to reward with a right hook.

Not that the thought of hitting a prick like Dermott didn't carry a certain appeal.

"I imagine I could drink you under the table too," Dermott said belligerently.

"Only one way to find out." David snatched up his trousers and shirt and began the awkward business of pushing grit-covered limbs into them. Tonight, the thought of going on a whisky bender with Dermott and his friends was about as appealing as the idea of swigging a snifter of seawater. His answer seemed to appease Dermott, though. The man squatted and began digging out a pit in the pebble-strewn beach with his hands. One of his friends grabbed a piece of driftwood and began to arrange it for a fire.

David expelled a frustrated breath. How to extricate himself from this mess? If he and Caroline were caught out alone at this time of night, and in such a state of undress, she would be ruined. And he couldn't offer for her, even if her reputation was shredded, even if there were some who would consider it the right thing to do. Being ruined was not the worst possible thing that could happen to an innocent like Caroline.

Being forced to marry someone like him was.

Besides, after their conversation this evening, he doubted the meager numbers in his bank account would qualify him as a respectable match, no matter that he was the second son of a baron.

"Where'd the other chap go?" Dermott tossed over his shoulder. "Hamilton here has an almost full bottle here he's willing to share."

David spared a glance for the gentleman with the bottle. It was the man who had provided Caroline's sister with the cheroot, unless he was mistaken. Such illustrious company he was keeping tonight.

"He is . . . er . . . already heading back to town," David improvised. From the corner of his eye, he saw Caroline sneak away from the rock, wrapped in the dark safety of his jacket. The thought of her damp, bare shoulders shrugging into it while she fumed about being called a "chap" brought a reluctant smile to his face.

Dermott's head swiveled to the left and he spent a long moment staring at something on the ground near David's feet. "Looks like he forgot something."

David glanced down too. Dermott was staring at Caroline's wadded-up gown.

He snatched it up, then tucked it into a ball beneath one arm. "I'll return it to him in the morning." David prayed they accepted his harried explanation. With any luck, none of the louts would notice he was holding a ladies' gown instead of men's clothing.

He went searching for his shoes. Found Caroline's corset instead. Cursing under his breath, he kicked the thing beneath a scrubby bush and prayed the group didn't decide go on a treasure hunt.

Behind the men, he could see a moving shadow that told him Caroline had made it to the western edge of the cove, where the footpath veered off. The quick flash of a long, bare leg extending below the hem of the coat drew his eye. He swallowed, willing his body to stop paying such close attention to her legs.

He had kissed her tonight for no reason other than to show her what a proper kiss could be, to shape her knowledge into something she could use in the future. His point had been made.

So why couldn't he stop thinking about her?

She finally disappeared from view and he could breathe again. He wanted nothing more than to follow her. To make sure she made it home safely, to be convinced she understood the experience he had offered had been just that: an experience, with no expectation—or promise—of anything else. The sounds she had made, and her body's eager response, had him worrying that she thought more of it than she should.

But he could not leave and risk this rowdy group following him. And so he sat cross-legged on the pebbled shore as the fire began to snap. Accepted the bottle of swill that Mr. Hamilton produced. Took a long, throat-constricting draught and tried *not* to think about her.

And proved a miserable failure at the exercise.

His body's reaction during their kiss had startled him. He had progressed from interest to full-bore lust in the space of five seconds. If she had not stopped him, he couldn't peg what the outcome of the evening might have been.

He was an idiot. She was a *friend*, for Christ's sake. It had been her proximity and state of undress, nothing more. Dangerous, to be sure, but explainable.

Her body wasn't even fashioned in a way that would normally interest him. He was more often drawn to women who were soft and pillowy, with curves one could ride into oblivion. He had always preferred breasts that fit in his hands, or better yet, that spilled over his questing palms. In contrast, Caroline was mostly lean muscle. He knew it by feel now as much as by sight; she had been devilishly hard to keep hold of when she had been squirming in his arms.

But despite his claims to the contrary, he hadn't felt just . . . *friendly* when she had sighed into his lips.

History didn't just poke a stern finger at him then, it clear kicked his feet out from under him. Tonight he had come very close to ruining an innocent young woman of gentle breeding. Had he learned *nothing* from his past? Dallying with her served no one's interests, and conjured up dark parts of his soul he was determined to keep buried.

Caroline Tolbertson was not the sort of woman available for a quick tup against a wall. She would not be interested in the type of hard and fast coupling he specialized in, a storm of emotionless energy that would leave both of them simultaneously satisfied and empty. She was bound for marriage, a family, a future.

In short, she was bound for everything he had already destroyed in another.

He struggled through these punishing thoughts for a good quarter hour while the surrounding conversation centered on the sorts of things soused young men talked about by firelight. Whose horse had made a better showing at the Brighthelmston Races last week. Which barmaid at the Rising Sun pub would serve up more than just a pint.

But then, it veered into dangerous territory.

"I say, that was good fun at the dinner party tonight." One of the men, who had been identified as someone named Branson, passed the whisky bottle to his left. "Shadow Buff is a brilliant game, Dermott. Wouldn't have minded a go on the terrace with Miss Baxter. Lovely bubbies, she has."

Dermott, who was sitting across the space of the fire,

raised his hands, palms up, as if squeezing a woman's breast in each. "More than a handful, sure enough. Which begs the question, Cameron. Why didn't you pick *her* when you had the chance?"

Three pairs of whisky-lidded eyes turned to stare at him. David's shoulders tensed. He recalled he had, for a moment, similarly weighed Miss Baxter's attributes when faced with the need for a quick decision earlier this evening. Now he felt guilty for having ever considered them. "I chose the woman I found most interesting."

Branson laughed, a harsh, flat sound. "Come on. You're putting us on. If given the choice between Miss Baxter and Miss Tolbertson, I wager any sane man would pick the former."

David raised a brow. "I promise you, I am perfectly sane. I would question, however, the intelligence of a man who might think the only thing worth admiring in a woman is the size of her tits. There is more to Miss Tolbertson than you might imagine."

Branson fell quiet, though his eyes widened in surprise. Dermott, however, was not silenced. "You have to admit, Cameron, there is something a bit unnatural about a girl whose shoulders are broader than a man's. She seems rather . . . *athletic*, after all."

David's lip curled up in a half smile. "Perhaps it is all a matter of proportion. For example, *my* shoulders quite eclipse Miss Tolbertson's." He should have stopped then, let the insult hang in the air, a well-deserved observation that the problem was less Miss Tolbertson's statuesque physique than Dermott's lack of one.

But then his mouth got ahead of his thoughts. "I like a tall woman," he said, though in truth he had never given it much thought before tonight. A memory flashed through his head, of Caroline's bare legs, just before she disappeared down the footpath. When they had been sitting in the surf he hadn't given her legs much thought, but now he couldn't imagine how he had overlooked them. They were pale and slim and had stretched a good half mile from hip to heel before disappearing into a shift so short it should be banned on several continents. "A tall woman has longer legs, certainly."

"You picked Miss Tolbertson tonight because of her legs?" Dermott sounded incredulous. "How could you even know what her legs might look like? She was wearing a bloody ugly dress. Never seen a frock so hideous."

David shrugged. "Use your imagination, man. You haven't seen Miss Baxter's breasts either, and yet every one of you here is salivating over them. Imagine how long Miss Tolbertson's legs are, beneath that ugly gown. Imagine what it would be like to be the one to discover them." He paused, something mean churning in his gut. He wanted to box these young men about the ears. He didn't want to imagine any of these three lusting after Caroline, but he also didn't want to imagine her continued torture at their hands either.

"Think about it," David told them. "When it comes to a partner, do you want someone delicate and fragile, or do you want someone who can handle a bit of bed sport without falling to a fit of the vapors?" He cleared his throat, realizing he might have gone too far. "Not that I have engaged in anything so improper as bed sport with Miss Tolbertson, mind you. She is a well-bred girl with proper ideas, after all. But she *is* the sort of woman a man would be proud to call wife. If she was on your arm, you'd never have need to look for a mistress."

All three mouths opened in wordless surprise.

It occurred to David that these inebriated men were hanging on his every word. In fact, they almost looked envious that it had been he who had taken Caroline out on the terrace this evening.

Perhaps he hadn't gone far enough.

And so he went on, telling them just what made Caroline Tolbertson so special, and what louts they were to not have seen it themselves. He couldn't provide her what she needed, but he could pave the way for others to see why offering for her was something worth considering.

She was going to make someone a passionate, though not biddable wife. And the man who had her, whoever he was, was going to count himself a lucky bastard.

It just wasn't going to be him.

Chapter 10

Caroline awoke to the sound of a low moan, coming from her sister's bed. Morning came early during the summer, but the sunlight pouring through the lace curtains held no resemblance to the cautious flow of dawn. It saturated the room she shared with Penelope, taking aim at the cracked space between her eyelids and bathing her face with agreeable warmth.

Penelope, however, seemed to find nothing agreeable about it. "Oh please, make it *stop*," she groaned, pulling the pillow over her face.

Caroline bit her lip to keep from launching into a well-earned lecture. Though her recall of her sister's antics last night did nothing to invoke a smile, knowing her sister was suffering this morning came close.

Although, if she were honest with herself, Penelope was not the only one who had acted out of character last night.

It all came back in a gut-twisting rush as she swung her legs over the side of the bed. Miss Baxter's dinner and the humiliating parlor game. The moonlit swim with David, and the soul-rending discovery that she had wanted the kiss he offered to mean much, much more. The profound mortification of being discovered by Dermott and his friends, though this was the one time she was grateful they had mistaken her gender.

And finally, the ignominy of sneaking home alone, stumbling through darkness, wrapped in David's jacket.

She spied that jacket now, lying in a heap on the floor. The black woolen garment had hung from her shoulders last night. Each step had sent the oversized hem tangling about her bare legs. She had felt small in that jacket, a singular experience for her. It had been a visceral, constant reminder of how large David was.

And how attractive she found him, blast the man.

She snatched the garment up and shoved it beneath the mattress. Her stomach churned as she trudged toward the water basin. She tried in vain to scrub the memory of her poor judgment from her skin, along with the film of seawater that had dried there last night. Her hair was an absolute mess, stiff and brittle and still damp around the roots. She brushed it out and then twisted it into a bun at the nape of her neck, a severe style she knew was less than flattering but which was adept at hiding damp tresses. She had long since gotten used to such necessities as a result of her clandestine activities.

But this morning her usual coiffure seemed painful to reconstruct. She didn't want to hide her hair in a plain style, or her body behind an unattractive dress. David Cameron had made her feel beautiful last night.

It hurt to return to her usual state of blandness.

She was still sorting through her raw emotions as she jerked her best dress from the meager tangle of gowns in her wardrobe. Best, of course, being a hopeful euphemism, given how the thing pinched beneath the arms and pulled across her chest. She eyed the frock's high-necked bodice and overskirt with embroidered sprigs of lavender flowers. "Pen," she called out, knowing she would need help getting into it. "I need you."

A muffled groan was the only response her sister saw fit to deliver.

Sighing, Caroline tried to find her corset. She nurtured

hope that wearing her best gown would divert criticism and questions from her mother. A good defense, after all, required an excellent offensive strategy.

And a good offense required a corset.

Unfortunately, she belatedly realized that hers was still lying on the beach as a result of her mad dash for anonymity. "Pen." She poked at her sister's reticent body, still curled under the covers. "I need to borrow your corset. And I need your help fastening it."

When her sister showed no sign of response, Caroline snatched the pillow still covering Pen's face and hit her with it. Sympathy was not chief on her list of emotions this morning. It felt good to unleash some of her annoyance in violence.

"Ow!" Penelope cracked open a reluctant eye. "I am tired this morning. C-can't you ring for Bess?"

Caroline glanced toward the window, where unapologetic bright light streamed in. Usually they would have been roused by a maid an hour ago. "I am sure she is downstairs helping serve breakfast. It appears Mama has instructed her to let us sleep in."

"Well then." Her sister yawned. "We shouldn't disappoint either of them."

Caroline leaned in and sniffed her sister. "Are you sure you want me to ring for Bess? Or should I call Mama? Presuming she has recovered from her headache, I am sure she would be interested in learning why you are still abed and smell like a cannabis cheroot."

Penelope shook her head, and then pushed herself to sitting. "No, I d-don't think that would be a wise idea at all."

Caroline put her hands on her hips. "I managed to get you into bed last night without attracting notice, but if we don't make an appearance at breakfast this morning, Mama will be in here in a thrice, determined to collect every detail of our night."

Penelope eased herself from beneath the embroidered coverlet. "Breakfast sounds like just the thing." She yawned, rubbing her eyes with a fist. "I wonder what we are having?"

A quarter hour's combined effort saw Penelope's face washed, her hair untangled, and Caroline's borrowed corset laced. Unlike Caroline's own stomach, which had declared itself resentful of any expectation of sustenance, Penelope's seemed none the worse for her brush with cannabis. She heaped her plate high with coddled eggs and sausage from the dining room sideboard, and indulged in at least three different varieties of jam on what seemed to be half a loaf of bread.

Caroline sat down at the table and contemplated the meager slice of toast with quince jam on her own plate. Breakfast was poised to be a precarious thing, with the inevitable questions that would come. Worse, last night's humiliation was tapping to be let out of its box. Her faithless stomach roiled in protest, and she wondered if the beef from Miss Baxter's dinner party would make a return appearance after all.

How was Penelope eating so heartily? Miserable, Caroline settled for a cup of tea, its warmth scalding her fingers as she lifted it to her lips.

The sound of a fork being placed on a china plate disrupted the stillness. The copy of the *Brighton Gazette* their mother had been reading crinkled ominously as it was lowered to the table. "Well?" Their mother's coiffure tilted as she regarded them, each in turn. "How was your evening?"

"Fine," Caroline said hastily.

"Quite memorable," Penelope added, impaling a fat sausage with her fork and inhaling it on a low, satisfied groan.

Their mother frowned at Penelope's plate. "I hope you didn't display such a rabid appetite last night, dear. We strive to make a *good* impression. A lady should display a delicate appreciation for food in the company of others."

The urge to protect Penelope hit Caroline as squarely as the first sip of tea on her apologetic, empty stomach. "Pen is just hungry this morning because she ate sparingly at the dinner party," Caroline said through gritted teeth. "As she knew you would want us to."

Although this line of questioning was preferable to the details of what *else* Pen might have eaten last night.

Her mother turned her vivid blue gaze in Caroline's direction, and probed the scant contents of her plate. "Then should I presume by your lack of appetite this morning that you indulged in heartier fare last night?"

Caroline pressed her lips together. As if she could remember whether she had eaten at last night's dinner party or not. Her entire capacity for memory was tied up in what had occurred *after* dessert had been served.

At her lack of response, Mrs. Tolbertson sighed. "This was an opportunity to shine, dear, to show everyone we are a family of substance, to begin the process of entering Brighton's social scene." She hesitated, then leaned forward. "Do you at least believe you made a positive impression with Lord Avery?"

Caroline curved her fingers around her cup, wishing she had just feigned a headache and skipped breakfast all together. "Er . . . I can think of no reason why he should have formed a poor impression." *Given that he was not in attendance.*

Mama's smile stretched wider. "Was Brandon Dermott present last night, perchance?"

Caroline sputtered into her cup. "I beg your pardon?"

"Mr. Dermott," her mother pressed, passing down a napkin as if her youngest daughter had merely hiccupped instead of spewing already-sipped tea. "Pen told me about the young man who asked you to go walking after church a few weeks ago. The Dermotts have been coming to

Brighton for years. I seem to recall he was a handsome youth. You could make a worse match."

Given that she was unlikely to make a match at all, Caroline doubted it.

She clutched her cup's handle as if it was a life ring. "I do not believe Mr. Dermott holds any romantic interest in me, Mama. He . . . only wished to offer his opinion on something." *Such as my kissing abilities.*

"She spent a long time speaking with David Cameron last night." Penelope's voice piped up with the efficiency of an arrow, finding its intended mark. "Mr. Cameron is the son of a Scottish b-baron."

"A *baron*?" her mother exclaimed. "Well, that is an interesting prospect. Is he the heir?"

"A second son." Caroline squirmed in her seat, realizing that she was admitting some knowledge of the man that went beyond a slight acquaintance.

A frown pinched her mother's face. "Is the elder son in town as well?"

Caroline inclined her head, exasperated at the merciless probing. "I do not know, Mama. He mentioned that he was accompanying his mother here while she convalesced after a long illness. Why does it matter?"

"The title, Caroline. Those Scottish baronies are a little murky, I'll admit, but it is usually the eldest who inherits the caput. Although I suppose a second son is better than naught. Where is he staying?"

"He mentioned taking rooms at the Bedford," Caroline said warily. "And he serves as the magistrate in the Scottish town where he lives." Why, of all things, could she remember such a trivial bit of information so clearly?

You know why. It was the last thing he had said before he kissed her the first time.

"Do you like him, dear?"

The question caught Caroline off guard. Yes, she liked him. She liked him very much. But her feelings on the matter were not the point in dispute. "It hardly matters, Mama. Mr. Cameron is not interested in me that way." She swallowed, desperate to halt this detour in the conversation. "He considers me a friend, nothing more."

The admission hurt, no matter that it was the truth.

Penelope sighed dreamily. "I am not sure Caroline is correct. He chose her as a p-partner during the parlor games, and Caroline spent a few lucky moments alone with him on the terrace. And he is almost as handsome as Mr. Dermott, if I might make the observation."

Caroline set her porcelain cup down with enough force that it should have cracked. David Cameron, after all, was far more attractive than Mr. Dermott.

"And what of the overlong conversation you had with the photographer, Pen?" she accused in return. "You seemed rather pleased with yourself when you returned from the terrace with him."

Mrs. Tolbertson's brows jerked upward. Her incredulous gaze darted between both girls. "Terrace? *Alone?* What sort of party was this? Honestly, I depend on you girls to chaperone each other."

"Mr. Hamilton is ever so nice," Penelope said. "He is not just a photographer, he reports on local events for the *Gazette*. He is knowledgeable about an astonishing number of things."

Like hashish, Caroline could not help but think.

"Did you know he produces d-daguerreotypes of the natural settings around Brighton? He exposes a copper plate to iodine vapor, and the resulting silver particles create the image we see. It is a marvelous invention, and I—"

"Penelope." Mama sounded stern.

"The p-potential for this process to revolutionize the printing industry—"

"Penelope!"

"Yes?"

"It is a rare occasion that either of you meet eligible men. I hope you did not subject Mr. Hamilton to such verbosity last night. A lady would have listened patiently."

Penelope looked down at her plate, a flush marring her usually pale cheeks. "I am sure I listened well enough, if I can recall the nature of the pr-process in such detail."

"True," their mother mused. "Although both of you have a remarkable capacity for speech that should be curtailed to some degree in the company of men." She took a determined sip of tea. "Well, we must capitalize on your start last night. Bess mentioned there is a band playing at the pavilion tonight. You will go and make an appearance." Her gaze penetrated the white lace of Caroline's collar. "And I believe I shall send Bess into town this morning and make an appointment with that new modiste on East Street. Madame Beauclerc, did you say her name was?"

"Mama, I do not believe . . . that is, the impression we may have made last night did not go quite as well as you think—"

Caroline was interrupted by Bess, who entered the dining room, bobbed a curtsy, and delivered a card to their mother. "There is a . . . *gentleman* caller here for Miss Caroline," the servant said, her voiced hushed in awe. "I left him in the foyer, although I could put him in the parlor if you prefer."

Caroline's mouth fell open. Her pulse began hammering in her ears even before the desire to bolt from the breakfast table set in. After the disgraceful way she had departed, she had not expected David to call on her today, and certainly not so early. Surely he wouldn't mention anything of their night in front of her family . . .

Her mother fanned herself with one eager hand. "Oh my!" she exclaimed. "A *gentleman* caller. Why, I still recall the day I received three gentlemen callers. That was a day to remember." Her eyes sparked with excitement as she took up the card and read it. Slowly, her hand lowered to the table, and she leveled a shrewd gaze in Caroline's direction.

"Well, my dear, you must have made a better impression than you realized, because someone named Mr. Peter Branson is here to see you."

Chapter 11

CAROLINE UNDERSTOOD WHY Mama would be vibrating with excitement, given the fact they rarely received visitors, much less ones of the gentlemanly variety. But she couldn't help but feel piqued by Bess and Pen's bold curiosity in the proceedings. The pair followed her out of the dining room as well, speaking in noisy whispers.

Mr. Branson was waiting in the foyer. He looked to be in his early twenties, with a straight arrow of a nose, sandy hair, and skin that showed the residual ravages of late adolescence. He was almost as tall as Caroline, and his brown eyes darted from right and left and seemed to settle, more than once, in the vicinity of her skirts.

Heavens. Was he trying to see *through* her skirts?

He was clutching a small bunch of flowers, which Caroline accepted with bewilderment before passing them to Bess. After all, she didn't know this man. She wasn't sure she wanted to know him. If she searched her memory, he looked a bit like one of the useless young gentlemen at Miss Baxter's dinner party last night.

Which wasn't a point in his favor.

"Thank you for receiving me this morning," he said. The voice sparked an unfortunate memory. The words had been slurred, but he sounded very much like one of the voices from the nightmare of her almost-ruin last night.

In lieu of a greeting, Caroline narrowed her eyes. What was this about?

"Mr. Branson." Her mother overcame Caroline's lack of manners and greeted the young man with a smile and an outstretched hand. "We are so delighted to make your acquaintance." She was reminded that her mother, at least, knew how to receive gentlemen callers.

"I am the one who is delighted, Mrs. Tolbertson," he said, offering what on the surface appeared to be a genuine smile. The gesture revealed uneven teeth, and Caroline shifted her uneasy gaze to the ends of his collar, which had been starched to attention. His clothing was the absolute height of fashion, with a necktie instead of a cravat, and a striped waistcoat that would have put Mr. Dermott to shame. No wonder Mama was fluttering about like a moth that had spied a newly lit bonfire.

Regardless of the state of his teeth or his skin, the man's clothing bespoke money.

"Would you care to step into the parlor?" Her mother launched into her role as hostess with practiced ease, as if her fumbling, stumbling daughters received callers on a daily basis. "It is early for visiting hours, but I could ring for some tea and an early luncheon."

Caroline gritted her teeth. For heaven's sake. They hadn't even finished breakfast yet. Neither could they afford to waste the perfectly good repast already laid out on the dining room sideboard.

Mr. Branson, thankfully, answered with a shake of his head. "No thank you. I came so early because of the day's temperature, you see. It promises to be devilishly warm later. I was hoping Miss Caroline would consider taking a walk with me this morning on the Marine Parade."

Caroline's mouth fell open. Her only prior experience with such a thing had been with Mr. Dermott, when he had invited her to walk the length of the Chain Pier after church two weeks ago. Given the way *that* fiasco had turned out, she didn't trust her voice to convey the appropriate sentiment.

Of course, Dermott had orchestrated that scenario to win a wager. He had not presented himself formally to her family, or asked her in such a charming, confident manner.

At the stunned silence that descended on the four women crowding the foyer, Branson shifted from one foot to the other. "I know this is sudden, and that you scarcely know me, but I hail from London. My father owns Branson's Dry Goods, a purveyor of fine—"

"She would be pleased to accept," her mother interrupted, already stepping to the small, ancient bureau they kept near the front door. She pulled out a pair of kidskin gloves from the top drawer. "Penelope, dear, is it all right if Caroline borrows your good sunbonnet?"

"I scarcely think—" Caroline started, but her objections were cut off as Penelope snatched the bonnet from the hat tree, reached up high, and plopped the straw monstrosity on Caroline's head. She tied the ribbons a bit too forcibly under Caroline's chin, then stepped back, tilted her head, and reached out to straighten the brim just so, as if Caroline was a china doll in need of dressing.

At that moment, a knock from the front porch echoed throughout the little foyer. They all froze, including Mr. Branson. Caroline stared suspiciously at the weathered wood. As surreal as the morning had already been, this latest development bordered on shocking.

Had there been a time in recent memory when the Tolbertsons had received not one, but *two* callers during breakfast?

Bess, bless her heart, had enough presence of mind to answer it. The stooped servant stepped back, her lips parted in surprise, to reveal the red-haired reporter, Mr. Hamilton, at the door. The new man's features darkened to a scowl as his gaze fell on Mr. Branson. "Oh, I say. I didn't realize you had planned to call on Miss Tolbertson this morning, Branson."

"I didn't realize you were either," Branson bristled.

Penelope was practically pulsing with excitement. "Oh Mama, this is Mr. George Hamilton. I t-told you about him, with the d-d-daguerreotypes."

Their mother smiled weakly. "Penelope was just mentioning your interesting work, Mr. Hamilton. Mr. Branson and Caroline were heading out for a walk, but perhaps you would like to come in and take tea with us in the parlor?"

Mr. Hamilton's cheeks flushed a suspicious shade of pink, which unfortunately clashed terribly with his hair. His gaze pulled between the two sisters and snagged a long moment on Branson. "I . . . that is . . ." He swallowed, and then offered a curt nod. "Of course. I would be delighted."

Penelope took Mr. Hamilton's arm and led him toward the parlor, stammering away at an impressive pace about silver nitrate solutions and the artistic merit of photographs and such.

Her mother stared after them, finally looking a little flustered. "Have fun, dear," she whispered to Caroline, squeezing her arm.

And then she shooed Caroline out the door with gentleman caller number one, the better to focus on the problem of Penelope potentially scaring off gentleman caller number two.

DAVID CAMERON DISCOVERED he was nervous as he knocked on the Tolbertsons' door. Not nervous enough to let the morning go by without calling on Caroline, but nervous enough to find his palms sweaty and his collar overtight as he stood waiting on the porch.

He'd had a hellish morning, starting with a whisky-induced hangover and memories of a night that left him with a good deal to regret. During breakfast, he couldn't help but notice his mother seemed worse, despite her apparent improvement of yesterday. This morning her lungs squeezed consumptively. The baroness shrugged off his recommendation to fetch a physician and instead insisted on making her way to her noon appointment at Creak's Bathhouse with only her ladies' maid in attendance.

Which left him with several hours alone, and nothing to occupy his time but the need to return Caroline's clothing. And so he had come here, the lost garments hidden in a leather satchel, sick at heart and worried about far too many things.

Would she even see him after how things had ended last night? It pained him to think of her stumbling home in the dark, turning over their kiss in her mind, second-guessing his intentions. He was struggling even to come up with an explanation for what must seem, on the surface, the most egregious sort of behavior.

One did not dally with friends.

Of course, as this was his first experience with a friend of the female variety, he was hard-pressed to enumerate exactly how many rules of etiquette had been breached. He was quite sure that in addition to a dalliance being off-limits, one was also supposed to avoid swimming at midnight with partially clothed female friends.

But some devil in his soul kept whispering he would not be averse to repeating *that* part of the experience.

If only she didn't make him feel so damned conflicted. One moment they had been sitting in the shallow surf, conversation flowing between them. He might have just as easily been with his good friend Patrick Channing, or any of a dozen military associates, sharing the same comfortable words and the same easy camaraderie.

The next moment she had confided her deepest fears and looked up at him with wide, doubting eyes, and instinct had simply taken over.

Well, if history had taught him nothing else, his instincts were not to be trusted.

A round servant with kindly gray eyes answered the door just as he was raising his hand for a second knock. "Yes?" She sounded vaguely suspicious, and David was struck by the sensation that she ought to be. After all, he was not convinced he had good intentions toward the woman's young mistress.

"I am here to see Miss Caroline," David informed her.

"Luh!" The maid's hand fluttered about her chest, and her eyes flew wide, spreading wrinkles far and wide. "I declare, this is a morning to end all mornings! I wonder what that girl's done to get so many young men sniffing about her skirts."

"I beg your pardon?" he managed to extricate from his mouth. The servant's colorful description about sniffing and skirts and such sent his instincts to blazing attention.

"Miss Caroline's gone out!" The servant sputtered a moment, clearly nonplussed. "First there was Mr. Branson, and then Mr. Hamilton. She's gone for a walk with the first one, along the parade."

David blinked, scarcely able to believe his ears. The servant's lack of formality he understood. He too had been raised with servants who were closer to treasured family than domestic help. But *he* had made an appointment to go walking with Caroline today. Yesterday, during their first meeting at the cove. Hadn't he?

He thanked the woman, took his leave, and stood at the bottom of the weatherworn porch steps, sorting out why the idea of Caroline walking with Branson made him feel so uneasy. Perhaps it was the man's drunken reference to Miss Baxter's bubbies last night, or the way he had practically salivated when David had waxed poetic about the merits of long-legged women.

Guilt burrowed its way beneath his collar then. Had

David's enthusiastic description of Caroline's merits last night brought the boys running this morning?

And moreover, why did it bother him so much if it had? Hadn't that been the very *reason* he'd done it, even going so far as to border on exaggeration?

Because, he was able to reason with the harsh insight of sobriety, they were most definitely boys. A man should have been able to see Caroline's positive attributes without a blow-by-blow description delivered by someone else.

And while it was inappropriate—hell, it was utter lunacy—to resent such a meager interaction as a morning walk, his gut told him he didn't want her doing it with anyone else.

Startled by the strength of this unexpected and unwelcome jealousy, David glanced behind him, staring up at the south-facing windows of the grand old house where Caroline lived. He wondered which room was hers. No doubt it would be one facing the ocean she loved so much. The house seemed a bit like her. Tall and narrow, it must have once been a commanding presence along Brighton's oceanfront, although it was now hard to see its raw beauty compared to the dazzling new homes going up in Kemp Town, farther inland and just to the east. Like her, the place lacked polish, but was full of possibilities.

It was the possibilities in the woman that sent his feet moving toward Brighton's center. If she was out walking with that spot-faced young fool Branson, one thing was certain.

He was going to be there to chaperone.

And there would be no sniffing of skirts on his watch.

Chapter 12

CAROLINE WALKED WITH Mr. Branson along the Marine Parade, swathed in such a frightening exuberance of shade-producing paraphernalia she was quite sure the sun was laughing at her.

Not that she could actually hear the sound. Who could, over the incessant nattering of her companion? The man hadn't stopped talking since they stepped out of the foyer.

So far she had heard all about his fourth term at Oxford, the pair of high-steppers he hoped to purchase for the fast new phaeton his father had promised him upon graduation, and the disdain he held for his brother, who might or might not be simple, but whom overall Mr. Branson felt to be a most useless sort of young man.

And so Caroline walked, keeping a weak smile plastered on her face and half an ear on the conversation. The focus of her thoughts pulled more toward her surroundings than Mr. Branson's words. To their right, the businesses along the Marine Parade were awash in cheerful awnings and colorful shutters. To their left, the ocean sat, bright and quiescent. A few miles to the east, her cove waited, the rough, murky surf a distant cousin to the sparkling azure landscape of Brighton's beach.

"My mother and sisters spent much of last winter knitting socks for the Children of Destitute Iron Workers," Mr.

Branson said, out of the blue. And then, for the first time all morning, he asked her a question. "Do you knit?"

She blinked. *Heavens.* Had they just devolved into a discussion about sock knitting? Or was this more of a conversation about women's philanthropic pursuits? She swallowed uneasily. This was what came of keeping half an ear on the conversation. She wondered what other scintillating topics she had missed.

Decided she didn't want to know.

"I am not as proficient at knitting as my sister, Penelope," she murmured in answer. She scratched at her collar with an inefficient, gloved hand, and wondered if it would be considered ill form to fan oneself during a discussion of socks and the like.

They turned onto Shop Street, and the view of the ocean shifted to their backs. Here, a profusion of brick-and-mortar bathing houses lay along the street front, each proclaiming the guarantee of a seawater cure on their painted walls. Just as prolific in number, the Shop Street taverns had their doors flung open, with scullery maids sweeping the stoops in preparation for the noon crowd. The soothing smells of the ocean were crowded out now by the odor of heated shoppers pressed into fashions designed for a more northern clime, and the equally stomach-turning smells of fried fish from street vendor stalls.

Caroline took one sluggish step, then another, and *still* outpaced the dawdling Mr. Branson. At the speed her companion seemed determined to set on this stroll, her hoped-for afternoon swim would not just be unlikely, it would be close to a mathematical impossibility.

Caroline ran through the options in her head, her thoughts chased by Mr. Branson's unending monotone. Allowing two hours to walk to the cove and back, she needed, at a minimum, a three- to four-hour window to attempt a decent swim. It was almost noon, and tea was at four, and she could feel her irritation rising from a long, slow simmer to something threatening to boil.

Why in the devil had Mr. Branson called on her this morning anyway? Not that she objected to a gentleman caller, per se. After all, one needed an occasional suitor to progress to the much-lauded stage of being affianced.

But she didn't like the idea of having to keep his time instead of her own.

And in a flash of insight that made her stomach reach for her knees, Caroline realized what it would mean to marry. There would be an expectation to *listen* to a husband, even if the conversation made her want to tighten the ribbons of her borrowed bonnet to the point of asphyxiation. The issue of whether she had time to take a clandestine swim would be a moot point: a husband could forbid her even to leave the house, particularly if he was keen on sock knitting as an appropriate wifely enterprise. Marrying someone like Mr. Branson, who lived in London and traveled to Brighton only for the occasional holiday, would mean she might never be able to swim again.

She drew in a deep, startled breath. How could she not have seen it before? And why was she seeing it now?

You know. Her conscience prodded her with a hot, gloved finger. Last night, for a few breathtaking seconds, she had glimpsed an alternative to such misery. David Cameron had shown her that, damn the man. And now the idea of the marriage she thought she had wanted felt like a chain-link noose about her neck.

Oblivious to her inner turmoil, Branson stopped in front of a small deserted shop and peered through the window, rubbing the dirty glass with a handkerchief he produced from somewhere in his jacket. "This shop is well positioned, isn't it? I was thinking of suggesting my father consider opening a small shop in Brighton. The city's recent expansion seems lucrative to the issue of dry goods."

It was the first intelligent group of sentences he had strung together this morning, but Caroline couldn't even applaud him for it because her attention was caught by an advertisement that had been plastered to the outside wall of a shop across the street.

She stepped away from the still-chattering Mr. Branson. Picked up her skirts and hurried straight over. Stood in front of it and stared.

43rd Annual BRIGHTHELMSTON
Swimming Competition
Monday, July 25th, Chain Pier
Interested Gentlemen Should Apply in Advance
Creak's Bath House, First Street
Prize: £ 500

The words swam in front of her eyes, familiar and terrifying, all at once.

The competition was held every year and attracted hopeful swimmers from all over England. It was not the first time Caroline had stared at such a poster, or imagined testing her mettle against the hard-weathered locals and soft-bellied London gentlemen who swaggered about the beach each July.

But it was the first time she had actually considered applying.

"See something interesting?" The words were whispered so close to her left ear that Caroline felt the puff of air escape David Cameron's lips.

A startled gasp escaped her. She whirled and knocked a boneless hand against the wall of the man's chest. "I . . . no . . . Oh! You startled me!" she hissed.

"It appears you have abandoned the young Mr. Branson in search of reading material. Did the conversation grow so stilted?"

She glared at him, pleasure and annoyance colliding in

the pit of her stomach at the sight of his tanned skin and curling blond hair. Unlike every other person on the street this morning, he wasn't wearing a hat.

Lucky beast.

He had a leather satchel over one shoulder and was wearing trousers, an old brown sack coat, and a white linen shirt with the top buttons undone. It occurred to her, as she took in his state of casual dress, that she still had this man's evening jacket shoved under her mattress.

"Have you been following us?" she whispered, keeping half an eye on Branson where he still hovered across the street. He was speaking now to the proprietor of the haberdashery located to the left of the empty storefront, and was gesturing to the man with a great deal of enthusiasm. As near as she could tell, Branson had yet to notice she had stepped away.

David shrugged. One rakish brow rose above eyes so blue the ocean looked drab by comparison. "Only to be sure Mr. Branson carries himself off as the gentleman he claims to be. Someone needs to look after you, lass, to make sure these boys stay in line. Who better than a friend like me?" He paused, then offered her a brotherly smile. "I stopped by your house this morning to return your . . . ahem . . . missing items." He patted the leather satchel. "Your servant told me you had already gone out and I dared not leave them with her."

The reminder of their illicit night sent something like gladness rolling through her, and she cursed her instinctive response, given that he seemed unaffected by the memory. *He considers you a friend*, she reminded herself, yet again.

She was becoming sick of the reminder.

"Mr. Branson stopped by and asked me to take a walk," she murmured. "I admit to being surprised by his interest." Why she felt the need to explain, she couldn't be sure. It wasn't as if David had intended to call on her for anything other than the delivery of lost clothing. She might have kissed this man last night, but he seemed unperturbed by the memory.

A thought flew in then, borne on the recollection of her folly. "Branson sounds like one of the men in the cove last night," she said, lowering her voice to the merest of whispers. "Is there any chance he discovered my identity?"

David's eyes narrowed and he considered the back of the man's head a moment before shaking his own. "No, I don't believe so. I stayed awhile after you left to make sure they did not follow, and they seemed convinced I was swimming with a fellow."

Relief flooded her veins. For once, her height and lack of curves had played to advantage. And she supposed it wouldn't have made sense for Branson to present himself so formally this morning if he had discovered her identity.

Indeed, it would make more sense for him to go sprinting the other way.

David jerked his chin toward the poster. "Does the boy Branson know you are considering entering the swimming competition?"

Caroline cast an uneasy glance back at the notice, realizing that if David had so easily guessed her thoughts, Mr. Branson might be able to as well. Not that the young man seemed to have thoughts centering on much beyond dry goods at the moment, but still, the danger was there. "He's not a boy, and I am *not* considering entering."

"It's as plain as the freckles on your nose that you want to."

She turned her back on the notice and glared at the smiling, golden man standing next to her. "Are you trying to ensure my ruin? Because, trust me, teasing me about it where others might hear would do the job as well as anything else."

David's smile faltered. "Ruin is the last thing I have in

mind for you. And I wasn't the one who was staring at the notice as if it was an iced cake."

"Staring at it carries far less potential for disaster than talking about it." She offered up a prayer Mr. Branson hadn't seen the poster, or her focused interest in it. She already had a floundering reputation, thanks to Mr. Dermott's casual insults over the past few weeks. And if she had learned nothing else from the unfortunate experience of her first kiss, it was that the summer set thrived on gossip and ill will.

But despite her agitation, Caroline's thoughts crept back to the newsprint.

The promise of a five-hundred-pound prize was a temptation so bright her eyes still stung from the encounter. The purse for the winner had increased remarkably from previous years. That, coupled with her astonishing moonlit conversation with David last night, shifted her thinking toward dangerous territory. She had promised her father she would take care of her family, and she had always imagined that she must do so through marriage.

Her mind wandered farther afield. Such a sum might grant her a reprieve from this distasteful business of finding a husband so quickly.

But the money wasn't the only thing. Swimming was a part of who she *was*, even if it was a part she kept hidden from the world. This was a man who not only knew her terrible secret, but was encouraging her to pursue it. The idea that she might share this part of herself with someone else touched an empty place in her chest.

She cursed the mad leap of her heart, and stomped across the wide swath of street. She pointed her feet toward Branson, who was still speaking with the haberdasher. David, damn his persistence, trotted along beside her like a stray bent on a handout.

He had no trouble keeping her pace, she couldn't help but notice.

"It would be a chance to demonstrate your swimming skills," he murmured, the words delivered in a breath so low it might as well have been the wind.

Her thoughts tumbled chaotically, but she managed to choke out, "No."

How dare David Cameron make her think? How dare he make her *hope*?

A woman would not be permitted to compete. The notice had been quite clear. Interested *gentlemen* should apply in advance. As if it was even necessary to specify such a distinction.

"Why not give it a go?" David asked, matching her stride for stride.

She gritted her teeth. He was being ridiculously persistent. While it might be an admirable quality in a magistrate, in a friend it bordered on just cause for murder.

They had almost reached the storefront and were coming within earshot of Mr. Branson. Fearing what else David might say, Caroline grabbed his arm and jerked him into the shadow of a parked hansom cab. Through the slats in one wheel, she could still see Branson's hunched back and flapping hands.

She settled her gaze on the far more delicious—but far more dangerous—man standing next to her. "Even if I possessed the gall to submit an application," she whispered heatedly, "and even if the race officials lost all sanity and permitted a woman to compete, such a public declaration of my abilities would be the death knell for any hope of a good match."

She lifted stern eyes to his, expecting to see sympathy there, or worse, amusement.

Instead, she saw only determination.

"Then teach me your swimming stroke," he said. "Let

me be the one to compete. And I will gladly split the purse with you."

HER LIPS OPENED in wordless surprise beneath the shadow cast by her bonnet. He had surprised her.

Good. She had surprised him too. He had thought her a sensible creature, after all, and then she had gone off walking with Branson, who possessed precisely two interests in his thick head: dry goods and bubbies.

"I am serious, Caroline." God knew he could use the diversion the swimming competition would provide, almost as much as he could use the prize money. Though he remained determined to spend every available second with his mother, the minutes the baroness had granted him so far were negligible, at best. And his mother would be occupied with recuperative treatments every afternoon of this trip, leaving him time to spare.

The idea had grown teeth almost since the moment he had seen Caroline staring at the poster with undisguised longing in her eyes. Despite his teasing, he knew it was an impossible idea for her to compete. But if Brighton refused to acknowledge the admirable young woman he was coming to know, it at least deserved to see the stroke she wielded with such skill.

He had no doubt of his capacity to win if he devoted himself to the exercise and Caroline showed him her secrets, and the Scottish side of him delighted in the idea of proving a foreign swimming stroke could outpace a perfectly constructed English crawl. It would also be a convenient way to remove Caroline from harm's way, given the fumbling interests of the boys of summer.

He promptly squashed the unwelcome thought that it would also permit him to spend more time with her.

Alone.

The only sticky part was convincing her. And at the moment, she looked far from convinced.

As her expression shifted from surprised to cautious, it occurred to him, like a sudden slap to the face, that she looked different today. The dress she was wearing this morning was not the reason—like all the dresses he had seen her in, it was cut in a less than flattering style, as if fashioned for a woman two inches shorter. But the bonnet on her head was trimmed with a pretty blue ribbon, and her white kidskin gloves looked utterly proper, if a bit too warm. There was even a reticule looped over one of her wrists, some beaded bit of frippery that would have looked at home on any of the other ladies prowling Shop Street.

Somehow, on Caroline, it all looked out of place. The image he carried with him, the image he preferred, was that of a woman in ill-fitting clothes, her freckled nose turned up to the sun, daring Mother Nature to do her worst. Had Caroline added these fashionable accoutrements for Branson, then? The thought sent his fingers curling, even though he had spent the prior evening drunkenly encouraging just such a possibility.

"You want me to teach you to swim?" she asked, her eyes wide.

He nodded, encouraged by the fact that she was no longer handing him a vehement no. "You've a brilliant technique. And I would like nothing more than to beat Dermott using it."

Her eyes flew wider still. "Dermott is entering again this year?"

David permitted himself a careful, casual shrug. "I would imagine. The man is quite the swimmer, to hear him tell it. The braggart challenged me to a race last night even though he could scarcely put one foot in front of the next. I cannot see him forgoing such an opportunity."

Caroline's jaw tensed. "The competition is less than a week away," she told him, though her voice had turned breathless. "That is not enough time."

"Lucky for you, I am a quick study." David chased his

words with one of his most rakish grins, enjoying the flicker of emotion that his words conjured on her face. He had offered her almost the same phrase last night, during the middle of their kiss—the kiss that, if he was brutally honest with himself, he wanted to repeat. The mere memory of it sent his body perking up in interest. He quelled it with a muttered oath. He needed to stop going down this perverse path. If she agreed to this bit of proposed lunacy, they would be engaged in swimming instruction, nothing more.

"We would have to practice every day," she warned, her lips finally tipping upward into a smile. "Including today, we would have only five opportunities until the day of the competition."

The tension ebbed from David's shoulders. She was going to do it. He had to reach for the bit of maturity it took to not rub his hands together in anticipation as he imagined the look on Dermott's face when he was bested.

Or the look on this woman's face when he provided her with the financial means to carve out an independent life.

"Given that I suspect you swim nearly every day, I can't imagine it will be too much of a hardship." He nodded toward Branson, who had ceased his animated conversation with the haberdasher and was now scanning the street in confusion. "Five lessons, including Sunday. We can start this afternoon, as soon as you inform your admirer his company is no longer needed."

Or welcome, he added silently.

"He's not my admirer." Caroline sighed, stepping out from behind the carriage and raising a hand to snag the man's attention. "I don't know why he wanted to walk with me in the first place. He seems far more interested in the potential of an empty shop than the thoughts I might keep in my head."

"He seems to be interested enough in you right now." David couldn't help but notice the way the boy's face lit up like Christmas morning as his gaze fell on Caroline.

"He will want to tell his father about the empty shop. I shall claim a headache and have him take me home, then encourage him to run along and speak with his father."

David nodded, his eyes fixed on the young man. As if summoned by David's stare, Branson began to walk toward them, the merest hint of a swagger infusing his stride. Damn it, the fop looked all of sixteen years old. No matter his encouragement of the young buck last night, this was not the man David would choose for Caroline. Hell, this was not a *man* at all.

And what sort of gentleman abandoned the lady he was walking with to peer moon-eyed through empty windows?

"Will you be able to meet me on the beach in an hour?" The thought of leaving her alone with Branson for even the quarter hour it would take for the man to return Caroline home chafed, but David could see no way around it.

She nodded. "My mother is used to me going for walks most afternoons. It will not be a problem to slip away. And with the store as an excuse, disengaging Mr. Branson's company should be a simple enough matter."

David forced himself to step away and put a more respectable distance between them as Branson rounded the side of the cab. Yes, it should be a simple enough matter. *Today.*

But as the sandy-haired swain approached Caroline with a bright, besotted smile on his face, David had a sinking suspicion that convincing this suitor to permanently cry off was not going to be anything close to simple.

Chapter 13

It soon became clear to Caroline she hadn't given proper thought to the mechanics of a swimming lesson with David Cameron.

Oh, she'd had an hour's hike to sort out how she would teach him. She intended to go about it the same way her father had taught her, starting him off on the rocky shelf about two dozen yards from shore, where he could get his feet under him if he ran into trouble. She would have David practice the overhand stroke first, then work on his kick after he became accomplished at the arm motions. Eventually, she would test his skills against the wrath of the ocean, working him first at low tide and progressing to deeper and more dangerous waters.

Only, in agreeing to this plan, she had neglected to consider the necessary matter of clothing. Or rather, the *lack* of clothing.

David was waiting, still dressed, when she arrived. But as she approached, he tossed the leather satchel he was carrying onto the shore and began to shrug first out of his coat, then his shirt. Seeing him strip on this very beach under the moonlight had been a lung-crushing enough experience. But seeing him emerge now, under bright sunlight, every glorious imperfection highlighted, was something else entirely.

Today she could see a small scar that traversed his left rib cage. The tiny lines at the corner of his eyes reminded her that this man was older than she, and far more experienced. The whorls of hair on his chest sent her imagination hurtling downward to where the trail disappeared into his trousers.

Trousers that even now were being unbuttoned.

"You should leave them on," she objected.

He offered her a tilted grin. "You saw me in my unutterables last night."

"Nonetheless. It was dark last night." Her voice pinched within her throat. "And you did not give me a choice."

His grin turned rakish, but his fingers fell away from the buttons. "So I'm to sacrifice a perfectly good pair of trousers to preserve your delicate sensibilities?" His voice softened, though his gaze remained sharp. "Clothing is expensive. You should know this isn't just a lark for me, Caroline. I need the money every bit as much as you do."

His admission of his financial state was jarring, but not enough to smother her desire to see him clad in something more than smallclothes. "When you win, you shall be able to afford a dozen new pairs of trousers," she pointed out. "But you shall not win without my assistance, and you shall not receive my assistance without some degree of modesty."

He heaved a sigh, and made a great show of stepping toward the ocean with his trousers on, hands up and out, offering his bare back as penance. "At the risk of pointing out the obvious," he called back to her, "how do you propose to teach me if you remain trussed up in a corset?"

"Do not worry about that," she shouted, startled by the thought as much as the blasted man's phrasing. The gown she had on buttoned in the front, at least, or else she never would have attempted this. She glanced toward David, who was standing, knee-deep in the surf. "Face the horizon. Stretch your muscles vigorously. Your body should be limber before you attempt to swim."

A low chuckle reached her ears, but he began to make a great show of flapping his arms.

When she was satisfied the lout at least knew how to follow instructions, she crouched to pick up the discarded satchel, turning over his words in her mind. Somehow, in spite of her mother's probing questions on the matter, she had presumed David solvent. Given her family's own precarious finances, she could appreciate his desire to pursue this opportunity.

But this was a lot of pressure to place on her shoulders, which were already weighed down by the promise she had given her father. Worse, his frank explanation of the matter established, in no uncertain terms, how unsuitable a match with him would be, no matter his father's title, and no matter how the sight of his bare chest made her body flush hot.

Not that it mattered. He had made it quite clear he was not interested in her that way.

She was here to teach David Cameron how to swim, not to convince him to offer for her. If he did not look at her with longing, there was little she could do about it. At the very least, he looked at her with respect, which was more than Dermott had ever offered. And so she would relish the moments of friendship he offered. She would try to be brave.

Or at the very least, try not to be nauseous.

Caroline stepped behind the large rock that dominated the shoreline and undressed down to her shift. She ran her hands over the fabric, testing the weight of the cotton and finding it woefully lacking. Her lack of curves might have been hidden by shadows last night, but there would be no missing their absence today.

Still, he was right. She couldn't very well teach David to swim while encumbered by crinolines and corsets. She would be dragged under the water the minute she stepped into the ocean.

Caroline opened the lid of the satchel and rummaged a moment. Slippers, gown, corset. Leftover reminders from a night that should not have happened. But she could not bring herself to regret the experience, not when David had guarded her reputation by gathering up her lost things, and not when she was here with him again.

She pulled out the navy serge dress in her hands, contemplating her options. It still bore traces of sand and crushed shells, remnants from her brush with stupidity the previous evening. It didn't even fit her properly, having been fashioned some years back before her shoulders had sprouted. She had worn the dress to Miss Baxter's dinner party like an unattractive shield, hoping it would protect her against the slashing talons of the summer set. The fabric was a winter weight, thick and substantial.

Even wet, David would not be able to see through it. And he *had* sacrificed his trousers.

"Do you happen to have a penny knife?" she called out to the man she prayed was still standing to his knees in water.

"In my coat pocket, lass." His brogue came rumbling over the sound of the waves, doing delicious things to her insides. She peeked over the top of the rock, and when she was satisfied he still had his back turned, she scrambled for the knife.

Wielding it in her right hand, Caroline set about removing as much excess fabric from the old dress as discretion permitted, then stepped into the ruined garment. It was still not ideal. The bodice was too constricting for deep breaths. The ragged hemline swung somewhere around her knees, leaving her legs free for the necessary movements but revealing too much skin for comfort.

But it was better than nothing, and nothing would not do.

Perhaps this, in the end, was why ladies didn't swim. Not because of a lack of ability, or a dearth of want, but because of a preponderance of fabric in all the wrong places.

As near as she could tell, a lady determined to swim in the presence of a gentleman had only two options: death by drowning, or expiration from embarrassment.

Either would do a girl in right quick.

HAD CAROLINE TOLBERTSON been born a man, she would have made a brilliant drill sergeant.

She wrangled David's limbs into ruthless formation as she barked her commands. She declared Britain's revered breaststroke "a waste of time and energy" and made him practice the new steps over and over again, pitting him against the hellish current, positioning him to meet the fury of the ocean head-on. It was exhausting work.

And yet, it was over far too soon.

He'd barely begun to wrap his head around it, barely begun to imagine he might be able to apply these skills in an actual race, when she nodded for shore. "That's enough for today. Your stamina is not quite up to the demands of open water yet."

David coughed, his chest burning as much from exertion as from the multiple mouthfuls of seawater that had found their way inside his lungs. He had only four more lessons to master this stroke, and he was beginning to realize that for all she made it look easy, Caroline's unique style of swimming required a degree of skill that he wasn't sure he possessed. "I'll have you know I can march twenty miles a day in full military regalia," he choked out.

"I would question whether such a skill is useful even on land." She began wading toward shore, leaving him to follow. "Endurance is the key to this race, David," she tossed over her shoulder. "Success in open water requires more than brute strength. It's more a matter of using the current to advantage than defeating it outright. And you've yet to experience the threat of this inlet at the point of high tide. If you're to have any hope of winning next week, you must be able to swim no matter the tide cycle."

David pushed after her. He couldn't deny the logic. They hadn't even left the rock shelf once this afternoon, and he had been grateful every time his toes scraped against the bottom. His arms and legs felt none too solid, and he found himself relieved she hadn't put him to the test.

Yet.

But there was no doubt that test needed to come soon. The more she had drilled him, the more hopeful he had become regarding the prospect of winning. His portion of the prize money would be the equivalent of two or more years' salary for someone like his friend Patrick Channing, who eked out a respectable living as Moraig's veterinarian. Or it would be six months' blunt for a London dandy like Mr. Dermott. That amount of money would not solve his financial problems, but it would carry him to a place where his investments began to pay out.

And now that he had met Caroline, now that he had brushed up against her innocence and been reminded so forcefully of his own shortcomings, he was more determined than ever to avoid the sort of hell that would come from marrying a naïve young chit to solve his financial questions.

"What comes next?" he asked as he dragged himself from the surf, half fearing she would direct him to perform more calisthenics while she jeered at his lack of endurance.

This time, she offered him a smile instead of an order. "I usually dry out a bit before attempting to dress."

David eyed the shingle beach at his feet. Surely she didn't stretch out and sun herself there. That mermaid bit was a jest, after all. Although, the thought of an hour's walk back to Brighton, with coarse sand and crushed shells rubbing beneath wet clothing was about as appealing at this moment as another go in the surf.

Caroline clambered up onto the big rock that rose up about ten feet back from the water. She pulled out her hairpins, shook out her damp tresses, and settled into a self-conscious sprawl, tugging her altered dress as low as it would reach. Then, with her eyes closed, she turned her face up to the sun.

And David, once he had fully recovered his breath, could do no more than stare in stupid wonder.

During this morning's conversation on Shop Street, he had enjoyed her company immensely. But much of that enjoyment had been cerebral in nature, the pleasure of sparring with her well-equipped mind. The ill-advised urge to kiss her again had been there, hovering below the surface, but it was easily tempered on a public street with Branson serving as a bloody spectator. During their swimming lesson she had been covered to her neck in water and her lips had been issuing such terse commands that more pleasant options for her mouth were the last thing on his mind.

But now, the barely clad creature sunning herself on the rock clear snatched every thought from his head save one: Caroline Tolbertson was bloody beautiful.

The water-soaked remnants of what had been a hideous gown skirted the contours of her lithe body, meandering along gentle curves that stretched the eye and the imagination. The sunlight dazzled his eyes, gathering momentum from the white cliffs and bouncing off the sparkling water. That light fell on thick, waving hair that he could now see wasn't just brown, but shot through with a hundred shades of gold and umber.

Had he a rope and enough nerve, he would have bound her hands, just to keep her from bundling those damp, vibrant tresses back up into the stern knot she preferred.

Then, of course, there was the problem of her legs. There were yards and yards of them, stretching from beneath the hem of her torn-off gown. As his eyes skimmed the neat indentation in one of Caroline's calves, it occurred to him that before last night, David had never given much thought to a woman's legs. He'd only blathered on and on about them to foster his drunken comrades' imaginations. Today, presented with such a delightful view of Caroline's, he found he couldn't stop thinking about them.

It was as if last evening's whisky-inspired soliloquy had brought this nightmare to life and now he was destined to think of nothing else.

Despite a reminder to behave, despite even a stern mental curse or two, his lower body stirred at the sight she presented. Damn his imagination to hell and back. He sent up a prayer of thanks that Caroline's eyes were tightly closed against the sun, because he was quite sure he would give her an eyeful should she choose to look.

David settled himself on the rock beside her, welcoming the distraction of the sun-warmed stone beneath his bare shoulders. He kept his gaze trained on the cliffs that stretched above him, counting the swallows and admiring their dizzying acrobatics, probing the crevices that peeked down from hundred-foot walls.

Anything to keep his eyes off her legs.

Gradually, the beauty of the place shoved its way in front of his humming awareness of her. His senses felt assaulted. The stinging warmth of the sun was eclipsed only by the pungent smell of salt and vegetation and the constant, earthy rumble of waves. His gaze settled on the high watermarks visible against the white chalk walls. He lingered there a moment, admiring the artistic contrast of dark against light.

But then he sat bolt upright as the meaning of those marks registered in his sun-fogged head. She had not been exaggerating when she said a high tide could be dangerous in this inlet.

He turned over onto his stomach and examined the cliff walls more closely. The bird's nests that dotted the haggard natural landscape were constructed no lower than five or six feet from the ground, suggesting the swallows understood the danger of the little cove far better than he had. He cast a searching glance toward the ocean. They seemed to be at a mid-point in the tide cycle at the moment. But in a few hours, he wondered if even this rock might be surrounded by roiling surf. Did she swim here at high tide too? The thought made his fists clench.

He was behaving well today, keeping her relegated to the status of "friend" that their circumstances required. He had not tried to kiss her again, though his thoughts had flown there on more than one occasion. During their lesson, he had not even tried to touch her, beyond what was necessary to the process of learning where to place his hands and feet in the water. He had reminded himself— several times—that she was not what he wanted, and he was not what she deserved.

But that did not make the thought—nay, the *fear*—of losing her any less staggering.

"I don't want you swimming here alone anymore, lass." The words ejected themselves from his mouth before he could think better of it.

Though he would have expected a far more visceral reaction—an uppercut, possibly—she struggled to sitting and gaped at him. "I beg your pardon?"

"It is too dangerous." He was going to be stubborn about this, apparently. He lifted an accusing hand to the watermarks along the cliff walls.

Her lips settled into a thin line. "I do not take unnecessary risks, David." Her eyes sparked at him, a thousand small mirrors reflecting the beauty and the danger of the place.

"That in itself is a dangerous, naïve presumption. Swimming alone, especially when you do not have to, is a completely unnecessary risk." The words pushed out of him, hard and unrepentant. They were true, even if they were not kind. "Promise you will not swim here without me."

Color suffused her cheeks. She shook her head. "I told

you, I think a person's word is one of the most important things they can offer. And while I appreciate the concern, I cannot make such a promise, especially to someone who is only here for another week or so."

Irritation made him imprudent. "I could reveal your activities to your mother."

But she was already sliding down off the far side of the rock, disappearing from sight. From the frantic rustling that reached his ears, he presumed she was getting dressed. Her voice, when it floated to him over the rock, was clipped and angry. "Yes, you could. But as she never leaves our house, there is little she can do to stop me either." She paused, then peered over the edge of the rock. "I have shared my secret with you, David, though it could easily ruin me. I hope you will not betray that trust."

Shame coursed through him then. But hadn't he warned her he was not a man to be trusted? History, certainly, had painted him as such, and he had come to believe it.

He jumped down from the other side of the rock and picked up his shirt. He shook off a small crab that was hiding in the collar before sliding his arms in the sleeves, one angry jerk at a time. He was still buttoning it when she stalked around the edge of the rock, her legs respectably covered in lavender sprigged muslin and her hair ruthlessly pulled back.

She paused in front of him, holding out a boot he had not yet realized he was missing. "I would have your word that you will not divulge my secret, David. As a gentleman."

He accepted the offering, his fingers tightening over the worn leather surface. "I thought we established such a title does not fit."

"There is honor in you. I feel it. And I would have it directed toward this matter."

David wavered, uncomfortable with her presumption, but unable to let her leave angry. He pulled his foot into the boot and started on the other. "I will not tell, if you will promise that while I am here in Brighton, you will let me swim with you." He did not add that he would discard whatever he was doing to accompany her and ensure her safety. He straightened and offered her a half grin, willing the suspicion to lift from her eyes. "After all, I need frequent practice if I am to win for us on Monday."

The tense line of her shoulders softened. "I suppose I could promise. But only until the race. I will not promise anything beyond that."

Relief settled over him, but it was tinged with regret. What was he doing? And what was she doing *to* him? Beyond the swimming competition on Monday, Caroline Tolbertson was not his concern. Or at least, she was not *supposed* to be his concern. They were committed to this course now, their futures pinned on the promise of a purse he could see he was going to have to work hard for.

But there was more at stake than money.

He knew he should limit his time with her. He was leaving for Scotland in ten—no, nine days now, for Christ's sake.

And yet, as he handed her the leather satchel containing the rest of her clothing, he found his treacherous heart asking, "Will I see you tonight? I hear there is a band playing at the pavilion. I would have you save me a dance, if you are willing."

"Oh yes. The band. I had quite forgotten about that." She sighed, and her mouth turned down in a frown. "My mother expects me to attend. I imagine she will be quite insistent now that Mr. Branson has declared some interest."

The reminder of how he had unleashed the swain on Caroline grated like sand in places best left unmentioned. "You know, when I win this race, you will have two hundred and fifty pounds," he offered as they began to walk toward the footpath that would carry them back to Brighton. "Perhaps you would not have to marry."

Indeed, he was banking on that same outcome for himself.

"When you win? That's quite hopeful of you, isn't it?" she asked in amusement.

David shrugged. "With your swimming stroke, I don't see how we can lose."

"Not to deflate such a hopeful sort of pride, but unless you improve significantly in both form and speed in the next four days, I very much doubt my chances for a reprieve from marriage."

"You don't think I can win?"

"I shall withhold judgment until I see how you progress in our next lesson." She offered him a resigned smile. "But even if, by some miracle, you are able to win this race, I cannot see how half the purse would be enough to delay my search for a husband. I am afraid I am still bound for the altar, David. And there is little you can do to change my course."

Chapter 14

THE MUSICIANS PLAYING at the open-air pavilion that evening wielded their French horns like weapons, aimed at the ears and hearts of Brighton's summer visitors. As if they too had been imbued with hopes of seeing the royal family, the band opened the evening's festivities with a rousing tune of "God Save the Queen."

Even if lacking an actual queen.

Caroline was beginning to wonder if Miss Baxter was either an outright liar, or just grossly misinformed.

Undeterred by the obvious lack of royalty in attendance, the crowd roared its approval, and the band responded by swinging into an infectious military rhythm that had couples pairing off to dance in short order.

Caroline stood on the outskirts of the pavilion's mayhem, a flute of champagne clutched in her hand. Though she still felt out of place, she felt better much here than she had at last night's dinner party. The salt-kissed breeze coming off the ocean soothed her discomfort, and the sheer volume of people in attendance made it easy to stand in the shadows. She did not yet see David among the crowd, though she had scrutinized every man on the dance floor taller than herself. The process had taken all of a minute, given how few men could lay claim to that bit of fame.

Mama had remained home again, depending on Penelope and Caroline to serve as each other's chaperone, although this time she had sent them off with stern instructions against forays onto darkened terraces. Penelope was pulled almost immediately onto the dance floor, and so there was no one to judge Caroline if she was not partnered for a dance, or if she indulged in one glass too many.

As if to test the theory, she tipped the flute to her lips and drained her third glass of champagne. She wondered if she should have a fourth. She was still feeling parched, and her first three glasses had rapidly fallen to the sort of desperate thirst that came from a too-long day of sun and swimming. Not that she regretted the day. It had been a revelation, both in the enjoyment of David's company and the realization that, despite his loutish delivery, he had cared enough for her to express a great deal of worry. Cared enough for her, even, to demand she swim only with him. It was hard to be angry with such a man.

He had made her hope again, even if that hope was a fragile thing, cupped in hands as likely to shatter the emotion as nurture it.

Caroline placed the empty flute on a nearby tray and scanned the crowd, looking for her sister's familiar face. *There.* On the far side of the pavilion, spinning around the room in Mr. Hamilton's arms. She had lost Penelope to the persistent red-haired reporter within minutes of arriving in the crush, and she had been pleased by Mr. Hamilton's apparent shift in affections. In fact, Penelope's behavior of the past few days was nothing short of astonishing if one considered the years of bookish intensity and painful stammering that trailed her sister like an unfortunate cloud.

But there was no cloud in sight tonight, either in the sunset-tinged night sky or in Penelope's bright, excited smile. Beneath the blazing lanterns that hung from the ceiling of the open-walled pavilion, Penelope looked more than happy—she looked transformed. Caroline could admit to herself that attending Miss Baxter's dinner party had been a good thing, for at least *one* of the Tolbertson sisters.

A rustling at her elbow sent her heart pounding, and Caroline turned, pleasure already loping ahead of her brain. But instead of David Cameron, a gentleman she didn't recognize stood a foot or so away. He had brown eyes and a crooked nose. Though he couldn't have been much older than twenty, his brown hair was already thinning on top, but it curled around his ears in a hopeful fashion.

"Good evening," he said, as if he approached too-tall wallflowers every day. "We have not yet had the pleasure of a formal introduction. My name is Gabriel Adams."

"Miss Caroline Tolbertson," she said, trying to push her confusion out of sight. He seemed familiar, and as she searched her memory, she landed on the disturbing image that placed him in her mind. Mr. Adams had been at Miss Baxter's house party.

And he had been taking a deep, appreciative drag on the end of a cannabis cheroot.

Before Caroline could recover her composure, which had quite flown to the far corners of the room at his unsolicited approach, he offered her a smile that had the misfortune of making him appear even younger. "Might I request the pleasure of your company in a dance, Miss Tolbertson?"

DAVID ARRIVED JUST as the band shifted from some sharp patriotic march to a high-stepping waltz. He craned his neck, searching for the woman whose head he knew would be easily visible among the rest of the crowd.

He spied her almost immediately. She was still wearing that ill-fitting dress with the little purple flowers on it, and it struck him that she didn't seem to own a single gown that fit. But then all thoughts of dresses and flowers disappeared, and the anticipation that had followed him to the pavilion turned to annoyance as he realized she was dancing.

To his surprise, given her general awkwardness at other social niceties, Caroline appeared to be quite a good dancer, sure-footed and quick through the intricate steps. David didn't recognize the gentleman she was dancing with, but he recognized the look on the man's face. A nearly identical expression was stamped on Mr. Branson's face, on the other side of the dance floor. The boy was staring at the couple, shifting from foot to foot, looking for all the world like a puppy without a stick to chase.

"Good evening, Mr. Cameron. You seem remarkably focused on the music, for someone not dancing."

David tore his eyes away from the vision of Caroline and her dance partner to find Miss Baxter standing next him. She too was staring at the couple on the dance floor. And she too had a perplexed and not wholly pleased look on her pretty face.

"The fact that I am not dancing seems less problematic than the fact that you are not, Miss Baxter," he pointed out. "How is it that so many gentlemen have squandered such a rare opportunity?"

"If you must know, Mr. Adams was promised this dance, although his mind seems to have deserted him on that matter. Not that I blame him. Miss Tolbertson appears to possess an unexpected degree of grace on the dance floor."

David's instincts marched toward high alert. Miss Baxter was, after all, a part of the summer set that tormented Caroline. "You sound surprised."

"Well, she lives in *Brighton*, Mr. Cameron. I would not have thought she had much opportunity to dance. And she is just so very tall. Mr. Dermott told everyone—"

"Mr. Dermott is an idiot who wouldn't know a diamond from a horse apple."

Miss Baxter's eyes widened. She regarded him a pensive moment before her mouth twitched upward. "I shall have to remember that," she said lightly, "because I am ever so fond of diamonds."

David's shoulders relaxed at the defused threat. Though her carefully coiled red curls came far short of his chin, Miss Baxter carried herself with confidence, a fact he could admire, even if the sentiment fell short of genuine attraction. She might not yet be an ally in his quest to change the summer set's opinion of Caroline, but that didn't mean she couldn't be.

He extended his hand. "Would you care to dance, Miss Baxter?"

Her cheeks went from pale to pink. She flashed one more pointed look toward the couple whirling by them. And then she placed her hand in his.

"I would be delighted."

He was a heartless brute, truly he was. Because Miss Baxter was indubitably the most beautiful woman in the pavilion tonight. She was the daughter of a viscount, and no doubt had a dowry that would solve every financial problem he had ever entertained.

And yet, as he took two turns around the floor with this vibrant woman in his arms, he could think of nothing beyond a simmering annoyance that he could not get closer to Caroline. He listened with half an ear cocked toward the stream of chatter Miss Baxter was feeding him. Something about who had done what with whom and why it was important that they *not* do it again. And the entire time he tried to maneuver closer to Caroline, employing every military tactic he knew so that when the music finally changed, he was positioned right beside her.

As the band transitioned into the lilting strains of a new song, he all but shoved a surprised Miss Baxter into Mr. Adams's arms, snatched Caroline up in his own, and set off at a determined clip. Caroline's body flowed into his arms, sending his mind careening in a very dangerous direction as they began their own sojourn around the crowded dance floor.

Her mouth, however, did not follow the steps as well as her feet.

"That was a bit uncalled for." There was a slight drawl to her vowels, telling David that whatever else Caroline was enjoying tonight, she had also enjoyed several glasses of champagne. "Mr. Adams was a pleasant dancer, and I was enjoying his company."

"You don't want a pleasant dancer."

"Don't I? Who are you to tell me what I want?" Her lips pressed against each other in irritation. It occurred to him, though he wished it had not, that he had kissed those lips the previous evening. They appeared harder now than the ones in his memory.

Then again, last night they had been framed by moonlight and murmuring his name.

David spun Caroline around with a tad more force than was necessary. "You spent the afternoon instructing me on technique, so turnabout is only fair. I offer my opinion on the matter so you do not make a mistake."

"I know how to dance, David. 'Tis the one thing my mother taught me that stuck."

He could find no disagreement with that. Indeed, she knew how to dance very well. He could feel her body moving in perfect time to the music, even through the layers that separated their skin. "Dancing is a bit like kissing. You can know the motions, you can even practice the steps, but choosing a partner who is your proper match makes all the difference in the encounter."

She raised a dark brow. "Mr. Adams knows how to dance as well."

"You described him as a pleasant dancer, which is not the emotion a good partner should conjure." He leaned forward, until they were pressed indecently against each other, muslin to wool, breast to chest. "For example, would you label me a pleasant dance partner?"

Her body quivered in his arms. She tripped over a step. Righted herself. Shook her head. "Not precisely."

"Mr. Adams knew the steps, but he didn't make *you*

forget them. You should be so caught up in the experience you don't even think about the placement of your feet."

She swallowed. "You seem to have mastered the effect."

He nodded, satisfied she finally understood what he was trying to tell her. "*That* is what you need to look for in a match, Caroline. Do not settle for bland. You need a partner who can match your spirit if you are to find the lifetime of happiness you deserve."

She searched his eyes, even as he did his best to ensure the room spun around them. "And if I believe I may have already found such a partner?"

This time, it was *his* turn to almost trip. Her words hit him in some deep, primitive part of his brain, but beyond the first glad flash of male-soaked pride, reason quickly took over. He realized, with sudden and startling clarity, that Caroline was staring at him with very much the same expression that Mr. Branson had on his face while watching her.

And while his pulse danced faster at her words, his head reacted in completely the opposite fashion. When Caroline was playing along nicely in the platonic role he had assigned her, it was easier to deny his own feelings. But now, when she was looking at *him* as if he might be an iced cake, his thoughts became panicked.

How could he not have seen it? How could he have so completely missed the sort of emotion she hoped for, emotions he could not admit even to himself? In the past eleven years, he had never let himself get close enough to a woman to risk this. He had convinced himself Caroline was a safe sort of danger to him, a friend with whom he could control his baser instincts.

Remorse didn't just nudge him then, it cuffed him over the head. *Goddamn it.* How had this progressed from a bit of not-quite-innocent instruction to something far more precarious? There was no mistaking her suggestion. She believed him to be her match.

And there was no mistaking his necessary response.

Chapter 15

"THEN YOU SHOULD be dancing with him instead of me," David told her as he maneuvered them across the pavilion floor.

Caroline blinked against the hurtful words. The light breeze coming in through the pavilion's open walls held not even a prayer to cool the sudden scald of humiliation that washed over her. "I . . . I thought . . ." she stammered, every bit as tongue-tied as her sister usually was.

He gave her hand a gentle squeeze. A *brotherly* squeeze. The blue eyes she had spent much of the afternoon staring into shifted to scan the other couples, a marked departure from his attentive gaze of just moments before. "Let us peruse the crowd for someone who might be a better partner for you than Mr. Adams or that slavering pup Branson."

The music from the brass band, which had shimmered with promise only moments before, tarnished in her ears. She didn't understand. Hadn't they been getting on well? Hadn't David kissed her, without any hint of duress, not once, but twice?

Hadn't he just wrestled her out of another man's arms, for no purpose other than having a go with her on the dance floor?

"I don't want to dance with someone else," she told

him. Her mind, which had been tied up in knots, began to slip free. In fact, it started sliding down the steepest of slopes, tumbling end over end, with only one possible outcome in sight. "I want to dance with *you*."

He shook his head, a notion that made him appear unexpectedly vulnerable. "Whatever you think of me, whatever misimpression I have fostered, I am sorry. Truly, I am." His voice had gone hoarse, and she latched on to the regret that hung in his words with all the finesse of a drowning woman. "But I am not a worthy partner for you, Caroline. I am just trying to help—"

"Help me?" she choked out. "How are you helping me? By commandeering a dance away from Mr. Adams, who was, by all accounts, a perfectly adequate dance partner? By challenging me to articulate what I want, whom I want, and then implying I don't know my own mind?"

His arms slackened about her, which made her want to howl in frustration. "By dancing with you to show the crowd how lovely you are. By changing their impression of you from someone worth tormenting to someone worth wanting."

Caroline stared at him, stricken by the explanation that was so unwanted, and yet made perfect, horrific sense. He didn't feel for her the same soul-crushing want that she did for him. He entertained a far simpler emotion in his regard for her.

He felt sorry for her.

The music shifted, signaling the end of the current musical number. David's palm fell away from her waist as if it could no longer bear the punishment. Caroline numbly followed him from the floor. Apparently, his comments about forgetting the dance steps applied to walking too, because she would have been hard-pressed to identify her feet over her kneecaps at the moment.

She liked to think she wouldn't have said anything, but for the effects of the three glasses of champagne. Surely that was the reason her tongue had gotten ahead of her. Now she was left facing the quagmire of her next decision, without the courage of a glass in her hand.

He pulled her to a quieter corner and levered her back up against one of the columns that held up the pavilion's roof. Steps away, the cool night air beckoned, as did a forgotten tray of champagne glasses, laid out on a receiving table.

What next? She could apologize for her presumption, she supposed. Tell him she had been joking, having a bit of fun at his expense. She could claim a fierce and sudden headache, or she could pretend to twist her ankle, or . . .

Or she could have another glass of champagne.

Caroline snatched a glass and tossed it back, not even caring that it appeared to have been half drunk by someone else.

David pulled the emptied flute out of her hand. "Do you think that is a wise idea?"

"I seem to be fresh out of wise ideas," she told him, welcoming the scald of her fourth glass, an indulgence she refused to regret. And least, not tonight.

Tomorrow might be a different tale.

The shadows from outside the pavilion seemed to reach for her, offering relief and anonymity. "I should go home," she said, seizing on escape as a new option worth considering. Of course, she couldn't leave without Penelope, and her sister was still spinning about the dance floor in Mr. Hamilton's arms, her cheeks flushed, her eyes sparkling.

David fixed her with a blue-eyed stare that might have been sharpened on a whetstone. "I hadn't pegged you for a coward. Let's address the problem, rather than avoiding the discussion."

"Oh yes, let's." Caroline half hiccupped, already questioning the wisdom of that fourth glass. Her head felt fuzzy, irregular. Her tongue, however, felt as free as the sparrows that performed dizzying acrobatic maneuvers on the air currents above her swimming cove. "I am the girl that people laugh about behind cupped hands. An almost-spinster, spilling out the secrets of her heart to a handsome, eligible gentleman. You do not think of me in a way that might be considered romantic. The problem is solved."

David sighed, and the sound cut through the fog of her brain like a beacon. He rubbed a hand against the back of his neck, assessing her as if she was a conundrum that required sorting out. "You mistook my interest, Caroline, that is all. I might have even encouraged it. But I am only here for a short time, and will return with my mother to Scotland in a few days' time. We would not suit as anything other than friends."

Caroline fought against a disbelieving snort of laughter, forcing herself to acknowledge the rational aspect of his words. Of *course* he didn't find her attractive. Of *course* this little game he had been playing hadn't been about any feelings of admiration he might harbor for her.

Why would he be any different from the other gentlemen in Brighton?

David's explanation and her own self-doubts sent Caroline reaching for a fifth glass, but he placed his big hand over hers and firmly tugged her fingers away. "And I had not pegged you as someone to embrace public drunkenness, given the verbal tongue-lashing you gave me eleven years ago for the same sin."

She glared up at him, the only gentleman she had ever had to look up to since attaining her full height. There was no way she could see herself clear of the hole she was digging beneath both of their feet. There was no way she could take her words back, no way she could erase such a glaring tactical error. She had just confessed the intensity of her feelings for this man, had given voice to an emotion that had permeated the very fabric of her life since girlhood.

Surely public drunkenness was her only remaining alternative.

HE HADN'T MEANT to hurt her. He'd never *intentionally* hurt any woman.

But Christ above, was he destined to do anything else?

She stood stiff-shouldered, fingering a remaining glass of champagne that had been left on a tray by a waiter who ought to be hunted down and flogged. She was going to regret such impulsiveness on the morrow, but short of tossing the entire tray on its end, he had no ability to prevent her from further overindulgence.

He needed to pull her attention away from the danger of the champagne, but far from finding some sort of resolution to the problem she presented, he found he could think of nothing cogent beyond how she had tasted last night, there where her hair lay against her skin. One tempting coil had loosened during their dance, and it now lay draped across the delicate column of her neck. He longed to loosen it and let it fall in its natural state, as he had seen it this afternoon: unleashed, damp, unruly.

And though he was in a public place, though she was angry as a wet cat with him, his body hardened with what was fast becoming a remarkable predictability around this woman.

"I do not want this to damage our friendship," he argued, trying to approach this as he would a dilemma presented to him in his role as Moraig's magistrate. The offending party would be expected to offer an apology, and he had done the offending tonight. "I admire you. Respect you."

"But not enough to offer for me." Her voice pierced his scrambling thoughts with the surety of an arrow.

David sucked in a breath. Hell, but she was a forward chit. "I cannot offer for anyone," he said, by way of the most inadequate answer ever crafted by man.

"Can you at least tell me *why*?" She turned now to face him, the glass of champagne finally forgotten in her apparent need for information.

Information he was not, under any circumstances, going to divulge.

David recoiled against the hope he saw etched on her face. He considered how much to tell her. Not enough to destroy all faith in him. But enough to convince her of how inadequate he was for the role of white knight she seemed determined to fashion for him.

He settled on a stilted version of the truth. "I am in love with someone else."

Her face drained of color, and he heard the ragged intake of her sudden breath. "But . . . but you *kissed* me."

He welcomed her well-deserved outrage. He *shouldn't* have kissed an innocent young woman, for all that he had meant to be helpful. He needed the reminder tattooed somewhere on his person.

"The person I love would not object," he told her, his stomach knotting up to describe it in such terms. "At least not in the literal sense. She died eleven years ago."

Caroline's lips parted in surprise, softening the tense line of her jaw. "Oh," she breathed.

"Her name was Elizabeth Ramsey, the vicar's daughter. We were both twenty-one. And I loved her very much."

Caroline's features settled into a sympathetic mask. It struck him, then, how little she actually knew about his past. In Moraig, any mention of Elizabeth Ramsey among the townsfolk there caused a far different reaction.

"You remind me of her, in some ways," he told her. "No doubt it has caused me to behave inappropriately in your presence at times, and for that I am sorry."

It wasn't precisely true. He had been naïve in thinking that Caroline reminded him of Elizabeth, yesterday on Miss Baxter's terrace. The physical differences were obvious, of course—Elizabeth Ramsey had been petite and fair, whereas Caroline was anything but. But in their innocence, and in his body's reaction to each of them, he had thought them quite similar.

He reconsidered that notion now. There was steel in Caroline, a core of strength that even now showed itself in the firming of her lips and the squaring of her shoulders, that Elizabeth had never possessed. If Caroline was a rock jutting out of turbulent water, Elizabeth had been the water itself. Her mercurial moods had been the near death of him, and had certainly been the death of her.

"If the woman you loved . . ." Caroline swallowed, as if the question pained her. "If she has been dead for so long, then why can you not see yourself offering marriage to someone like me? We get along well enough, I think."

David let out his bunched thoughts on a long, slow slide. The noise of the crowd, which had receded to the point of silence, began to creep back in. This, then was the crux of his problem. Most men would have buried their loss years ago, moved on to find another love. But he was not most men.

And penance was a matter best kept private.

"Elizabeth Ramsey took my heart with her when she died, lass. I am not free to give it to another, and do not imagine I will ever be."

Her uncertain gaze dropped to a level that would have been shocking had it not come from someone who had already seen him in smallclothes. "Are you . . . *celibate*?" she whispered.

"No." He permitted his lips to turn up, though it seemed somehow less than appropriate. "Although I am stretched to understand how you even know such a word."

"Penelope has a book that I read—" Caroline exhaled noisily, then waved her hands about as she searched the crowd, apparently for her sister with a penchant for naughty books. "It does not matter. None of this matters. I am sorry I said *anything*. I didn't know . . ."

"Of course it matters." David's body still felt coiled tight, but this, finally, was getting at what this conversation ought to be about. It would pain him to see her happy with someone else—he was man enough to admit that. But he needed to do this for himself, as much as for her.

His palm twitched, wanting to brush a wayward wisp of hair out of her eyes. He curled his traitorous fingers into a fist instead. "That is what I have been trying to tell you, Caroline. I found my perfect match, once upon a time. I wish the same thing for you."

Her gaze jerked up to meet his. "You would subject me to this sort of pain?" She met his gaze with a doubtful, arched brow. "Your whole body tenses up when you speak of the girl you loved. It looks as if a lifetime of shuttlecock would be more enjoyable, if you will forgive the observation."

David welcomed the return of the sharp tongue he admired to the conversation. "I was unlucky to lose my match, but it does not mean you will be. There is a man somewhere in Brighton, and quite possibly on this dance floor, with whom you might have a happy future."

He swallowed his regrets, and let his smile stretch higher, false though the sentiment might be. "And while I cannot be that man, I can promise to help you find him."

Chapter 16

So THIS WAS what four glasses of champagne felt like the next morning.

Caroline woke to a vicious pounding, not unlike church bells on Sunday, clanging in her skull. Except she was quite sure it wasn't Sunday. It was Thursday.

The world shifted. Tilted. Slid back into place.

She opened one protesting eye to sunlight streaming across her headboard. It was morning, which meant her hellish night was finally over. But it also meant she must face the day, and that was a thought worth haggling over.

She slid a glance toward Penelope's bed. "Pen?" she whispered. There was no answer.

Indeed, there was no Pen. Her sister's bed was neatly made up, the pillows tucked away beneath the smooth, uncreased coverlet. What time was it, if Penelope had risen before her and already tidied her bed?

Caroline buried her face in her pillow, breathing in the familiar smell of the lilac sachets she helped Bess make for the linen closet. The feeling in her head came again. Less of a pounding than a knocking. She should not have had that fourth glass of champagne.

But then the memory of what had driven her to consume the last glass reinserted its ugly head, and she wondered if four had been enough.

Because despite the drinks' clear effects on her head, they hadn't erased the memory of her painful conversation with David. Or how she had felt afterward, when he had encouraged her to go on laughing and dancing and—dare she acknowledge it—flirting with other gentlemen, as if he had not just inverted her world and tossed it onto the rubbish heap.

The last glass of champagne and David's departure soon thereafter had freed her. There had been offers to dance. So many she lost count. She had thrown herself into the remainder of the evening, convinced that nothing else that might befall her that evening could be worse than what had already happened. For the first time in her life, she hadn't cared what kind of an impression she was making, or whether her eccentricities might scare off a potential suitor.

Anything to prevent her from thinking of David's heart-wrenching past, and his inability to move on from the woman he had loved and lost.

More knocking interrupted her thoughts. She groaned. Burrowed under the covers. Willed it to stop. It was curious how the sensation ebbed and flowed. She would have thought post-alcohol misery to be a constant thing, like a hammer chained to one's bones.

The sound of the bedroom door slamming proved the worst possible accompaniment to the racket that would not loosen its grip on her skull. "Caroline!" Pen's excited voice reached beneath the covers. "You have to s-s-see!"

Caroline pulled down her coverlet and blinked up at her sister's flushed, pretty face. Penelope was still wearing the same gown she had worn to the dance at the pavilion last night, a sea foam green silk had been remade from an old evening gown of Mama's. Had she been to bed at all?

"Fl-flowers!" Penelope snatched up Caroline's hand, tugging harder now. "Delivered this morning. An entire h-house full of them."

Caroline let Pen pull her to sitting, though the movement sent the room into a nauseating pitch. "From Mr. Cameron?" Her heart began to match the rhythm in her head, foolish, *stupid* organ that it was.

Although, now that she considered it, her head wasn't actually knocking. The sound came again. Someone was knocking on the front door that sat right below her open window.

Pen shook her head. "Not that I saw. The first two deliveries were from Mr. Branson and someone named Mr. Adams." At Caroline's bleary-eyed gawk, she flushed. "B-but Mama and I stopped reading the c-c-cards after that."

Caroline stared at her sister, aghast. None of this made sense.

The knock below her window came again, more insistent this time, and Caroline could hear Bess muttering something from the porch below. Mama's higher-pitched, excited exclamation soon followed.

Penelope's blue eyes danced over the commotion. "Heavens, it sounds like there's another deliveryman at the door."

Caroline swallowed. "*Another* deliveryman?"

"The sixth so f-far."

Caroline contemplated pinching the skin on the underside of her wrist just to see if the pain might be real. The circumstances called for something drastic, because nothing else about this morning could be distinguished from a dream.

"And there's more." Penelope rattled a newspaper in front of Caroline's eyes. "You, my d-dear sister, have made the social section of the *Brighton Gazette*."

A HARSH COUGH tore David's eyes from the heap of coddled eggs on his plate.

He gripped the edge of his chair as he watched his mother set down the paper she had been reading and labor to draw a proper breath. Hers was a battle he could not help her with, though he would have gladly given one of his lungs had he the ability to make the sacrifice.

"I'd like to fetch a doctor this morning," he insisted when his mother leaned back against the mountain of pillows. "You seem a good deal worse than when we arrived last week."

She shook her head, setting limp gray curls bouncing on either side of her nightcap. "I am fine. Just a little tired."

"But perhaps one of the Brighton doctors could—"

"*No*." Another cough racked her frail body, but she fought through it. "By my bones," she gasped, "I would rather expire on the spot than be bled again, David."

He absorbed her words, contemplating his choices. He could fetch the doctor against her express wishes. Insist she suffer through whatever archaic treatment the man recommended. Demand she put off this foolishness and return home to Moraig, where she had a bevy of household servants and David's father to dote on her.

But none of those choices would make her happy. By bringing her to Brighton, David knew he had pleased her, even if he wasn't making her better. And the memory of the last doctor, who had chased his poor prognosis with a recommendation to bleed her every other day until she either improved or succumbed, kept David's arse settled in the chair.

His mother dabbed her mouth with a napkin, some delicate bit of frippery embroidered with the Bedford Hotel crest. "Let us finish our breakfast without talk of such unpleasantries." She picked up her crumpled newspaper again. "And please," she said, nodding toward his plate. "Eat your eggs."

David stared down at his plate, his stomach objecting to the very idea. He had been eating breakfast with his mother every morning since they arrived, both as a way to spend precious time with her and to surreptitiously sort out whether she showed any signs of improvement. But between the emotional thrashing he had subjected Caroline to last night and the worry he felt for his mother this morning, food was the last thing on his mind. The Bedford boasted an excellent kitchen staff, but even the most accomplished of chefs would have found it difficult to bring life to his appetite this morning.

His mother was visibly, painfully ill. Caroline was probably sick at heart.

And he didn't see how eating his eggs was going to mend either of them.

He pushed the jiggling yellow mess around on his plate until his mother made an odd noise.

"Is something wrong?" David looked up in alarm.

There was no immediate answer. From the position of the *Gazette* in his mother's hands, he could see that the upcoming swimming competition was featured on the front page, the headlines declaring it the "Race of the Decade."

David drew in a sharp breath at the reminder. He didn't even know if the competition was still a possibility. He had no hope of winning without Caroline's instruction, and after the muddle he had made of things last night . . . He had done his best to patch things over before he took his leave, but he would not have been surprised to learn that she had returned home and given in to a good cry into her pillow. He hoped she would still want to continue their clandestine swimming lessons.

But he wouldn't blame her if she changed her mind.

His mother's voice intruded on those troublesome thoughts. "I see you've made the social section."

David shifted in his chair. Why did his mother sound so accusing? *She* was the one who insisted he traipse about Brighton's social scene when the sun went down.

"It says here you danced with Miss Julianne Baxter." The baroness leveled a shrewd glance in his direction over the top of the paper. "And that you danced with someone named Miss Caroline Tolbertson. I've met Miss Baxter, of course, and she is a lovely chit. But when were you going to tell me about Miss Tolbertson?"

David caught his breath. "She . . . is a lovely chit as well," he finished, unsure of what else he could say. He shoveled a forkful of eggs into his mouth and swallowed the curdled mass far more easily than he swallowed the latest twist to the conversation.

His mother's lips turned up into a faint smile that seemed at odds with the shadows haunting her eyes. "Well, you'd best move fast if you've an interest in that one, dear. Because according to the newspaper, Miss Tolbertson is the surprise sensation of the summer."

Chapter 17

Yᴇᴛ ᴀɴᴏᴛʜᴇʀ ᴅᴇʟɪᴠᴇʀʏᴍᴀɴ knocked on the door by the time Caroline made her way downstairs. She stared in amazement. Bouquets sprouted from every conceivable vase, and even an old, chipped pitcher Bess must have scrounged from a forgotten kitchen cupboard. The fragrance of all those hothouse blooms was dizzying in and of itself, but the knowledge that the combined cost of those already-wilting flowers would have been enough to feed Caroline's family for at least the next month made her stomach turn.

Her mother looked up from where she was admiring an arrangement of pink clematis and calendula. Her sharp blue gaze settled on the frayed cuffs of Caroline's sleeves, and her mouth turned down. "Please tell me you are not planning on wearing that gown today, dear."

Caroline looked down, belligerence welling up inside her. The faded blue print of her dress wasn't much to look at, she knew. But at least it didn't pinch her about the shoulders, or squeeze about her neck. "I haven't another clean dress, Mama."

"What about your navy serge gown?"

Caroline winced. That ruined garment was tucked under a bush on the beach at her swimming cove. It had seemed safer at the time to keep it there for David's daily lessons.

She searched her mind for an appropriate explanation. "Er . . . I believe it is ripped."

Her mother pressed exasperated fingers against both temples. "By the stars, child. Must it *always* be so difficult with you? Go upstairs, right now, and change into something of Pen's. Her yellow day dress, I think."

Caroline snorted. "Pen is at least six inches shorter than I am."

"But she has more of a bosom, dear. Surely that extra fabric will balance out somewhere around your feet." Mrs. Tolbertson clapped her hands together. "Quickly, as fast as you can. I have a feeling—"

Before her mother could finish the thought, a knock came at the door. Bess peered through the front window. "Heavens," the servant exclaimed, wiping the window with a corner of her apron and leaning over for a closer look. "It's a gentleman caller!"

Her mother's hand crept up to smooth soft, blond curls back from her temples. "So early, these boys are. Why, when I was being courted, no one would have ever dared call before two o'clock."

"We *are* in Brighton," Caroline pointed out. And according to the clock she had passed in the upstairs hallway, it was a few minutes past eleven o'clock. Given the predictable heat of the day, the trend of paying early social calls in summer made good sense.

"I am very aware of the fact that we live in Brighton," Mama said, her voice sharp as the thorns Caroline could see on the nearest bunch of roses. Her mother's brows pulled down in thought. No doubt she was trying to weigh whether it was better for her youngest daughter to be seen in an unattractive dress that fit, or a prettier one that gaped about the chest and showed far too much ankle.

A regretful sigh escaped her as she eyed Caroline once more. "I suppose the blue will have to do for today. But I declare, our appointment with Madame Beauclerc cannot come soon enough."

"Mr. Gabriel Adams is here for Miss Caroline," Bess sang out from the door. The servant stepped back, a surprised hand fluttering about her chest. "Gor, and Mr. Branson too!"

The walk to the parlor would have been awkward enough with one man to deal with, but with two it proved a veritable gauntlet of stilted discourse. Caroline chose her wingback chair out of habit, while Pen cleared three books and a leather-bound journal away from her usual spot. This left the settee for the two men, who sat stiff-backed and bristling on the delicate piece of furniture, trying not to touch each other.

"Thank you for the flowers," Caroline said, trying to ignore the sight of Mr. Branson's elbow catching Mr. Adams somewhere in the vicinity of his liver.

"The roses are mine," Branson said, pushing the words through gritted teeth. "Not that you can find them in that circus of a foyer," he added under his breath.

"*I* sent the clematis," Mr. Adams grunted, rubbing his chest and shooting Branson a glare. "Roses are far too predictable."

The two men began to argue about the merits of choosing flowers. Mr. Branson was of the opinion that garden-reared flowers were superior in form and fragrance. Mr. Adams felt that hothouse flowers conveyed a more appropriate sentiment of worth.

Penelope took advantage of the bickering to lean in close. "Mr. Adams is the c-cousin of a marquess," she whispered.

Caroline choked back a startled gasp. She at least recalled dancing with the brown-haired young man last night, which was a miracle considering that by the end of the evening, the dances had all started to blur together. Then again, she had danced with him *before* the muck she had made of things with David. But good heavens. What had possessed the cousin of a marquess to ask her to dance last night, much less call on her this morning?

And when had Penelope become such an authority on the lineage of the summer set?

"How did you know that?" she hissed.

Pen's eyes lit with amusement. "The social section of the *Gazette*, of course."

Caroline studied the gentleman beneath her lashes as he was battered by Branson's lengthy verbal discourse on how to select a rose based on the length of its thorns. Mr. Adams had moderately straight teeth. Better than Mr. Branson's, though not nearly as nice as David Cameron's.

A wicked voice—her own, not Pen's—whispered in her ear. *What does it matter how straight they are? Those teeth belong to the cousin of a marquess.*

Bess popped her head through the parlor door. "Oh my heavens, miss," she squeaked, wringing her hands. "Another gentleman has arrived. You'd best come out here for this one, though."

Caroline excused herself and stepped out of the parlor with a far-too-curious Penelope in tow. She could immediately see why the newest arrival had not been escorted to the parlor to join the others. He was a bit younger than the other men who had called this morning, twenty if she had to hazard a guess, with a thick black mustache and matching sideburns. But despite his tender age, he looked to have been cleaning his plate for most of those years.

His addition to the foyer took up the space of two or three men.

With a great deal of effort, Caroline resurrected the barest memory of waltzing with this bear of a man. The recollection took shape and filled with color and texture. Ah, yes. He had stepped on her toes four times. And asked her for another dance soon after, which she had side-stepped on the grounds of propriety.

Her mother's wide smile offered a brilliant contrast to the worry line drawn between her brows. Caroline would have laughed, had her still-rolling stomach been up to the task. Apparently her mother's experience with managing multiple suitors was a matter of quantity, not density.

Pen leaned over to whisper in Caroline's ear. "Mr. Duffington is the third son of the Earl of B-Beecham."

Ah. Duffington. The name clicked into place. Caroline stared in wonder and amazement. Not at Duffington, who, despite his impressive bloodlines and expensive clothing, was not much to look at.

No, Caroline stared at her sister.

An interest in the *Gazette* was something Pen had in-herited from their father, but she spent most of her time reading the editorial section. Never once had her sister showed the slightest bit of interest in a social section. Heavens. Caroline wasn't even sure she realized there *was* a social section in the *Brighton Gazette*.

"Where shall I put the new gent?" Bess asked Mrs. Tol-bertson, a bit too loudly. Even as she spoke, Branson and Hamilton tumbled into the foyer, no doubt determined to catch a glimpse of their newest competitor.

Their mother tossed a harried look around the tight space. "The parlor, I should think."

Bess squawked her objection. "The parlor's a mite *small* for this many men, don't you think? They'll be like a mob of cattle in a curiosity store."

"Duffington should come back tomorrow," Mr. Adams interjected. "He was the last to arrive, after all."

"Yes, and I feel sure he won't want to miss luncheon," Mr. Branson added.

"At least I can *afford* luncheon," Duffington shot back, his dark mustache twitching. "Miss Baxter told my mother that your father's cut you off again, Branson."

Branson's chest puffed up a full three inches. "That wouldn't be the first rumor Miss Baxter's gotten wrong. And I am surprised *your* mother even let you off leading strings this morning."

The temperature in the foyer rose, a consequence of too many bodies, three male egos, and not enough space. Caroline's temper begged to follow suit. She wanted nothing more than to return to the simple bit of knocking that had roused her from bed. How had the morning devolved into such mayhem? She couldn't imagine what she had done last night to garner the attention of so many young men. If anything, emboldened by so many glasses of champagne, she had leaned toward being indecorous.

"Perhaps they c-could all go for a walk. Much as yesterday, only as a group," Penelope piped up.

Six pairs of eyes stared in Pen's direction, Caroline's included. The line between their mother's brows deepened to a furrow.

"But this time I'm g-going as well. I'll serve as a chaperone." Pen was already setting her sunbonnet over her fair hair and tying the blue ribbons.

Their mother lifted a hand to flutter about her throat. "I am not sure that is wise with so many—"

"It seems a logical solution," Caroline interrupted, warming to the idea. If she was to erase the memory of David's rejection from her mind, she needed to fill her thoughts with other men. In fact, given David's jaw-gritting insistence that she needed to find her perfect match, she was quite sure he would encourage this activity.

Three gentlemen callers were standing in her foyer, each of them a fine potential match, each one an opportunity that could not be squandered. She had no reason to dislike any of them, save the fact that none of them was David Cameron. And going for a walk was a means of entertaining the lot of them *and* escaping the scent of flowers that threatened to crowd them all out of the foyer.

"It's a capital idea," Duffington agreed. "Mother always says a bracing bit of ocean air in the morning does her a world of good."

Her mother's creased forehead smoothed out a fraction. "Well," she said hesitantly. "If the countess enjoys a nice morning walk, I suppose it might be all right."

Caroline's fingers closed around the blue silk fabric and the stiff spines of the parasol Penelope held out to her. Her sister's brave smile reminded her that Penelope's future was as tangled up in this charade as her own. She was fortunate these men had not been put off by her champagne-drenched antics last night, but she could not afford to make that mistake this morning.

Duffington offered Caroline his arm, clearly determined to be first in line. She placed a tentative hand on the man's sleeve. His arm felt thick and solid beneath her fingers, but the sensation did not send her senses spinning in the same manner that touching David Cameron's arm did.

Well, she didn't need her senses to skitter. She needed to convince one of these fine young men she was someone worth considering.

With her stomach in knots, Caroline forced herself to step out the door on Duffington's arm. She *and* Penelope needed to make a good impression today, so that one of these men—any of them, really—might be smitten enough to offer for her, and, by necessity, bring her sister along for the keeping.

For her future's sake, she needed to behave.

Even if all she wanted to do was bolt.

DAVID STEPPED INTO Creak's Bathhouse just before noon and wiped a hand across his already perspiring brow. After his mother's rough start to the morning, he had insisted on delivering her to her daily appointment himself.

He was relieved to see the place boasted a crisp, medicinal aura. Two white-aproned attendants greeted his mother warmly and answered David's questions about the risks and benefits of her treatments with a knowledgeable air. There was nothing of the place to send him running for a physician. Indeed, he was left with the thought of whether it might not be prudent to take a restorative bath here himself. His muscles had been bunched and knotted ever since his mother had informed him of Caroline's stunning success of last night. Apparently, after he had gone home, she had taken him at his literal word and gone off looking for her match.

What did you expect? Caroline had a role to play. A husband to find.

And there was no doubt he had shoved her in that direction, with a stinging rejection and a few glasses of champagne to hurry her along.

As his mother hobbled through the door into the depths of the stone-walled spa, David turned to the front attendant who was busy behind a counter. "Excuse me."

Truth be told, he felt a bit silly. Creak's Bath House was geared toward a female clientele, from the floral print curtains on the window down to the selection of helpful creams beneath the counter, several of which guaranteed an end to unsightly blemishes. Did they even have facilities to accommodate men? He didn't see a cream that promised to improve a man's prowess anywhere under the glass.

The bespectacled attendant looked up, a businesslike smile on his face. "Have you come to register for the swimming competition, sir?"

David hesitated. This was something he had not anticipated when he insisted on bringing his mother for her appointment. "Today is the last day to sign up," the clerk offered. "The larger purse this year has drawn swimmers from all over Britain."

David's eye fell on the list the man pushed toward him. As suspected, Dermott's name was first on the list. A memory came to him, of Caroline admitting how Dermott had kissed her, then spread the tale far and yonder. Something dark twisted inside him as his finger hovered over the man's proud, boastful flourish.

"Promises to be quite a race," the clerk said helpfully. "Mr. Dermott won the purse last year, if memory serves."

"Did he indeed?" David's finger curled into a fist. Manners prevented him from smashing Dermott's face without good cause. But perhaps there was another way.

With a vehemence that startled him, David picked up the pencil and signed his name with a determined scrawl. He placed the pencil down with a firm *snick*, gripped the edge of the counter, and leaned closer. "Well, should you see him, you can tell the duffer I shall enjoying thrashing him in such a public venue."

The clerk's eyes widened, and the sound of the clerk's chair scooting back a half inch reached David's ears. "Yes. Er . . . certainly, sir."

All thoughts of a medicinal bath vanished as David offered the man a curt nod and strode toward the door. His decision cemented into place, courtesy of the competitive avarice Dermott conjured in him. No, he was not going to waste his time this afternoon being pampered in mineral salts. If he was going to take a dip today, it was going to be somewhere he could hone his swimming skills.

David stepped out of the bathhouse and headed east. His body felt stretched like leather over the barrel of a drum, taut and eager and ready for action. A renewed desire to compete in this race settled in his gut, as much for the pleasure of besting Dermott as winning the purse. But to have any sort of a chance, he knew he needed a great deal more practice with the new stroke he had just started to master.

Yesterday, when things had still been easy between them, Caroline had agreed to meet him at the cove at one o'clock every day. David wasn't sure if such a promise held water anymore after last night, but if he was to make it there by the appointed time, he needed to leave now. He turned toward the white cliffs that ran like a chalk line to the east, but just as he passed Broad Street, his attention was snagged by a crowd of young people near the Marine Parade. The mob appeared mostly male, but at the center towered a familiar head of brown hair beneath the shade of a blue parasol.

His knees locked up tight at the sight of Caroline in the middle of all those men. The group was pointing west on Madeira Drive, walking in the opposite direction from where Caroline was supposed to be heading to meet him. The evidence of her rebuff felt like a blow to the head. Or maybe that was just the breath-robbing sight of her. Her hair was pulled back in that severe knot she preferred, and she was wearing a cotton print dress that did nothing to highlight the sensual body he now knew lurked beneath the yards of fabric.

But judging by how they hovered at her elbow, the men around her seemed all too aware of the potential she hid from the world.

Last night he had encouraged Caroline to consider other gentlemen. Hell, he had pushed her back out on the dance floor. But the full repercussions hadn't seemed so clear at the time. Now that she was surrounded by a jostling group of young men, men who were no more trustworthy than he, his feelings on the matter shifted.

He, at least, held honorable intentions toward her. And he, thank God, was no longer a twenty-one-year-old youth incapable of self-control.

Did she even understand the potential danger? Not that he could be sure any of these men might have plans for her beyond the afternoon walk, but they were men. He, of all people, knew how their minds worked. If he was to both win the race and protect her from fops who were contemplating how to toss up her skirts, he needed to speak with

her and convince her that it was important to continue
their lessons.

But how to gain a private moment if she was caught in
this snarl of suitors? The wolves were circling, even if they
were of the fumbling, juvenile variety of predator.

And for all that she was hiding beneath an ugly dress,
Caroline Tolbertson was tempting prey.

Chapter 18

As the sun slipped past flush overhead, Caroline's feet started to itch.

This was the time of day she usually gave serious consideration to whether a swim might be possible. Not today, though. Today she was accompanied by three solicitous gentlemen and a sister who spent much of the half-hour walk scribbling notes in a leather-bound journal.

Best behavior, Caroline reminded herself. There was too much at stake to even flirt with the idea of swimming. One of these men might be her future husband.

Or her next failed kiss.

But the stern reminder couldn't stop her from stepping away from the group of men when their collective attention was caught by a vendor selling paper kites. She stared out at the sailboats dotting the horizon, the heated breeze brushing the damp curls on her neck. A short distance to her right, the Chain Pier rose like an ominous black spider, stretching out to deeper water. She studied it for a moment. The packet boat to Dieppe was docked alongside it, boarding passengers to France, but it was the water beneath the pier, not the well-dressed passengers on top, that pulled her attention.

This section of ocean, from the western side of the Chain Pier running east to the Stone House, would be the site of Monday's swimming competition. It looked to be a calm piece of surf, with no visible eddies or rocks to snag an unsuspecting swimmer. However, the water rushing in a circular motion about the iron pilings of the pier brought to mind the current in her cove.

Most competitors, she knew, would stay far to the right of that turbulent bit of water in their sweep around the pier. If she were swimming, she would hug the line of the pier on the way out, both to avoid the frenzied rush of the other competitors and to gain a few yards' advantage in the race to the finish line.

Of course she *wasn't* swimming. It was an exercise in futility to even imagine it.

And after the way things had gone last night, she had to question the sanity of continuing her lessons with David Cameron. No matter his reassurances to the contrary, she had thrown herself at his feet, while he had made his lack of intentions quite clear.

Not the sort of situation that lent itself to platonic swimming lessons.

"Fancy a swim, Miss Caroline?"

Caroline jumped at the words that threaded into her left ear and reached for her throat. Duffington had broken away from the others and now stood but a few inches away.

"I beg your pardon?" Caroline searched her memory with an increasing degree of panic. Had she said something inappropriate to Duffington during their dance last night?

Surely she wouldn't have forgotten *that*.

He waved a fleshy hand toward the wooden bathing machines that littered the lower shoreline. "It is the same with Mother. The day warms up, and all her thoughts turn to sea bathing and the pleasures to be found there."

Caroline unclenched her fists, one finger at a time. He was talking about sea bathing. *And his mother.* He seemed incapable of engaging in conversation without some mention of the woman.

"Indeed." Caroline forced herself to stand fast and not take the instinctive step away her feet demanded. Of all the suitors this morning, Duffington had been the most persistent, hovering near her arm, monopolizing the conversation to the point that even the vociferous Mr. Branson appeared something close to mute.

She fastened her reluctant gaze on the row of small, wooden houses lurking in the shallows, their giant wheels mocking the very idea of deep water. The thought of four solid walls crowding in from every side was the farthest thing from pleasure in her mind.

Not that she could let Duffington know that.

"C-Caroline quite enjoys swimming." Penelope's broken voice intruded on the moment. Her sister had an innocent smile on her face and held her pencil aloft, as if she had just written that same titillating bit of slander down in her journal.

Although Caroline supposed it didn't count as slander, given that it was true.

Still, how could Pen say such a thing? How could she even *know* it? Caroline felt a bit as though Pen had taken her parasol and given her a good whack about the head. She had never mentioned her swims to her sister. Not even once.

Caroline reached for a bit of plaster to repair this new crack in the wall that housed her secret. "My sister is mistaken." She laughed, fluttering a dismissive hand in the direction of the bathing houses. "I've never even set foot in one of those terrible machines." She affected what she prayed to be a weak, frightened look, although she suspected she looked more like a biting midge was stuck in one eye. "Why, I am quite done in by the thought of them."

There. The solution was at hand. If Pen would be quiet about this, Caroline still might salvage the morning. Although there was no question she was going to give her sister an earful when next they found a private moment.

Duffington's fingers plucked at Caroline's sleeve. "'Tis not a frightening experience, truly. They are said to be good for the constitution, even for those of delicate strength. Mother takes a sea bath at least once a week while we are in Brighton." He leaned in, warming to the topic. "Why, you won't even get your clothing wet, because they provide a robe. Permit me to call one of the machines up for you."

Caroline blinked at the large man. Out of all the suitors, his status as the third son of an earl made him the man who could most easily save her family. And he was a nice enough fellow, she supposed, if a bit hairy and attached to his mother.

How to encourage his interest, while discouraging this ridiculous idea?

"Thank you, but I think not." She searched for another reasonable explanation, given that her facade of fear didn't seem to be working. Sea baths cost money. Not *much* money, perhaps two or three shillings. But extra shillings were something the Tolbertsons didn't have.

Not that one admitted such a thing to a prospective bridegroom.

Caroline patted the edge of her empty reticule. "I'm afraid I neglected to bring any coins with me."

A hearty laugh shook Duffington's frame. "Nonsense, Miss Caroline. It shall be my pleasure to purchase a day's ticket for you. Why, if you like it, I would strive to procure you an entire month's subscription."

She was quite sure she gaped at him then. Was that even appropriate? A gentleman might purchase a lady flowers, or even a light refreshment while out for a walk.

But a subscription for sea baths?

The sound of arguing made itself heard over the din in her head. The other two men had left the kite vendor and were crowding closer. Mr. Adams had a green paper kite beneath one arm. Mr. Branson's hands were empty but he sported a thunderous look on his face.

He shoved his way in front of Duffington and offered Caroline a stiff, proprietary arm. "This morning's walk has become a bit crowded for my tastes, Miss Caroline. Why don't we take a private turn on the Chain Pier?"

Mr. Branson's unexpected demand sent her head spinning. As backdrop to her first lackluster kiss, the Chain Pier was not somewhere she wanted to visit on the arm of a gentleman.

"Good God, man, have you not been following the conversation?" Duffington blustered. "She is going to take a sea bath with me."

"Not *with* you," Caroline protested. The houses were segregated by gender, and men and women bathed on different sides of the beach.

Mr. Branson's cheeks flushed red. "Perhaps she would prefer to take a walk with *me*, Duffington." The two men looked close to fisticuffs.

Adams crowded closer, clutching his kite. "I was hoping you would want to fly this kite with *me*, Miss Caroline," he objected.

Caroline looked between the three young men. The itching of her soles turned into a full-fledged burn. And was it any wonder? The genial group walk Penelope had proposed as a solution to the problem of too many suitors had come to a flaming end. Dousing it in water seemed just the thing.

"I suppose I should choose the sea bath over the pier or the kite," she muttered. That, at least, promised a measure of privacy.

Anything to get away from the lot of them.

Duffington raised an eager, beefy hand and snapped his fingers in the direction of the bathing machine attendants. Branson and Adams began to bicker over which part of Brighton's beach was better for sea bathing.

"The eastern beach is too close to the outflow for the sewer line," Mr. Branson argued. "It muddies the water, especially after a hard rain."

"'Tis still better than the western beach, where the day-trippers down from London tend to congregate," retorted Mr. Adams. "The eastern edge is closer to the Steine and therefore preferable among the fashionable crowd."

"But she'll be swimming in *shite*," Branson protested, seeming to forget their mixed company.

Penelope looked up from where she was scribbling something down in her journal. She placed her pencil in the seam and closed the leather-bound edges with a decisive snap. "Do take note of whether you see any of *that*," she said. "I might like t-t-to write about it."

That severed the last of Caroline's thin thread of control. She grabbed her sister by the arm and dragged her several feet away. "How?" she whispered to Pen, anger heating the very word. "How did you know that I swim?"

Pen offered Caroline a smile that lacked any hint of apology. "I am more observant than you give me credit for. You c-come home quite damp most afternoons. So there is no point pretending you do not swim."

Caroline took a step backward, stunned to temporary silence. She felt as if her cloistered world was being ripped apart, board by board. "Do not say anything more," she begged. "We need these men to *like* me if I am to have any hope of an offer by the end of the summer."

Pen's mouth pulled down. "Why must it be this year? Or one of these men?" She leveled an assessing stare toward Duffington, who was counting out money to a white-frocked bathing attendant. "You cannot tell me you love any of them."

"I do not need to love a prospective bridegroom. Such a fantasy has no place in real life." Caroline swallowed, refusing to acknowledge that she believed there was the potential for it with David Cameron, if only he was free to love in return. "I just need to find the man tolerable."

"Tolerable. Like boiled p-pudding, you mean, when you could have a nice strawberry tart." Penelope crossed her arms, her journal clutched in one hand. "How romantic."

"I don't have time for romantic," Caroline snapped as Duffington arrived with the attendant in tow. "I have a sea bath to take."

The bathing attendant escorted Caroline toward her designated box, all the while explaining the pertinent details of sea bathing. The machine would be pulled out into deeper water by a team of horses. Caroline would have a half hour to bathe in privacy, and then the machine would be brought back in.

"Some women are quite frightened by the ferocity of the waves, miss," the attendant explained as he opened the door to the yellow box. Up close, the bathing machine appeared even less hopeful than it had from a distance. The paint was peeling off in large swaths, revealing tedious, weather-beaten wood beneath.

Even the horses hitched to the front appeared bored.

The man motioned to a red flag that lay against the outside of the house. "If you become overwrought, you needn't stay out your entire allotted time. Just pull on the rope inside to signal the flag, and we'll send the driver out, straight away."

Oh dear heavens. The man was quite serious. Caroline chanced a fidgety look back at the group along the parade. Was there any chance of backing out of this now, before she became "overwrought" by a few meager waves? Branson appeared to be pacing the shoreline in a positive snit, and Mr. Adams was working to get the kite aloft. Penelope was conversing with the red-haired photographer, Mr. Hamilton, who had materialized from somewhere along the Marine Parade. She noted with a frisson of gladness that the man seemed quite interested in what her sister was saying. Perhaps there was something positive brewing there.

But Duffington, the man who was sponsoring this ill-considered excursion, the man who Caroline *ought* to place high on a list of potential bridegrooms, was leaning over the iron railing that divided the Marine Parade from the beach, watching her. When she caught his eye, he nodded, as if in encouragement.

Caroline sighed in resignation, handed her reticule and parasol to the attendant, and then clambered up the steps of her assigned bathing machine. The back door swung shut, and her eyes began a slow adjustment to darkness.

So *this* was how ladies were required to enjoy the ocean. It almost made her glad not to be a lady.

The only light came through a small, unglazed window, but it was enough to see the squalor. There was no hint of the hopeful yellow paint on the inside of the box. The contraption smelled of mildew and rot, and condensation shone against the peaked ceiling. The planks of the wooden floor were spaced several inches apart, and it appeared the water would flood the lower space of the machine as it was pulled out into the surf.

Apparently a concession for people who were too afraid to venture out into the real ocean.

"Brilliant," she muttered, just as the machine gave a jerk and she was tossed against one slick wall. She righted herself to the sound of splashing and the firm chirrup from a driver, and then the box began to move.

With some difficulty, given that her dress buttoned up the back, Caroline slipped out of her dress, shift, and stockings and placed them on a high shelf as water began to seep up through the floor. On that same shelf, she found a gray flannel robe, as damp and musty as the house itself. She examined it a full half second before pushing it back on the shelf in disgust.

It wasn't as if anyone was going to see her. She wasn't going to set foot outside this thing, for heaven's sake, not with Duffington straining for a glimpse of her from shore.

The machine's forward momentum stopped, and the

sounds of the horses being unhitched reached her ears. Cold water lapped around her bare waist, sending chill bumps along her arms. She could see why the attendant had mentioned difficulties. Every so often a large wave smashed against the wooden frame, setting her pulse pounding and the house rocking.

How did Duffington's mother consider this pastime pleasurable? She tried to imagine a countess enjoying her time in such a depressing, fetid space. What, pray tell, was so fashionable about sitting in the dark, waiting for a rogue wave to smash one's shelter to bits?

There had to be a more enjoyable way to go about attracting a suitor. And yet, wasn't she trying her best? Duffington was the son of an *earl*, for heaven's sake. Rebuffing him was not an option.

Caroline stared at the door in front of her as another wave rocked the machine. This wasn't where she wanted to be, and neither Duffington nor any of the other gentlemen waiting on the beach were whom she wanted to be with.

At that moment, the front door of the bathing machine gave a mighty rattle. She blinked, wondering if a wave had damaged the bolt somehow. But then the sound of creaking hinges assaulted her ears, and she realized with horror that the door was swinging open.

Caroline's eyes jerked against the bright spear of sunlight that breached the small, wet interior. A dark shape, backlit by the sun, stood in the open doorway. The danger of her situation sent her arms flying up to cover her bare chest. Surely Duffington hadn't been serious about swimming with her—she might not have paid proper attention to the attendant, but she was *quite* sure this was not part of the intended experience.

The shadow shifted sideways to fit through the narrow opening, and Caroline filled her lungs in a desperate whoosh, preparing to let loose a scream. She had a sudden sense of wet linen sleeves and muscular arms. Straw-colored hair that threw off droplets of water as the man loomed ever closer.

And then her breath was cut off as David Cameron's hand covered her mouth.

Chapter 19

DAVID HAD IMAGINED Caroline would be sitting in the bathing machine, gritting her teeth against the uselessness of the endeavor. Even from his distant vantage point along the Marine Parade, there had been no mistaking the tense line of her shoulders as she had climbed up inside.

But no matter how he had imagined her mood, he had thought she would be clothed.

He was now being punished for his naïveté.

David spun her around, keeping his right hand over Caroline's mouth even as her curved backside made excruciating contact with the front of his saltwater-soaked trousers. In this manner, at least, he could no longer see the bare skin that had greeted his eyes like the stiff drink he hadn't known he needed.

But unfortunately, he could still *feel* her ocean-slicked body, and he had a fearsome imagination to fill in the visual gaps. He was quite sure something approximating a breast writhed dangerously close to his left hand.

His cock, which had protested the cold shock of water only moments before, stirred to vigorous life.

A strong wave rocked the entire structure, knocking them both off balance. As she was tossed against him, he was stung by the precariousness of their situation as much as her lack of clothing. He had risked both their reputations to come here, but the sudden appearance of all those suitors had quite smashed all resolve to behave with honor.

Then again, was there anything of honor in him?

David drew in a deep draught of air that had the misfortune of being laced with her unique scent: salt and vanilla, scented bath soap and humid ocean air. As if in response, Caroline pushed a muffled stream of words between his fingers.

"Shh." He leaned in close to her ear, inhaling her heady scent and trying in vain to keep her from rocking *that* part of her anatomy against *that* part of his. "Are you trying to get yourself ruined?"

In answer, her teeth closed around his fingers. That, finally, made David jerk his hands away.

She lunged forward, giving him a lung-piercing view of her backside as she reached high to snatch something down from a shelf. He had two seconds' time to register that her freckles extended across the whole of her body, and then she pulled on a shapeless gray garment that swiftly and regrettably covered her like a blanket.

As she whirled to face him, he blinked, trying to chase the last fantastical image of her bare arse with a good dose of hard-edged reality.

Damn, but that robe was hideous.

"Are you deranged?" Her voice ricocheted off the peaked rafters, two shades below panicked.

David raised his still-smarting finger to his lips, pantomiming the need for silence. "If you rouse the hue and cry and force our discovery, you'll have no one to blame but yourself."

She fell silent and pulled the robe closer around her. "Could anyone have seen you?" she finally whispered.

He shook his head, sending sprays of water pelting the walls. "I entered the ocean from the men's beach east of the pier, and swam under water the last bit." He grinned at her. "My best swimming stroke, as it turns out. Perhaps I ought to use *that* on Monday."

She seemed to shove that around in her head a moment before giving voice to the question that haunted them both. "What are you doing here, David?"

"I . . ." He paused, searching his brain.

What *was* he doing here? He still wasn't sure what had prompted him do this. To understand if she still intended to teach him her swimming stroke? To demand if she was seriously entertaining ideas of a romantic nature about one of the swaggering bucks who had trailed her all morning? Her sudden and startling popularity had made it deucedly hard to find the private moment either of those conversations demanded.

Her eyes smoldered across the heated space. "You went to a good deal of trouble to just stand there mute."

He tried to think of something—*anything*—that would make sense. "I . . . I signed up for the race this morning, and I still need your help to win."

A sharp burst of laughter escaped her lips. "You expect me to continue to instruct you, after . . . after last night?"

"Yes. I mean, no. I do not *expect* it. I would hope you would want to continue."

Her pointed chin came up in synchronized harmony with her brows. "You risked my reputation for that? Honestly, David, you could have just sent a note. Last night, you pointed out why you were not a suitable match for me, and in fact, encouraged me to dance with other gentlemen. And yet you have shown up here, uninvited, threatening to destroy the interest of others who might make an offer."

David was chastened. He was also enthralled by the way that flannel robe rose and fell with her every breath, as if it wanted to slide off her.

As if it wanted *him* to slide it off her.

But damned if she wasn't right. Last night he had reacted poorly to her shiny, polished view of him and the avalanche of self-loathing her words had triggered. He had focused on his own feelings instead of Caroline's. That was not fair.

He would make it right now.

"Then let me apologize again. Do not let last night's discussion change the nature of our friendship. I still intend to compete in Monday's race, and I would very much like to continue our planned instruction."

"Do you think it is wise to spend so much time alone together, after all that has passed between us?" she asked, catching her lower lip between her teeth in an innocent gesture that, regrettably, made his cock stiffen with renewed interest.

"Probably not," he admitted.

She tensed beneath that heavy robe, and he could not blame her. He had, after all, given her good reason to fear for her virtue, bursting into the little bathing machine without even first stopping to check that she was clothed.

"But if you will do this for me, if you will see our lessons through, I promise to behave honorably," he added. "To keep our interactions strictly impersonal. You have nothing to fear by continuing your instruction. I give you my word."

DAMN DAVID CAMERON *and his gilded tongue and devilish grin.*

One word, one rakish smile, and the sliver of hope that Caroline had forced herself to bury last night had already begun to work its way back toward the surface.

No matter his monkish stance, no matter his patent denials from last night, he was not immune to her. The hard, defined length of his arousal had just been pressed against her bare back, for heaven's sake. He could deny his interest all he wanted, but he could not hide it.

Last night, on the dance floor, David had instructed her

on what to look for in a dance partner, claiming his unsolicited tutoring was fair turnabout in exchange for her swimming instructions. That memory breathed new life into what
was probably a foolish idea. Caroline lifted her eyes to meet
the intense blue gaze that hovered a mere two feet away.

She might not be able to capture David Cameron's
heart, but mayhap she had set her sights too high.

"I *might* be willing to continue your swimming instruction," she told him, her stomach churning. "Given the right
incentive."

He did not even hesitate. "I would gladly give you the
entire purse, if you wanted."

She shook her head, although the generous offer surprised her, given his admitted need of the prize money.
"You misunderstand me. Splitting the purse, should you
win it, is more than fair. But there is no guarantee you will
win, and that might leave me without recompense."

His jaw tensed. "What do you suggest as payment?"

The suspicion in his voice near dragged her under, but
Caroline shrugged it off, determined to see this through.
She might not have a future with *this* man, but if she had
to marry someone else to keep the promise she had made
to her father, didn't she at least deserve a taste of what she
was giving up?

"You showed me how much possibility could be found
in a kiss, David. I want to learn more, before I marry. And
I want to learn it from you."

He jerked backward as if she had struck him. "If I win
this race for us, you'll have enough money you won't *need*
to marry."

"I appreciate the gesture, but such a boon would only
delay the inevitable. I've my sister to support, and my
mother as well. I am still bound for marriage, David. And
the longer I wait, the poorer my chances."

His face flushed scarlet. "I cannot offer for you, so do
not ask me."

His words stung, for all that she was now prepared to deal with them. Caroline crossed her arms across her flannel-clad chest and tried to hide her shaking fingers. "As you pointed out last night, we would not suit. I am not seeking an offer of marriage from you."

And she wasn't. He had made it quite clear his heart was otherwise engaged. But given that the love of his life had been dead for some eleven years, he could not argue that other pertinent parts of his anatomy were not available.

And though her motives tended toward selfish, she might be able to help him as well. It struck her as a terrible waste that a man capable of such strong feelings had spent eleven years loving someone who could no longer love him back. He seemed unwilling to even consider an alternative to that cycle of mourning, but perhaps he had not found someone who could help him see that his life might be more. Even if he could not see a future with her, Caroline was willing to prove he should at least consider a future with *someone*.

Oblivious to the machinations of her mind, David raked a hand through hair that already stood in a damp, golden tangle. "If not marriage, then what, in the name of all that is holy, are you asking me for?"

Caroline took a deep breath for courage, and flexed her fingers against the suffocating cocoon of her flannel robe. This next bit would require some finesse. "I require only your expertise in matters of a physical nature."

His eyes narrowed on hers. "That sounds like an indecent sort of proposition."

"You told me last night you weren't celibate. That means you grant your favors to other women." Her stomach churned, whether from the constant, shuddering movement of the bathing machine, or the nature of what she was asking, she couldn't be sure. "I want you to share some small measure of those favors with me. One friend to another."

He began to pace in the narrow confines of the bathing machine, although circling might have been more apt description. Two steps carried him from one end of the house to the other. His movements set the timbers of the little house shaking.

"Have you not heard a word I have said?" His words swung wildly, but still found their mark. The honor she sensed lurking beneath David's skin, the honor he denied he possessed, insinuated itself front and center. "You are more than 'other' women to me. You are asking me to ruin you, and then wrap it in a nice bow as if it's some kind of perverted gift."

"Don't I deserve to know what I should be seeking in a husband before I make the wrong choice?" she countered. "And I have not asked you to do anything of the sort. I do not require the whole of the experience. Just enough to properly inform my decision."

He paused facing away from her, trapped in one narrow corner of the box that seemed to have shrunk about three sizes. She heard him swallow, even over the rush of the ocean. "How much of it?" he rasped.

"Not *all* of it. But more than kissing." She had already had that from him, and while she was looking forward to repeating the experience, she wanted to know more.

His shoulders tensed beneath the wet fabric of his shirt, and she could see his fists clench and unclench. "You do not know what you are asking of me."

"I do." And she believed, with every fiber of her being, that he was the only man who could accomplish it. "I want this, David."

"You want the experience." He swung around to face her. "It does not have to come from me."

Caroline studied him, frustration shaking her with sharp teeth. She did not want to marry someone like Branson or Duffington without first exploring the sort of emotion that made her heart spin on its axis. "Are you suggesting I should ask someone else to show me? Mr. Branson, perhaps?"

He took a heated step toward her, his eyes flashing. "God, no. Do not even consider taking such a careless risk to your reputation."

Her knees locked at his terse reminder. He was right—she was skirting ruin here, and not just in the physical sense. She considered what had happened as a result of her single, ill-considered experience with Mr. Dermott . . . and *that* had been nothing more than a kiss. If someone found out about this, her reputation, fragile thing that it was, would be shattered. She did not want to disappoint her family, just to find some narrow piece of happiness.

But she also wanted a memory that would buffer her through the increasing likelihood of a cold, loveless marriage. And she wanted that memory to be shaped by David Cameron.

Despite his claims to the contrary, there was honor in this man. She trusted David to preserve her reputation. Who better to protect her than a man so determined not to ruin her?

And who better than she to show him what potential lurked in his heart?

Caroline shook free the misgivings that sat heavy on her shoulders. "I do not want to ask another man to show me this, David. I want it to be you, precisely because I know my reputation is safe with you."

And then, before he could lodge another protest, before he could shove her, once again, into the realm of mere friendship, she stepped forward and kissed him.

DAVID FOUND HIMSELF knocked off balance, this time by Caroline herself. The impact of her body and their wild tumble against the salt-slicked wall left him so stunned that for a moment he wondered if she had hit him with something more solid than just her frame.

Not that he wouldn't deserve it.

But then her fingers tangled in his hair and he was pulled, quite forcibly, down to meet her lips.

Had he ever met a girl so determined to be ruined?

He tried to remain unmoved by her sweet assault. Kept his lips closed as she pressed her lush mouth against him. Forced his fingers to stay pressed flat against his own thighs, when what he wanted to do was lift his hands to grip her hair and yank her closer.

She gasped against his mouth, a small, feminine mewl of frustration.

He lost the battle for apathy with that sound, which so perfectly echoed how he felt. Lifting his hands to cradle her head, he scraped his fingers through her coiled hair and loosened an army's worth of pins in the process. An astonishing array of scents greeted him as her hair came down, scents he was coming to associate with Caroline: ocean salt, vanilla, and something undefinable that went straight to his gut.

Even as he fought to retain some base measure of control, his body flared to life around the familiar, stinging taste of her. His cock rose up to greet the collision of flannel and wet wool, softness and heat. He coaxed her mouth apart and ran his tongue along the seam of her lips. Showed her the rhythm that set up its inescapable beat in the primitive part of his brain. And then, though he knew he should not, though he had told her he *would* not, he gave her the moment she sought.

But he didn't just draw her into in a sweet, sheltered embrace.

No, he cupped her arse, pulled her against his throbbing erection, and showed her why it was not a good idea to tease the beast he kept chained.

She ignored the warning. If anything, she pushed back against him.

Her flannel-clad core settled dangerously close to part

of his body that wanted to bury itself in her. The friction of their bodies caught against the edges of that hateful robe, and it gaped open in places he suspected he would dream of for some time to come.

It proved an impossible invitation, one he didn't have the intelligence or presence of mind to refuse. He lifted a palm to one of Caroline's breasts, and she sighed into his mouth with pleasure. She might be small-breasted, but there was no lack of response. Indeed, it was as if every nerve ending was concentrated in space and time, straining for the touch of his thumb. He stroked her nipple, reverently at first, and then turned his touch harder, rolling the peaked nub between his fingers until she gasped, this time with pleasure instead of frustration.

The sound unearthed an answering, rumbling growl deep within his chest. He hitched her legs around his waist, where they wrapped, impossibly tight. He pushed her against the opposite wall, intent on providing her with the instruction she had demanded. But as his hands groped for leverage against the damp wood, his fingers caught on a rope of some sort.

A sound reached his ears then, a scraping along the outside wall. The kiss ended on dual gasps of surprise, and they both stared at the rope where his left hand still rested.

"Flag up, yellow box!" The distant shout echoed from shore, just discernible above the sound of the water and their own labored breathing.

His right hand, which had still been pressed against her breast, was greeted with a rush of cool air as she jerked away from his touch. Caroline exploded in a flurry of limbs and flannel, pulling the edges of the robe around her. "You've pulled the flag!" she accused.

"What flag?" He couldn't think of anything except that in this moment, he would have agreed to any terms she wanted, if only she would kiss him again.

"The flag to call the bathing machine back in." She pushed against him, her hands firm. "Go. *Go.*"

"Go where?" he asked, feeling trapped. He was confused by the sudden shift in atmosphere. Her lips were still swollen, and the skin along the collar of her robe was flushed pink. She still hummed with passion.

But a hint of panic had been inserted into the mix.

She reached a hand up to the shelf and dragged down a bundle of blue print fabric, then turned her back on him. He stared, transfixed by the sight of her curved spine as she shrugged off the robe and pulled her white shift over her bare shoulders.

Christ, but she was lovely.

"To the shore," she snapped over her shoulder. "To the cove. Anywhere. Just . . . don't be seen here, for God's sake!" She yanked the shift down to cover her hips, not even pausing as it skimmed the water and became soaked through.

He started to turn toward the door, but paused. His thoughts were tumbling, but they were all pointing in the same direction. "You'll meet me at the cove? In an hour's time?" Despite the risk of discovery, his hand refused to turn the latch until he achieved an understanding.

She paused, her fingers halting in the process of pulling on her dress. "Do you agree to my terms?" she asked warily.

He strained against the demands of his conscience. Had she left him any choice? Hers was a reckless sort of spirit, and she seemed to either not understand or care that ruin hovered around this corner she was demanding to turn. Could he do what she asked? He needed only to ensure her virtue remained intact. He was no longer a lust-addled youth. Surely he could show her a taste of her body's potential without taking the ultimate prize.

And if it kept her out the hands of a fumbling fool like

Branson . . . well, mayhap there was honor to be found in that.

"Aye." He turned the latch. "I agree to your terms. But only through Monday's race, and no more." He would not survive if she insisted on daily lessons through his leaving.

"Then I promise I will meet you there." She chased her words with a brilliant smile that he was quite sure would have damned him to hell, had he not already surrendered that part of his soul eleven years ago.

The danger ratcheted up as David heard the sounds of splashing outside the box. The whinny of a horse reached his ears, followed by the snap of reins. He reached for the front door of the bathing machine, but paused as the house gave a lurch and started to turn.

Water swirled around their legs as the house strained against the current.

"Not that way," she said, whispering now. She motioned toward the back door as the box gave another shudder and began to move forward. "The driver is on that side. The back door is now pointed toward the ocean."

And then he was pushed out of the machine's rear door, preparing his lungs for a long, underwater swim and an hour of frustration until he could see her again.

She had promised she would come. There was unfinished business between them.

And he had never wanted to finish something so much in his life.

Chapter 20

Λ THRUMMING BEAT STILL shimmered at the juncture of Caroline's thighs a quarter hour later. If that had been her first lesson in the pleasures to be found beyond kissing, she could not imagine what her second lesson might reveal.

If David hadn't pulled the flag, how much more might she have learned? She wanted to imagine he would not have taken her there against the wall of the bathing machine, but the urgency of his kiss and the primitive, vital response of her own body had quite shocked her.

How could she expect him to guard her virtue if her own feelings on the matter were so easily swayed?

Mr. Hamilton had joined them for the long, sticky walk home, drawing Penelope into a private conversation and leaving Caroline to fend for herself among the three remaining men. She breathed a grateful sigh of relief as they made their way up her porch stairs and came to a disorderly halt. At last she could count this ill-designed exercise at an end and find a way to slip out and meet David at the cove. She was already late, but there had been no choice but to return home first. The three men remained glued to her side from the moment she climbed, damp and disheveled, out of the bathing machine.

"Might I call on you for a walk tomorrow?" Duffington's booming voice jerked her back to the hard reality of the parting niceties.

Branson elbowed his way closer and lodged a swift protest. "*I* was hoping to call on you tomorrow, Miss Caroline."

To her surprise, given his seeming focus on Penelope, Mr. Hamilton was the next to pipe up. "It isn't sporting to monopolize her time when there are also others who would enjoy a chance to call on her. I would like to call on her tomorrow, as well."

Caroline tried to summon a smile, but it was hard to find one that fit the moment. The infantile verbal sparring between the men was starting to remind her of the gulls that squabbled over crusts of bread on the beach. Worse, they imposed on time she needed to preserve for David. She was going to need every second to teach him what he needed to know in order to win against Brighton's more seasoned competitors on Monday.

And she was going to demand every second he owed her in return.

"I really must beg *all* of your leaves on the matter of a walk tomorrow," she hedged, fanning her face. "I am unused to such . . . strenuous exercise." She saw Penelope's eyes round at bit at the lie. Not that she blamed her. After all, her sister was usually the one who had to explain the long walks Caroline took most afternoons to their mother.

When the last man had taken his leave and trooped off the porch, Caroline exhaled in frustration. "I am sorry, Pen. I do not know why Mr. Hamilton said he would call on me. He seems much more interested in you, truth be told."

Penelope gave her a probing look as she opened the front door, her blue eyes serious beneath her shaded straw bonnet. "That is really neither here nor there. Not an hour ago you insisted that these men represented your b-best chance at finding an offer of marriage. That romance and love held no place in your decision. Yet you c-c-could have been contemplating which serving of spoiled fish to eat just now."

Caroline held her breath against the dizzying scent of flowers that greeted her as she followed Penelope inside to the foyer. A great deal had changed in that hour, including, it seemed, the arrival of several more bouquets. But by far the most important change of the past hour had been her agreement with David.

Not that Penelope knew anything of that.

"They seem like fine young men, but the prospect of courting one of them is a bit daunting," she admitted.

"Do you find any of them appealing?" Pen asked curiously as she placed her journal on the foyer table and began to remove her gloves. "Mr. Adams is p-passably handsome. And I admit some partiality to Mr. Hamilton's red hair."

Caroline shook her head as she tossed the hated parasol into the umbrella stand. "Not really," she admitted. Indeed, based on the way these gentlemen made her feel, even Mr. Dermott might be a better choice. At least he had nice, straight teeth and made her feel a little light-headed, even when he tormented her. "But as I must marry," she mused with an increasing sense of discomfort, "I can't see my way around it."

Penelope untied the ribbons of her bonnet and fixed Caroline with a stern look as she lifted the straw hat from her hair. "*Why* must you marry?"

The question startled her. "To ensure our futures. To return our family to respectability." Her father's last words teased at the scant edges of Caroline's memory. "To take care of you and Mama."

Pen shook her head as she placed the bonnet on the hat tree. "I refuse to be the reason you marry. I am c-capable of making my own way."

Caroline stared at her sister in surprise. "But . . . I made a promise."

Penelope threw up her hands. "To whom? To *Mama*? I cannot believe that. I d-do not believe she intends you to be unhappy. She married Papa for love. She would not d-deny you the same opportunity."

Caroline's toes twitched inside her half boots. Could Pen be right? She thought back to recent conversations. Mama had been fixated on the matter of a suitor's title and financial security, sure enough, but it was also true she wanted to know how Caroline *felt* about things.

The noise of heels sounding on the floorboards overhead proved an unwelcome distraction. She glanced up, examining the old plaster molding that threatened to come apart with every footfall. No matter Pen's claims regarding Mama's intentions, Caroline wanted to deal with her mother's scrutiny right now even less than she desired to have this conversation with Penelope. But she needed her sister's help if she was to provide their mother with a logical excuse.

"I forgot I have an appointment this afternoon, Pen. Will you give Mama my apologies and tell her I shall miss afternoon tea?"

"An appointment with whom?" Pen's voice rang in suspicion.

Caroline's mind scrambled for purchase on some idea, and came up blank.

"I am not sure why you won't confide in me. Haven't I always k-kept your secrets? I did not tell Mama about that matter with Mr. Dermott, and I would not tell her about this."

Her sister's probing made Caroline squirm with guilt. "And what of *your* secrets, Pen? You have not confided in me either. When did you progress from reading about the world to writing about it?"

"Perhaps I have something t-to write about for the first time in my life," Penelope retorted, her face flushing a virulent shade of pink. "And d-do not try to turn this around. You are going to swim. Do not deny it."

Caroline curled her fingers in empty frustration. The only way to keep Pen quiet on this was to make her an ally.

Then they would *both* catch it if Mama found out.

"Yes," she admitted, wondering if she wasn't making the biggest mistake of her life. Well, perhaps not the *biggest*.

She had kissed Dermott, after all.

"I am going to swim. In the cove where Papa used to take us to gather seashells when we were small."

There. She had given voice to this terrible, clandestine part of her life. It felt oddly comforting to confess the truth to her sister. But she was not, under any circumstances, going to tell her sister whom she was going to swim *with*.

"Isn't that a tad reckless?" Penelope asked, her eyes rounding to the shape of marbles. "I recall the current there being ferocious."

"Oh, it is quite safe," Caroline rushed to assure her. She did not, under any circumstances, want Pen to feel compelled to take this information to their mother. "Nothing to worry about. Why, even the most novice of swimmers could manage it, if only they knew where to find it." She laughed, negating the potential danger with a flippant hand. "I enjoy going there because it reminds me of Papa. Swimming was something he encouraged me to do, you know. Much like he encouraged your interest in books and the newspaper."

Pen's mouth opened wordlessly, then closed again. "Oh," she said, before her face softened in understanding. "I s-s-suppose I could tell Mama you have gone to an appointment with the modiste on East Street."

Caroline nodded, although new clothes were the furthest thing from her mind. "Thank you, Pen. I . . . well, I shall owe you." She took a step toward the front door and the freedom that hovered just beyond. By now David would be pacing along shore, wondering where she was, and she still had an hour's hard walk ahead of her.

A firm rapping on the very door she was aiming for sent Caroline's stomach churning. It could be just another bouquet of flowers, she supposed.

Or it could be another blasted gentleman caller.

She cast a wild glance around the foyer, preparing to slip down the hallway and make her exit through the scullery door. Of course, that would put her in Bess's path, which would be almost as bad as stumbling into Mama's. But Penelope didn't give her time to formulate a plan. She was already stepping around her and pulling open the door.

A smartly dressed woman stood on the porch. Her hair was the sort of vivid orange that could only come from a chemist's shop, and her generous bosom was showcased by tucks and gathers in places Caroline would have never considered sending a needle and thread.

She regarded Caroline with a shrewd, assessing air, her eyes running the length of her frame from heel to hair. "*Bonjour, chérie.*"

"*Bonjour?*" Caroline replied.

Bess appeared from the hallway that ran to the kitchen. "Oh, Madame Beauclerc!" The servant wiped her flour-covered hands on her apron. "I'll fetch Mrs. Tolbertson straight away." She headed up the stairs, muttering about pies and fittings and too many gentleman callers.

"Did you know about this?" Caroline hissed to Penelope.

Her sister shook her head, though her eyes sparkled with anticipation. Caroline couldn't begrudge her that. It had been at least three years since either Caroline or Pen had been gifted with anything other than a made-over gown.

But why did it have to be *today*, of all days?

"I came as soon as I could," the woman said, her French accent slipping as a hint of London's East Side snuck in. She recovered well, though, affecting a very cosmopolitan sniff. "Mrs. Tolbertson's missive on the need for my services seemed, *comment vous le dites . . .* frantic?"

The sound of Mama's heels on the top of the stairs made Caroline's insides shrivel. She could see the remainder of her afternoon coming like a runaway wagon down a narrow alley, and yet she could not steer herself clear of the pending wreckage.

Still, she had to try. David was waiting for her. And she had *promised*.

But Madame Beauclerc's large frame blocked any hope of easy egress. "Um . . . please," Caroline breathed, motioning with both hands. "If you could just step a little to the side . . ."

The dressmaker took a single, dramatic step to one side, one penciled brow cocked upward in amusement. "Are you sure, *chérie*?" She was trailed by a shopgirl bearing an armful of fabric samples and a covered basket with ribbons and lace peeking out of the top. "By the looks of that dress, I suspect you might be the one I have been summoned here to help."

"Perhaps another day," Caroline said, preparing to bolt through the open door like lightning.

But even as she gathered her skirts, her mother's voice floated down from the last step of the stairwell. "Caroline Rebecca Tolbertson! If you take one more step toward that open door, you shall live to regret it."

Caroline blinked up. Why, oh *why* couldn't this be the day that Mama was confined to bed with a headache? "I have to go," she protested. "Surely this can wait?"

Her mother descended the final step, her blue eyes flashing in excitement as much as annoyance. "No. I am very much afraid this *cannot* wait. There is not a minute to spare."

Caroline looked between her mother and the modiste. "I don't understand."

Her mother's skin flushed a pretty pink against her widow's weeds. "Penelope was correct, it seems, in the matter of one invitation leading to more. You've both received an invitation to a ball tomorrow night, sponsored by Lord and Lady Traverstein. So I am afraid your afternoon walk will just have to wait."

Chapter 21

CAROLINE WAS HAULED into the parlor and stripped down to her shift. Mama and Penelope settled on the settee to study a book of fashion plates. Tea was ordered, a poor sign all around. And then the shopgirl began taking Caroline's measurements with the pace of a tortoise.

Quite possibly a *deceased* tortoise.

Madame Beauclerc circled with a critical eye, her magnificent bosom bouncing with each step. She brought her fingers together, as if considering pinching some part of Caroline's misshapen anatomy. "Those shoulders . . . I have never seen the like. I shall have to cancel the rest of my afternoon appointments to deal with this problem."

"Will that cost more?" Mama asked, her face pulling into worried creases.

The modiste shook her head. "It shall be my charitable pleasure. Such great need, after all, cannot be ignored."

Caroline groaned. So now she was a "problem," a philanthropic venture for Brighton's newest modiste to show the town what an excellent seamstress could accomplish under dire circumstances. She could almost hear the gossip now, from Miss Baxter's all-too-ready lips.

If Madame Beauclerc could turn that Caroline Tolbertson into someone passable, imagine what miracles she could work on the rest of us.

And all the while, David was waiting. She had promised him she would be there, and a promise was something one did not break. But as painful as the memory was, another promise she had once made demanded its own recognition. She had promised her father, all those years ago, that she would take care of Mama and Penelope. And a small, reluctant part of her could not deny that standing here and suffering this was a step toward fulfilling that promise.

Madame Beauclerc turned toward Mama and Penelope on the settee. "You mentioned in your urgent summons we must work within a limited budget, *oui*?"

Mrs. Tolbertson's face settled into a determined mask. "Yes. We must set up both of my daughters with a new, more fashionable wardrobe, for thirty pounds or less."

"Mama!" Caroline gasped. By her mother's own admission, they had, in total, less than a hundred pounds. They needed that money to live should her mangled efforts to produce a well-heeled husband fall through. "I have three . . . er . . . two perfectly good dresses," she protested, now cringing at the memory of destroying her navy serge gown. "I do not need more."

"It is money well spent if it procures a betrothal within the month." Her mother straightened her small but stern shoulders. "We cannot afford a trousseau. Best to focus on the outer garments."

Caroline wanted to shake her mother into rational thought. If they spent such a substantial portion of their savings on this desperate gamble, they would have nothing left to fall back on should the price of bread go up.

Or should the ceiling cave in.

"Please do not do this," Caroline begged. Time was already racing by for her, time she resented losing. If this money was spent on clothing, she would have no choice but to strongly encourage one of her current suitors to consider a scandalously short courtship, despite the fact that none of them made her heart do more than push the usual amount of tepid blood through her veins.

Her mother raised a determined brow. "You had three gentlemen callers this morning, Caroline, and now have an invitation to a ball."

"Four callers," Penelope chimed in. "Mr. Hamilton joined the group later," she added, and though her sister's voice offered no hint of resentment, Caroline squirmed at the reminder.

"*Four* gentlemen callers," her mother corrected, her eyes widening. "It quite taxes the imagination. This is a time for action, not frugality. I want two new day dresses made for you, but first we must focus on a ball gown that is in the absolute height of fashion. Penelope's day dresses are in better shape, but I think at least one new dress for her, as well as a new evening gown."

Madame Beauclerc burst into enthusiastic motion, clapping her hands. "I must see what accessories you have, so we know what to work around. Bring them all to me here. Bonnets. Slippers. Evening gloves, shawls, reticules . . . anything you have. I must see the colors of these items, the workmanship. Only then can I know which direction to go, and what can be made over." She motioned, once again, toward Caroline's shoulders. "But the ball gown for this one must be made from new. Her form is very difficult to show to advantage, *oui*?"

"Caroline's shoulders," said Mama, shaking her head, "are the bane of my existence."

"I shall bring everything we have in our room," Pen said, already heading toward the parlor door.

"And I have a trunk full of things left from my own come-out in London," her mother added, rising from the settee. She touched Caroline's chin, though she had to reach up several inches to do it. Tears swam in her blue eyes. "Oh, how I envy you this experience. This is your chance to shine, dear. You might as well smile and enjoy it."

"I do not want to enjoy it, Mama." It was the honest truth, even if it sounded petulant, framed in her hoarse, strangled voice.

Mrs. Tolbertson shook her head. "Then you must bear it instead." She turned to Madame Beauclerc. "Might I borrow your assistant to help carry the items downstairs?"

"Of course." The dressmaker motioned for the shopgirl to follow.

When the room fell quiet, Madame Beauclerc turned to Caroline with a mysterious smile on her rouged lips. She tilted her head, making Caroline feel as if she was the subject of some fascinating mental dissection. "Now that we have sent the chickens pecking for scraps," the modiste said, "why don't you tell me what *you* want, *chérie*."

Caroline shuffled her feet beneath the woman's scrutiny. What *did* she want?

One answer came to mind. She wanted a reprieve, a chance to explore passion before she tied herself in marriage to an amiable husband who would expect her to spend all her time on charitable knitting.

But surely a dressmaker would not be referring to anything so esoteric.

"I . . . I am not the person to ask," Caroline stammered. "I have no sense of fashion."

"Perhaps you want more than pretty dresses?" Madame Beauclerc circled again, appraising. Judging. She leaned in, so close Caroline could see the pearllike powder caked in the crease of the woman's ample cleavage. "Those shoulders give you away. I have seen others like you. I have made them . . ." She waved her hand, as if searching for the right word in French, and then abandoning the effort. "*Dresses*, if you would, that are better suited for water and still provide some modesty. I could do the same for you."

Caroline stared at her with stricken eyes. Her throat felt squeezed from within. "I am not sure what you mean."

The dressmaker raised a brow and touched a finger to the fabric covering Caroline's skin. "Your shift is wet, *chérie*."

Caroline exhaled. Well, that was easily explained. "I went out in one of the bathing machines this morning. I must have gotten it damp."

The modiste shook her head. "I do not think you are a woman who spends much time in bathing machines." She gestured to Caroline's thigh, just below the hem of her shift. "Your skin is brown in places the sun should not touch. How do these men in Brighton stand the sight of your wet shift without falling to their knees in desire?"

Caroline's pulse proved a roaring counterpoint to the dressmaker's pointed silence as the woman waited for an answer. "I . . . only swim in private," Caroline said, unable to believe she was admitting this for the second time today.

Madame Beauclerc shook her head and clucked her tongue. "Well, is it any wonder? Plain white cotton leaves nothing to the imagination when wet. And the flannel robes they give you in the bathing machines would send even the bravest of us to the bottom should we attempt to swim in deep water. You need *proper* swimming attire, *chérie*. Then you could grace the public beaches, as your body was fashioned to do." She leaned in again. "I could create you an ensemble that will turn you into a goddess."

Caroline stared, her eyes probing every corner of the dressmaker's frame and finding only ample, female curves. What kind of modiste was Madame Beauclerc, to offer to make such an improper item of clothing?

Perhaps the woman really *was* French.

Penelope staggered into the room then, her arms full of undergarments and shawls. "I br-brought everything I could find," she said, almost quivering with excitement. "Although now that I see how few quality accessories we actually own, it seems hopeless."

Madame Beauclerc smiled at Pen. "I shall make you both spectacular, *chérie*. Do not doubt it."

"Spectacular seems a bit of a stretch for me, given that the garments must also *fit*," Caroline objected. "My shoulders are so broad—"

"It is the fashion that makes them appear so," the dressmaker interrupted. She lifted a hand to tug at the cotton fabric near Caroline's shoulder. "The dropped sleeve that is so popular plays against you. It highlights the length of your shoulder too much. If we put more fabric here . . ."

"I wish her to be in the height of fashion," Mama reminded as she came into the parlor bearing her own armload of frippery. "She shall need bishop sleeves on her ball gown."

"Bishop sleeves are a fleeting fancy," countered the dressmaker, her bosom heaving with conviction. "We must make our own fashion for this one." She returned her hands to tug at Caroline's chemise. "Lower here, at the neckline. Delicate sleeves across the center of your shoulder, not below it. Even just a ribbon would suffice, to draw the line and break up the appearance of all that skin. Light green silk, I think, to accentuate your unusual eyes."

Her mother tilted her head and ran her eyes along Caroline's shift-covered frame. Slow understanding bloomed across her face. "I had not considered before how the current fashions might be downplaying her attributes."

"She has a long, lovely line to her neck," Penelope pointed out, making Caroline feel like a prize heifer at a parish fair.

The modiste nodded. "*Oui.* And excellent posture."

Her mother began to look excited. "Might we have Caroline's ball gown by tomorrow night?"

Madame Beauclerc pursed her lips. "We shall need an additional fitting tomorrow, after I assemble the piecework. And that would leave us little time to finish the gown."

"There must be a way," protested Mrs. Tolbertson. "If we covered the cost of another seamstress to work with you . . ."

Madame Beauclerc's doubtful expression softened at the mention of additional funds. "*Oui*. For an extra three pounds, I believe I could produce a gown by tomorrow evening."

Her mother beamed, even as Caroline's world began to splinter into wreckage around her. "It shall be no problem for the extra charge, Madame Beauclerc. Because I have a feeling our fortunes are about to improve."

As DAVID PICKED his way over the last few hundred yards of the footpath, he ignored the coming sunset and focused instead on the worry simmering in his gut.

He had waited for Caroline all afternoon. The first hour had passed with his body still hard with want, a by-product of their ill-advised romp in the bathing machine. Eventually he had napped on the sun-heated rock while the swallows flitted above him, laughing at his dilemma. When the shadows started to lengthen, he had spent a fretful half hour pacing the shoreline, worrying that something had happened to her. A twisted ankle. A tumble off the narrow footpath, or falling rocks from the high cliff face. Those thoughts sent him hurrying back, his worry a hard lump in his throat.

But as the lights of Brighton came into view and he thankfully caught no sight of her body prostrate along the path, he turned himself over to other disturbing possibilities. Had she come to her senses and realized that the experience she sought with him wasn't just ill-advised, it was downright dangerous?

Or—and he was desperate enough to admit this thought was far more troublesome than the first—had she decided to take him at his word and save her breathy sighs and soft, bare skin for a partner who could offer her the betrothal she sought? The thought of her kissing someone like Branson sent his mind careening in regrettable directions, and made it difficult to focus on the simple task of just getting home.

As the treacherous footpath fell away to reveal the wide shingle beach that defined the outer limits of Brighton, David found he could no longer ignore the sunset. The brilliant evening sky had pulled hordes of fashionable beachgoers from their hotels and houses, and they were scattered about, facing the color-splashed horizon. With a muffled curse, David sidestepped an older couple sitting side by side on folding chairs, then almost tripped over a small boy who was darting about with chubby fistfuls of seashells. Several people had brought their dogs down to the water and taken them off lead, and one exuberant retriever shook its coat, spraying salt water all over David's trousers.

Bloody hell. No wonder Caroline preferred the isolation of her cove. As he shook the errant droplets of water from his jacket, David's gaze was pulled to the first row of houses that lined the eastern edge of Brighton. Damn it, why hadn't she come?

And what was he going to do about her?

Even now, his body tightened in response to the memory of that kiss. God, that kiss. So unexpected, the complete opposite image of sweet innocence that he had been trying to pin on her shoulders. He had wanted to inhale her. To take her, right up against the wall of that bathing machine, with the damp, slick boards at her back and the motion of the waves pushing him into her. She did regrettable things to his body, things that made it difficult to keep one foot on a field of honor. She did regrettable things to his brain, as well. Turned him stupid. Made him agree to things no sane man would consider.

But heady as those feelings were, and as tempted as she made him feel, he had naïvely thought he could keep those feelings chained. After the frustration of the afternoon, and after the panic he had endured at the thought of her injured, or worse, in someone else's arms, he could no longer claim his heart was immune to the enigma that was Caroline Tolbertson.

And that made this a much more dangerous game they played.

The tall Georgian with the red shutters pulled him as surely as if strings had been attached to his feet. At this time of evening, Caroline's family would either be preparing to sit down for dinner, or more likely finishing it. Manners dictated he keep going, head for the Bedford, apologize to his mother for arriving late to their own evening meal.

Well, he had never been one to let a few manners stand in his way. And right now, if he couldn't have Caroline in his arms, damp from a swim and squirming in need, he at least wanted an explanation for her change of mind.

He was still several dozen yards away, moving in relative anonymity among the evening beachgoers, when a small party burst out of Caroline's front door in a flurry of excited feminine chatter. David recognized Caroline's tall, lean frame and dark hair, wrapped as it was in evening light. He thought he recognized her blond-haired sister, as well, although the other women milling about the porch did not seem familiar to him.

A cultured voice reached his ears, higher pitched than Caroline's, but carrying the same rich tones. "We shall expect you tomorrow, a little before noon, for Caroline's next fitting, Madame Beauclerc," the woman in black said.

"*Oui*. We shall work as hard as we can to have her gown finished in time."

David's gaze arrowed in on Caroline's face. There was no protest from her lips, no negotiation for another time, no mention of another engagement. If anything, she nodded her appreciation.

And the edges of his vision turned black.

David turned away, his body's stiff-shouldered reaction predictable, even if it wasn't sensible. His fingers curled into tight fists, and he knew in that instant that if Branson or Dermott had happened to walk by, he would have been hard-pressed to keep himself from exploding with flying fists and battered ego. Had he been in Moraig, he would have sought out his friends and raised a pint or three at the Blue Gander. But he wasn't in Scotland.

And his one friend in Brighton had just spurned him.

David forced himself to head west, toward the Steine and the Bedford's excellent, attentive staff. To his mother and his waiting dinner and, if he was lucky, his erstwhile sanity. He dodged the revelers and the families and the happy, laughing couples. And all the while, he fumed.

This was the same girl who had once told him that keeping a promise was the most important part of a person's character. Today, Caroline had kissed him. Convinced him to agree to her outrageous proposal, promised to meet him. And then she had not come. Not for anything reasonable. Like a coastal invasion by the French navy. Or a raging case of smallpox.

No, she had rejected him for a dress fitting.

And he couldn't understand why it disturbed him so much.

Chapter 22

THOUGH SHE HAD told herself she would close her eyes for only a moment, Caroline awoke to a thick, gray dawn threading its way through the lace curtains of her bedroom. She sat bolt upright, cursing even as she tumbled from the bed.

It was Friday morning. She had intended to pen David a note last night apologizing for yesterday's missed afternoon. But she had fallen asleep in something akin to a narcotic haze, a side effect of the past two late nights. She recalled Penelope and Bess wrangling her out of her clothes and tucking her feet into bed.

And then . . . nothing. Not even her usual state of dreams. And that meant not only had Caroline broken her promise to David yesterday, she had done it without a single note of explanation.

She needed to deliver a note to the Bedford this morning, before her mother awakened and before Brighton began to stir. She and David now had only three days left to practice before the race, and she was desperate enough to demand every one of them.

She opened the door to the wardrobe, quiet as a dormouse. Her hand paused over the skirt of her lavender gown, the bodice of which was still awaiting Bess's miraculous laundry skills. It was to be the same blue print dress as yesterday, then. But as she ran through the meager contents of the wardrobe, she noticed with surprise that Pen's yellow day dress was missing. She turned an inquisitive head toward her sister's bed, and that was when the first threads of anxiety began to attach themselves for the day.

Pen's bed was not just empty. Her pillow was still perfectly squared, with no indentation where a head would have rested.

Caroline reached back in her mind. She had awoken alone yesterday too, and had thought it odd at the time that when Pen had appeared, she was wearing the same gown she had worn to the pavilion. What was her usually biddable sister up to?

Mired in this unwelcome distraction, she made her way to the window and pulled the lace curtains to one side. The morning was just emerging from its cocoon of darkness, and through the warped glass she could make out little more than the vague shape of the pebbled beach and, farther out in the ocean, the occasional white-tipped wave.

"Where in the devil are you, Pen?" she muttered. Her sister's disappearance didn't make sense. Penelope was the *proper* Tolbertson girl, the one who always followed the rules. Caroline was the one who snuck out and met gentlemen by moonlight.

She turned back to the room, looking for clues. Her search uncovered only one promising lead: Pen's leatherbound journal sat on the bedside table. Caroline's fingers twitched over the embossed cover. She had never violated her sister's privacy before. But worry for Pen quickly overcame any compunction she felt over prying.

She turned up the lamp and opened the notebook to the last page, determined to rifle through as little of her sister's secrets possible. But as she examined the ending page, and then the one before, and the one before that, she only grew more perplexed. The journal was not filled with Pen's yearnings, or poetic nonsense about the color of some gentlemen's eyes, as Caroline had expected.

No, the journal was filled with notes about *her*, in Penelope's tight, neat script. And the notes were about the most mundane sorts of trivia one could imagine.

> *July 20th. Caroline walked along the parade with Mr. Branson.*
> *July 20th. C—danced with ten different partners tonight.*
> *July 21st. Caroline took a sea bath. Looked flushed upon her on exit, but did not smell like shite. Note: Ask her what the inside of the box was like.*
> *July 21st: Caroline and I received invitations to the Traversteins' ball. New dress ordered.*

She hovered over the entries, more confused than ever. Clearly, she wasn't going to find a clue to Penelope's whereabouts within these pages. Only *her* comings and goings seemed to earn a space in her sister's journal, which made no sense at all.

The sound of the bedroom door being opened jerked Caroline from her focused thoughts, and she jumped like a five-year-old caught filching pies from the larder. Pen stood in the doorway, her slippers in one hand. "What are you d-doing with my journal?"

Caroline closed the thing with a guilty snap. "I . . . I was just . . ." She heaved a frustrated sigh, knowing she had been caught. "Where have you been?"

Pen pushed her way inside the room, dropping her shoes in a pile on the floor. "I couldn't sleep, so I went out for a w-walk." She stalked over and extracted the journal from Caroline's fingers. "And that d-doesn't answer my question," she added, before putting the journal in the drawer of the bedside table.

Through the window, Caroline could see the first red

streaks of morning on the horizon. Her own time to get a note to David was slipping away, but her worry for her sister kept her rooted to the floor. "You must admit, it is an odd time for a walk," she pointed out. "It's only a little after dawn."

Pen turned back to face her, her blue eyes flashing in the light from the lamp. "You, of all p-people, have no right to lecture me about taking a little walk." She sat down on her bed and began to unhook her stockings from her garters.

That shook Caroline from her shock. "If you went to bed at all last night," she told her sister, crossing her arms and trying to look imperious, "then I am a garden fairy. Who were you meeting? And why did you feel the need to do it under cover of darkness, instead of inviting them for a proper sit-down?"

Pen flushed. "I was meeting Mr. Hamilton." She paused over the unrolling of one stocking and lifted guilt-hooded eyes. "But we only t-t-talked."

Caroline shrank back, stunned. She did not begrudge Penelope a few stolen minutes with a gentleman. But Penelope had snuck from the house under cover of darkness to meet a man who had publicly declared his intentions to court her sister.

"That throws a questionable light on Mr. Hamilton's character, wouldn't you say?" Caroline demanded. She hoped Penelope had only walked with the man, and not engaged in anything more serious. She wasn't very happy with him, given that he was obviously playing fast and loose with both their affections.

Not that the esteem she held for the man resembled anything close to affection.

Penelope rose and began to undress, ill-hiding a yawn in the process. "He is a decent sort of gentleman, Caroline. Do not d-dismiss him out of hand. I know his teeth aren't quite as nice as Mr. Adams's, and his family is not as distinguished as Mr. Duffington's, but he quite outshines Mr. Branson, d-don't you think?"

"I suppose," muttered Caroline. She sat down on the edge of Pen's bed as her sister slipped into her night-clothes. Penelope had just returned from a clandestine meeting with Mr. Hamilton, and now she was pushing *Caroline* toward the man?

Caroline really wasn't very happy with *either* of them.

But what could she do about it? Not tell Mama . . . Pen had kept Caroline's secrets, after all, and covered for her long afternoon walks on more than one occasion. She ought to stay and press Penelope for more information. By all appearances, Pen was doing something potentially dangerous, and Caroline had promised Papa she would take care of the family.

But the urgency of penning a note of explanation to David also poked at her. Dawn appeared quite serious in its intentions now. A definite shaft of light speared the lace curtains and twisted onto Penelope's unused coverlet. No matter what business had taken her from the house, Pen was back, safe and sound. Caroline had, at most, a half hour before the rest of the house began to stir, and she hadn't even finished dressing yet. Her morning's mission to send a note to David, explaining her conflict and letting him know she would meet him closer to two o'clock today, was becoming more compromised with every new inch of the sun on the horizon.

Still, she had to try, or he would think she had abandoned him for a second day in a row.

"Pen—" she began, only to be interrupted by their mother gliding through the open bedroom door. Caroline stared openmouthed, unable to recall the last time her mother had risen before eight o'clock in the morning.

"You should both be dressed by now," Mama exclaimed, though she herself was still in her night rail and wrapper. She surveyed them both like a queen considering which peasant to flog. "We need every minute to get you ready."

Caroline shrank against Pen's mattress. "Ready?" she echoed, dread boring its way through her initial confusion. "Ready for what?"

"You have a fitting with Madame Beauclerc today. Your first ball is tonight. And let us not forget, there is *always* the possibility of additional gentlemen callers. And so you, my dear, are going to take a bath this morning."

As if conjured by her mother's words, Bess appeared in the open doorway, still in her nightclothes as well. She hid a yawn behind one weathered hand, and then said in a sleepy voice, "I've set the hip bath up, Mrs. Tolbertson."

Caroline froze at the mention of the copper hip bath that occupied a permanent place downstairs in the scullery. Her mother wasn't referring to any usual method of washing then, a quick swipe of a cloth while hunched over a china washbasin. "I don't have *time* for a bath this morning," Caroline objected. The errand that had pulled her from bed this morning was slipping further from her grasp. "I have . . . an appointment."

Bess grinned, showing the familiar gap between her two front teeth. "Aye. That you do. An appointment with a washcloth and a bar of soap."

"But I could take the bath tonight, before the party, so I don't see—"

The servant fisted both hands on her wrapper-clad hips, a bristling foot soldier refusing an order to retreat. "I've already set up the water, Miss Caroline, and I won't have you wasting my time when there's breakfast to cook and laundry to get on. And 'tis more than just a bath, child. We're going to wash that wild mane of yours."

Caroline gaped at the servant, who looked a little too pleased with the prospect of such early morning torture. Hair washing was a Saturday evening activity, not a Friday morning event. And she *couldn't* wash her hair this morning, not when she was poised to douse it in seawater this afternoon.

As if she could read her unspoken thoughts, Mama leaned in close, her blue eyes sparkling in the increasing light of dawn. "And after that," she added with maternal enthusiasm, "Bess is going to set your hair up in rags to get it to curl for tonight."

Caroline no longer wanted to just shrink against the covers. She wanted to wrap the edges around her body and sew herself inside. She hadn't sat to have her hair put up in . . . well . . . in ages. Her body refused to be still for the length of time such nonsensical preparations required. And any curls Bess managed to get up would be destroyed by the afternoon swimming lesson.

"I don't want my hair curled" was all she could think to say.

"I know." Her mother spoke soothingly, but her fingers closed over Caroline's wrist in a definite statement of fact. "But your opinion on this matter does not count, because your appearance tonight *will*. So you are washing your hair, Caroline, even if Bess needs to hold you down to do it."

Chapter 23

DAVID WAS ABOUT to give up on Caroline for the second day in a row when she appeared around the patch of scrub grass that guarded the entrance to the cove.

He tried not to smile as she picked her way across the pebble-strewn beach, an hour later than promised. Her tall frame was recognizable, but the closer she came, the more she looked like someone he didn't know. Today her hair had been tied up in a hodgepodge of mismatched rags, giving her the appearance of a very frustrated hedgehog. She was wearing that old blue print dress again, the same one she had worn yesterday. Only this time she had added an apron that in no way disguised the gown's obvious ill fit. To add insult to injury, she was scowling in a ferocious manner that would send small children and wildlife scurrying, should they be unlucky enough to cross her path.

That is, if her hair alone wasn't enough to do the job.

"You are late." David slid off the rock as she pulled up in front of him. "*Again*." He tried to remind himself that he was angry with her. It was a little difficult to maintain a solid hold on his irritation, given the distracting way his body was already stirring to life at the sight of her.

Which was a very concerning thing, given how bloody ridiculous she looked.

Caroline blew a stray wisp of hair out of her eyes, the

lone straggler that had somehow escaped the noose of rags the rest of her tresses had been subjected to. "I owe you an apology, David. I had intended to send you a note explaining it. Mama scheduled a dress fitting for me and then all but chained me to the chair."

"You didn't look chained when I saw you yesterday evening, on your front porch."

Her eyes widened beneath the caricature of her hair. "You saw me last night? But . . . why didn't you say anything?"

"You seemed busy." He tried to sound nonchalant, even as he cursed his stupidity in all but admitting he had watched her in secret. His was not the behavior of a man determined to help her find her match.

"Not so busy I didn't worry about disappointing you." Muddled green eyes met his over the few feet that separated them. "Given my morning, 'tis a miracle I've made it at all."

He pursed his lips and permitted his gaze to meander across her. He decided in an instant that the apron was the thing he hated the most about today's fashion monstrosity. It bisected her chest, but came nowhere close to delineating her waist. "Yes, I can imagine. You look as though you've been playing dress-up with a three-year-old."

All hint of her earlier remorse vanished, and her chin notched up. "Shouldn't *you* be undressed? I've an hour to devote to this, at most. Mama has declared that it shall take three hours to get ready for the ball I am expected to attend tonight. What could they be planning, given that I have already been scrubbed halfway to Sunday and had my hair wound tight as a bobbin? I could swim to France and back in less time."

David fought a smile. There was something wrong with him. This was, after all, the girl who had rejected him for a dress fitting yesterday, and then made him wait in the heat of the sun today. He ought to be mad as hell.

Funny how at the moment he leaned more toward snorting in amusement, instead of giving her the dressing-down she deserved.

"Are you referring to the Traversteins' ball?"

"Yes." She wrinkled her nose, no doubt weighing the displeasure of the event against a game of shuttlecock. "A little faster with those buttons, if you please."

He began to unbutton his shirt, but gave voice to the niggling hurt that still plagued him. "You seem rather enthusiastic about hurrying me along, given that it was your tardiness today that has made us so pressed for time. I think an hour devoted to the task of swimming is enough time to accomplish the day's lesson."

She drew in a sharp breath, and he couldn't help but notice how the motion made her breasts, small though they might be, strain against the confines of her misshapen apron. "Are you forgetting we have a bargain?" she demanded. "You promised to teach me a few things as well."

David froze, arrested in the very motion of shrugging off his shirt. Her words reminded him like a punch to the gut of what else beyond swimming she intended to accomplish this afternoon. The last time he had removed his shirt in this woman's presence, he had entertained only one objective: learn to swim using her overhand stroke. But today, the act of undressing carried more weight. There were two stated goals to the lesson this afternoon, and he was reminded of the second one as Caroline's eyes swept over his bare chest in open admiration.

"I had hoped you had changed your mind about that," he told her. *Liar.* His heart was even now lunging against the end of its tether. "Are you sure you would not prefer to pass the hour focused just on the swimming lesson?"

"We shall divide the hour up, a half hour each." Her gaze settled behind his shoulder, on the ocean. "And . . . and I cannot swim today." She gestured to her hair. "Not like this. I shall have to instruct you from the shore."

Whatever remaining wisps of anger he harbored fell away at that. That she had come, when she couldn't even swim herself, told him how important this exercise was to her.

David tossed his shirt upon the rock, then hurried to dispense with his boots and socks. He didn't even consider removing his trousers given her admonishments about time, just dove into the cool water with the fall still buttoned. The wet, heavy fabric created extra drag against the current, but there was no way on God's good earth he was going to spend the afternoon teaching Caroline . . . *things* . . . without his trousers on.

Not if he needed her virtue to stay intact.

CAROLINE WAS GRUDGINGLY impressed when David finally dragged himself back to shore a half hour later.

"That was really well done." She meant every word. It had gone remarkably well, all things considered. He had retained most of the salient points of Wednesday's lesson, and had performed well in the rougher water today.

And tomorrow, by God, she was going to swim with him, the indignity of curled hair or no.

"Still not well enough to guarantee a win on Monday, I'd wager," he said, shaking his head and sending a spray of water all about.

"I think you will acquit yourself well enough." She touched her tongue to a drop of water that landed near the corner of her mouth, reveling in the familiar taste of salt, imagining she could taste the essence of the man in it as well. "You'll be the only one using this stroke, which gives you a decided advantage." She held out his shirt, which he took and began to rub with brisk, efficient strokes over his chest and arms. "That and the fact I shall be cheering you on from shore."

He grinned at her, and his rakish smile sent warmth curling through her abdomen. "'Tis good to hear you say that. Last night I was convinced you had decided to cry off."

Caroline shook her head, surprised by how her thoughts spooled up tight at the thought. When he had first suggested this course of action, she had been hesitant, true enough. But now that she had committed to this path, she would not let him down. The inability to race herself would sting, she suspected, but cheering David's attempt come Monday would be no hardship.

"I promised I would do this." Her mind whirled in protest as he began to shoulder his way back into his shirt. "But you promised me something as well. Surely you remember our agreement—"

"Aye." He set his fingers to the buttons, even as his mouth worked its way to a grim line. "I have not forgotten. You shall have your half hour."

Relief flicked through her. "Wouldn't this next bit be aided by a continued lack of clothing?"

He seated the last few buttons with slow, deliberate motions. "Clothing was not discussed as part of our bargain. I prefer to keep my shirt on."

Caroline huffed a frustrated moment. She felt coiled up inside, a child's toy that had been wound up too tight and was now being held without the opportunity to spring free. Her eyes locked on a droplet of water as it escaped his damp hair and ran down his neck to catch in the collar of his shirt that was now, regrettably, buttoned. She wanted to trace its path with her tongue, to show him what an apt pupil she was prepared to be.

Then again, they had at most a half hour left. A casual exploration would need to wait for another day.

Aware only of the march of time, Caroline took three steps forward, stood on her toes, and pressed her lips against his. His hands came up, hesitant at first and then growing in pressure, to span her waist.

Yesterday's failure, and her morning's frustrations, all

fell away as the taste of the ocean met her lips again. He felt large and damp and solid beneath her hands, which had come up to fist his buttoned shirt. Her body unfurled. She felt like one of the waves she loved, building in momentum, and she wanted to crash down hard into him.

"Slow down," he murmured against her mouth, as if he could feel the precarious emotions building there at the point where they were joined. "There is no need to rush this lesson." He stepped back, forcing a few inches of reluctant sanity back between them.

He was, she noticed with some satisfaction, breathing almost as hard as she was. Nonetheless, she battled a moment of hurt at his rejection. She had hoped that David might seem a bit more enthusiastic about his role as instructor, but she was curious—and greedy—enough to wait and see what he offered.

She studied him a moment, trying to sort out what was different today. He had seemed more susceptible to her in the bathing machine, but that had been a different day, and a different set of boundaries. No doubt he wanted his shirt on to ensure he kept her at some safe, respectable distance.

Well, if he insisted on adding a layer of clothing, she had every right to take one away.

Caroline turned away to face the white cliff walls and presented him with the row of buttons that ran up the back of her dress. She waited, training her eyes on the familiar cliff wall instead of his terse features. "I'll need your help getting out of this," she prompted.

She swore she could hear him swallow, and for a second she basked in the pleasure of it. But then he cleared his throat and said, "I have some rules to put down first."

Caroline looked over her shoulder and raised a brow. "You are not in a position to negotiate the terms of this next half hour."

"You negotiated the terms of the swimming lesson," he pointed out, making no move to come closer and help her out of her clothing. "And then you provided today's instruction from shore, a distance of some two dozen yards or more." He smiled, and it was a wicked sight to behold. "I offer the same to you. Our clothes remain on. And a kiss, while nice, is a bit more physical contact than what I have in mind."

Caroline jerked back around to face him, irritation making her restless. "If you'll recall, you promised to show me far more than just a kiss."

"Aye. And you'll not discover what I intend unless you take yourself up on that rock like a good lass and wait for my instructions."

Caroline sucked in a breath, at a loss to explain why his words, far from making her feel angry or unwanted, sent a sudden, forbidden thrill snaking through her veins.

"What would you have me do?"

"You instructed me from a distance today. Turnabout is only fair." He crossed his arms, still making no move to touch her. "Up on the rock, if you please. Skirts pulled up high."

She regarded him for a long silent moment, aware of the accelerating bump of her pulse. This didn't seem anything close to what she had petitioned him for yesterday. How could she help him overcome his aversion to emotional intimacy if she was not to be permitted to touch him? "This was not our bargain."

"On the rock," he said, more sternly this time, "or I shall presume you do not mean to have this lesson today."

Caroline turned and scrambled up on the rock. The warmth that had earlier percolated in her abdomen now bloomed along her cheeks. "I instructed *you* from a distance because I could not risk getting my hair wet," she objected over her shoulder, but she clambered up the sun-warmed rock face anyway. "And you did brilliantly out there on your own," she added as she threw herself down in a puddle of skirts.

"I suspect you will acquit yourself well enough," he

replied. His choice of words sent her embarrassed anticipation soaring even higher. She had no idea what he was
about, or what was in store for her.

She only knew the threat of not finding out was untenable.

When he did no more than watch her, their precious
seconds sliding by, she felt her ire rise. "Are you going to
join me over here, or stand there like a lout?"

The low rumble of his laughter made the fine hairs on
her neck stand at attention and she responded with a glare
she was quite sure could have singed the sun.

"Neither. Skirts up," he reminded, looking every inch the
smug seducer, for all that he stood at least ten feet away.

She inched them up, wincing as she caught sight of her
freckled legs. This was not the day to eschew stockings,
it seemed.

"Higher. I want to see your legs. *All* of your legs."

She jerked her skirts up to the vicinity of her waist,
wanting to sink beneath the stone surface in mortification.
She pulled her shift down as low as it would go, but it only
stretched to mid-thigh. Oh, but this was not what she had
in mind when she had negotiated this devil's bargain. She
had imagined tangled limbs and closed eyes and the feel
of his hands on her body.

Bright, revealing sunlight, David's unfettered scrutiny,
and squirming mortification had been the farthest thing
from her mind.

He stared a long moment, his eyes roving the regrettable
length of her legs. She concentrated on breathing through
her nose, reminding herself that she had made this deal,
pointing out to the rational parts of her brain—the parts
that objected to such a bawdy display—that David Cameron had already seen her legs, and likely more, through
her wet shift several nights ago.

It didn't help. Her thoughts still ran wild, and her mind
refused to reassemble into something lucid.

"Aren't you even going to kiss me again?" she asked crossly.

"No, lass. I am not going to kiss you. Now lie back," he commanded. "And close your eyes."

DAVID WAS NOT just hard at the sight of Caroline lowering her body down upon that cursed rock.

He was raging hard.

He could not recall having ever experienced this degree of arousal before, and all from the simple act of sparring with a girl who had her hair tied up in rags. A girl who, he was beginning to suspect, was determined to see herself ruined, and whom he was going to do his damnedest to deliver to a future husband with her innocence mostly intact.

But God's teeth, the little hoyden deserved a sliver of the frustration she meted out so freely. And he could not deny a perverse sort of enjoyment in knowing he was not only going to be the one to deliver her set-down, but also be the one to instruct her first taste of pleasure.

He stepped closer to where she lay, staring down at the offering he had demanded of her. If one focused on her body instead of her hair, she looked like a sacrifice to some pagan god of fertility, her lips parted in the sweetest of invitations, and her skirts rucked up around her hips. His fingers itched to tangle up in her.

So did his cock. In fact, it was quite insistent.

Go easy, he cautioned himself. This was not meant to be a lesson he enjoyed.

"Keep your eyes closed," he growled down at her from his new, closer vantage point. "Or the lesson is over."

She nodded and her lids stayed closed.

He had the freedom to look at her all he wanted. He took full advantage of the gift. He stood, two feet away, and stared. With his eyes, he traced the freckles along the column of her neck, imagined pressing his lips against the tempting hollow of her throat. He regretted now refusing to help her remove the damned dress, as the only thing he could imagine sweeter than the current picture was also seeing her nipples peak beneath her shift.

But there was nothing to be done for it if he was to maintain any kind of hold on his sanity.

David permitted his gaze to settle lower on the worn, white cotton undergarments that peeked out at him from beneath her bunched skirts. He swallowed. "Have you ever touched yourself, Caroline?"

Her eyes scrunched tighter at the question. She shook her head once, the perfect picture of a woman shocked by a man's lewd words. But something in the way her lungs filled with air and strained against that ugly apron gave her away.

If she was appalled by his bold suggestion, he was a thirty-two-year-old virgin.

"Liar." A delicious bolt of lust swept through him at the thought. "I can imagine you running your hands across your body. Slipping between your legs. For today's lesson, I want you to show me what pleases you."

"I don't know what you are talking about," she protested, her cheeks now a slash of crimson below her tightly squeezed eyes.

"No?" he drawled. "Pity. It will be a short lesson then, I am afraid."

She made a sound of frustration that echoed how he felt inside. "How is this supposed to show me what to look for in a partner?"

"A good partner will care about what pleases you." David forced his voice to soften, deepen. "Trust me, Caroline. This will help him see what you want, which is a first necessary step toward providing it for you himself."

He waited to see what she would do. He could see the war she waged, the desire to slide off that rock and run, pitted against the desire to remain compliant and see where this might lead. All the while, she kept her eyes carefully shuttered, and he had to admire her restraint.

God knew he wasn't feeling very restrained at the moment.

She had no way of knowing how she looked, laid open for scrutiny, with the halo of afternoon sun splashing across her bare, freckled calves. He dared not breathe, lest the moment be shattered by his impertinence.

And then, impossibly, she lifted a hand. Rubbed a tentative finger across the skin of her inner thigh.

Simultaneous to his own shocked inhalation, he saw her face relax into the pleasure of her own touch. The urge to follow her lead and press his lips to that same tempting place where she placed her fingers almost sent him scrambling atop that rock himself.

Instead, he anchored himself in place, gripping his fists in the bunched wet wool of his trousers and using his own torso as ballast.

It was the hardest thing he had ever done.

"Higher," he whispered, wanting to pull her hand northward himself. "Move your hand higher."

Slowly, as if she could not quite believe what she was doing, she obeyed.

"The place there, at the top of your woman's mound. That is where is it feels the best, doesn't it?"

She nodded.

"Focus there."

David held his breath until his lungs reached an agonizing peak of pain, watching as she brushed a tentative finger across the shadowed space between her legs. He imagined her growing moist beneath the cotton hemline, secret scents driven by her rising passion. He wanted to press his lips there, wanted to watch her face as he introduced her to the wonders of a well-practiced tongue.

Instead, he was forced to wait for her fumbled explorations, bound by what damned little honor he possessed to do no more than stand and watch the combination of frustration and dawning passion stretch across her face. Her fingers slipped beneath the cotton fabric and disappeared into the place where David wanted to lose himself.

He stared, committing the act to eager memory, knowing he would be tortured by this scene for the rest of his unnatural days. Eventually, he saw the hitch of her shoulders that told him she was close, felt the strain of her breathing as she flew closer to oblivion.

And then she stopped, a groan of frustration on her lips.

"Don't stop, lass." His words came out ragged. "There's more, if only you'll trust me."

She opened her eyes, shattering the moment. "'Tis not a matter of trust. I just don't know what you are trying to have me do." Her hand fell away, clenching empty air. "I want . . . something. But I know not what."

David gritted his teeth, knowing the reward, once abandoned, was now out of easy reach. "Our time is up anyway," he said, readjusting his body's interest against the prison of his wet trousers. "It takes a bit longer the first time."

"What takes longer?" She struggled to sitting.

David permitted a smile to steal across his face. Could she really be this naïve? He reminded himself that two weeks ago she had been gifted her first kiss at the hands of a rakehell like Dermott. She might touch herself on occasion, but it seemed clear she had never *found* herself. "You . . . er . . . might want to consult that naughty book of your sister's."

Her eyes narrowed. "Which naughty book?"

"The one that taught you the word 'celibate.'"

Her lips finally pursed around the edge of her own smile. "It is a medical text, David. My sister is a proper sort of lady. She does not have books of that nature."

David raised a brow. "If you insist."

"And if there *had* been a section on this," she ground out, "not that I know what 'this' is, I would most assuredly have not just failed my first lesson."

At her miffed retort, David's whole body shook with

suppressed laughter. God help him, he wanted nothing more than to stretch her back down on the rock and dive in and not come up for air until she was thrashing about, lost in her pleasure.

But he could not help her with this.

If he did, he would be bound for hell, dragging her there alongside him. It was not a path he was going to take her down today, no matter how much he wanted to be the one to break her apart and watch her settle back down to earth.

She took an inordinate amount of time rearranging her skirts before fixing him with a fresh, accusing glare. "I demand a full hour's lesson tomorrow." She blew that stray wisp of hair out of her face. "And I want to be able to touch *you*. I shall not offer you a single minute of swimming instruction without your full promise on this."

"Then you'll have to meet me earlier, at noon." He offered her his hand, but she shoved it aside and slid down the rock herself, pushing her skirts down to modesty in a move that came very close to the tantrum of sexual frustration that David himself felt like throwing.

"And if you are late tomorrow, you'll have no one to blame but yourself," he teased. He might not have brought her to completion, but he could at least take her back to Brighton. He suspected the bruising walk would be good for some part of his anatomy beyond his feet.

He was still throbbing from the release he had not been granted. And she was demanding a full hour tomorrow. He wasn't sure he could survive it.

He had thought it would be safer to avoid touching her, but he had underestimated the power of watching her reach for oblivion. He *wanted* to help her find her heaven, even as he wanted to throttle her for putting him in this position.

And God help them both, he still had two more days to go.

Chapter 24

THE TRAVERSTEINS' BALL was the sort of crush that made Miss Baxter's dinner party look like a small family gathering. The house itself was a jaw-dropping affair, with a lavish chinoiserie interior no doubt inspired by the nearby Royal Pavilion.

Not that Caroline had ever seen the interior of the ostentatious, round-spired estate that occupied such a central place in most Brightonians' minds, but if this was as close as she ever came to living like royalty, she knew she would never forget it. She stared up at the rounded domed ceiling of the Traversteins' foyer, amazed that not only did the Traversteins own a home so fine, but this was nothing more than their summer home, inhabited for a mere month out of every twelve. Her eyes slid down the gilded framework and dodged the beams of light refracted by the chandeliers.

"So many c-candles," Pen whispered beside her, a wide-eyed mirror of how Caroline felt. It was hard not to think of what such luxuries must cost when they often struggled to afford a week's worth of tallow.

"We must not appear too dazzled," Caroline reminded her sister. "We've every right to be here." And they did.

She had the invitation folded up in her reticule to prove it. Just in case someone challenged their audacity.

Caroline strained for a glimpse of David's tall, blond head above the other partygoers, and her stomach churned when she could not find him. He had mentioned he was coming, though they had not spoken of it again, and she could admit to a sick sort of anticipation at the thought of seeing him here tonight. The memory of her astonishing, frustrating afternoon sat inside her like fermented cider left in the sun. She had gone to see him today with her hair up in *rags*, for heaven's sake.

Well, she wasn't wearing rags any longer and she was looking forward to erasing that last image he must have of her. Madame Beauclerc might not be French, but there was no denying her skill with a needle. The gown covering Caroline's frame was the most beautiful confection she had ever seen, much less worn. Made of a lightweight moiré silk, it brought to mind the color of the ocean at noon, and seemed to change in color and texture with every subtle movement of her body. True to her promise, the modiste had fashioned tiny, capped sleeves that, while not in the height of fashion, suited Caroline's physique far better than the dropped shoulders and rounded sleeves adorning the other women in attendance.

But the fact that she stood out amid the crowd, that she was not only different, she was *purposefully* different, made Caroline want to run. With her first hesitant steps into the ballroom, heads turned, tracking her progress. Whispers grew in volume behind artfully placed fans.

And Caroline faltered.

To her right, Penelope's gloved hand touched her elbow for support. "Smile," she murmured. "You look as if you have t-tasted something unpleasant."

"They are whispering about me." Caroline scanned the faces that surrounded them. She was grateful for the worn fabric of her old shift, tucked up against her skin beneath the layers of new silk. But a thin cotton shift could not shield her from the pointed looks and barbed comments that threatened to skewer her tonight.

"They are looking at you, I'll admit." Pen's gaze seemed to travel all the way through her fashionable layers. "B-but they are not *laughing* at you. You look lovely. Well enough to meet the queen."

Caroline gasped. "Is the royal family here?" Somehow, the thought of seeing the queen seemed less nausea-inducing than the thought of fending off Miss Baxter or Mr. Dermott.

Pen pursed her lips and smiled. "No matter the recent conjecture on the matter, I d-d-do not think the queen is in Brighton at the moment, or that she will even visit this summer. But the Countess of Beecham appears to be in attendance."

Caroline twisted around. "The Countess of Beecham?"

"Duffington's mother." Pen took a deliberate step away. "And Duffington besides," she added before melding into the crowd. Caroline affixed a smile she hoped looked pleasant on her face, and turned toward the pair who had sent Pen scuttling away.

If she were to be wholly objective, she had to admit Duffington looked well tonight. At least, he looked well for *him*. He was splendidly attired in a formal jacket with black velvet lapels, and a waistcoat of red and purple. There was just so . . . very much of it. He brought to mind a bear that had been stuffed into doll's clothing.

The woman accompanying him seemed to subscribe to the London school of thought that more is better, and that a holiday climate was no reason to shirk a duty to fashion. She was swathed in yards of sweltering taffeta, draped to disguise a figure that might have once rivaled even her son's robust proportions. Emerald earbobs the size of small bird eggs threatened to split what remained of her stretched-out earlobes, and a necklace of equally terrifying proportions lay against her wrinkled neck.

Lady Beecham tolerated her son's exuberant introduction, then fixed Caroline with a stern look that sent her toes curling into the soles of her flat-soled slippers. "So *this* is the infamous Miss Caroline Tolbertson, whom my son has not been able to stop talking about for even one hour out of the last twenty."

Though the accusation in the woman's voice made her want to follow Pen's trajectory across the crowded room, Caroline refused to let her smile slip even a fraction. "That suggests more a title of famous than infamous, I should think."

Lady Beecham offered a twitch of her lips in an upward direction. "Haven't heard him go on about anything like that since the Christmas dessert buffet we put out last year."

"*Mother*," Duffington protested, but his objection was cut off by an exaggerated thump from his mother's walking cane on the tile floor. He fell silent, as any well-trained terrier might.

"I am not familiar with the surname Tolbertson," the countess said, shuffling closer and peering up at Caroline through rheumy eyes. "Tell me about your family, child."

"My grandfather on my mother's side was the Viscount Ashemore." Caroline hesitated, unsure of how to explain the rest of it. She might be speaking with a countess, but she refused to relegate her father to something less than valued in this woman's eyes, just because her parents' union had been a love match. "My father was a prominent local businessman who founded the *Brighton Gazette*. He died when I was twelve. I have lived in Brighton my entire life."

"Your mother was Miss Lydia Birch?" The countess sounded surprised. "The viscount's daughter?"

Caroline nodded. "My grandfather's title went to a distant cousin, however, and we are not close with the new viscount's family."

"Good bones though. I knew your mother when she was a young woman, in London. She made quite the headlines the year she came out." The countess's face softened. "I took tea with Miss Baxter yesterday, and by her limited description of you, I confess I had expected someone a bit different. Your gown is quite cunning, if I do say so myself."

"Thank you." It was a miracle Caroline managed that, because what she really wanted to do was snarl something disparaging about the far too loose-lipped Miss Baxter.

The countess shifted her cane from one hand to the other. "Harold mentioned that he purchased you a voucher for a sea bath yesterday. Did you enjoy your first experience with the ocean?"

Caroline's cheeks heated as she considered what improper things she had done with David Cameron inside the bathing machine's sheltered walls—walls that had, in fact, been rented by this woman's son. "I found it quite diverting," she said by way of an answer, hoping the warmth flooding her cheeks was not visible.

The countess nodded approvingly. "Improves the circulation, soothes the constitution. When Harold told me he had found a woman who seemed to appreciate a good sea bath, I insisted he introduce us this evening."

They spoke another minute or so, and then as Lady Beecham made her excuses and drifted away into the press of people, Duffington offered Caroline his arm. "Would you like to take in a breath of air on the terrace?" he asked, his booming voice competing with the sounds of the stringed instruments that had started to warm up on the far end of the ballroom.

Memories of another terrace, and another night, had her shaking her head. "Perhaps later. I have just arrived, and do not yet find myself in need of . . . er . . . air."

"Perhaps a dance, then?"

"The band has not started up yet in earnest," she pointed out, distracted.

Duffington's jowls worked around the ends of his quivering black mustache. "I had hoped for a more private place to have this conversation, but I find I cannot wait now that Mother has given her approval."

A small, steady beat of denial began an indelicate rhythm between Caroline's ears as she swung her attention back to the problem that was Duffington.

"I hope you will not consider me too forward if I say that it is my fervent wish to see us betrothed and married before the New Year."

Caroline's thoughts curled around the edges of Duffington's proposal. *No, no, no,* her internal compass moaned. This could not be happening. Not this evening. Not when she still had two promised days left to explore passion on her own terms, with the man of her choosing.

She fumbled for an appropriate response. "I . . . that is . . . I mean . . . that is so kind. If a bit unexpected." She fell silent, unable to find a single other word to articulate how his offer made her want to grab the nearest decorative vase and toss up the contents of her stomach into it.

"I understand this is sudden, of course. But now that Mother has met you, I wanted to be the first to declare my interest."

She covered her mouth with a gloved hand. He had his mother's approval. Caroline wanted to laugh. Either that, or weep. Had she known this was the test she was taking, she might have tried a little harder to make a poor impression with the countess.

"Might I have a few days to think on it?" she whispered through the hand still clasped to her mouth. The words seemed to get stuck in her throat as much as her fingers.

Duffington straightened his waistcoat with a determined pull. "I would wait until midsummer next, but for the pleasure of your smile."

Caroline permitted Duffington to claim a dance on her card, making sure it was some innocuous thing that involved facing him across a row of partners. Then she breathed a desperate sigh of relief as he lumbered off into the crowd.

Duffington wanted to be the *first* to declare his interest? It quite stretched the limits of her imagination that he believed she would receive more offers. She couldn't see anything beyond this moment and this proposal. Her future yawned before her, bleak and depressing, one long luncheon punctuated by the occasional sea bath.

She drew a deep breath, wondering if she might actually need a turn on the terrace now, only to choke on the sharp, pungent scent of Watson's hair pomade. She whirled to find Mr. Dermott standing but a few inches away, a studious expression on his handsome face.

For a fear-filled moment, she wondered if Dermott had overheard Duffington's proposal. She was not yet ready to share news of this offer even with Penelope, much less a gentleman who rivaled Miss Baxter's skills in the area of rumormongering. But instead of commenting on the nature of her recent conversation with Duffington, Dermott's mouth stretched wide to show the teeth that had once so beguiled her as to permit this man to press his lips against her own.

"You look quite fetching this evening, Caroline. I must say, this style of gown suits you."

Caroline considered her response. She *did* look lovely tonight, at least by her usual standards, and her gown was only partly the cause. Thanks to the busy meddling of Bess and her mother, her hair hung in soft ringlets about her face in a manner she had to admit was more becoming than the severe style she usually favored. Her dress might not look like anyone else's here tonight, but it was, inarguably, the finest garment she had ever owned.

But she had not taken pains with her appearance to impress *this* man.

"Thank you." She did not comment on his own appearance, though Dermott was wearing an emerald waistcoat embroidered with tulips or some such flower. He outshone Duffington, true enough, with his lean body and aristocratic features. Why, his profile alone had been known to stop foot traffic along the Marine Parade.

But compared to someone like David Cameron, Mr. Dermott could have been transparent.

"It seems you have caught the notice of some influential people since we last spoke," Dermott mused. "It makes me wonder what I have been missing these past few weeks."

"I am the same person I was two weeks ago," Caroline informed him, her voice ringing in suppressed challenge. That wasn't true, though. She was no longer that awkward girl who had been surprised to catch the notice of anyone, much less someone as popular and handsome as Dermott. Now she was a woman who had been properly and thoroughly kissed by moonlight, a lady who had just received a proposal from the son of an earl.

Not that Mr. Dermott knew any of that.

The sounds from the orchestra shifted, coalescing into a more defined pattern of notes. "It sounds as if they are winding up for the opening dance. Would you care to join me?" Dermott extended his gloved hand, palm up, fingers all but twitching. "That is, if Mr. Duffington has not claimed all your dances for himself?"

Caroline stared at the hand as if it might be an adder's head, poised to strike. David was not here to guide her, but a memory of his past words poked at her. Why *did* she care what this fop thought of her? What did it matter whether she was barely polite to him, or if indeed she chose to be less than civil?

She was seized with the sudden, freeing, dizzying notion that it *didn't* matter.

Not in the slightest.

"Why?" She chased the question with an exaggerated upsweep of brow. "Are you here to reconnoiter my dancing skills? Perhaps ascertain if I insist on leading, just so you can spread the rumor far and wide?"

Her tormentor's mouth fell open, though it was hard to discern whether he was startled more by her pointed questions or by her newfound confidence. She had never spoken this way in polite company before. At least, not while sober. There was a dizzying sense of freedom that accompanied her speech, the knowledge that she could say these things, could be this person, without the crutch of even a single glass of champagne.

The fingers on Mr. Dermott's still-outstretched palm fisted, and the hand dropped to his side. "I imagine I deserved that. Would you grant me this dance as a way to redeem your opinion of me?"

Caroline met his gaze, unrepentant. Indeed, unamused. "And what of how you have shaped others' opinions of *me*?"

He shifted uncomfortably. "I imagine that dancing with me will dispel any unfortunate rumors that may have started." A flush crept along the edge of his collar. "Please, Caroline. I would like this chance to start again."

She expelled the breath that was cramping her lungs. Her head felt fuzzy, whether from her new boldness or Mr. Dermott's unexpected apology, she could not be sure. A part of her—a surprising part—was tempted to take a turn around the dance floor with him, if for no other reason than to quiet the crowd's rumors and show him he could not affect her.

"Miss Tolbertson," she told him.

His confused blue eyes lifted to meet her own. "I . . . beg your pardon?"

"If you wish to start again, you will address me as Miss Tolbertson." She managed to gift him with a tight smile. "Then I would know you mean to start anew. And it should not be the crowd's opinion of me you seek to reform, but the opinion they hold of you."

He broke into a dazzling grin that stretched from one tip of his *en pointe* collar to the next. His hand lifted again, a long, slow gesture ending in the renewal of his earlier offer to dance. "Thank you, Miss Tolbertson. I shall endeavor to restore your faith in me."

Caroline found she couldn't look away from the sight of those gloved fingers reaching for her. Not an adder, then. They were venomous, certainly, but their bites were not often fatal. No, Mr. Dermott's bright, eye-numbing smile and outstretched fingers brought to mind another sort of snake. She had read about cobras in one of Penelope's omnipresent travel books, a snake indigenous to India that mesmerized its victims with slow, beautiful movements before striking with deadly efficiency. She had laughed at the time, wondering how stupid a victim would have to be to fall for a dancing snake.

She didn't have to wonder any longer.

Because her hand was sliding, almost of its own accord, into Mr. Dermott's. And then she was stepping onto the dance floor.

Chapter 25

Dᴀᴠɪᴅ ᴡᴀᴛᴄʜᴇᴅ Cᴀʀᴏʟɪɴᴇ walk out onto the floor with Dermott with a sensation akin to falling. Only not from a fine, tall height, where he had time to get his feet under him.

No, David felt as if someone had kicked his feet out beneath him, and he had fallen a short, heavy distance onto shards of glass.

He had arrived late, shouldering a plan to keep a wary distance from Caroline for the entirety of the evening. It was a calculated strategy for self-preservation, because every time his mind wandered in her direction, it settled on the image of her stretched out on a rock, skirts rucked up, her face flushed with pleasure.

Not the sort of image that lent itself to stale conversation or the polite company of peers.

In addition to his own instincts for survival, he had also assembled this plan for her benefit. Hovering at her shoulder and glaring at her potential suitors would not help Caroline discover which gentleman here tonight was worth setting her sights on.

But almost immediately, he spied Caroline bowing to Dermott in the opening strains of a quadrille, and he could no longer recall why removing himself from her vicinity was a sane idea.

She was luminous, drawing the eye of every available male in the room, and quite a few of the unavailable males, to boot. Her gown, some miraculous creation he had never seen before and could not quite remove his eyes from, bordered on indecent. Not in the amount of cleavage it displayed, because, after all, this was Caroline.

It was more the manner in which the dress cut away from her shoulders to reveal her curved upper arms. It was an elegant thing, proper in its construction, but it also made a man want to press his lips against the tanned indentation of her collarbone. Tonight, finally, she had relented in her choice of hairstyle, and he sent up a prayer of thanks for those silly rags she had so hated this afternoon. Her hair fell in soft ringlets around her ears, and with each movement of her shoulders those waves moved like a lazy fallen halo against the endless column of her neck.

And Dermott, blast the man, had the best view in the house.

Even if he had to look up to see it.

Every proprietary instinct in David's body, every possessive urge he had been fighting to suppress, surged to the front of his emotional queue. He paused at the edge of the dance floor. Pulled a frustrated hand through his hair. Considered tugging at the roots, just to remind himself this was all his fault.

Yes, he had encouraged Dermott and his friends to open their eyes. Yes, he had wanted them to see Caroline for the potential in her eccentricities rather than just the perceived oddity of her actions. But he also wanted to haul that smiling bastard off the dance floor and plant a fist somewhere in the vicinity of his leering mouth.

What did she see in the man? Surely Caroline couldn't be interested in such a disingenuous soul, especially not one who seemed as intent on spreading gossip behind her back as swooning at her feet. Even Branson would be a better choice than Dermott, and Branson fit her about as well as a ladies' left slipper fit his own right foot.

David wanted Caroline to be happy, truly he did. He just wasn't sure he wanted her to be happy with someone like Dermott.

As the dance finally came to its conclusion, he could see, in a flash of unholy annoyance, that a single dance with Mr. Dermott appeared to have done Caroline's reputation a great deal of good. Within seconds, she was swarmed by a crowd of young—and some not so young— men, like ants discovering a nice cherry pie at a country house picnic.

A possessive drumbeat struck up a rhythm in David's veins, insistent on taking a piece of this pie for himself. He began to shoulder his way toward the crowd. From across the room, he could see Branson start toward her as well, a determined look on his face. Apparently the boy wanted the next dance. Well, the love-struck swain was going to have to wait, because while David might not be her perfect match, he was quite sure Branson wasn't either.

Caroline's face broke into a smile as David covered the last few feet, then fractured around the edges, no doubt when she caught sight of his glower. He was stalking her with the terse focus of a predator, but she did not move away.

If anything she leaned toward him.

"It is a pleasure to see you tonight, David." She used his given name without hesitation, setting the stage for the evening with her chosen informality. He supposed, after the trick he had pulled on her this afternoon, he should be glad it was not a more derogatory name she chose to use.

"And you, as well." David's body reacted unfortunately to the low timber of her voice. Then again, he was used to his body hardening at the sight and sound of her by now.

But he wasn't used to this concurrent, unexpected stirring in the region of his heart.

"I believe the second dance of the evening is mine," he told the gentlemen hovering nearby, eliciting a series of groaned protests and sending the remnants of what had been a very good plan up in smoke.

It wasn't his dance, of course. He had just arrived, had not even completed an entire circuit around the periphery of the ballroom, much less devolved into penciling his name onto young ladies' dance cards.

But she offered him her hand anyway, as he had known she would.

And then it was his turn to dance. His turn to admire the beautiful curve of her neck.

His turn to be the object of other men's ire.

It was a waltz, of course, the same dance that had set off their unfortunate conversation two nights ago at the pavilion. Only this time, it was a slower melody, better suited for an elegant string orchestra than a brass band. She seemed more rigid than his memory, or less pliant. Though David had told her two nights ago that a proper dance partner would make one forget the steps, he could almost hear her counting.

One, two, three. One, two, three.

Clearly he was not doing his job if she was so focused on the placement of her feet.

He pulled her a little closer then, and she moved into his arms with a slight, wilting sigh. She stayed quiet, and the silence surprised him. This was, after all, a girl who tended toward chattering, especially when she was nervous.

David searched his mind for something to say that would pair well with the strains of the music. Though he had more than once been accused of having a silver tongue, the poet in him seemed to have been cannibalized by a growling, primitive beast who had trouble stringing two coherent words together.

The only thing that came to mind that made any sort of sense matched the rhythm of the music in fine, terrifying fashion: *Mine, mine, mine.*

He swallowed against that inappropriate thought. "You look lovely tonight, Caroline."

She raised her eyes and offered him a peculiar smile, once that carried a hint of discomfort rather than pleasure. "Thank you."

He set his sights on the target of her mouth, given that there was nowhere else he could look that did not cause his body to tighten. She might be unusually quiet, but that also meant her lips were not moving, and that was an opportunity that invited closer scrutiny.

Her lips looked . . . mouthwatering. Like a plum at the peak of flavor, placed temptingly atop a bowl when the rest of the fruit had yet to ripen.

He dragged his eyes from the temptation of her mouth to the crowd beyond, only to spy Dermott watching them with hooded eyes. He wondered in that telling moment if her discomfort had anything to do with the man. "Did Mr. Dermott say something to upset you?"

David half hoped he had. Hadn't he been looking for an excuse to pull the man outside for a good, old-fashioned thrashing?

"No. It was something Mr. Duffington said."

His gaze jerked back to hers. "Who in the hell is Duffington?"

"The Earl of Beecham's son." She inclined her head toward a nearby couple.

David looked in the direction she indicated. He spied Miss Baxter dancing in the arms of a dark-haired gentleman he recognized as being part of the crowd that had followed Caroline about on the Marine Parade yesterday. Duffington looked as though he might maim his slightly built partner with one misstep.

"What did he say?"

Caroline's lips settled into a straight line he felt to his bones. "He asked me to marry him."

David felt as if the floor tilted. Indeed, it may have. He struggled to maintain a facade of calm reason through his rising disbelief. "And did you accept?"

Her eyes darted a moment to their spinning feet. *One, two, three. One, two, three.* "I told him I would think on it."

"You cannot seriously consider him a viable candidate."

Her gaze pulled back up. "He is the son of an earl, David. I shall not entertain an improved prospect. I am not even sure why I delayed my answer, given my family's dire financial straits. It has to be yes, I think."

A stubborn denial set up in David's brain. "He is too short for you."

"If I am to use height as a guide, I would have to exclude an overwhelming majority of men in attendance tonight. I don't think I can afford to be so particular."

"Well then, he's about four stone too heavy."

She raised a brow. "Better me as his partner than the imminently crushable Miss Baxter, don't you think?"

"Well then, he's too bloody young for you!" David snapped, exasperated by her inability to see reason. Blood pushed through veins narrowed by panic, seeking an outlet and finding none. There was no one he could pummel, no exertions at the ready to calm his ire. "Duffington is not your match," he ground out, so there could be no mistake.

That, finally, brought a flash of spirit to her features, which had tended toward stone for most of this conversation. "Should I set my sights on Mr. Dermott, then? Although if we are to be quite strict about it, he doesn't meet your height requirements either."

"Did Dermott offer for you too?" David demanded, incredulous at the man's balls-up bravado.

Then again, hadn't Dermott proven himself, on more than one occasion, a competitive fool? If Dermott believed the son of an earl was interested in Caroline, he might renew his twisted interest in her on that basis alone. David's hands tightened involuntarily about her waist. Perhaps he should have encouraged Dermott to take that drunken swim the other night, after all—the world would now be a safer place.

Her cheeks had gone pink at his question. Or was that becoming color a by-product of their afternoon on the beach? He regretted it now. He had left her simmering with frustration, and then turned her over to a ballroom full of randy young men.

What had he been thinking?

"No." Caroline gave her head a slight shake, setting the gentle curls around her face in motion. "He did not ask me to marry him. But he offered me an apology. And I believe it was sincere."

"You thought his intentions toward your first kiss were sincere too, and look what happened." David's lips tightened around the obvious. "Dermott does not have your best interests at heart. You must trust me on this."

Her color ran higher at that. "Well I *don't* trust you. Not on this. The objections you raise disqualify every man of my acquaintance except one: *you*."

Her words sounded small. Or it might have been their negligible volume, juxtaposed against the vacuum they created in his chest. *One, two, three. One, two, three.*

Her fingers tightened on his hand against his silence. "Do you know what I think? I think your reasoning on the unsuitability of other interested gentlemen has nothing to do with logic, and everything to do with denial. Mr. Duffington might not be my ideal, but he is at least a living, breathing person who cares enough about me to see to my future. You, on the other hand, seem to care very little about what becomes of me."

Her words fell like carefully constructed blows, designed to tear him apart from the roots. "How can you say that?" he demanded, recalling the unholy restraint it had taken to prove very much the opposite, just this afternoon. "How could you think I don't care for you?"

She licked her lips, looking the very opposite of a wounded creature. "You send a good deal of mixed messages in this regard."

"Where would you be if I permitted you the kind of ruin you seem so willing to embrace? It is my worry over your future that guides me in this."

She shook her head, her eyes near glinting sparks. "You speak of my ruin as if it is some kind of inevitable conclusion to our relationship. Well, spending the rest of my life married to the wrong man seems every bit as ruinous as falling for you."

"Then don't fall," he told her. "Because I do not welcome the burden."

Chapter 26

𝐷AVID STARED DOWN at the woman frozen in his arms, his chest thundering with turbulent emotions. Caroline's eyes were wide with hurt and her feet had stopped moving.

At this moment, he would have given anything for a whispered "one," much less the obligatory "two, three."

Escape from the dance floor and the summer crowd's prying eyes emerged as the most pressing immediate concern. Anyone watching them would know they were arguing. And he would be very, very surprised if everyone in the room wasn't watching them, given how the sparks practically rose in the air above them.

David pulled her from the dance floor even as the couples went on twirling around them, an inexcusable display of manners that was sure to cause more gossip than any mere argument would. He jerked her behind the nearest refuge, a potted palm with fronds the size of a park bench.

And then he faced his reckoning.

"I should not have called you a burden," he admitted, though what he should have called her was still a point of debate. Obsession seemed a bit harsh of a term, but there was a glint of that hidden beneath his churning thoughts. "I care for you. I would not have you thinking I do not value our friendship."

Caroline's eyes shone almost green under the chandeliers. "This is more than simple friendship, and you do us both a disservice to gloss it over in such terms. Do you remember that day when we first met?"

"Aye," David acknowledged. And he needed to remember it better, if he was to have the courage to carry this through. Every memory, every regret, bade him to let her go and just keep going. But she deserved more than the rose-tinted history he had given her two nights ago.

She deserved the entire truth.

"I never forgot you," she said. "Not once, in those eleven long years. I thought of you nearly every day. Wondered who you were, where you were from. *You* are the man I think of when I close my eyes at night. So do not stand before me and tell me I still need to find my perfect match!"

Her confession burrowed beneath David's skin, a pulsing knot demanding excision. "You are describing a girlhood infatuation," he said, though the sentiment sounded meager to his own ears. "Life is still an open possibility for you. You know not what you say."

"I am not a child," she snapped. "Is that how you see me? As some silly chit, pouring out her secret yearnings?"

"No." David expelled a frustrated breath. That too had not been fair of him. There was nothing childlike in the stormy set of her jaw, or the punishing way her hand tightened in his. She deserved the truth, and he would not lie about this.

He had ceased to think of her as a little girl the moment he saw her again on the beach, after so long an absence from Brighton. But thinking of her as a woman, and giving her the hope that he might think of her as *his* woman, were two different things.

His instincts told him to gather her up in his arms. But for her own good, he needed to shove her off this cliff instead.

"I am not the man you imagine me to be." He shook his head. "You are infatuated with a falsehood."

"This is not an infatuation." Her face flushed red. "I know what I want, and whom I want. I want *you*."

"I explained why I could not—"

"You explained about your past. About Elizabeth, and the tragedy of her death. That you are leaving soon, to return to Scotland. I understand all of that, David, truly I do. But none of that explains why you refuse to consider a future with someone."

"I cannot, Caroline. There are things you do not know."

"I know that you are a man worth loving. I can help you, if you would but let me. You need to stop living in the past, tied up by a love that no longer makes sense."

Escape beckoned but a few feet away. It would be an easy matter to slip out of the room and not look back. But the challenge in Caroline's eyes kept his boots anchored in place. She looked stern and powerful and, yes, even knowing.

But she did not know. Not the whole of it.

"You know nothing about me, or what I have done. You cannot want me," he told her. "Not because of what you think happened eleven years ago, but because of what actually did."

She blinked, confusion crowding in. "How can you say that? That day was one of the most important in all my life. I was a child on the brink of womanhood, not knowing who I was. My father had just died, but because of you, I found hope. Because of you and your encouragement, I continued to swim."

Christ. She didn't understand. This wasn't about swimming. How old was she now, twenty-two? Twenty-three? Older than he had been at the time.

But far more innocent.

He hesitated, knowing there was no easy way to say it, knowing there was no going back once he had. But for the first time in eleven years, he wanted to give voice to his terrible past, to admit his mistakes.

Because if he didn't, Caroline would never understand why he was the most inappropriate man in all of Britain to set her sights on.

David felt as close to shattering as he had that day, when the posted letter had arrived at Preston Barracks bearing the news of Elizabeth's death. "That day, eleven years ago, I had just received a letter informing me that Elizabeth had died." His voice might have belonged to a different man, so gruff and coarse did the words sound. "*That* is why I was in the water."

He could see her start to reshape the events of that day in her mind then, twist it from the fantasy she had been nurturing into the far more adult understanding it required. "I . . . I thought you had been drinking."

"I *had* been drinking. That is the usual way of things when you cannot face the world through sober eyes. You see, I didn't just lose Elizabeth that day. She was carrying my child when she died."

"Oh my God." Caroline went still, her face drained of the color that had just been flying high only moments before.

David stared down, seeing Caroline again as she had been that day. A twelve-year-old innocent chastising him for circumstances she did not have the power to understand. Even now, she *still* didn't appear to fully comprehend what he was saying.

Then again, how could she? He wasn't sure *he* understood. Eleven years had passed since he had turned himself over to these memories, and he found himself struggling to wrap his mind around the enigma that had been Elizabeth Ramsey. He could still taste the swirl of emotions that had come with his first taste of love.

God, he had been such an idiot.

"Her father was the town rector. Hell, brimstone, dam-

nation. But that did not stop my desperation to have her."
David hovered on the edge of his confession, trying to remember. His very soul objected to dredging up the messy
business, but he owed Caroline a more complete explanation than he had previously provided at the pavilion, given
that she seemed to have imprudently decided his was a
soul worth redeeming.

"I was brash, bound for the army. It took scarcely a kiss
to coax Elizabeth to send me off in style. I offered for her,
after. Not that a mere offer could make it right. But it was
a conversation we should have had before we tumbled into
bed, because Elizabeth had no intention of becoming a
military wife."

Caroline studied him, her eyes needle-sharp. "It sounds
as though it was her choice, if she declined your offer.
Why do you blame yourself?"

"Because I failed her." He recalled the pain Elizabeth's rejection had wrought, as acute as the slash of a
saber, but it had been tinged with the slightest bit of relief
too. That, even more than her senseless death, was what
had tormented him all these years. There had been no
reckoning for him to face, no choice to make. He had not
been required to abandon his dream of joining the army,
even though in his heart he had known it was the right
thing to do.

Elizabeth had made the decision for him. He had been
too selfish to insist.

And he had lived with that guilt now for eleven long
years.

He drew in a deep breath. "I killed her."

That, finally, brought a bloodless gasp from her lips.
"Surely you jest."

David shook his head. "This is not a joke, Caroline. I
left Elizabeth in Moraig when I bought my commission,
even though I knew the possible outcome of the choices
we had made. I killed her through my neglect, as surely

as if I had strangled her with my own hands. I told her to write to me if she found herself in difficulty, and I would come. But I did not understand that letters from home were held by the commanding officers until our initial six weeks of training was completed. I received Elizabeth's letter telling me she was with child, and the letter from my mother informing me she had taken her own life, on the same day."

Beyond her shoulder, David could see that Branson had spied them. The man was even now threading his way toward them around the edge of the ballroom. David plowed on, knowing he had but seconds to finish this. "I am no saint, no gentleman, lass. You may think you see honor in me, but I assure you there is far more to fear than to admire. I came very close to killing myself that day, but I did not even possess enough decency to manage *that*. Living with the knowledge of what I had done, of what I had lost, proved a more fitting penance in the end."

Branson rounded the potted palm, a hopeful smile strung on his face. David extracted his hand from Caroline's. He hadn't even realized she had still been gripping it. "So now you know why I cannot love you. Even if I tried, I would destroy what is beautiful in you, the same way I destroyed it in Elizabeth. *That* is why I am not the right man for you."

He pushed her toward Branson. Toward a future she might not believe she wanted, but which was undoubtedly better than the one she sought with him.

"That is why I am not the right man for anyone," he added.

And then he walked away.

DEAR GOD, SHE was in love with him. Completely, ir-revocably, stupidly in love.

And he was in love with a ghost.

Caroline watched him leave through the open doors of

the ballroom, and all the air seemed to be sucked from the room with him. Her pulse was still bounding in her throat. She had laid her heart bare, not caring that he was a man of meager means, or that in choosing him she might be letting her family down. She could think of nothing beyond the fact that the man she had loved for eleven long years had just held her in his arms on the dance floor, and made her tremble with a want so sharp it hurt to draw breath.

And then that same man had also just confessed a past so sordid, any sane woman would bolt for safety.

"Is everything all right?" Mr. Branson peered up at her, his brown eyes round with concern.

Caroline tried to smile, though she feared the gesture came out more as a grimace. "I am fine," she assured him. "Just a minor disagreement with Mr. Cameron."

"It appeared to be more than a minor disagreement." Branson's jaw worked sideways, as if testing the veracity of an idea. "Shall I speak with him? Call him out?"

Caroline smothered a hysterical laugh. "That will not be necessary, thank you."

She felt no compunction to expand on the nature of the argument. Indeed, she felt protective of David and his terrible secret. How must he be feeling? God knew she felt raw from the encounter. Even Mr. Branson's confused gaze burned like an open flame. David claimed he had killed the woman he loved.

How did one respond to a confession like that, particularly when she had just ignorantly petitioned to be the *next* woman he might love?

He hadn't been merely drunk and foolish. He had tried to kill himself, that day in the surf. She could not regret saving him. Never that. But in those moments before he had turned away from her, in the seconds it took to explain why he could never love her, she had glimpsed the stunted and scarred nature of his soul.

She loved him desperately—she could see that now,

how the seeds of infatuation had begun to change into something far more adult, almost from the point of seeing him again. She understood how rash mistakes could happen, particularly in areas of the heart. Her body's own wild response to David's touch told her there were primitive undercurrents to her soul that might be nigh on impossible to control.

And so she did not blame him, not to the degree he blamed himself. He could claim he lacked all honor, but the fact he had spent eleven years in purgatory showed her the truth. But if he would never permit himself to move beyond the pain of his past, Caroline couldn't turn that into a future.

In that moment, she hated Elizabeth Ramsey. The girl had rejected David's offer of marriage and then taken her own life. How peculiar to feel such a knife's point of jealousy for someone eleven years dead, a woman who had fallen to such tragedy. But there was no doubting the emotion wrapping its green, strangling tendrils around Caroline's throat. Elizabeth Ramsey might have died young, but she had taken David's very soul with her to the grave.

"Would you care to dance, then?" Branson asked, treading on her thoughts.

There was no denying she needed a distraction of some sort. And yet tonight, the thought of spinning in Mr. Branson's arms felt about as appealing as splinters in her stockings. She didn't want to dance. She wanted to follow David. She wanted to dissect the conversation, to remember how it had felt to dance in his arms when she had still believed he might want her.

But it was clear, in the manner in which he had removed himself and in the way he had pushed her toward Mr. Branson, that David wanted nothing of the sort.

No, dancing was not to be recommended, not with her feet so numb and her stomach tied up in knots. "I believe I might prefer a glass of punch," she told Mr. Branson, chasing her words with what she hoped was an encouraging smile.

The young man nodded eagerly and offered her his arm. "Shall we, then?"

She placed her fingers lightly against the smart woolen fabric of his evening coat and let him pull her toward the nearby room where the refreshments were being served. It felt wrong to be here, a suitor on her arm. Somewhere in the night, David was mourning the love of his life.

And here, in the brightly lit ballroom, with the vibrant music hammering her senses, Caroline was mourning the loss of her ignorance. Because if only she could skip back in time, she might still believe she could capture such a man's heart.

Chapter 27

For the third day in a row, Caroline woke alone in her room.

Though she had slept a few hours, she felt anything but refreshed. The ball had stretched on until two o'clock in the morning. But it was last night's argument with David, rather than the late hour, that had her feet dragging as she went about her morning ablutions. She had thought she could help David overcome his tragic past, but now she realized his reasons for refusing her were more complex than a simple case of mourning his first love.

David blamed himself for the girl's death.

And Caroline reminded him of her.

She would have liked to talk things through with Penelope, to use her sister as a sounding board against the tumult of emotions that tossed inside her. But Pen's bed was as neatly made as it had been yesterday, and it seemed clear that whatever else her sister might have done, it had not included sleep.

This time, she did not need to pick up Penelope's journal to sort out where her sister was. Pen had danced twice with Mr. Hamilton last night, although she had also danced with a handful of other gentlemen. And while Caroline found she could not begrudge her sister a few stolen moments with the man, she *did* resent being left to explain her absence to their mother.

Because Penelope had not arrived by the time she made her way down for breakfast either.

"What do you *mean* she's gone out for a walk?" her mother sputtered over the rim of her floral-patterned porcelain teacup, the one with the chip on one side. "It's only ten o'clock in the morning!"

"She mentioned wanting to take in the sunrise." Caroline looked down at her plate, her thoughts still swirling around David's revelations of last night. She tried to distract herself with the more looming problem of breakfast, which this morning consisted of toast made from the remnants of last week's loaf of bread and a single poached egg. The egg had been placed on top of the bread, preventing any attempt to dress the ensemble up with jam or butter. Caroline sighed as she recognized the telltale signs of Bess's creativity to stretch the family's food budget. Apparently the expense of her new gown was already showing up through the loss of breakfast staples.

"Which doesn't explain why she's missing now." Mama's mouth turned down. "The sun came up several hours ago."

Caroline squirmed in her chair, unable to come up with anything more logical to explain Pen's glaring absence from the breakfast table. And then she breathed a sigh of relief as the sound of the front door slamming reached her ears and Penelope came barreling into the dining room, a newspaper tucked under one arm.

"Morning, Mama." She kissed their mother on one cheek, then placed the paper down on the table before taking her seat. She bowed her head a quick moment, muttered something like a prayer beneath her breath, then opened her eyes to blink at her meager plate. "Er . . . where is the rest of br-breakfast?"

"The more pertinent question is where were *you*?"

Mama prompted, a hint of steel in her voice. "It is not like you to be gone so early."

Pen passed the newspaper down the table before reaching for the teapot. "I went out to get a c-copy of the *Gazette*. I thought we all would enjoy reading the social section. It is sure to mention Caroline, after her success at the b-ball last night."

Caroline looked at her sister with a rising sense of unease. Clearly, Pen had come prepared, with a ready excuse tucked up under her arm like that. There was much to admire in how neatly her sister, who was new at this process of subterfuge, deflected her mother's questions. Then again, hadn't Caroline provided her ample room to practice, asking Pen to cover for her afternoon walks?

Mama's expression softened to a more tolerable state. "That was thoughtful of you, dear. But we can't afford to spend our money on such luxuries as the *Gazette* anymore." Their mother pushed the unread paper back across the table. "I am afraid things are going to be tight around here in the near future. Our bill to Madame Beauclerc is due next week, and we still have several dresses planned for both of you. Purchasing a copy of the paper merely to read the *on-dit*s is an indulgence we cannot afford."

Pen swallowed the bite of dry toast she had taken and offered a tight smile at their mother's rebuke. "I shall try to r-remember, Mama." She picked up the paper. "But as long as we have it today, why don't we take a look?"

Caroline paused, her bite of egg halfway to her mouth. Her memories of last night were not ones she cared to revisit in the company of her family. Had word of her disagreement with David found its way into the *Gazette*? Or worse, what if someone had overheard their conversation, and printed something about David's past?

But there was nothing to be done, because Pen was already opening the paper. "Oh my g-g-goodness! It says here that Duffington proposed to Caroline last night!"

"What?" Their mother snatched the paper out of Pen's hands in a display of sharpened claws that quite belied her common claims to having been born a lady.

Caroline slid down in her chair. How had a *Gazette* reporter found out about Duffington's proposal? Her stomach had already been feeling a bit off, but what little she had consumed threatened to make a return appearance now. Clearly Mr. Duffington was a man who could not be trusted to keep any sort of counsel.

"Oh my word." Mama's blue eyes met hers. "Is it true?"

"Er . . . yes." There was little Caroline could do but admit it. Because wishing he hadn't wouldn't make it go away.

"Oh, I *knew* the investment in Madame Beauclerc's services was going to be our salvation." Mama's cheeks shone pink with excitement. "That dress was divine, if I do say so myself. Have you decided whether you shall accept him? Imagine, if you did, you would be potentially in line to be a countess, Caroline."

Caroline opened her mouth to say she didn't want to be anything of the sort, only to be interrupted by her sister. "She should w-wait to give him her answer." Pen busied herself refolding the paper with great care.

"Why? Duffington would be excellent choice. Provided she gets on with him, of course." Their mother's blue-eyed gaze turned probing. "Do you like him at all, dear? I mean, enough to contemplate marriage? He isn't the most handsome of your lot of suitors, but there is more to life than the way a man looks."

"Mr. Duffington is nice," she hedged.

"And his family is wealthy," her mother prompted.

Caroline studied her hands, examining the ragged beds of her nails. "I suppose."

"Mr. Branson d-danced with her last night too, after . . . well, after the first waltz." Pen paused for breath, before plunging back into her stilted speech. "She never lacked for a partner, not once during the evening. And Mr. Hamilton mentioned to me he was looking to take a wife within the year." Penelope fixed Caroline with a look. "She should not make any rash d-decisions where Mr. Duffington is concerned."

"But I thought *you* liked Mr. Hamilton," Caroline protested, her head swirling from the rapid volley of conversation that threatened to unseat her.

"I have more of a b-business interest with him," Pen said matter-of-factly. "He told me just last night that he was thinking of asking you to accompany him to the race on Monday."

Caroline narrowed her eyes at her sister. She could well imagine what kind of business her sister had with the young, red-haired, cheroot-smoking photographer, and she was not going to have any part of him.

"I wasn't the one who danced with him last night," Caroline told Pen. *Or snuck out to meet him this morning*, she mentally tacked on to the statement.

"He couldn't get on your dance c-card." Penelope offered her a sly smile. "Something about it being full."

"But—"

Bess bustled into the dining room, chattering like a magpie whose nest had been turned over. "Oh, Mrs. Tolbertson, there are two gentlemen, and they are both insistent on seeing Miss Caroline right away. I tried to explain you were eating breakfast, but Mr. Dermott just walked himself back to the parlor and—"

Caroline pushed back from the table, her knotted stomach loosening. "Mr. Dermott is here?"

Bess nodded, wringing her hands. "And Mr. Branson too."

Caroline picked up her skirts, determined to sort this out. At the least, the morning's new event promised a ready excuse to avoid finishing her miserable bit of breakfast. Branson she might have expected, but Dermott's presence was an admitted surprise, given they had shared no more than a single dance last night.

Well, and that single, unfortunate kiss two weeks ago.

Both gentlemen were waiting in the parlor, pacing on opposite walls. Their heavy masculine footsteps sent her mother's glass figurines rattling on the mantel, and their presence bristled above the feminine frippery, as if seeking which delicate thing to tear down first. Caroline pasted a smile on her face as she walked in and put a steadying hand on the fragile sculptures. "Good morning. What brings you here so early, gentlemen?"

Branson lunged toward her and extracted a copy of the newspaper from an inner pocket of his jacket. He shook it in a hard fist. "The *Gazette* brings me here."

Caroline sighed. "Is that why you have come? To speak ill of Duffington?"

"The man is brash in the extreme to offer you marriage after only two days' acquaintance. Why, I have admired you for far longer."

Caroline inclined her head. Branson was correct. He had known her for all of *four* days.

Branson clasped Caroline's hand and fell onto one knee, bringing to mind a wounded soldier trying valiantly to prove his worth. He pressed a fervent kiss to the top of her hand. "Caroline. My heart is wounded by the turn of events. I had wanted to offer for you, but my friends argued it would be prudent to wait a week."

"A week?" Caroline echoed, incredulous.

"But he who hesitates is . . . well . . . suffice it to say I cannot wait anymore. Would you do me the honor of becoming my wife?"

Caroline felt as though the blood drained from her head. Indeed, she felt as if all the blood drained from her body. This could not be happening again. She extracted her hand from the sandy-haired young man's strong grip. "It is very kind of you, Mr. Branson. Truly. But . . ." Her mind searched for some deterrent. "Don't you have another year at university?"

He rose unsteadily. "We could have a long betrothal."

Caroline sighed, trying to pick through an appropriate response. A long betrothal would not solve her family's financial problems, and the thought of marrying this boy-man made her feel about as hopeful as a long march to the gallows. Honestly, between Branson and Duffington, she wasn't sure of the worse choice.

Dermott stepped forward then. She had almost forgotten his presence, so quiet had he been through the awkward exchange. "Mr. Branson was a bit eager in his offer, I think. Might I inquire first whether you have accepted Mr. Duffington's offer?"

Caroline shook her head, blinking under the somewhat mesmerizing spell of Mr. Dermott's rumbling voice. He had a way of asking a question that suggested he already knew the answer, and used his voice only to hypnotize his prey. She recalled now that he had spoken in just such a way in the moments before he had kissed her on the Chain Pier.

She flushed at the unfortunate memory. "I have not formed a decision yet."

Dermott smiled up at her, and she was reminded that she had, for a time, thought the man quite handsome. Their first physical interaction had ended disastrously, but their dance last night had gone better. A quivering hope sprang free. She could not deny that Mr. Dermott, at least, made her blood hum in some degree of awareness. It was not the body-spinning attraction that David Cameron brought out in her treacherous veins, but it was at least something beyond the mild case of peptic upset that Duffington and Branson inspired.

She reminded herself that this was the man who had all but ruined her life with his thoughtless words. The man who had stalked her, kissed her, and then jeered at her.

But he wasn't jeering right now. In fact, though she had treated him with only the stiffest sort of courtesy last night, he had presented himself at her home this morning, respectful intentions in hand.

One of Dermott's hands played about the lower edge of his waistcoat, and Caroline's eye darted toward the motion. Poppies today, unless the bit of enlivened embroidery was playing tricks on her eyes. His voice pushed through the rolling fog of her thoughts. "I am glad to hear you are carefully considering your answer. I hope that means you will consider my own suit."

"Your suit?" Caroline asked, still staring at the bloodred poppies, lined up like soldiers against the black woolen background.

"I have come to admire you, and although I would normally wish to us time to become more closely acquainted, the rash behavior of others forces me to quick action." He shot Branson a heated look. "Given that my family has visited Brighton for many years, and given that I have, in fact, graduated from university some five years past, I hope you will consider me favorably."

"Oh, I say, that's a little unfair," Branson protested.

Caroline met Dermott's unswerving gaze then, abandoning the poppies for the distraction of his smile. The man was brilliant. In one smooth sentence, he had managed to make Branson seem panicked and immature, and cast a logical suspicion on the rationale behind Duffington's two-day proposal.

"What are you saying, Mr. Dermott?"

He straightened his waistcoat, and offered her again that stunning, cunning smile. "I would take this opportunity to lodge my own proposal there beside the others. Miss Tolbertson . . ." He drew a breath, and then continued, "Caroline . . ." This time her name did not sound so grating to her ears. "I would be humbly honored if you would consider becoming my wife."

Chapter 28

SHE WALKED EAST, of course.

She could do nothing else, after leaving the circus of her house. Her mother was beside herself with excitement. Penelope seemed pensive. Poor Bess busied herself changing out the water in all the flower arrangements.

And so Caroline had taken the walk she had known she would take from the moment her eyes had opened this morning. If nothing else, it gave her a solid hour to think.

Three proposals. Three opportunities to help her family.

Three chances to get it completely, miserably wrong.

She almost, *almost* turned back around on the threshold of the cove. But the painful memory of David's parting last night and the wretched, abraded surface of her heart, pushed her forward through the final stretch of scrub grass. She did not know which gentleman's offer to accept, but she knew she could not consider any of them without taking this next, necessary step.

Her conscience was doing its best to tell her this decision was wrong. Not the wanting of David—she suspected she was going to be caught in that trap no matter her final decision on which offer to accept. She could no more stop loving him than stop the tide from coming in. But wanting the man and acting on her desires were two different things.

Was it a sin to seek physical passion from one man when she had a bona fide offer of marriage from another? If it was, she was about to be a sinner three times over.

He was already in the water when she arrived, a fact Caroline found vexing. He had coaxed a promise from her that she would not swim here alone on account of the danger, and yet here he was, sluicing through the waves. He was swimming away from her, facing the eastern edge of the inlet, and Caroline took advantage of his removed concentration to study him.

Although she tended to have a critical eye when it came to swimming technique, she could find little fault with his movements today. He had improved since their instruction began, and her gaze moved appreciatively from the motion of his arms to the spray of water his feet kicked up. She noted a few things they could work on. His hand tended to cup on the downward arc, which, when corrected, would lessen the drag. And his legs tended to kick too wide apart, when a narrow, scissorlike kick worked better for propulsion.

Caroline stepped behind the rock and set herself to the task of removing her dress, but she hesitated at the point of putting on the altered navy gown. Her fingers skimmed the lower edge of her shift, pausing at the scalloped lace edge. Yesterday's experience in self-exploration had been . . . frustrating. Incomplete.

Maddening.

Why had he chosen that particular lesson? Truth be told, David had been far more physically engaged during the interlude in the bathing machine. And to her mind, the main difference between those two experiences had been the amount of clothing involved. Warmth pooled in her abdomen, heat that had nothing to do with the sun or the blinding light from the cliff walls. She recalled the appreciative gleam in his eye when he had kissed her under moonlight, remembered the heady feel of his hand on her bare breast a mere two days ago.

But this was not a moonlit night, nor a dimly lit bath-house, with shadows to hide her flaws. The midday sun hung overhead, bright and glaring and inescapable. Her doubts tried to dissuade her, jeering at her as loud as any crowd, but she refused to be guided by those old fears.

She did not want to release David from his promise, no matter their argument last evening, no matter the shock-ing details of his confession. He would not be outside the bounds of logic—or decency—if he refused to honor their arrangement today.

But to Caroline's mind, these lessons had been negoti-ated and executed primarily on the basis of her curiosity, and that had not abated in the slightest. If anything, faced with the mind-rattling choice of the three men vying for her hand, her desire to seize this moment with David had swollen to a fearsome size. And if she gave him the choice to bow out now, she would not merely be denying her own chance at pleasure. She would be giving up on him.

She wanted to prove to him that he was more than his history. She wanted to lie down on the rock beside him, run her fingers through his hair, and extract the hurt he carried inside him. And if she were truthful, she wanted him to understand what he was forcing her to offer an-other, so that he might feel a fraction of the envy that she felt when she thought about Elizabeth Ramsey.

The navy serge gown dropped to the rocky shore, for-gotten. She had two days left.

And she refused to spend them as frustrated as he had left her yesterday.

DAVID HAD BEEN swimming for the better part of an hour, pushing his body, testing his strength. He had slept poorly, tossing and turning and waking in sweat-soaked sheets, plagued not by nightmares of the girl he had lost, as he had expected, but by feverish dreams of the girl he could not permit himself to have. He had come to the cove early, determined to drive all carnal thoughts of Caroline out of his head the only way he knew how: with a good, punishing dose of exercise. It had nearly worked too. He was exhausted, struggling for air, and swimming in water that reached several feet over his head when he saw her.

Caroline Tolbertson was standing at the water's edge, clad only in her shift.

His mind was none too clear, having reached that place where survival outweighed the need to think. His muscles were numb, both from the physical exertion and the constant, cold waves that battered him. But his brain was not so muddled that it did not hone in on the sight of her lithe body, stepping into the water.

He sucked in a breath and seawater flooded his mouth, making him cough and sputter. Eleven years ago he had nearly drowned in this very spot, paralyzed by the knowledge that he had failed someone he loved. And as Caroline waded out farther into the waves, he was struck by the sudden realization that in a scant few seconds, he was going to be poised to do it again.

Because if he held her in his arms, with only the futile barrier of her wet shift between them, his failure to preserve her virginity wasn't just a possibility.

It was a bloody foregone conclusion.

He had hoped his exhaustion would have calmed that part of his body. He had never been a man prone to good fortune. The sight of her dampening shift, and the shadows that emerged to visibility beneath the translucent fabric, proved more than enough to send his cock straight to attention, the cold water and exhaustion be damned.

He made his way toward her, wary and weary, slogging his way through water that lessened in depth with each step. And then she was inches away in hip-deep water, peering up at him with ocean spray in her eyelashes. He wanted to crush her to him and kiss her till her knees gave way beneath her. It would be wrong to take that advantage, though.

He briefly entertained the idea of shaking her senseless, if kissing was not going to be an option. She had clearly come for their lesson, dressed as she was. Any sensible girl would have kept her distance, given that he had admitted to something just short of murder last night.

Of course, hadn't Caroline proven on more than one occasion that she had far more substance lurking beneath her surface than any merely sensible girl?

"You started without me." Her voice sounded accusing, and he wondered how long she had been watching him battle the ocean current.

"I did not expect you," he admitted. "Not after last night." He ran a hesitant hand through his hair. "Christ, Caroline, you twist me up in enough knots to do a sailor proud. What do you *want* from me?"

"Our bargain." She licked her lips, and the motion shot straight to his groin. "I am not inclined to release you from the promise you made."

David groaned out loud. Couldn't she see how dangerous this was? He had no way to win this game she played. He preferred his odds of surviving the inlet's high tide. While weighted down with paving stones.

Tumbling down drunk.

Suddenly she was in his arms, and he was knocked off balance by the sweet, terrible surprise of her. They tumbled into the water, and then they were under, their lips of an accord on the matter of kissing.

Salt water stung his eyes, and the power of the ocean roared in his ears, but it was no match for the wicked sting of lust that snaked through him as her mouth moved against his. And then her tongue touched his own, and he was lost to all coherent thought, save one:

This woman was both his reward, and his greatest punishment.

He had timed the morning's brutal exertions to temper the keen edge of desire. Had swum an hour in this ferocious current for no other purpose than to banish the need to claim her as his. How ironic to discover that far from serving its intended purpose, his exertions had instead left him too exhausted to resist her.

They bobbed back up to the surface, gasping for the air in each other's lungs. He cradled her head in his hands, threading his fingers through her hair. The beast in him, the one he tried so hard to keep chained, raised its head to roar. *Mine*.

But the gentleman in him, the gentleman he hadn't quite believed existed, placed an authoritative hand on the beast's head and pushed it down for the breadth of a second.

"Are you sure this is what you want?" He all but snarled against the sweet temptation of her lips, because God help him, he was failing the test he had laid for himself.

"With certainty." She answered with a breathless moan he could not refuse.

Scooping her up in his arms, he staggered to the shallows, his lips refusing to leave hers for even the second it took to draw a new breath. She wrapped her legs around his waist, and he could feel her bare calves rubbing against his own skin where his trousers met his torso. Implausibly, his brain registered the obvious before his cock did.

They were here alone, an hour or more from civilization. She was almost naked. And the scandalous press of her legs about his waist was pushing her core flush against his bare skin.

The trouser-encased part of his anatomy that wanted to bury himself inside her jerked toward the promise of her body. He thrust upward, a deliberate stroke that left nothing to either of their imaginations. She gasped into his mouth.

And then, unbelievably, she said, "More."

He obliged the lady's request and thrust again. Slower this time. A delicious promise of friction that sent his fin-

gers curving about her cotton-clad arse, there at the point
of no return.

"Think hard on this," he growled into her mouth, even
as they splashed down to earth at the water's edge. "Because there is no going back."

Caroline landed on top of him, a heavy burden he could
not bring himself to regret. The relentless current swept
them backward toward shore, and pebbles and shells
scraped across his bare back, but he held her about her
waist as she straddled his chest, the feel of her woman's
mound against the bare skin of his abdomen the most agonizing sensation of all.

"I *have* thought hard on this," she told him, her eyes
glittering down. "And eleven years is a long time to think."

He thrilled to her response, even as he pulled her down
to meet his lips. David kept his touch gentle, though his
body ordered he set a different pace. He ignored his cock's
demands for the moment. He'd endured a great deal of
practice ignoring that most insistent part of his anatomy,
a part that hadn't even, at first, realized the treasure it was
pointing him toward.

Five more minutes' restraint was not going to kill him,
not if he could stoke the fires of her enjoyment first.

He forced his body into compliance and kissed Caroline a long, leisurely moment, enjoying the sharp, salty
taste of her. The tide was coming in, the waves rolling
into oblivion around them, but he ignored them for the
moment. He ran his tongue along the edge of her lips, a
sensual slide that belied the building frustration he felt
for this slow, careful process he was determined to construct for her. His hand had found her breast at some point
during the kiss, and he rubbed his thumb deftly over her
peaked nipple, back, forth, and back again.

She responded by rocking against him and gasping into
his mouth. "More," she murmured again.

He grinned into her kiss. For such a loquacious person,

it seemed the woman in his arms was reduced to the same primitive, one-word responses that he felt in this moment. "Tell me what you want." He let his hand drift lower, teasing at the edge of her shift. "I am good at following directions."

She pulled back and stared down at him, breathing hard. Her skin was flushed, marring the usual prominence of her freckles, and her lips were beautifully swollen from his kisses. "Liar," she told him, rocking against him again in a movement that suggested either a damned fine instinct, or a great deal of time spent studying her sister's book. "If you had followed proper directions, we would have done this yesterday."

Chapter 29

DAVID FELT AN answering grin spread across his face. "Tell me what you want *today*, then."

"You." Her eyes glinted down at him, framed against the sunlight by the wild halo of her hair. She lifted her palm to cup his face, and her touch felt like silk, pulled across sensitive flesh. "This." She breathed out, and the sound was like a balm to his soul. "Us."

David pulled her down and rolled with her so they were lying side by side, the water rushing around them. He let his eyes roam down the exquisite length of her, from her pert brows to the pink toes that flashed at him amid the ebb and flow of the shoreline waves. He recalled the water had felt cold to him this morning, but there was none of that in this moment, only an intense, burning heat that seemed to suffuse every pore.

Her eyes met his across the space of the few inches he had created with his repositioning, and he seized upon an adequate description for their color.

Abalone. The most incredible mixture of colors, but defying any single label. She was unique, like the shells that littered this beach, like the storm of emotion that littered his mind. And while he did not know that the next hour might bring, for this moment, at least, she was his.

His gaze drifted down to the tempting, wet edge of her

shift. He wondered if she knew that he could see every part of her through the fine, thin cotton. The dark patch between her legs, in particular, stood out against her skin like paint beneath a transparent canvas.

He reached a finger down as he met her eyes once more. Brushed against the curls that waited for him there. Knew he had found her hidden pleasure point when those beautiful eyes widened and she arched up to meet him.

"Is this what you want?" he asked, though it was a question she had already answered with the push of her body against his questing finger.

"You know it is." She caught her lower lip between her teeth, and her obvious frustration urged him on.

He settled into a rhythm, testing her reflexes, finding them open for his touch. He focused hard on that spot that made her thrash beside him, challenging her to go further, reach higher, than she had yesterday. He offered words of encouragement, carefully skirting any mention of that messy business of love.

And then, in response to her strangled cry, David added the "more" she was begging for, slipping his finger inside her. The blazing heat of her passage was like crossing the surface of the sun.

"I . . . *oh.* It didn't feel like this yesterday," she exclaimed, closing her eyes and straining toward the push of his hand.

He took her lips in a kiss then, drowning in her words as much as her heat. "It wasn't meant to," he found the presence of mind to say after a moment. "It was a lesson to teach *me* what you wanted, not a lesson for you to find it."

"Then you are an apt pupil," she gasped, "because . . . I . . ."

And then she was gone, shattering around his hand. She bucked upward through the surf, her cry of release the most beautiful sound imaginable. Her body pulsed around his finger, an invitation his cock readily accepted as its well-earned due.

But still, David hesitated. She was falling back to him now, her wings momentarily clipped. They could stop this. Somehow, some way, he had survived it, though he was about ready to spill in his trousers like an inexperienced schoolboy.

And then she opened her eyes. They were glazed. Brilliant.

Begging.

"More," she whispered, her drugged smile the most compelling of invitations. And then he was unbuttoning his trousers.

He rose over her, his mind focused on her beautiful face, the primitive echo of "mine" roaring in his ears. He was about to take her, here on the open beach, her invitation unmistakable, his own body more ready than it had ever been.

Only one thing stopped him, a single terrible thought that flashed through his mind and threatened to asphyxiate him far more quickly than any convenient drowning.

What if she had already accepted Duffington's offer?

Remorse spun through him, all the more confusing because it was tempered by a desire to harm a man he had no cause to dislike, much less want to kill.

But he couldn't do it. He couldn't go through with this, couldn't give her the experience she sought, not if she was promised to another man.

David hauled his objecting body off her pliant one, settling into the grit and small, smooth-shaped rocks that lay all around them. He was shocked to his core by how close he had just come to taking her virginity. It did not matter if it was a gift she gave freely. It did not matter if he wanted it more than his body's next breath. It did not matter if she asked for "more" ten times over.

He was leaving for Scotland with his mother, in just

over a week. He had been about to ruin her life forever, on the cusp of an inevitable parting.

And he, of all people, knew what it was like to live with that kind of regret.

She struggled to sitting, her eyes a perplexed shade of amber and green. "Why did you stop?" she asked in confusion.

David swallowed against the trembling note of confusion in her voice. "I think," he said, struggling to form the words he needed to say, instead of the words he wanted to say, "that before we go any further with this lesson, we need to have a serious talk."

STUNNED BY THE abrupt shift in mood, Caroline pulled the edge of her shift down as far as it would go. She had found her senses again, and the reality of the moment lay like hot coals beneath her skin.

David had just . . . and she had felt . . . well, she didn't know what he had just done or what she had just felt, but she was quite sure there was a word for it somewhere in Penelope's book.

And "celibate" was not it.

"What do you want to talk about?" she asked, struggling to a sitting position and curling her legs up beneath her. She was confused by the new note of censure in his voice. Moments before, he had been urging her into oblivion.

Now, he seemed determined to yank it out of her grasp.

"Did you accept Duffington's offer?"

She sighed into the directness of his question. "No. Not yet." Caroline felt as if she were a ship that had sighted land, only to flounder in the shoals. She did not want to think about Duffington's offer in this moment. Or Branson's or Dermott's either. She wanted to return to the distraction of David Cameron's mouth and busy fingers.

But judging by the dark glower he was tossing her way,

she suspected she wasn't going to get out of the conversation by kissing him again.

"Do you plan to?"

"I don't know," she admitted, forcing her mind to the pertinent question at hand. "You raised some excellent concerns about Duffington last night, things I had not considered." In fact, now that a certain part of David's anatomy had been almost introduced to a certain part of hers, she was rethinking the wisdom of Duffington's size. "He is not a good fit using weight as the criterion, I'll admit."

A hint of relief touched David's smile. "I am relieved to hear you say that."

"If I am to go by height," she mused, reaching a hand to brush away the silver grains of sand that clung to the thick, blond hair on David's chest, "I think Mr. Branson would serve better than Duffington. But if I am to rely on instinct, I must admit Mr. Dermott has made an excellent case for me to place his offer first."

David reared back as if she had grasped one of those hairs and plucked it straight out. "What are you talking about?"

Caroline dropped her hand and battled a twinge of guilt. She knew she had been negligent in not admitting as much earlier, but a frank discussion of her choices had seemed a poor preference to kissing, at the time. "Mr. Branson and Mr. Dermott both presented me with offers of marriage this morning."

David pushed up and away from her in a single, fluid motion. "Bloody hell, Caroline."

She did not object to the obscenity. Indeed, it was a phrase she had been dancing around uttering herself all morning. As far as expressions went, she doubted she could find a more apt one to describe the absurdity of her week. She, Caroline Tolbertson, Brighton's most established wallflower, had received three offers of marriage in less than a single day, one of them from a man believed by many to be the most handsome of the summer set.

Bloody hell, indeed.

David fastened the buttons of his falls with a series of jerks, buttons she hadn't even realized had been undone. When he had finished, he glared down at her. "Were you going to tell me before or after I tupped you on this beach?"

Caroline lifted her chin. "That depends. Is tupping still an option?"

He reached down a hand to pull her up. He felt hard, vibrating against her skin like the blade of a sword, swung against granite. "Are you seriously considering any of them?" he demanded.

Caroline spent a long moment scraping the grit and crushed shells from her shift. There was no doubt she was going to find the tiny particles in places best left unmentioned, after David's bold exploration of her body. And no doubt she was avoiding answering the question.

Finally, she found her voice. "I imagine I would be mad not to, don't you think? I must marry someone. And I cannot marry someone who hasn't offered for me." She allowed her eyes to meet his, wincing as she took in the stone-set cast of his jaw. "Ergo, I must choose one of them."

David looked ready to explode. "You don't need to marry anyone, at least not in the immediate future. And you deserve someone better than Dermott."

"He has quite redeemed himself." Caroline thought back on Mr. Dermott's expression from the morning. He had looked desperate for her answer, crushed when she had offered him a delayed response. He had been serious in his offer. Either that, or the man was the most accomplished actor she had ever had the ill fortune to come across.

And unlike Branson, Dermott's offer, at least, had made her pulse wobble, just a bit. If she was to take David's own advice on the matter, wasn't *that* what she supposed to be looking for in a husband? Only two men had ever made her body hum enough to seek their kiss. One of them, of course, was Dermott. It had ended poorly, but she had not known what she was doing at the time. Logic argued that next time around would be more pleasurable.

The second man, who was even now stalking over to the rock and snatching up her discarded dress, had made his feelings on the nature of their relationship more than clear. Though he was upset over Mr. Dermott's offer of marriage, he was not going to make a counteroffer. She realized, in that moment, a part of her had been hoping he might. Her heart came close to crumpling in her chest.

David thrust out the gown as if the very fabric burned his hands. "Dermott does not deserve redemption. I should know. I am an expert in the cause."

Caroline met David's gaze, anchoring herself to the chink that had appeared in his armor. She accepted the dress from his clenched hands. "*Everyone* deserves redemption, David. Yourself included."

David fetched her slippers next. "I do not like the man."

Caroline stepped into the gown and pulled it up over her shift, wincing as the fabric turned dark with damp. "You don't have to like him," she retorted, working to reach the buttons between the back of her shoulders now. "*I* do. He has a nice bank account. Lovely, straight teeth. There is no doubt he would be my preferred choice over either of my other two offers."

She risked a glance at her glowering companion, wondering how far she was prepared to needle him. David was rapidly approaching the end of what appeared to be a very short rope. The only question was, did he care for her enough to prevent what she was honest enough to admit might be a grave mistake?

"I am three-and-twenty, David. Falling off the shelf. And Mr. Dermott is considered an excellent match."

"He does not appreciate you. Not the *true* you, at any rate."

Caroline exhaled, praying for patience. Was this really the same man who had just touched her so intimately? He looked angry enough to scale the white cliff walls using only his teeth for leverage. "What do you mean, the 'true' me? I'd say he does, if he is offering to marry me. It is not as if I have a dowry to tempt him."

"Perhaps he is responding to the myth, rather than the woman. Or perhaps he feels the need to best Branson. But he doesn't know you, not like I do. You would never be happy married to someone like him."

The first niggling shards of doubt lodged in Caroline's mind. "What myth? What are you referring to?"

A muscle ticked near David's right eye, and his face reddened, making the bright, golden color of his hair seem even lighter by contrast. "I might have encouraged Dermott's thoughts toward you along a more flattering path. Tuesday night, after our moonlit swim."

Caroline's thoughts flung wide at his admission, and settled on an inescapable truth. "Branson was there too, wasn't he?" she asked, horrified.

"Aye." David at least had the grace to look discomfited now, blast the man. He picked up his shirt and slipped it over his broad shoulders. "Branson was there," he admitted. "Hamilton too. But not Duffington or Adams. You cannot blame their interest on me."

Caroline stared at David as he buttoned up his own clothing. How could she not have seen it? It was so obvious now . . . The interest. The offers. Why would any of these men be interested in her, unless they had been spun a string of lies? Caroline swallowed the painful lump of her throat. "What did you say to them? What did you *do*?"

"I didn't want your reputation hurt any more than had already been done, and so I spun a little fancy over a shared bottle. I encouraged them to think of you in a more feminine light, I suppose. Distracted them from their incorrectly drawn conclusions. But I only wanted them to leave off with their heckling. I never expected it to result in all this stir."

The newfound confidence Caroline had discovered during the past few days dissolved into nothingness, displaced by the same self-doubts that had plagued her all her life. "Did you lie? Say something about me what wasn't true?"

He opened his mouth, a look of swift surprise flaring across his face. He shifted his weight from one foot to another. Guiltily, to her mind. "No," he finally said. "I can honestly say that nothing I said that night was an untruth."

But he had not believed it at the time. That much was clear. Her understanding of the situation settled from a vicious churning to a dull ache. She felt a bone-deep sense of who she was, a social plague that would not be cured, no matter the skill of her modiste, no matter her potential choice of husband. "What you are saying," she said slowly, "is that I was not good enough for them as I was."

David's gaze jerked down to meet hers. "That is not what I am saying at all."

"You had to convince them of my worth, and even that was a facade strung out of sympathy."

David shook his head. "You are twisting my words. I wanted . . . I *want* . . . to protect you."

"But you do not want to marry me." Caroline caught the sob in her throat, forbade it to escape. "So much so that you invented a story, just so others might remove the burden of my admiration from your hands."

David spread those very hands to which she referred, reaching for an answer he apparently could not give. Even now, even with all that had passed between them, his expression skirted an emotion that looked suspiciously like sympathy. "I am not the right man for you, Caroline."

A welcome rage settled in her gut. "So you keep saying,

but given that I have already accepted the man you are, what you *mean* is that I am not the right woman for you."

She waited for him to protest. To assure her she had the wrong of it.

He did none of those things. Instead, he nodded.

"What you mean," she continued, her certainty a terrible thing, "is that I am good enough to almost tup in the waves, but not good enough to pledge a troth. Well, let me tell you something, David Cameron. We are through with these lessons. I don't need your pity, and I don't need your proposal. It turns out I have plenty to sort through on my own."

Chapter 30

Sunday church service was a painful affair.

Caroline sat stiff-backed in her family's pew, dressed in her gown with the lavender flowers, her mind on anything but the sermon. She felt hollow inside, David's words running through her mind again and again. Her attention was snagged only once, when a blessing was offered for those who would compete in tomorrow's race. And then it was noon, the church crowd was gossiping about the latest news in the *Gazette*, and Caroline was stepping out into bright sunshine, Penelope walking several yards ahead.

Dermott intercepted her as she made her way down the church steps. He looked devilishly handsome, as always, and she could see at least two girls making moon eyes at him across the street. She knew she was lucky to have such a charming smile directed toward her, but as she summoned a smile in return, it occurred to her she had more than that.

She had an offer of marriage from this perfect specimen of a man. And even if Mr. Dermott's proposal was more calculated than romantic, even if his interest was based solely on some image conjured by too much whisky and David Cameron's exuberant description of a make-believe woman, the choice was now in *her* hands.

And a choice was something David had never permitted her.

"Good morning, Caroline," Mr. Dermott said, bowing at the waist. "I was waiting for you, hoping for a word about my proposal."

She eyed him, her stomach jumping like oil in a heated skillet. His nearness did not spark the same violent feelings in her that standing close to David did, but if her recent experience with David had taught her anything, it was that it was far more tenable to be the partner who was adored than the one doing the adoring.

David Cameron didn't want her. This man did.

Why was she even hesitating?

"I have been thinking hard on your offer," she told Mr. Dermott, her teeth trembling on the answer she knew she must give. "You make a favorable argument for my acceptance."

He looked pleased. "Favorable enough that you will have me?"

Caroline nodded. "I think," she said, willing herself to keep breathing, "that my answer is yes. I will marry you."

White teeth flashed at her. "Well, that's brilliant." His eye fell eagerly on a crowd emerging from the depths of the church. "Oh, there's Duffington and his mother now. And Branson behind them. Should I tell them our happy news?"

Caroline shook her head, alarmed at the thought of involving Mr. Dermott in such a delicate matter, given the way his chest was already puffing up. "I'd rather do it myself, if you don't mind. I shall tell them now. I do not want to string them along."

Dermott's smile slipped, ever so slightly. "Shall I call on you tomorrow then?"

"Aren't you competing in the race tomorrow?" she asked, inexplicably hesitant to plan tomorrow, much less the rest of her life, with this man she had had just accepted.

"The race is at eleven. But maybe after? We can tell your family, and also celebrate my win together."

Caroline raised a brow at his bravado, but she wrangled her instinctive retort into submission. "That sounds lovely," she said. "Come for tea. That seems as good a time as any to share the announcement with my family."

Dermott left whistling a bright, airy tune that seemed at odds with the task Caroline had before her. The business of putting off Duffington and Branson was the work of but a moment, but it left her drained and shaking. It had less to do with disappointing them than the realization she was cutting her safety net, as if by declining their offers, she was making her acceptance of Mr. Dermott's proposal seem more real.

It was almost one o'clock by the time she arrived home. If yesterday had gone differently, she would have been meeting David at the cove right about now. But she couldn't see herself facing him now, even if that made her a coward. The words they had exchanged, and the fact that he had failed to even consider offering for her, sat like yesterday's breakfast high in her stomach. Whatever promises they had made each other were through. She had told him their lessons were finished, and that had released him from all obligation.

It released her from obligation too, including the promise she had made him not to swim alone. David no longer required her instruction. He was ready for tomorrow's race. And she was ready for a hard, fast swim, without the distraction David Cameron had become.

The two o'clock hour came and went before she felt comfortable setting off, presuming David would finally be finished with his own practice. She could tell from the way the ocean lapped at the edge of the footpath that it was approaching high tide, and indeed, she felt the pounding of the waves reverberating beneath her feet, even before she rounded the last turn. It occurred to her, belatedly, that she might have come too late to swim today. At the point of highest tide, when the water surged up along the south-ernmost edge of the cliffs and obscured the rocks beneath the surface, her refuge was transformed from something enjoyable to something potentially deadly.

But as the little beach she knew so well came into view, she stopped, horrified, at the sight spread out in front of her.

The ocean, while high, was not the only thing contrib-uting to the roaring in her ears. The narrow shoreline was crawling with two dozen or more Brightonians. Women in gauzy white dresses. Children with kites and sailboats. Men in shirtsleeves. A couple had spread a blanket on top of the rock—*her* rock—and were laying out a picnic feast from the depths of a wicker basket. Behind them, two ado-lescent boys climbed the chalk cliffs, dislodging clumps of sea grass and knocking the sparrow nests down with pointed sticks.

A shudder racked her as she thought of the baby birds she had watched this summer, not yet fully feathered, tum-bling down into the teeming water below.

The danger of this inlet, and its lethal, hidden cur-rents, sent Caroline's feet running toward the crowd. She grabbed the nearest person she could find and shook the man's shoulder with a rough palm. Mr. Hamilton turned around, his red hair sticking out beneath the brim of his cap. The surprise of seeing him here paled in comparison to the fear crawling up her spine.

"What is happening?" she demanded. "Why are all these people here?"

"Didn't you see the article in the *Gazette* this morn-ing?"

"No." Caroline shook her head. She had eschewed breakfast this morning, preferring to mope in her room.

"It mentioned this swimming beach. Called it a hidden gem, where the summer residents could escape the clamor of the London day visitors." Hamilton tossed a dubious eye toward the boys climbing the white cliff walls. "Not that we seem any better behaved."

"But why would you write such a thing?" Caroline demanded. Hamilton had been one of the men who had stumbled across the cove Tuesday night, and her mind flew to the only logical conclusion. "This is far too dangerous of a beach for the public. These people are in great danger!"

"I didn't write it," he protested. "It was in the *Gazette*'s social section."

"But . . . *you* write the social section." An echo of confusion clamored in her head. "Don't you?"

"No, I don't." He looked a little put out. "I am a serious reporter, Miss Caroline."

Caroline eyed the young man uncertainly. "You didn't write about my proposal from Mr. Duffington yesterday?"

He shook his head. "No. I write about sporting events. The Brighthelmston horse races, the swimming competition, that sort of thing."

"Well, who writes the social section?" she demanded.

"I can't reveal the paper's sources, Miss Caroline. You know that. It was one of your father's rules, after all." Hamilton spread one hand out, panning the crowd, and then held up a heavy black box in the other. "Now that the secret is out, I feel obligated to photograph it. I am thinking of making a book, you know. *Photographic Treasures of Brighton*. Perhaps they'll even sell it in London."

Caroline felt as if the whole of the beach was sliding sideways beneath her feet. This was the cove that provided a cherished connection to the father she had lost, a place that served as a refuge from Brighton's brighter, noisier scene. Swimming here was one of her few pleasures in life.

Her *only* pleasure, now that her lessons with David Cameron were over.

And Mr. Hamilton was going to take a picture of it and share it far and wide.

"You can't do something so irresponsible," she protested. "If Londoners learn of this beach, then the people who come down for the day will come here instead of Brighton." She swallowed the lump in her throat. "And they'll destroy everything that is beautiful about it."

Hamilton shrugged. "I'd say it's a little late for that. Might as well record it now, while it is still of a piece. This crowd here will destroy it, soon enough." He offered her a searching glance. "About the swimming race tomorrow . . . I am slated to cover it for the paper. If you haven't accepted Duffington yet, would you like to come with me?"

Caroline blinked at him in surprise. "I . . . that is, no, thank you. I actually accepted Mr. Dermott's proposal this morning, so it turns out I am not free to accompany you."

"Dermott?" Hamilton sounded surprised. "I hadn't heard he had asked you."

"Yes, well, it all happened suddenly."

Too suddenly, truth be told. Even now, the thought sent her blood slowing in her veins. Caroline panned the crowd, wondering if Dermott was here too. She found him almost instantly, holding court among the summer set along the eastern edge of the cove. It occurred to her, as she watched him manipulate the rapt attention of his followers, that he was at home among that crowd in a way she would never be. Her gaze snagged on a familiar head who hovered near the edge of the group, her blond hair bent over a leather-bound journal.

"You might ask Penelope to accompany you to the race," she murmured, distracted by the way Pen seemed to have attached herself to that group. Did she want to be accepted by the summer set so much then? Didn't her sister feel the slightest twinge of nostalgia, of anger, at the loss of this private place? After all, Papa had brought her to this beach too.

Hamilton followed Caroline's gaze. "I tried. Believe me, I did. But your sister wants little to do with me that way, I'm afraid. She was the one who encouraged me to ask you." He shouldered the camera, holding it steady with one hand. "Well, best of luck to you, I suppose. Dermott's a fortunate man."

Caroline stared after him as he slogged off across the shingle beach, carrying his load. Penelope had turned Mr. Hamilton down? The pieces of this puzzle lay scattered around her, and she was sick of trying to force them into holes that did not fit. Only one thing was clear.

She was not going to get the swim she came for. Not today, and likely not ever again.

As Caroline contemplated whether to stalk Penelope and demand some answers, or spend a moment hauling the gleefully destructive boys off her beloved cliff walls, her thoughts became tangled in the sound of a child's scream. Shading her hands to scan the surf, she searched for the origin of such a terrified sound. *There.* A dozen yards off shore. Some well-meaning family had brought their children, no doubt lured by the article in the newspaper.

And one of those children was caught in the current.

She could already see a man who appeared to be the father wading out, his own anxious shouts mixing with the pounding of the waves. She could see the danger the man faced from the water, though he appeared oblivious to the risk.

Then again, she *knew* these waters. Knew their spinning force, and their potential to drag an unsuspecting body in the exact opposite direction of where you intended.

"Stop him!" she shouted to the clustering crowd. She picked up her skirts and ran as fast as she could, but she was too far away, and he was too frantic, and within seconds the man was as doomed as his son. A woman's screams joined the mix then, and they built in scale and volume until Caroline was quite sure her eardrums had perforated twice over.

"Stop *her*, then!" Caroline commanded as she skidded to a stop at the point where water met land. A desperate certainty grabbed hold of her as she took in the two struggling swimmers.

One of them was going to drown. She couldn't save them both. Not at high tide, with only one pair of arms, and her skirts dragging her under. She was risking her own life just to contemplate the saving of one.

She panned the crowd with desperation, and her eye fell on Dermott in the crowd of gawkers. He had won last year's race, marking him as the obvious choice. But he stood inert, making no move to help either her or the drowning family. No doubt he was reconsidering the sanity of being tied in marriage to someone who would.

Well, *she* was not going to stand by and let a small child drown, not if she had even the slightest chance of saving the boy.

Caroline lifted her skirts, preparing to dive in.

And then her knees nearly buckled with relief as David Cameron materialized beside her. His hair was damp around the edges, telling her he had swum these waters earlier today.

"Take off your boots," he ordered, the command issued in a precise, military fashion despite his apparent exhaustion. "Your stockings, crinolines, anything that might weigh you down."

She scrambled to follow his instructions, though the lessening of her load was still not nearly enough. "This will be too much for you if you've already practiced today," she objected as he began to strip off his own jacket and shirt. She knew he could swim. Hadn't she taught him herself?

But he had not been tested against the inlet's high tide, with exhaustion from an earlier swim weighing him down. "I tackle these waters at high tide with some regularity, David, and it is hard enough when a body is fresh."

Truly, even *she* would have thought twice about going in today.

David's face darkened at her admission. "And the only reason I am not going to scold you for such a risk is that we don't have time. If I don't go, one of them will drown." He glowered at her with a steely determination that made her want to follow his lead, no matter what. "What kind of a man would I be if I didn't at least try?"

She knew what kind of man he was. She always had.

But it was heartening to hear *him* acknowledge it.

"All right." Caroline pushed into the first line of waves. They tangled in her skirts and almost brought her to her knees. The cold sting of the water made her teeth ache. "You take the father," she gasped. "I shall rescue the boy. He is farther out, but his weight will be easier for me to manage."

Beside her, David hesitated, and then he jerked her toward him, his hand a vise grip on hers. The heat of him blazed across the spare inch of space. "If you find yourself in trouble, if your skirts prove too great a hindrance, don't try to make it to shore."

She nodded, breathless with panic and awareness of this man. She thought, for a heart-blinding second, that he was going to kiss her. He smiled grimly at her instead. A promise, that.

Or perhaps a good-bye.

"Take the child to the rocky shelf," he said hoarsely, "and then wait for me to come to you."

Caroline nodded, though she knew the shelf David referred to was several feet over her head at this point in the tide's cycle. Instead of correcting him, she squeezed his hand. "Go!" she urged. "I'll be right behind."

Within moments the current had David in its grip. He handled it well though, sustaining the calm, steady stroke she had taught him as the fearsome current pulled him out.

Then again, going out was not the difficult part.

Caroline dove in and set off toward the child, reaching him in twenty solid strokes. The little fellow was still conscious and he clung to her like a nettle, his eyes wide with fear. To her right, she saw that David had reached the panicked father and was already making good progress back. Breathing a sigh of relief, she started to swim back to shore, then froze as she confronted a new reality.

The mother's faint screams still echoed from the beach, but now that Caroline was facing north again she could see the woman had started to wade in and was standing in knee-deep water. The woman's idiocy sent Caroline kicking for shore in a panic. If she came out any further, the woman would be dragged under by those wet skirts.

Caroline ought to know. She was battling the very possibility herself.

"Do not come any closer!" she shouted. But she could barely hear herself over the rush of water. There was no way the woman could hear her.

Caroline looped her arm around the boy's shoulders and began the battle back to shore. She had never attempted to swim this stretch of water in a dress with full skirts before. The water sucked at her limbs, pulling them both under, and for a moment she felt the boy's own panic lick at her skin. As water filled her mouth and threatened her lungs, a memory flashed through her mind, of Papa explaining the mechanics of the tide.

Though it took every bit of trust she had, though her body screamed for her to fight, she rolled onto her back, sent up a prayer, and let the current pull her and the boy out toward the horizon.

DAVID REACHED THE shore with his sputtering burden, only to watch with horror as Caroline and the child drifted out to sea. He finally understood her warnings about the strength of the current here at high tide. It was something monstrous and terrifying and beautiful, all at once.

And right now it had hold of the woman he loved.

Why hadn't she headed toward the rocky shelf, as he had instructed her? Because there was no doubt if she had, he would not now be grappling with the bone-chilling certainty that he was about to lose the second woman he had ever loved.

David tossed the sputtering father onto the shore and wrenched himself back toward the waves, his muscles' protests damned. But as he turned, he realized definite progress was taking place in the water. Caroline was free of the outgoing current, although she now had twice the distance to swim as before. She was swimming toward shore, one arm looped around the boy's neck, the other reaching out in a one-handed parody of her usual stroke.

He waded out, ready to share the burden the moment she let him. His heart filled with pride, not only for the sheer physical strength of this woman, but her strength of character as well. She had much to lose in this astonishing demonstration of skill.

And there was no doubt she was putting on quite the display.

Behind him, pushed from the shore, he heard snippets of awed voices.

"Do you see her swim?"

"One of the Tolbertson girls. The tall one."

And then there was this one, which seemed to get stuck and rattle around for a good minute in his skull: "Dermott says she accepted him this morning."

The last comment sent a wave of nausea rolling through David's gut. It seemed Caroline had been busy since they parted ways yesterday. Could he blame her? She had never lied to him about her intentions to marry, had made it clear that he was forcing her to a decision she didn't want to make. No, he couldn't blame her.

But he could certainly blame himself.

David forced his eyes to the horizon and the more immediate problem of Caroline's progress toward shore. He had never been so grateful to see the moment when her feet met the ocean floor. He staggered out to relieve her of the tiny, frightened bundle in her arms. The child began sniffling and hiccupping into the cradle of David's neck, letting him know that whatever else ailed the boy, a small set of lungs filled with seawater was not the primary worry. Children were resilient.

Of Caroline, however, he was a little less certain. She hitched over at the waist and coughed up a great deal of water.

"Are you all right?" he asked, his eyes raking her for visible signs of injury.

She breathed in, through her nose this time. She braced her hands against her wet skirts and took three more breaths in rapid succession. "I am," she rasped. "Could you take him to his mother, while I catch my breath?"

David carried the boy to shore, his pulse settling into a more even rhythm. Although the danger had passed, a new worry set in, one that had more to do with who she was than what she had done. He might be proud of her—hell, he was in utter awe of her—but he doubted this current turn of events was going to endear her to Mr. Dermott.

And he didn't know whether to be worried for her future or pleased for his.

He tried to deliver the boy to his mother, but the boy's arms tightened about David's neck. Not that he blamed the child. The woman was still making an unholy racket, although her screams, thank God, had reduced to a rhythmic wailing.

He pried the little chap's fingers free and then deposited the child on the ground. The mother collapsed beside him, her noise subsiding to a more tolerable level. Sobs punctuated by hiccups. Much preferable.

He couldn't help but think, a bit uncharitably, that if the mother had learned to swim half as well as she screamed, she wouldn't have to rely on others to save her offspring.

Within seconds, a drenched Caroline had joined him. Her color had improved, as had her breathing, and he reached out a hand to take hers up, the crowd and propriety be damned. She had just risked her life to save a child, goddamn it. She deserved better than hushed whispers and pointed stares.

But there was no denying they were growing in volume and audacity.

"You can see right through her skirts. Scandalous, really."

"Not the most circumspect of chits, is she?"

"Hold, everyone!" Hamilton was bent over a black box, some fifty feet away, and his voice rang out clear over the din. Most in the crowd stilled, pleased with the idea of having the moment recorded, but Caroline cringed, her hand squeezing his in panic. David fought against the urge to pull her into his arms and shield her. But there was no hiding it now, no matter how she might pray to return to a state of anonymity.

Hamilton was taking a bloody picture.

He met her gaze, the eyes so changeable, resisting definition. His heart swelled around the sight of her. Not that the intensity of his body's response made any difference. She had accepted Dermott.

Once Hamilton shouted the all-clear, a blond head shouldered her way through the crowd, and then Caroline's sister reached out for her. "Oh, I was so scared when I saw you swimming out there!" Her sister's eyes shone with tears. "But you were brilliant. Absolutely br-brilliant."

"Mr. Cameron had the harder task," Caroline objected, threading her hand out of his and leaving him bereft. "The boy's father was the heavier load."

"I didn't swim it with thirty pounds of skirts tangling about my legs," David answered. "Your sister is right. You did well, lass. Better than well. You saved that boy's life."

"I think," Penelope said, stepping back and regarding

him with a watery, blue-eyed gaze that seemed to miss little, "that you were b-both brilliant."

From the corner of his eye, David caught sight of Dermott, standing a few feet away. He looked a little green, truth be told. Or perhaps it was just the sun's reflection off the man's damned waistcoat.

"Is it true?" David asked Caroline, low under his breath so her sister could not hear. "You've accepted the duffer then?"

Caroline's eyes darted to Dermott, and she paled again. "If you mean Mr. Dermott, yes." Her voice was still hoarse from her battle with the waves. "Just this morning, in fact."

David felt the impact of her words as if they were bullets fired at close range. All that was left was the ribbon of smoke and the gaping wound in his soul. She was betrothed then.

He shook his head, more disgusted with himself than her. Why, of all people, did it have to be Dermott? She was going to marry a man who had stood on the shore with his hands in his damned pockets while a child almost drowned not two dozen yards away.

He was hit by the chilling realization that despite his intentions, despite his best efforts, Caroline had circled back around to the very place he had been trying to avoid. She was pledged to marry a man who did not deserve her, and *he* had pushed her there. Whose fault was it, if not his own? David had repeatedly rejected her, convinced he was doing the right thing, believing he wasn't worthy of her. But confronted with this moment, he could recognize his error. He hadn't turned her away because he couldn't love her.

He had done it because he already did.

"I just hope you know what you're doing, lass," he sighed as Dermott turned his back on them and walked away from the scene. "Because it seems clear your future husband doesn't know quite what to think of you."

Chapter 31

CAROLINE AWOKE TO her mother's upset voice, echoing up the stairwell and through the open bedroom door. Bright daylight streamed through her window. Penelope's bed had not been slept in. Familiar things, all of them.

None of them worth waking up for on a Monday.

She rolled over, wondering what had set her mother off. Perhaps Mr. Dermott had come to break off their betrothal. Caroline was expecting something of that ilk, given the outcome of yesterday's unplanned adventure and Dermott's cold response. Although, given that her mother did not yet even know of the betrothal, she supposed that couldn't really explain her mother's angry words.

She shut her eyes tight, only to have them startled opened again by a very definite, very deliberate clearing of a throat. Bess was standing in the open doorway to the bedroom clutching a piece of dark fabric.

Caroline blinked, trying to ascertain what had the servant's color so high.

Bess shook her hand, setting the fabric flapping. "Do you mind explaining what a man's evening coat was doing under your mattress, Miss Caroline? I found it when I was changing the sheets yesterday."

Caroline struggled to a sitting position, finally awake enough to feel fear. "Is that why Mama is upset?" she asked, recognizing David's evening jacket. Her fingers twitched against the servant's unfortunate discovery. She had forgotten it was there.

A mistake, that.

If she were Pen, she supposed, she would have a ready-made excuse. But she wasn't Pen. And she had more to worry about than the little matter of explaining away David Cameron's evening coat.

Bess clucked her irritation. "Who knows why your mother's upset?" she muttered, tossing the jacket onto Caroline's bed. "Probably because your sister spent good money on the newspaper again, I would imagine. Best get up quick, now. I won't mention it to your mother, I suppose, given that she's already riled up this morning, but I will say this. It's a fine muddle when you start wearing men's clothes, Miss Caroline. You're a right pretty girl. You've nothing to be ashamed of, no matter which way your inclinations lean. I just don't recommend dressing as a man. That's a sure trip to Bedlam, if you ask me."

Caroline choked back a sob of laughter as Bess bustled off down the hallway. Oh, if only her secrets were so simple.

Her lavender-sprigged gown was still damp with seawater, a reminder of its brush with infamy, and so Caroline dressed in her blue print day dress, as her new dresses had not yet been delivered by Madame Beauclerc. She splashed clean water on her face. Bundled her hair up into a tight knot at the nape of her neck.

And then she went to face her mother.

"How could you," Mama wailed, rattling the paper before Caroline even found her seat at the table. "It's all in here. Swimming like a man. Like a *foreign* man, at that." She slumped against the high back of her chair and stared at Caroline as if she had two heads of hair, both of them in need of curling. "Oh," she breathed, shaking her head. "What would your father think if he were here to witness this?"

"I think," Pen said, calmly scraping a burned section off her piece of toast, "that Papa would be pr-proud of what she did. She saved a child's life, and has likely boosted the ratings of the paper to boot."

Caroline's gaze narrowed in on her sister. A trigger was pulled on a thought. The late nights. The meticulous notes. "Pen . . ." she said slowly, her mind reaching toward its inevitable conclusion. "Are you the *Gazette*'s reporter for the social section?"

Pen smiled up at her, the perfect picture of blue-eyed innocence. "No. Of c-course not."

Caroline deflated. She had no explanation for her life's curious turn of events, then. If the reporter for the social section wasn't Mr. Hamilton, and it wasn't Penelope . . .

"Which isn't to say I wasn't," Pen added, returning to her toast with a slight upward curve of her lips. "But as of yesterday, when I turned in the st-story of your rescue and they decided to run it for the front p-page, I was promoted to a position as an associate journalist."

"So *you* are the one who called Papa's cove a delightful hidden gem?" Caroline demanded, pride in her sister's accomplishment and aversion to such a breach of trust colliding in fine shower of sparks. "A child was almost killed because of that article!" Her eyes stung from the magnitude of her sister's betrayal. How would she live with this necessary piece of herself destroyed? The privacy of the cove was the only thing that made swimming possible for her.

Pen placed her toast and utensil down on her plate, and took a deep breath. "I am sorry about that. I did not intend for that to happen, but I needed a more dr-dramatic story about Brighton than who had d-danced with you at whose b-ball, or they would have grown suspicious."

"Suspicious of what?" Caroline countered, still reeling from the realization that she would likely never be able to swim at her cove again. "And how did you know about

Mr. Duffington's proposal? I hadn't even had a chance to tell you yet."

"Suspicious of *me*, of course. I admit, I've b-been using my influence with the newspaper to help the town see how special you are. And I overheard Mr. D-Duffington tell Miss Baxter he asked you to marry him." Penelope flushed pink, whether due to her confession of eavesdropping to gain a story, or her admittance of meddling, Caroline couldn't be sure. "'Tis nothing nefarious, I assure you."

Caroline stared at her sister, her mouth hinged open. Why did people keep doing this to her? First David had betrayed her by talking about her to the summer set, and now Pen was manipulating their interests.

Only—and this was definitely a sticking point— Caroline knew Pen loved her. Though her methods were flawed, Caroline didn't doubt her sister's motives. Pen's attempts to be helpful were born out of love. But they also mirrored David's, and that had Caroline's thoughts spinning off in a new direction.

She had accused him yesterday of spreading lies about her, had assumed that Dermott's renewed interest could have only been influenced by David's bold exaggerations. But now that she realized Penelope had been working toward a similar cause, and indeed, that the town's residents were so susceptible to influence, she had to wonder if she had been a bit harsh in her judgment of David.

Not that it mattered. She had set a torch to that bridge, and there was no going back.

"I am sorry about your beach, Caroline. I . . . d-didn't think of what the article might mean for you." Penelope sighed. "I've been frightfully selfish, haven't I?"

Caroline's throat closed on a spasm. "It is all right, Pen. Someone was bound to discover it eventually." Through the lingering haze of anger, she could reluctantly acknowledge that her sister's betrayal was not the end of all future happiness. After all, swimming was not the only thing that defined her. This summer had shown her she was more than a girl who was as comfortable in the water as she was on land, more than the girl who invited ridicule and speculation among Brighton's summer visitors. She was passionate and desirable and increasingly comfortable in her own skin.

David had helped *her* see that, even if he seemed unable to realize it himself.

"Well, *you* are the one who t-told me it was a nice swimming b-beach," Pen added, picking up her toast. "I had no idea that you have been sneaking away to swim in such a d-dangerous place."

A fresh wail escaped their mother. "You've been sneaking away to *swim*, Caroline? And Penelope is working for the *Gazette*?" Her lips trembled. "Sometimes, I think you are trying to thwart my efforts to fulfill the promise I made your father."

Caroline and Penelope swiveled their heads toward their mother in perfect, shocked unison. "What?"

Their mother mopped a sheen of moisture from beneath one eye with a long, aristocratic finger. "I've done what I felt he wanted. I have tried to guide you as proper ladies. But look how it's all turned out. You are in the paper, Caroline. Not just the social section, which I am pained to admit might have worked, but splashed across the front page headlines. And Penelope"—she gasped, waving her hand in the direction of her fairer daughter—"is the one who put the evidence of your impropriety there, for all of Brighton to see!"

"The child I saved is fine," Caroline said dryly.

"I *know* the child is fine," Mama snapped. "I read Penelope's article." Her breath hitched downward on the last syllable, as if the mere act of admitting that news item had come from her daughter's hand was a secret to be stashed away.

"You speak of propriety as if it is something I have

squandered. As if I chose to behave poorly. Would you have preferred I let an innocent young boy drown then?"

"No," their mother said, shaking her head. "Of course not. Saving a life was the Christian thing to do. But can you not understand why I am upset? It isn't just the matter that you swam yesterday, in front of half of Brighton. It is that you have been swimming, all these years, and hiding it from me. And Penelope, with her secrets, is no better!" She lifted a shaking hand to her temple. "Your father would turn over in his grave if he realized the true extent of my failure to fulfill the promise I made him, of that I have no doubt."

Caroline gritted her teeth. "What did Papa ask of you, precisely?"

"He asked me to take care of you, that awful day when he lay dying." Their mother slumped back and gave a shuddering sigh. "Terrible, dear man that he was."

Pen's chair scraped against the floor boards. "B-b-but . . . *I* promised Papa I would take care of you b-both."

"That can't be right, dear." Mama shook her head. "You were scarcely more than a child."

"He asked it of me, nonetheless. And once you t-told us about the state of our finances, I knew I had to do something. I met Mr. Hamilton, and he mentioned the opening at the paper. I thought it would provide us with some small amount of income. I was happy to finally have a way to help, and fulfill Papa's dr-dr-dream." She paused, and then added with a touch of guilt, "As well as fulfill my own dream, of c-course. I have wanted to write for the *Gazette* since I was a little g-girl. Papa always told me I could do anything I set my mind to."

Caroline leaned back in her chair, stunned. She had spent over a decade feeling as if she was the only one who could make things right. And yet, her father had not singled her out to bear up his burdens. He had ensured that each of them looked out for the other.

"He extracted the same assurance from me, as well," she said, her mind racing. "I thought by marrying well, I would be fulfilling the promise I made him."

Her mother raised a hand to her throat. "*That* is why you have been so keen on marrying one of these young men?"

Caroline nodded. A dull throbbing had taken up behind her eyelids, whether due to the revelations of the morning or her own regrets, she could not be sure. "And . . . and there's more. I accepted Mr. Dermott's proposal yesterday."

"B-but *why*?" Pen demanded. "You d-don't love him."

"I accepted him because I cannot see an alternative." Although that wasn't precisely true. She hadn't needed to make such a rash decision. She could have muddled over her choice for days. Her pride, however, and David's rejection, had hurried her along to a rash decision.

Pen regarded her with solemn blue eyes. "What about your feelings for Mr. C-Cameron?"

"He doesn't want me." Saying it out loud made it somehow more tangible, and that made it more painful. She knotted her fingers in her lap. "So it's to be Dermott or no one."

"Then choose no one," Pen demanded. "You don't need to marry. I have a job now. We d-don't *need* you to provide for us."

Caroline sighed. She had spent the last few days mired in the certainty that she needed to make this sacrifice for her family's financial security. The realization that she didn't was hard to accept. "Money is not the only reason I wanted to marry," she admitted, realizing for the first time that it was true. "I would like a husband, and children." Indeed, the problem wasn't that she didn't want to be married.

It was that she wanted to marry a specific man, a man who made her feel cherished, a man who made her forget how to dance.

But that man had not asked her.

"There will be repercussions if I break off the betrothal now. I told Mr. Duffington and Mr. Branson about my decision yesterday, and they will have told others." She shook her head, facing the impossible and realizing she might be too much of a coward to tempt fate. "If I call it off, I am quite sure I would never receive an offer again."

Mama leaned forward, palms spread wide on the table. "There are worse things than being a spinster, Caroline Rebecca Tolbertson. And marrying the wrong man is one of them."

"You mean, the way you married Papa?" Caroline said, her throat closing around the question. "Do you regret us so very much?"

Her mother bristled beneath her black bombazine. "What kind of poppycock is that? I made the right choice in your father, and I have never regretted it." Her eyes narrowed across the space of the table. "I think I need to come to the race today."

Caroline gaped at her mother. "You . . . you would come?" She mentally tried to ascertain the last time her mother had willingly left the house. Came up alarmingly blank.

"I have not yet had the pleasure of meeting this Mr. Cameron that Penelope speaks of, and I would like to judge for myself if you are making a mistake in marrying Mr. Dermott. We didn't have much, your father and I, but we *did* have love and respect. And that is the one thing I know he would wish for you."

CREAK'S BATHHOUSE WAS closed for the day, due to its role in organizing the annual swimming competition, and so David had no easy alternative to his mother's suggestion that she might like to watch the race.

He helped his mother down to Brighton's eastern beach. Evidence of the competition and the townspeople's enthusiasm swirled around him like leaves caught in a gust of wind. Almost overnight, the bustling seaside town had taken on a circuslike air. Food vendors lined the Marine Parade and Madeira Drive, their sharp cries mingling with the smells of meat pies and fried fish. Chairs had been set up in rows along the wide swath of beach. And the London visitors that Caroline had so decried appeared to have come out in droves, their thick, common accents mingling with the softer sounds of the Brighton locals.

As they made their way toward the section where the spectators would be seated, his mother was struck by a sudden fit of coughing. As he held up her frail body and felt the bones in her arms shift beneath his hands, David questioned anew the wisdom of exposing his mother's failing lungs to the moist air.

"Perhaps it would be better to return to the Bedford, Mother," he offered, worried.

"I can't see a thing from the window of my suite." She shook her head. "No, I want to do this. The newspaper claims it is an event not to be missed."

"You are too ill for these types of exertions," he pointed out. "The doctors said—"

"The doctors might be concerned with the state of my lungs," she interrupted, wheezing slightly. "But I am more concerned with the state of my mind."

David tilted his head, staring down at his small, stern mother. She seemed entirely lucid. Perhaps too lucid, given her propensity toward stubbornness. Indeed, he suspected she would be far easier to manage if it was her mind that was giving her fits. "There is nothing wrong with the state of your mind."

"If I am healthy in that regard, it is only because I refuse to live in the past, clinging to the doctor's recommendation. I didn't ask for this affliction, or such a dire prognosis. But I also refuse to lock myself away and just give up on the business of enjoying my life." She offered him a glance that appeared both shrewd and maternal at the same time. "One shouldn't stop living, just because of a little hurt, David. You would do well to remember that."

David drew in a breath at her unexpected insight. "Why do you say that *I* need to remember that?" he asked, guiding her to an empty chair, and shooing away a pair of seagulls that seemed intent on guarding their perch. "I am not ill or injured."

"Perhaps not physically. But you've been living a stilted version of life since that unfortunate business with Elizabeth Ramsey, David. Don't think your father and I haven't noticed."

David's lungs funneled shut. The murmuring crowd and the distant sound of the waves receded to a dim point on his internal horizon. His mother had never spoken of this to him, not once in eleven years, though he had always suspected that she, along with everyone else in Moraig, believed him at fault for Elizabeth's death.

Why did she bring it up now?

His mother's long-fingered hand reached out to clasp his own suddenly clammy skin. "You're a fine man, David. You rescued that family from the ocean yesterday, as selfless an act as I've ever seen."

He drew back as if his frail, reed-thin mother had struck him with a pugilist's fist. "How did you know about that?" He hadn't told her. In fact, he'd made a point of *not* telling her, being averse to having her worry any more than she already did.

Her fingers tightened on his wrist. "It made the front page of the paper, David. My lungs are failing, but I assure you my eyesight is as keen as ever."

"I didn't do it alone," he protested. "Anyone would have—"

"Anyone would *not* have," his mother interrupted, shaking her head. She released his wrist. "And according to the paper, no one else did, except that girl Miss Tolbertson." She lowered herself into the chair, settling in with a relieved groan. "You just don't seem able to see what the rest of us have always known. The man who dove into the water to rescue that poor family yesterday is the same man you were during that business with Elizabeth. You have a good heart, David, and if you had been given an opportunity to save her, there is no doubt in my mind you would have."

A hard lump formed in David's throat as he crouched down beside his mother and fussed with the blanket around her feet. "I *had* the opportunity, Mother. But I chose the wrong path."

She shook her head. "I know she turned down your offer of marriage, son. And I also know something else that you do not. She had already set her sights on James MacKenzie, before you even made it out of town."

David drew in a sharp breath. Elizabeth was rumored to have turned to his former best friend, James MacKenzie, for comfort in those final days. He had gleaned that much from the undercurrent of gossip that percolated through Moraig like the Highland wind. But he had always presumed he had driven her into the man's arms, not that she had gone there willingly.

"How do you know that?" he demanded.

"Mothers talk, David. You know that James has recently come to a better understanding with his own family, and he clarified some of those facts with his mother." She shaded her eyes with a hand and peered out at the horizon, as if she was not talking about the single most agonizing event in David's life. "Terrible thing, the choice that girl made. A *selfish* choice. Elizabeth could have come to us. We would have gladly seen to her welfare."

Her hand lowered slowly, and he could see tears shimmering at the corners of her eyes. "It hurt us too, you know. That was our grandchild. You wouldn't talk about it, and we could only watch your suffering and trust that time would heal us all."

David busied himself adjusting the lower edge of her blanket, trying to think of something to say. No wonder his mother was so fixated on seeing him marry and holding a blond-haired granddaughter. Until this moment, he had not considered she might have been dealing with her own version of loss.

When he trusted his throat to work again, he said, "I didn't realize you knew so much about what happened with Elizabeth."

"Yes, well, you were away on your army assignment. Your father and I didn't realize quite how much it affected you either. But since you've come home to Moraig, it has become all too clear that you are still living under that shadow. We both decided you needed a little shove to start living again." She shifted in her seat, but refused his help when he tried to adjust the back of her chair higher. "This trip was intended as much for you as me, as I am sure you have surmised."

David's lips firmed. He had suspected some degree of plotting afoot, certainly. But he had presumed the journey was about finding him a wife, not helping him to heal. His mother's insistence on Brighton as their destination made more sense now. She had known he was stationed nearby, and must have suspected that geography would play a role in his reckoning.

David swallowed hard, pushing the gratitude that threatened to well up in his throat down to a more proper depth in his chest. He hadn't truly understood his need for forgiveness, or his mother's determination to deliver it to him, until now.

"Thank you," he murmured.

His mother reached out a bony hand and squeezed his again. "You spent ten years in uniform, sacrificing your own healing for God and country. Whatever mistakes you made as a boy, whatever role Elizabeth herself had in those mistakes, don't you think it's time to forgive? And if not forget, at least move on?"

David expelled a long, shuddering breath. It was as if his mother had picked up a loose thread and pulled, and now he was unraveling. He could not deny that if Elizabeth's letter had reached his hand sooner, he would have returned to Moraig in a thrice, hang the consequences and the displeasure of his commanding officer.

"I can promise to try," he told his mother. With his mother's understanding, the facts of that day were already shifting about in his head. His past and his future coalesced smoothly, as if they had always fit up against each other and he had just been too distracted to realize it.

If he permitted himself to think of a future—and it was jarring to do so, after eleven long years of self-denial—his thoughts flew to only one destination.

He wanted Caroline. And bugger it all, against all odds, against all *logic*, she wanted him too. She knew everything there was to know about him, had absorbed his confession and accepted his past and still offered him her love.

But he had pushed her away, and now it was too late. He had shoved her toward Dermott and she had made her decision, and now he feared he was going to spend the next eleven years mourning *her* loss.

His mother scanned the crowded beach. "Now, according to the social section, you've met at least two nice young ladies since we arrived in Brighton. I see Miss Baxter over there." She pointed to the young red-haired woman, who was walking some distance away, a tiny dog in her arms. "You should go and say hello, in case there is any hope there."

"I am not sure—" David started, but then he fell silent. No, he was actually *quite* sure. There was no hope there. Not even the slightest possibility of it.

Miss Baxter, while lovely, was not where his intentions lay.

"I've no interest in Miss Baxter that way," he told his mother.

"Hmmph. How about this Miss Tolbertson, the one I've read so much about in the paper?" She craned her neck, searching the crowd. "I've no idea what she looks like, of course. Do you think she'll swim today? The *Gazette*'s description of her was quite scandalous."

David choked on his surprise. "She shall attend, I think. But the competition does not permit women to swim." He paused, then added, "She has been teaching me to swim using her unusual stroke. I am competing today."

Shrewd eyes raked his. "When were you planning on telling me this?"

"Well, I had hoped you would be occupied by your daily appointment at Creaks. You should know that if I win, I am planning to give half the purse to her."

His mother's eyes lit up. "What do her suitors think of that? According to the social section she's received scads of proposals. Has she accepted any?"

"Aye, she has." David felt as though his mother had found a wound and was now poking about to see what she might find in it. "But I really don't care what her suitors think. If I can win today, she will have earned it."

"Oh." A beat of silence passed and then his mother's eyes narrowed. "Is she pretty?"

David sighed. "Aye. There are some that think so." And he counted himself among that small but discerning group. "But it doesn't matter. She's going to marry someone else."

"Well," his mother said, settling back against her chair and adjusting the brim of her bonnet against the advancing sun with a delicate, blue-veined hand. "If she has taught you to swim even half as well as the newspaper claims she can dance, I imagine this will indeed be a competition to remember."

Chapter 32

Caroline finally found three empty seats near the water's edge, and waved Penelope and her mother toward them. Queen Victoria was clearly not visiting Brighton this summer—further proof that Miss Baxter was not to be trusted—but it seemed as though everyone else was. Ladies in fashionable dresses and men in smartly cut coats sweated in the late morning sun, and she had to elbow at least one surprised gentleman aside to procure the chairs. It was worth it, though. From this position, they would be able to see the swimmers as they made their loop around the edge of the pier and began the hard crawl toward the finish line.

It was a beautiful morning, with clouds like carded cotton and a sky so blue an artist would have been hard-pressed to duplicate it using any normal palette of colors. Red and purple pennants flew from the iron spires of the Chain Pier, adding a cheerful wash over the scene. She wanted to stare out at it forever.

Except she couldn't. Because try as she might, she couldn't shake the feeling that everyone else was staring at her.

"Isn't that the girl from the paper?"

"Were you there? Did you see her swim?"

Caroline could have laughed. She would never have

predicted that a story more shocking than the circumstances of her first kiss could ever snag the attention of the
summer set.

Apparently she had been wrong.

"Mama, are you sure this isn't too much for you?" Caroline asked as her mother settled into one of the wooden
folding chairs. "The sun is very strong, and your skin is
not used to it."

"As I explained at length, I want to see the swimming
competition," her mother said, arranging her skirts carefully. She swiveled her head, studying the beach's other
occupants. "Now, Penelope. In your recent position writing the social column you must have paid very close attention to the activities of most of the young people here.
Would you be so kind as to point out these individuals
who have been less than kind to your sister? I am thinking
I might like a word with their parents."

Caroline groaned. Her mother claimed that this, her
first real social outing to somewhere other than church in
eleven years, was because she wanted to attend the race,
but hadn't she suspected that Mama had ventured out for
a different reason?

Pen looked down at their mother and grinned. "Well,
Miss Baxter has said some mean-spirited things on occasion." She paused, and then pursed her lips. "Of course,
she has also said some nicer things. Rather an enigma. I
c-can't figure her out."

As if called by the very direction of Pen's thoughts,
Miss Baxter walked by, her pert face shaded by a sunbonnet whose brim threatened to eclipse the entirety of the
sun. A small white dog rested in her arms.

"You look lovely today, Miss B-Baxter," Pen called out,
waving as if they were the best of chums.

Miss Baxter shifted her dog from one arm to another
as she stopped and turned to regard them. "And you both
look . . . pleasant enough." The girl sauntered closer and

glanced down at their mother. "You must be Mrs. Tolbertson. I am Julianne Baxter." She waited a beat, and when their mother did no more than raise a haughty brow, she added, "The daughter of the Viscount Avery."

Mama's face settled into a practiced smile. "Oh. Of course. I believe my father and your grandfather were roommates at Eton together. I knew your father well, many years ago, during my come-out in London. Please do pass my condolences on to Lord Avery. I am sorry I could not make it up to London for your mother's funeral."

Miss Baxter's mouth fell open. "I . . . er . . . that is, you could pass those wishes along yourself." She blinked, regrouping. "He has come down from London for a few days."

Their mother nodded. "I shall do that. It will be nice to reacquaint myself with an old, dear friend."

Miss Baxter was, for once, effectively silenced. She chewed—in a most unladylike fashion—on her lower lip, no doubt trying to decide if this was a problem or a boon for someone in her social position.

"Miss B-Baxter," Penelope said, breaking through the awkward moment. "Did you know . . . your d-dog matches the exact shade of your gown."

Miss Baxter colored up, although Caroline would not have put it above the toothsome girl to match her pet to her dress. "Why, thank you. I have always admired the color of Constance's coat." She rubbed one cheek against the little dog's fur. "Madame Beauclerc made the dress. She is quite brilliant with a needle, isn't she? It is surprising to find a seamstress of such talent in such a *quaint* little town like Brighton."

Caroline narrowed her eyes at the slight to the city she loved. She searched her mind for an appropriate rejoinder, but could find no fault with Miss Baxter's elbow-length gloves or the sash around her small waist, a splash of pink embroidered with tiny pink roses.

Not that she liked roses, per se. Given that the Tolbert-sons' foyer was still sporting a few dozen of the dubious flowers, Caroline was developing an intense dislike for the thorny blooms.

"Can we help you with something?" she prodded. "Directions to the reserved seating area, perhaps?" She wished Miss Baxter would move along. The race would be starting in less than a quarter hour, and she still hadn't seen David in the crowd yet.

Miss Baxter's perfect nose wrinkled in thought. "I wanted to offer my congratulations, of course. News of your engagement to Mr. Dermott is spreading. You appear to have attracted the imagination of the entire town, and without the help of a single word from me. Few in London can claim such notoriety."

Caroline gritted her teeth. It had not escaped her that the man to whom she was supposedly engaged appeared to be avoiding her this morning. In fact, she could see him beyond Miss Baxter's shoulders, near the sign-in table, warming up his muscles with a series of windmilling arm motions. The movement had the misfortune of exaggerating the inelegance of the shapeless woolen swimming costume he had donned for the day's race.

She returned her annoyed focus to Miss Baxter, who, unfortunately, was not showing any signs of moving on. "Er . . . thank you. Was that all you needed?" She wondered if a good, strong shove might facilitate the situation.

Miss Baxter touched a white-gloved finger to her lips. "Well . . . there is one more thing. You see, I am trying to decide if I believe the rumors about your little ocean adventure, given that I have been denied the pleasure of starting them." She leaned in conspiratorially. "Do you really swim as well as a man?"

Mama gasped at the girl's audacity. Caroline's tongue seemed sewn to the roof of her mouth. Everyone in Brighton already knew about her swimming abilities, of course, thanks to Penelope's front page headlines. But it was a sensation entirely too close to drowning to have a discussion with Miss Baxter about it.

Pen was apparently emboldened with a different response. "I suppose it d-depends on the man, Miss Baxter."

The red-haired girl's eyes narrowed on Pen. "It is my experience that the truth has a way of being distorted when *amateurs* recount the events at hand. I know I would not want to risk my reputation by repeating such gossip in London without first seeing it with my own eyes."

Caroline finally found her voice. "How fortuitous, then, that such stories shall not be bandied about London."

"Perhaps she could provide a demonstration for you." Pen's voice rang out, shockingly clear and devoid of any discernible stammer. "At today's swimming race."

Caroline turned to stare at her sister, her voice once again hobbled. She swallowed, searching for whatever air remained in her pinched lungs. "The posted rules were quite specific, Pen. Gentlemen only."

Miss Baxter's bow-shaped lips pursed in wicked thought. "My father is one of the primary sponsors of this year's race. He has put up half the money for the purse, and has some sway with the judges."

Caroline's stomach twisted cruelly, whether in hope or fear, she couldn't be sure. "That doesn't mean they will let a girl compete."

Miss Baxter drew herself up, probably reaching all of five-foot-three. "I assure you, if I ask it of him, *he* will ask it of the race officials. And if the request comes from my father, you can be sure they will bend the rules." She paused for breath, and her eyes softened, ever so slightly. "I can ask him if you like."

Caroline stared at Miss Baxter as if seeing her for the first time. Perhaps she was. Despite her quick tongue and her showy exterior, there was a hint of iron beneath the girl's skin. That hint of iron now settled dubiously on Caroline, in the form of narrowed green eyes. "Provided, that is, you can produce a swimming costume that is less offensive to fashion than Mr. Dermott's."

A thousand thoughts vied for supremacy in Caroline's head. Could she do it? Could she swim in front of all these people, pit herself against seasoned competitors, for a chance at something she had always dreamed of?

Could she not?

Some proportion of the town had already seen her swim. The rest had read about it, even if they couldn't quite believe it. For the first time in her life, she had nothing to lose by stepping out of her shadows.

She turned down to look at her mother, who was watching the exchange with sharp eyes. "What do you think, Mama?" she asked.

A slow, unexpected smile spread across her mother's face, something quite different from the practiced smile she had displayed during the earlier exchange with Miss Baxter. "I think," her mother said, "that it would make your father proud to see you swim. If Lord Avery can arrange it, I think you should compete."

Caroline's decision was reached in a half second. "Then I would be much obliged if you make this request of your father," she told Miss Baxter, already turning toward the Marine Parade and shops that waited beyond. "And now, if you will excuse me, I've an errand to run."

DAVID HEADED TOWARD the check-in table and the line of competitors that waited there. He made a wide berth around Miss Baxter, who was standing beside the table with a pleased smile on her pretty face. An older man he presumed to be her father was conferring with one of the race administrators, and this negligence left Miss Baxter to her own meddling devices.

"Oh, Mr. Cameron," she called out, waving him over. "Could I beg a moment of your time for Constance?"

David sighed at the distraction he did not need, but he dutifully responded to the summons. "Who, pray tell, is Constance?"

"My sweet little girl." Miss Baxter rubbed her cheek against the white bundle of fur in her arms. "Papa brought her down from London with him, but she refuses to walk more than a few steps on her lead this morning. I wonder if I could trouble you to take a look at her."

David raised a brow at the ruse to attract his attention. "Why would you think I could help?"

She fluttered her copper-colored lashes. "The *Gazette* claimed you had a miraculous way with small children, after the way you saved that little boy yesterday. I assure you, she is just like a child to me."

Miss Baxter held out the beast, clearly used to having men jump to do her bidding. The white mongrel—because indeed, this dog resembled no breed David had ever seen, reminding him of a cross between a very hairy rodent and a Siamese cat—promptly held out its right foot.

Good Lord. Did it expect him to shake its paw?

"You know, I was not the only one there yesterday, Miss Baxter," David said as he accepted the proffered burden. "Miss Tolbertson swam out to save the child." He held the dog up, meeting it eye to eye. "I did no more than deliver the boy into the arms of its mother."

"My biggest regret is that I was not there to see such a thing myself." Miss Baxter pouted a moment. "Father has kept a close eye on me since he's come down from London, I'm afraid, and wouldn't let me go to the new beach yesterday."

"I can scarcely imagine why," David drawled sarcastically, recalling the dinner party she had thrown not a week ago.

"Well, *I* can scarcely imagine a woman who swims. She's going to compete, you know."

David looked up from his halfhearted inspection of

Miss Baxter's pet. Here, at last, was a reasonable explanation for the girl's creative attempt to engage him in conversation, given that there was nothing at all wrong with her dog except for the fact it was quite a hideous-looking creature. "Miss Tolbertson?" At Miss Baxter's nod, he said, "I was not aware that they would permit a woman to compete."

"My father is arranging it at this very moment." She inclined her head. "I thought I would warn you, so you would not be disappointed at the starting line."

"Why would I be disappointed?" This was an unexpected pronouncement, coming from Miss Baxter as it was, but not disappointing. In fact, David's first instinct was to scratch his entry. But what good would that serve? If both he and Caroline competed, their odds of having one of them win against Dermott were improved. Then again, Dermott was now, for better or worse, Caroline's fiancé. Would she permit herself the win, if it meant besting the man she planned to marry?

There was also the small matter of the five-hundred-pound purse, a prize he still planned to share. David's need for it had not diminished in the slightest just because Caroline had accepted Dermott's proposal. But none of that mattered in the face of the most important fact of all.

David could not bring himself to abandon the hunt just because his prey had been claimed by another.

"There are some impressive wagers being laid down among the summer set," Miss Baxter continued. "I thought you would want to know now, rather than later."

"Well then, I'm much obliged." David returned his attention to the squirming bundle of fur in his hands. The dog blinked up at him, no doubt in response to the hard edge of his voice. The little thing offered its paw again. This time David shook it solemnly, only to discover a small thorn, lodged in the thickened pad.

"Ah, there's the trouble." He picked it out of the poor

creature's paw and returned the dog to its owner. "I imagine that might account for some of Constance's behavior this morning."

Although having a busybody mistress who paid more attention to the latest gossip than to her own pet might explain the rest.

Miss Baxter's eyes shone with admiration. "You've quite a way with animals, Mr. Cameron."

David shook his head. "No. 'Tis actually my friend Channing who has a way with beasts. The thorn was just a lucky find."

"Channing? Do you refer to Mr. Patrick Channing, from Yorkshire?"

"Aye," David said suspiciously. He supposed, if he reached far back in his memory, he could recall that Patrick had claimed his family hailed from that part of Britain. "Are you acquainted with him?"

"Our fathers are good friends." Two green eyes narrowed on him in a manner he was coming to associate with this woman's nose for natter. "Is he in Scotland, then?"

David's guard went up in an instant. "Mr. Channing is just Moraig's veterinarian," he said, shaking his head. "Nothing to worry about."

At least, nothing for *her* to worry about. He could not claim the same for himself, or his friend. Patrick had been quite closemouthed about his family since arriving unexpectedly in Moraig last November. If Miss Baxter's prurient interest was any indication, Patrick Channing was hiding in Moraig for a reason.

And he was quite sure he didn't want to know why.

CAROLINE WAS BREATHING hard as she burst through the door into Madame Beauclerc's shop. The modiste rose in alarm as the door slammed shut, a tinkling bell the only indication that the door could, on occasion, herald the arrival of a more composed sort of patron.

"Have you come for the new dresses, *chérie*?" she asked, her painted brows drawn down in confusion. "We agreed this afternoon to finish them, *oui*?"

"*Oui*. I mean yes. I mean *no*." Caroline shook her head against the trio of answers, none of which was the real reason she was staggering into this East Street dress shop so out of breath. "I'm here about the other thing." She lowered her voice to a ragged whisper. "The *swimming* thing."

"Ah." The dressmaker's face spread into a smile. "Wait here a moment, *s'il vous plaît*."

She disappeared through a curtained door, where the dull murmur of other voices could be heard. Caroline refilled her lungs with the sharp, rich scent of a dozen types of fabric, wool and cotton and the peculiar dull odor of silk, and tried not to think about whom those voices might belong to. If she was to go through with this, she was going to have to be brave. The thoughts and opinions of a few shopgirls were going to be the least of her worries.

And then her heart began to pound as Madame Beauclerc returned and held out a . . . shift.

Not even a particularly pretty shift. It was starched stiff, and lacked all ornamentation. No ribbons, not even a lace border. It had longer sleeves than the shifts she was used to wearing, but in all other ways it might have been something she pulled from her own bureau at home.

Caroline groaned. The hope that had borne her feet all the way to East Street faltered. "I can't wear that," she said, shaking her head. "I thought . . . I thought you had fashioned something different. Something appropriate for swimming in public."

"This is far more appropriate than those silly robes they give you for the bathing machines," the dressmaker huffed. "There is no chance of this gaping in the front, or floating up at inopportune times. Of course, if you prefer something prettier, I might add a ribbon about the neckline."

Caroline gritted her teeth. "Unless you are going to put an entire army of ribbons here"—she pointed to the chest area—"and here," she added, gesturing lower, "I am afraid it will still be quite hopeless. I cannot swim in a shift today, not in public."

She was willing to pit her skill against a group of men. She was even willing to flash an arm or show a bit of calf. But she was not going to present herself on Brighton's eastern beach—the beach where all the fashionable people strolled—in a shift that when wet might as well be made of glass.

"This is no ordinary shift." Madame Beauclerc's lips turned down. "'Tis duck cloth. They will not be able to see through." She held it out. "See?"

Caroline rubbed the fabric between two fingers. "Oh," she said, understanding dawning. What she had presumed to be muslin was actually a thick, substantial linen. And whatever else it had been treated with, it wasn't starch. "What has it been painted with?"

"Linseed oil, among other things. This seems to hold up to the seawater better than other things I have tried. The fabric is stiff enough so it will stand away from the body when wet. No one will be able to see through this." The modiste smiled. "I told you, *chérie*. You will be a goddess."

Caroline held it up against her, measuring it inch for inch against her own dress. It came down longer than her usual shifts, almost to mid-calf, and provided far more coverage than she was used to while swimming, but that didn't keep it from being utterly scandalous. "It is a bit short, isn't it?"

"You need the freedom to kick, *oui*?"

"*Oui.*" Caroline sighed. "I mean yes. I do. I . . . I am just not sure I am brave enough to be seen in this."

"Are you worried about what the women will think? Or the men?"

"Neither. Both. I don't know—"

The modiste patted her arm. "Let me tell you a secret about women. We are our own worst enemies. Do you think men object to the length of a woman's skirts? The other women on the beach, they may gossip about you. They may turn their backs on you. But inside? Secretly they will want to *be* you."

Caroline clenched the swimming costume in her hands, mesmerized by the dressmaker's silken tones. "And the men?" she breathed.

"The men, *chérie*? That is a simpler matter altogether. Not a man who sees you in this will think poorly of you. Indeed, they shall be unable to tear their eyes away."

Chapter 33

"IT IS NOT to be tolerated! Why, I would rather withdraw my application than swim against a . . . a . . ."

"*Fiancée?*" David broke in, enjoying the view of Dermott's bulging eyes. The race officials had just announced their decision, and while a few of the competitors were uneasy, Dermott had chosen a more infantile response. "I believe that is the word you are looking for."

"Woman!" Dermott barked, spittle flying. "I shall not compete against a woman." He pointed at something, just behind David's shoulder. "And most certainly not *that* woman."

David turned around. Caroline was pushing her way through the crowd, which parted before her with an audible gasp. Her hair was up in that tight bun he was coming to dream about in his sleep. Somewhere, a sailing vessel was missing its foresail, having given it up for the purposes of dressing this woman today. She looked as if she might toss up her accounts at the slightest provocation. But God help him, she also looked beautiful.

The crowd found its predictable voice.

"It's Miss Tolbertson!"

"What on earth is she wearing?"

"Swimmers, on the ready!" the race official shouted.

"You can see her ankles," Dermott sputtered as Caroline took her place with the row of swimmers. He gestured to the crowd of onlookers lining the shore behind them. "There are ladies watching today, ladies whose delicate sensibilities should not be subjected to such a spectacle. It is unseemly!"

"We can see your ankles too," David said, taking his own place in line. Truly, he had never seen anything like the costume Dermott was strutting about in, a suit of shapeless gray wool that, if one had the misfortune to peer too closely, was embroidered with some sort of songbird around the neckline. David had chosen to wear his trousers, though he had retained a shirt today for those delicate sensibilities Dermott was sputtering about.

"*My* ankles do not call my character into question," Dermott said.

David turned on him. The man's antics were getting tiresome now. "What is bothering you here, Dermott? The fact that her swimming costume is more attractive than yours? Or that she might best you today?"

Dermott's face turned a mottled shade of red. "This is my betrothed, and I will not stand by and permit her to—"

"You shall not have a say in the matter," Caroline interrupted. She might look bloody nervous—hell, David was nervous for her—but her voice rang clear. "I *want* to race. And when this day is over, I am still going to want to swim. So you shall either have to accept me as I am, Mr. Dermott, eccentricities and all, or you shall stand down."

"On your marks!" the official said, raising a pistol above his head.

She turned toward the ocean, the skirt of her costume bunched in her hands.

David crouched. Water lapped at all of their feet as the line of competitors tensed, staring out at the buoy that marked their mid-way target. Finally, Dermott took his place in line, still grumbling about rules and women and ankles.

Then came a terrible noise as the pistol fired just over their heads. The race was on.

CAROLINE DOVE INTO the first row of breakers a few steps behind the rest of the swimmers. She held herself back, wanting to avoid the inevitable jostling that she knew from long observation of this annual event came at the start of the race. The group of swimmers pulled away in a fearsome froth of water, arms working like pistons, chests rising above the water only to come crashing back down.

David, clearly visible on account of his white shirt, was caught near the back, and was struggling to employ the stroke he had worked so hard to perfect. That was something they hadn't planned on, the need for space to accommodate the full of extension of his arm. She could see now how a breaststroke might be preferred, at least until the swimmers started to scatter out a bit more.

Determined to avoid getting caught in that snarl of arms and legs, Caroline hugged the western side of the pier. The overhead shadows gave the water a dark, ominous appearance, and the motion of the waves against the structure pulled against her, but her experience swimming in the cove, with its underwater currents and myriad hidden hazards, served her well. Her lungs were burning as she broke out of the shadow of the pier and aimed for the bright red buoy tied off shore. Her fingertips brushed the hard, solid surface, and then she was past.

Now began the real race as the swimmers started toward home. She was five yards behind the last swimmer, a large distance to close. Her hesitancy at the start of the race now proved costly, and she wondered, for a moment, if she had the strength to do this. Pen and Mama were watching from shore, and the thought made her lungs squeeze tighter. She thought of Papa. What would he say, if he were here now?

Probably something wise. Something poignant.

Caroline smothered a smile. No, he wouldn't. She had raced against her father, more than once, during their lessons in the cove. He had never let her win, not even once, urging her to try harder, reach deeper inside herself. If he were here now, he would not waste his words on gentle reassurances.

He would tell her to hurry it up.

Caroline kicked harder. She passed the first five stragglers, their mouths gaping like fish on land. Then another five. Where was David? She couldn't see, couldn't breathe, but the thought—the hope—that he was near the lead, battling it out with Dermott, drove her on.

It proved impossible to keep her thoughts focused on her stroke when Dermott was still ahead of her. The self-righteous prig. Could she bring herself to marry a man like that? Her muscles screamed at her, but her heart screamed louder.

Her mother was right. There were worse things than being a spinster.

And one of them was losing to the wrong man.

The shore seemed to loom above her now, and another six swimmers fell to her determined progress. Her brain felt fuzzy, but her gaze locked with certainty on a white shirt and a gray swimming costume, barely visible as their wearers sluiced through the water. She aimed for them, swimming harder than she had ever done in her life. Time was suspended, counted by strokes, not seconds.

One, two, three.

Breathe.

And then she was past them and the crowd was on their feet and cheering and Caroline staggered ashore, alone.

DAVID EMERGED A few seconds behind her.

She had done it.

Christ above, but he was proud of her, his own second place finish be damned.

He surged toward her, the crowd falling away around his determined stride. And then she was in his arms and he was kissing her, really *kissing* her. And she was kissing him back, her hands tangling in his hair and anchoring him to her as if she might drown should he let her go.

The roar that had erupted from the crowd when she had won the race paled in comparison to the noise that rose above them now. But beyond the excited shouts and whistles, Dermott's angry voice rang out, bleeding through the haze of pleasure. "Get your hands off her!"

David pulled away from her with a reluctance he felt to his bones. He was, after all, kissing the woman Dermott still counted as his betrothed. A woman he had no right to touch, much less maul in such a suggestive manner, in such a public venue.

"Is this what you want?" David asked her, searching her eyes. "Is *he* what you want?"

Caroline shook her head. "You are whom I have always wanted. I love you, David Cameron. Whether you want me to or not."

And then she was in his arms again, her lips finding his in a hard, quick kiss that nonetheless stole what little breath he had left.

"I love you too." The words near tumbled out of him, tired of being denied for so long. He had not thought to ever love again, had thought himself unworthy of such a sentiment, and such a partner. But now that it had found him, despite his best efforts to the contrary, he didn't want to ever take it back.

He raised his hands to frame her face, reveling in the privilege it was to touch her. "Every word I offered to Dermott and the others on the beach that night was true . . . I just didn't want to admit it to myself. You are a woman worth holding, a woman who inspires loyalty and passion and deserves such things in return. You are my match, Caroline. My *true* match. I was an idiot to pretend you were not."

A smile broke out on her face, a smile so luminous his body tightened around its brilliance. "Yes. Well. If I love an idiot, so be it."

She pulled away and turned her attention toward the man who stood glowering at them two feet away. "Mr. Dermott, I am ending our betrothal because I love this man. I presume you have no objections?"

Dermott's face darkened, if such a thing were even possible against the dusky rage that already held him in its grip. "Yes, I have an objection. You . . . you . . . you cheated during this race!"

"How did I cheat?" David heard the edge in Caroline's voice. It was an edge that Dermott seemed to miss entirely.

Then again, the man didn't know her the way David did.

"You *both* cheated," Dermott's face shone a mottled red. "That wasn't a proper swimming stroke. No self-respecting Brit would swim like that. Why, at Oxford, that would have been an automatic disqualification."

"This isn't Oxford." A woman's voice rang out. A lady who could only be Caroline's mother emerged from the crowd. Her blue eyes flashed indignantly, and she held her chin up with every bit as much spirit as he had come to expect in Caroline. "'Tis Brighton. And there is nothing wrong with that."

"Indeed." The voice came from behind them, and David turned to see Lord Avery, his daughter close by. The man offered an authoritative smile, but his tone brooked no argument. "There are no rules requiring a particular swimming stroke for this competition. I should know. I wrote them." He paused, and then inclined his head toward Caroline's mother, who turned a suspicious shade of pink at the viscount's attention. "It is good to see you again, Lydia."

Dermott sputtered another short moment, then careened off into the crowd. David waited to see which of

the summer set would follow. He was, after all, their veritable leader.

No one moved except Lord Avery, and he only held out
a stack of five-pound notes, neatly tied in a bundle. "It is
my pleasure," he announced, "to present Miss Caroline
Tolbertson with this purse of five hundred pounds, and
to declare her the winner of Brighton's forty-third annual
swimming competition." He shook her hand. "Congratulations, young lady. That was quite the show you put on."

CAROLINE ACCEPTED THE money with trembling hands.
In the confusion of her last-minute entry, she had nearly
forgotten about the purse.

"I've never seen anything like it," Miss Baxter declared, bouncing with excitement at her father's elbow, the
small dog similarly bobbing in her arms. She beamed, the
very picture of someone with a secret too delicious not to
share. "Oh, I cannot *wait* to go back to London and tell all
my friends I met Brighton's famous lady swimmer."

Caroline opened her mouth, prepared to correct the
girl's misimpression. After all, she was no lady, just
the daughter of a Brighton businessman. But before she
could form the necessary words, Caroline caught sight of
her mother. She and Lord Avery had drifted to one side
and Mama was laughing at something the viscount was
saying.

And Caroline realized that while she might be the
daughter of a businessman, she was also the daughter of a
lady. A smile spread across her face. She would leave Miss
Baxter to her gossip, and even her misinformed truths. She
supposed, in some way, she had the girl to thank for this
incredible turn of events. Not that she was inclined to acknowledge even a single positive outcome of Miss Baxter's meddling.

One did not encourage bad behavior, even when applied to a worthy cause.

Caroline turned to David, the money heavy and reassuring in her hands. "I am giving half of this to you."

David's eyes crinkled about the edges, and he burst out in a hearty chuckle that had some in the crowd laughing along, though they clearly had no idea why. "I cannot accept it, Caroline. You earned it, ten times over."

"Sharing the purse was our agreement all along. And you need the money every bit as much as my family does," she protested. "I want you to have it."

"Give it to your family," he said, more gently now. "All of it. We don't need it."

Caroline's thoughts narrowed on a single word, out of the handful he uttered. "We . . . ?"

He canted his head, his eyes warm. "There were some lucrative wagers placed on the outcome of this race. And I bet on *you*, lass."

The air in her lungs seemed to leach out of her skin. "You bet on me?"

"Aye. We've no need to worry about money, not anymore." He lowered himself to one knee, there along the shore, with the crowd pressing in and Penelope looking on with one hand clamped over her mouth.

David grinned up at her, sending her stomach into an inspired free-fall. "I know this is but one of a hundred proposals you have received this week, Caroline. And I cannot offer you the fine social connections or the extensive selection of dry goods that your other suitors have no doubt promised you. But I *can* offer you my heart, unencumbered by my past. So if it's not too much trouble . . . and if you feel even a fraction of the love I feel for you . . . would you do me the honor of becoming my wife?"

Chapter 34

DAVID KNEW CAROLINE was anticipating a wedding night on the renowned Bedford Hotel linens. And she surely deserved one, after the hellish wait they had both just endured. If they had been in Scotland, where an irregular marriage could be had on any street corner, the deed would have been done two weeks ago.

But he had wanted their vows to be said in Brighton, the town she loved so much. Had insisted on it, in fact. He had filed a notice with the civil registrar, knowing it was faster than posting the banns, but even then they had to wait the required fifteen days. Invitations had been penned. A reception planned. His father and brother had come down from Scotland on a Friday train. It was all a bloody circus.

And now he was a married man. He wanted nothing more than to lay his new wife down on a bed of crisp, white linens and run his hands over her lithe body. But while Bedford linens were indeed high on his list of things to show her tonight, first he had a surprise.

He pulled her down a path he knew she would not recognize, heading east along the high edge of the chalk cliffs. From this dizzying height, the wind howled in his ears, and the promise of the ocean was but a distant memory below. The half-moon offered a sliver of light to guide them, not nearly as much as the last time he had ventured out at night, and he had to rely on the lantern in his hand for much of the way.

Though she seemed content to let him lead, she was not silent a single moment of the half-hour journey, suggesting her nervousness over the coming night might match his own anticipation.

"Did you like my gown?" Her voice floated up over his shoulder. "Madame Beauclerc spent an entire week sewing seed pearls onto the bodice."

David nodded, wondering if it would be ungentlemanly to admit he had scarcely noticed that she still wore her wedding dress. He still felt dazed by his good fortune, unable to wrap his head around the fact that not only had she married him, she *loved* him. It had been difficult to appreciate what was covering his new wife's body when all he could think of was discovering what she looked like beneath.

"It was kind of Lord Avery and his daughter to attend the wedding."

"Yes," he murmured, still distracted.

"He and Mama seem to be spending a great deal of time together. He's gotten her to go walking with him on the Marine Parade twice in the last week."

David nodded, thinking about another possible use for Caroline's busy mouth.

"And I was pleased to see that the Countess of Beecham came to the wedding, even if Mr. Duffington didn't. Mama was thrilled to have such a prominent guest."

"Mmhmm." He listened with only half an ear, though he was achingly aware of every syllable. He reveled in the husky sound of her voice, imagined the glow of her skin as he undressed her, one agonizing inch at a time.

Mine, the beast whined, scratching at its cage.

Soon, he reassured it.

David shone the lantern to the right, looking for the landmark he had come to know so well over the past two weeks. Caroline leaned over his shoulder, peering into the scrubby growth of trees that had caught his attention. The press of her body felt like the softest of caresses, and he leaned back into her a long, simmering moment. It was the most thorough contact he had permitted himself in sixteen excruciating days, and he savored it, committing each of her breaths to memory.

"Why did you stay away from me before the wedding?" Caroline whispered, breaking through his thoughts. Her voice rang faintly with hurt, and he smiled into the night to hear it. A husband liked to know that his wife wanted him.

It stood to reason that a wife would wish to know the same.

He set down the lantern and pulled her into his ready arms. "Didn't you know, lass?" He cupped her face in his hands. "I couldn't resist you. One touch, one kiss, and I knew I would be ruined."

"I had been hoping you might ruin *me*." She tilted her cheek into the palm of his hand and wet her lips in a gesture that shot straight to that most neglected part of his body.

"I wanted to wait for our wedding night." His new realization that he was, in fact, a man of some honor demanded a principled path. Waiting wasn't just something he had wanted to do.

It was something he had *needed* to do.

He brushed the pad of one thumb across the smooth texture of her cheek. He could not see her freckles in the meager light, but he knew where each one lay, and his lips longed to trace their path. But first there were things he needed to say.

"I didn't do that with Elizabeth, and I regretted it. I told myself there would be time to get it right later, a lifetime of exploration to make up for my fumbling lack of acuity." He swallowed, looking down on his beautiful wife who stared so trustingly back from his cupped palms. "I know now not to take such a thing for granted."

"I think I can understand that," she whispered. "As long as you promise to ruin me soon."

She lifted her mouth, seeking his, but he angled higher, brushing a kiss to her brow instead. At her sigh of frustration, he dropped his hands, fighting a smile. "Come," he told her, picking up the lantern and pulling her under the branch of a small tree that had a "No Trespass" sign nailed to its trunk. "I have something to show you first."

"What is it?" Concern tempered the sensual exasperation that still simmered in her voice. "We cannot go this way."

"Trust me." He tugged her deeper, starting down the steep path that angled away into blackness.

"But this is someone's land, and we cannot just—"

"Caroline," he said sternly. "If you would just hold your tongue and follow me, I promise that in two minutes' time I will offer it a more pleasurable use."

She fell silent at that. He led her down a good two hundred feet, the scent of the ocean and the sounds of the waves growing stronger as they descended. When they finally came to a fence with a chained gate, David pulled a box from his jacket pocket, his fingers surprisingly steady against the black velvet.

"I have been waiting two weeks to give you this wedding present. I trust you will agree it was worth the wait."

She looked down at the ribbon-wrapped box. Her mouth opened in a perfect O that had him thinking of very unladylike uses for it. Not that he wanted a lady tonight. No, David wanted the wild temptress she kept loosely bound inside her. He was determined to unlock her pleasure, and this gift was only part of his plan.

She untied the ribbon, and he held up the lantern so she could see what lay inside. "You have given me a key." She sounded perplexed.

"It opens the padlock." When she hesitated, he took it from her and removed the chain from the fence. "Go on," he urged.

She pushed a few feet in, and then her gasp echoed against the high cliff walls. "Why, it's the cove!" she said, a delighted hitch in her voice. "But . . . we didn't walk nearly far enough. And I never knew there was another entrance!"

David joined her, taking up her hand. "There wasn't. I made this one. Hacked the footholds out of the cliff wall. And surprisingly, the distance to the cove was never that far from Brighton. The old seaside route just took twice as long because of the irregular coastline."

"So this is what you've been doing the last two weeks?" She looked up at him, one dark brow raised high.

"Aye." He chuckled. "A man has to spend his frustration somewhere. It's yours, lass. The beach, the cliffs, the land above . . . all of it."

She stared at him, her ever-changing eyes dark pools in the light from the lantern. "How is that possible?"

"'Tis a wedding gift from my family." David grinned, recalling how excited he had been when he had discovered the land above the cliff was for sale. "My father arranged its purchase for us. I covered over the old seaside entrance and put up the new fence, so no one else can find their way here without this key."

He kissed the top of her head, breathing in the warm, vanilla scent of her. "You do not have to worry about others using it, not anymore. You can swim here, whenever you want, dressed however you like." Although if he had anything to say about it, naked would be the preferred state of dress tonight. "We can build a summer house overhead, once my investments begin to pay out."

She reared back, her eyes searching his. "But . . . I thought we had decided to live in Scotland." She was squeezing his hand so tight his fingers had started to tingle, along with other neglected parts of his body.

"Who is to say we cannot have two homes?" He chuckled. "Scotland in the spring, Brighton in the summer. Now come." He tugged on her hand. "There is more."

He drew her in further and her second gasp echoed in his ears. He held the lantern up high and could see his instructions had been followed to the letter. A bed had been prepared, there on the rock. A profusion of pillows lay at the ready with the Bedford Crest embroidered on the cases. A picnic basket sat nearby, a bottle of good Highland malt peeking from the rim.

He turned to her, and smiled. Everything was ready. *He* was ready.

He only hoped she was.

"Welcome to your wedding night, Mrs. Cameron."

SHE SHOULD HAVE told him thank you.

Somehow, he had known. Known who she was, and what she needed. He did not expect her to knit socks, or require her to be someone other than who she was. He had given her the most perfect gift imaginable, and a proper thank you was the least she should give him in return. But the sob that caught in her throat left her literally unable to form the words the moment required.

She flung herself against him, and he caught her up in arms so strong they made her knees buckle. He chuckled against her hair, seeming not to care that she was proving herself an unmannerly sort of wife. She lifted her lips to his, seeking the joining her heart had been missing for two long weeks.

But once again, he avoided her kiss.

Caroline wanted to gnash her teeth. What was the matter? They were married. They were alone, surrounded by nothing but moonlight and ocean. It was dark, for heaven's sake, so he could not see her too-long legs or her too-flat chest. It was *perfect.*

Unless . . . unless he thought she was too forward. That

sobered her a bit. After all, she was beginning to realize she was a woman who reveled in physical pleasure. His lessons had taught her that far more effectively than any book, and her curiosity over the last two weeks had fueled thoughts so wicked she was afraid to give voice to them, even in her head.

But that was who she *was*. Surely he understood that such a woman lurked inside her, every bit as much as the fearless swimmer.

"I have wanted to do something since I saw you standing in this very spot three weeks ago," David said. His voice was a rumble, and at the sound, Caroline felt as if the waves on shore were actually tumbling in her chest. His hands came up and curved around her head, fingers stretching through hair that Bess had spent an hour putting up, just this morning. Pins dislodged like flying artillery, raining down as his fingers tugged gently against her scalp. And then her hair was down, and he was busy searching for the last remaining pins, his fingers taunting her with their bold strokes.

Finally he stood back, admiring his handiwork. "Beautiful." He smiled at her, and she could see in that smile the rake he had once been. "You still are owed a lesson, I think. Turn around, Caroline. And face the cliffs."

Her lungs seized up, but her feet, thankfully, retained their function. She turned as her husband instructed and waited to see what he would do next.

Her inability to see him only heightened her want. His fingers brushed against her neck in a slow, tantalizing sweep, smoothing her hair to one side and making the fine hairs on her arms stand at attention. And then his lips replaced his fingers, there along her nape. Her skin crackled beneath the blazing touch of his tongue and she sagged against him, feeling the insistent press of his erection notch against her backside.

Relief caught her up in its arms. She might be forward, but clearly, he wanted the same thing she did.

The strong band of his arm snaked around to pin her waist. Cool air met the skin of her shoulders as he used his other hand to unbutton the row of buttons that marched down the back of her wedding dress. Seed pearls scattered beneath his fingers, but she could not bring herself to care as he slid it down off her shoulders.

She started to turn around, but the wall of his arm prevented her. "Stand," he warned, nipping her earlobe with his teeth.

She stood with her back pressed against him. Trembled as he unlaced her corset and sent it the way of the beautiful gown. Obeyed when he instructed her to kick out of her slippers.

But when he reached around and untied the ribbon that closed the front of her shift, she placed a hand over his.

"Can we not leave it on?" Thoughts of her body's inadequacy made her fingers tremble. Divested of the protection of her gown and corset, she could feel his hard length, seeking her core through the thin layer of cotton. Her shift posed no barrier to physical intimacy, as his earlier lessons had already taught her. But it did relieve her fears, a thin shield that guarded her vulnerability.

His chuckle slid down her spine and centered with remarkable alacrity on that place between her legs that had grown moist with want. "Oh no, love. This is the other thing I have wanted to do, ever since you tortured me in the bathing machine with that hideous robe. Modesty has no place in a marriage. And I will not be denied my rights."

Chapter 35

THE MINX THOUGHT she could spend their wedding night in her shift.

Clearly, there was more here to teach.

David pushed her protesting hand away. Grasped the tie that haunted his dreams.

Pulled it free. Her gasp told him he was heading in the right direction, even if she couldn't bring herself to admit it.

He slid her loosened shift off one shoulder, then the other, then knelt to slide the filmy piece of fabric the rest of the way down. He permitted his fingers the luxury of trailing her bare skin as he went. When he finally had her free of the thing, he placed his palm against her soft calf. "No stockings?" he whispered, swallowing in anticipation.

"I do not wear them in the summer."

Her voice teased down at him, reminding him that he held a very long length of leg in his hands. His lips begged for the privilege of charting its contours, and he gave in to the demand, delivering a series of tiny kisses upward until he reached the hollow behind her knee. "I believe summer may have to become my favorite season, lass."

Her body shook, whether from amusement or want was difficult to tease out. "I like it when you call me lass."

"I wonder if you'll still like it when you're seventy." He hoped so, because he was planning on calling her that for a good, long time.

He was concentrating on the taste of her thighs now, and he swirled his tongue ever closer to where his instincts demanded his mouth go. Her labored breathing was painting a very clear map, but he reminded himself that she was still innocent. One step at a time.

He was fast losing his hold on the tenuous restraint he had been gripping most of the evening. He rose and stripped off his clothing faster than he could have ever imagined. And then his arms were reaching around her again, this time to cup her breasts. He brushed his fingers over her nipples, thrilled by the shudder he could jerk out of her with little more than a touch. Her gasp of surprise told him he had made the right choice in keeping his lips to a more conventional purpose. If a mere touch from his hand sent her trembling like this, anything more would have been too much, too fast.

The feeling of her bare back pressed against his own heated skin had him groaning against the nape of her neck. He pressed another kiss against the impossibly soft skin there, and then slowly released her. As difficult as it was to hold himself back, there was one more thing he wanted to do.

He stepped around her. Turned. And stared.

The moment stuttered to a stop, and David knew he had a new vision of this woman, to be held in miniature and tucked away for special occasions. Her skin glowed white against the meager light of the half moon and lantern. Her hair tumbled like a dark curtain over her shoulders, a riot of curls and waves that he wanted to wrap around his hand. The ocean lay at her back, the half-moon reflected on the horizon. It occurred to him that she belonged here, uninhibited, untamed.

And moreover, that she belonged to him.

"I love you, Caroline. I shall never tire of looking at you, I fear, so you'd best get used to the idea of swimming without your shift."

Her lips curved up, an open invitation that made the picture she offered that much more poignant. "Are we to swim, then?"

He nodded, his chest squeezing tight against the thought of even a moment's additional delay. "Aye. Among other things I have planned for tonight. But not the first."

He lifted her up and hooked an arm beneath her bare legs, carrying her toward the bed that had been laid out on the rock. "I think," he said, his voice gone hoarse with the want that threatened to consume him, "that it is time to finish this lesson."

DAVID LAID HER down on a pile of linens so luxurious that in another time and another place, Caroline would have been tempted to roll over and bury her face in them. But he scarcely gave her time to contemplate the feel of it because in what seemed like an instant, he was kneeling between her legs and running his hands up and down the length of her nude body.

It was unbearably dark. He had left the lantern where they had been standing, and now she had only moonlight to see him by. But it proved enough, given that at the moment, her eyes wanted only to flutter closed. Her skin caught fire at his sure, deft touch, licking along her limbs to center with delicious promise in the juncture of her thighs.

Yes. This was what she had been wanting, this pleasure-pain that the sight of him promised, but couldn't quite deliver. She arched up against him, trusting him to show her what she needed, convinced that if he didn't hurry, she might expire on the spot.

And then he was lowering himself on top of her and taking her lips in a kiss that left her panting. His tongue danced against hers, teasing, withdrawing, coming back again. He kissed her a long, long time, seeming to take pleasure in her rising passion. But it wasn't enough. She wanted to throw off her skin and meld into him. She wanted a touch from this man so sure, so deep, it would bind them as one breath, one thought.

She moaned into his mouth. "More," she gasped.

And he obeyed. Notched his hips against hers. Slid inside her ready body an agonizing inch and . . . stopped. Caroline opened her eyes in frustration. The moonlight seemed brighter now that her eyes had adjusted to the dark. She could see his large body looming over her, a look of pained uncertainty on his face. Surely he wasn't going to stop now. She was lying beneath him, her legs wrapped around his waist.

If he stopped now, she was going to kill him.

"I want more." She was demanding now, not asking.

"And you shall have it," he told her through gritted teeth. "Just . . . kiss me, lass."

She pulled his head down, her mouth open and willing, and then, at the moment when their lips met, he pushed into her body, making a raw sound of need that quite covered up her squeak of surprise.

While the brief flash of pain was distracting, the aftermath of it was not . . . unpleasant. Far from it. She adjusted to meet him. To welcome him. She might be innocent, but her body seemed to know the movements as if they were imprinted on her soul. When he began to rock her gently, she responded with an instinctive arching of her hips.

"Better?" he asked, his words a breathless question.

"I still want more," she gasped against his lips.

He chuckled and moved faster, apparently satisfied that she wasn't going to break or run shrieking into the night. Caroline's soul strained upward, reaching for that spark he had previously shown her, realizing, in that moment, how powerful she was with him.

How perfect they were together.

Whatever momentary discomfort she had felt on their joining dissolved. She reveled in the building storm. She felt no hesitance this time, no resistance to launching herself toward those swirling emotions. She knew her final destination now, and she *trusted* him. With her heart, her body, her pleasure. He had learned her body well, and she could sense he guided her toward that place, as skillfully as a captain at the helm of his ship.

And then she was there, breaking over the crest of that wave, shattering like the water against the nearby rocks. She felt bounced against the stars, lobbed high against the stark black canvas of the night. Dimly, she realized David was right behind her. He gasped against her neck, straining into his own release.

Falling back to sanity took nearly as long as the falling apart. She became aware, in slow degrees, of the cool night air and the perspiration on their bodies. David shifted so his weight fell beside her, and then she drifted in the beauty of his arms, sated and happy. She experimentally stretched her toes, to see if they still worked. Her body felt disjointed, as if he had taken her apart piece by piece. She wondered if she would ever be set back to rights.

"How did you find the final lesson?" His voice reached out to her through the shadows, curling about her thoughts and sending a frisson of warmth through that place on her body where they had just been joined.

Caroline opened her eyes to see this man who was her match. A smile worked its way onto her face. "Surely that wasn't the *final* lesson." She knew there was more to discover, knew it as surely as she knew how to breathe. Her innate curiosity about things of a physical nature, her athleticism, those things that had always set her apart and marked her as an oddity bound for gossip and ostracism, had finally found a place where they belonged in this man.

"I suspect I may need more practice, if I am to acquit myself well in the future."

A low chuckle reached her ears. "We've the whole night, lass."

Caroline lifted herself on one elbow. She was this man's wife. The thought filled her with awe. They could do this whenever they wanted, and there was no doubt in her mind she wanted to do it again. She skimmed a questing finger down his chest, and repeated the motion when he shuddered beneath it. He had taken great care with her, of that she had no doubt. She felt a little sore, but nothing to the degree that she had expected.

She reached out a hand and touched the length of him through the darkness. He felt soft in her hands, a man well spent.

Caroline permitted herself to give voice to the wicked idea that had plagued her ever since he had stood in front of her, glorious in his own nakedness, even as he had stared down on hers. "Would you like me to put my mouth on you?"

A beat of silence followed her question, and then she heard his unsteady response. "Where did you learn about that?"

"Pen's book," she admitted, fitting her fingers around him in an experimental fashion.

"I thought it was a medical text."

"Well, it *might* be a medical text. About Far East practices. My father collected travel tomes. Some of them are rather . . . revealing."

Another long silence. "Well lass," he sighed, though it was a happy sound, "not that I do not find the idea pleasing, but the truth of the matter is that such a thing works better before the act. It shall take me a few minutes more to recover to the point of being ready."

"How many more minutes?" she asked, genuinely curious. She tightened her fingers, and his body, which had been so quiescent only moments before, stirred to life in her hand. "Because I confess, I want more. And it seems to as well."

He rolled her onto her back and reared up over her, a dark, tortured prince come to life. "Christ, you are a surprise, wife." He leaned down and caught her lips in a gentle kiss, but now that she knew where gentle kisses could lead, now that she knew she could force him to that place where he lost his mind and became as much animal as man, she did not mind his careful restraint. "More, is it?" he asked, his breathing already becoming ragged.

She nodded, quickening again in that place where her body arched up against his.

"Well, Mrs. Cameron. You are a woman in luck, because it just so happens there is *much* more. And given that you are such a quick study, I think I can manage another lesson."

Epilogue

CAROLINE KNEW SHE would never forget her first journey by coach—even though she desperately wanted to.

The leather-lined interior carried hints of the sweat and cigar smoke left by the previous occupants, who had thankfully disembarked in Ullapool. The wheels found every rut in the road, making her joints unhinge with frightening regularity. The cramped wooden cabin brought to mind a coffin, being pulled at the mercy of wild-eyed horses that might or might not stop when ordered.

All solid arguments to stay in Brighton.

Of course, as Caroline and David's primary home was to be in Scotland, at least for the foreseeable future, the torturous coach ride was proving unavoidable.

They had spent a memorable two months in Brighton, swimming every day, exploring the fashionable parts of the city. They'd visited the theater. Walked in the botanical gardens. Gone to the Brighthelmston Races and bet on a losing horse. She was now thoroughly introduced to the wonders of a marriage bed, and was blushingly aware of the more daring guidance in the book she had once studied for inspiration.

But with the arrival of October's gray skies and colder weather had come the inevitable. The baroness had returned to Scotland weeks ago, and Caroline knew David worried about his mother's health. In the end, Caroline had not just wanted to come to Moraig—she had insisted upon it. She only prayed that what awaited them in Scotland held the same degree of happiness they had left behind in Brighton.

However, judging by the dreary view out of her window of endless hills and towering pines, Scotland's change in scenery was proving a disappointment, at best.

"Just another few miles now, love. The view opens up over this next ridge."

David's voice near her right ear pulled her from her thoughts. Given the option of viewing her new husband's smile or another few miles of pine-topped forests, the choice was clear. She turned away from the window and tilted her face up to welcome a quick kiss. "I'll feel better once we've stopped."

He went a step further than the chaste brush of lips she thought he would offer, lifting her bodily onto his lap with her back to his chest as the coach began to lurch up yet another hill. "I've a mind to use the last half hour to put that worried frown to rest," he whispered in one ear. His words were stern, though his voice was wrapped in warmth. His fingers traced a wicked pattern between her shoulder blades. "What has you so tied up in knots, lass? Are you missing your family so very much?"

She leaned her back against him, enjoying the way the word "lass" lingered in her ears. "No." Mama and Penelope had seemed happy enough to see her off, and they were planning to visit Moraig in the spring. She reached up a hand to finger the starched edge of his necktie where it pressed against her hair. "You are my family now, and I am content as long as I am with you."

"Is it *my* family then, who has that worry line etched between your eyes? You know they love you too."

She laughed. "They scarcely know me, David. We spent little more than a week with them in August, after the wedding. Surely 'love' is a little too strong a sentiment to apply here." Although, she knew they liked her. Against all expectations—against all logic—they seemed to accept their son's eccentric choice of wife with open arms, a fact for which she was grateful.

"Well, they shall learn to love you as much as I do. Given that we shall be staying with them until we find a place you like well enough to purchase, I imagine you shall get to know each other very well."

Caroline fit her lips around a smile. "It's not that either." She focused her nervous fingers on a loose thread along the edge of his collar. "I've never spent any time away from the ocean," she admitted, embarrassed to admit it out loud. "In fact, I've never traveled farther than an occasional day trip to Lewes. I am worried I shall miss it."

This time, it was David's turn to laugh. "Why should *that* be what is bothering you?"

Irritation flared, and she wiggled around to face him. She grabbed on to the edges of his open jacket and tugged. "'Tis not funny, David." It had taken courage to admit her fear.

He merely smiled, his eyes crinkling in amusement. "I suppose I didn't explain very well, did I?"

"Explain what?" she said, more crossly now.

He peered out the window, craning his head. "I think it shall be evident all too soon. Ah . . . yes. There it is." He spread his hands. "Behold, mermaid. Your kingdom awaits."

Caroline peered distrustfully in the direction he indicated, and then her breath tangled in her throat. As they rounded the crest of the hill, the endless forest seemed to fall away in front of them. A sparkling azure vista rose up to take its place. Her stomach turned over, pushing her thoughts tumbling along with it. Everywhere she looked she saw water. Brilliant, sky-reflecting blue, framed by dark rock cliffs. And farther on, almost a whimsical notion on the horizon, a thin, dark line where the freshwater merged with the ocean.

"Loch Moraig." David grinned at her. "And farther on, the Atlantic. The very same waters that touch Brighton, albeit much, much colder. You shall not miss the ocean, Caroline. I promise."

She blinked, scarcely able to believe what a ninny she had been. She hadn't even thought to ask. Then again, this man near robbed the very logic from her brain.

Using the edges of his coat still gripped in her hands, she pulled him toward her and buried her nose in the fabric of his shirt. She breathed in once, twice. "Will anyone think it odd if I swim in that lovely loch?" she murmured against the solid rock of his chest.

His big body shook with suppressed laughter. "Only when it snows, love. Only when it snows."

And then he was tilting her chin up with a gentle finger. The last thing she saw before her lashes fluttered shut was the brilliant blue of her husband's eyes, searching her own. She welcomed his kiss with a grateful sigh. His lips coaxed her own apart, and then he was breaching her fears and worries with a calm assurance that sent her squirming on his lap.

After that, it was but the work of a moment to shatter her preconceived notions regarding coach rides. Caroline quickly discovered that for consenting adults, the tight four walls and roll-down shades offered some hidden pleasures. The heady sandalwood scent to be found around the edge of David's collar banished the malodorous cabin to a state of nonexistence. And the rocking of the springs beneath the carriage floor and occasional ruts in the road made sitting on her new husband's lap interesting, to say the least.

With his busy fingers, he kept her so distracted she scarcely had time to dwell on the rest of the ride. In fact, she would not have minded if the coach traveled on forever, heading for that thin blue line where freshwater met the ocean. It was true she did not know what the future might bring, or what manner of pleasures awaited her in Scotland.

But with this man beside her, and the promise of summers spent in her beloved Brighton, she discovered she was very much looking forward to journey.

Want more? Keep reading for
a sneak peek at the next fabulous romance
from Jennifer McQuiston,
MOONLIGHT ON MY MIND

THOUGH IT WAS a thought she should have entertained far earlier, Julianne Baxter wondered if she ought to become a brunette before she became an accessory to murder.

It had been a hellish trip, first by train from London to Glasgow, then by four-horse coach with stops in Perth and Inverness. Now she was rattling into the little town of Moraig via a poorly sprung two-horse mail coach that was far better suited for hauling parcels than passengers. As the scenery outside her coach window shifted from pine forests to blurry, shop-lined streets, her mind twisted in this new—if belated—direction. Three long days spent hiding beneath the brim of a hat designed for fashion over comfort was enough to make even the kindest of souls cautious, if not cross.

And Julianne was admittedly not the kindest of souls.

Or, regrettably, the cleanest. The pretty green silk of her traveling gown was now a dull grey from the journey's accumulated dirt, much of it from the interior of this squalid little coach and the unhygienic Highlanders who used it for transport. She yearned for a hip bath full of steaming water, and a maid to brush her hair until she collapsed in a stupor on her feather mattress. But her comb was packed in her travelling bag, and that was loaded on the top of the coach. Her ladies' maid and her feather bed were in London, where *she* was supposed to be. And while she was indeed bordering on a stupor from lack of sleep, she doubted a proper bath was something she would see this side of the next sunrise.

Julianne eyed the coach's only other occupant, a portly man of middling years who had thankfully spent most of the five hour trip from Inverness sleeping. When he gave a reassuring snore, she plucked at the ribbons holding her bonnet in place and pulled it from her head, intending to let her scalp breathe.

According to her well-placed inquiries in Inverness, Moraig was a small fishing village of perhaps two thousand people. She hoped the town's negligible size would mean her business here would take no more than a few hours, but at the moment, the thought of even five more seconds spent in the chokehold of her bonnet was too much.

She enjoyed two heavenly minutes of freedom before the man sitting across from her sputtered awake. He blinked a slow moment, his eyes settling on her like an arrow centering home. And then he grinned, revealing teeth stained yellow by age and things best left unconsidered.

"Well, there's a pretty sight," he leered with a sleep-filled voice, filling the narrow space inside the coach with breath that suggested one or more of those teeth might be in need of professional care. "I dinna often see hair that bright, bonny color. Are you traveling alone, lass? I'd be happy to show you around Moraig, personal-like."

Julianne narrowly withheld the curt reply hammering against her lips, choosing instead to let silence speak for her. She was on a clandestine mission, after all. She was seeking one of England's most wanted fugitives, though she had little more than snatched bits of rumor to guide her. She was risking a great deal by coming here and following this lead without first contacting the authorities, but the shocking circumstances of the past week demanded it.

Still, she did not relish the thought of discovery, or the potential damage to her reputation should word get out. No sense giving this stranger a voice by which to recognize her, on top of the copper-colored curls from which he seemed unable to detach his eyes.

When the passenger continued to ogle her, she determinedly settled the hated bit of straw and silk back on her head, this time leaving the ribbons untied. Deprived of his entertainment, the man finally looked away and turned his attention to a newspaper he pulled from a coat pocket, but the implications of his bald interest were not so easily defused. She hadn't given her hair much thought upon setting off on this journey—although, to be fair, she hadn't given *any* part of this journey a proper degree of forethought. She couldn't jolly well depend on a bonnet to keep her safe from recognition for the length of this trip.

But she didn't have to *have* red hair.

Indeed, for the purposes of this mission, it might be better if she didn't. That the man she sought—truly, the man half of England sought—was rumored to have disappeared into the farthest reaches of Scotland suggested he didn't want to be found. If he was warily watching over his shoulder, determined to avoid the gallows, the sight of her familiar red hair—the hair he had once declared robbed him of all decent thought—would give him a running head start toward escape.

Which meant her first stop in Moraig really ought to be a chemist's shop.

As the idea firmed up in her mind, Julianne cleared her throat. Her traveling companion looked up from his rumpled newspaper. "Excuse me," she said, remembering almost too late she was trying to avoid recognition. She readjusted her voice to a lower pitch and leaned in conspiratorially. "Perhaps I could use your help after all—"

A piercing blast from the outside horn cut her words short.

A sickening thud soon followed.

The coach lurched sideways, tilting Julianne along with it. Her head knocked against the latch to the door, making her teeth ache with the force of the blow. The vehicle hung in awkward indecision a long, slow moment, and then swung back to center before rolling several more feet to a stop. For a moment there was only the sound of her panicked breathing, but then a quick rap at the window sent both occupants jumping.

"Is everyone all right?" The voice of the coachman pushed through the thin glass.

"Yes, I think so." The gentleman folded his newspaper, as if this sort of thing happened all the time. "Struck another one, have we, Mr. Jeffers?"

Julianne rubbed her throbbing head, realizing with dismay that her untied bonnet was now lying in a disgraceful heap on the filthy coach floor. Her eyes reached for it, but her fingers refused to follow. She could not imagine placing it back on her head. It bothered her to even set her boots upon those sticky floorboards.

The coachman opened the door and peered in, his eyes owlish in concern. "Are you injured, lass?"

She drew a breath, unsure of her response. Her head ached liked the very devil and her stomach felt tossed by gale force winds, but she could feel no pain in her limbs suggesting an injury of grave magnitude. The dust-covered coachman leaned further in and his eyes fell on her hair, which, judging by the disruptive curls that swung wildly across her field of vision, had lost several hairpins in addition to the bonnet. Predictably, the driver's lips tipped up in empty fascination.

Suddenly, she was *not* all right. The strain of the three-day journey, her fear of being recognized, and the past few pulse-churning seconds coalesced into a spiraling panic.

Dear lord . . . no one knew where she was. If she had died here today, her head dashed against the Scottish dirt, her body crushed beneath the wheels of this fetid little coach, her father would have . . . well . . . her father would have *killed* her.

Her stomach clawed for a foothold up her throat. She shoved past the driver, not even caring that she was abandoning all decorum along with her bonnet. She tumbled out into late afternoon sunshine, dodging the boxes that had come loose from the top of the coach. She swayed a moment, breathing in the fresher air, willing her roiling stomach to settle. All around her, the town moved in an indistinct smear of browns and blues and green, storefronts and awnings and people swirling in the maelstrom of the moment.

She almost missed it. In the end, it was the *lack* of movement that pulled her attention back for a second look. She squinted at the image, trying to make it out. A small, still form lay in the street, perhaps twenty feet away. Her imagination filled in the gaps left by her regrettably poor eyesight, and her lungs promptly funneled shut.

They had struck someone.

She clapped a hand to her mouth, willing the cold beef pie she'd eaten at the last posting house to stay put. A few feet to her right, she could make out the hands of strangers already helping to heft the scattered boxes and trunks back onto the coach. She caught snatches of conversation on street corners, and the sound of clattering dishes and laughter trickling out of the open door of a nearby public house. No one seemed to care the afternoon coach had just mowed down one of their citizens, or that the body lay broken and unclaimed in the street.

The coachman approached. "If you dinna injure anything, I'll ask you to step back aboard, lass. We're running late."

Julianne lowered her shaking hand and glared at the

man, who, despite his kindly face and high, perspiring forehead was showing a frightful lack of regard for whomever he had just struck. "I am not getting back on that coach," she enunciated, "until someone calls the doctor."

"Help will be here soon enough." The man lowered his voice to a more soothing tone, the sort she often heard used on frightened horses and recalcitrant toddlers. "No sense getting overwrought."

He thought she was overwrought? Perhaps she was. *Someone* ought to be. The apathy of the coachman—and indeed, of Moraig's citizens, who seemed to just be going about the business of their day—made her want to strike someone.

As if sensing the threat of imminent violence, the driver twisted his hands in supplication. "'Tis a sad sight, I know, especially for a lady like yourself. But it's common enough round Moraig. Why don't you take yourself back inside the coach? We'll only be a moment to get the last of these boxes back up."

Julianne blinked away an angry haze of tears, and gestured fiercely toward the blurry form lying so still on the street. "A body's been struck down beneath your wheels," she hissed, "and you are worried only about the state of the *luggage*?"

The coachman drew back, his broad brow wrinkled. "Can't do anything for it myself."

Her thoughts flew around the driver's words. *It.* So uncaring as to not even assign the poor victim a gender. The panic she had held at bay surged forward, toppling the thin dam of reason she had hastily erected in the aftermath of the accident.

Dear God in heaven . . . it was her coach. Her hurry. *Her fault.*

Hadn't she asked the driver to cut short their time at the last posting house, going so far as to press a sovereign into the man's palm?

This could not be happening. She had come to Moraig find a murderer, not to turn into one herself.

"Might as well take the coach on to the posting house, Mr. Jeffers." A new voice, startling in its familiarity, rubbed close to Julianne's ear. Her hand, which had come up earlier to catch the threatened return of her breakfast, now stifled her gasp of surprise.

She whirled around. She couldn't breathe, could only stare up, and then up some more. An awful sense of sureness settled over her, a sense that someone, somewhere, was having a hearty laugh at her expense. In fact, they probably had a stitch in their side.

Because Julianne had discovered Patrick Channing— the accused killer she had traveled three days to find— within minutes, not hours.

And it was a little too late to find a chemist's shop.

"No sense waiting when your pay is docked for every quarter hour's delay," Channing continued to the coachman, as if they were old friends who might occasionally share a pint.

"Very good, sir." The coachman's voice echoed his relief. "I've a letter for you as well. Would you like to take it now?"

"No, I'll retrieve it later. After I see to the dog."

Dog? The word bounced about in Julianne's skull for three long seconds before settling into something coherent. She eyed the still form lying in the street again, and this time caught the flash of blood—hard, red, and unforgiving.

The body was not human then. Embarrassment washed over her, though it was tempered by sadness. That the coach had injured an animal was still hurtful, even if it explained the town's disinterested reaction and the coachman's rapidly retreating figure a bit better.

Behind her she could hear the crack of the driver's reins and the creak of the wheels, but she scarcely registered the fact that her bonnet and bag were rolling away with the coach. Instead, she suffered an almost painful awareness of the man towering over her.

He didn't much resemble the charming rogue she had once waltzed with at a Yorkshire house party. He looked . . . common, she supposed. And thin. She could see the angular edge of his jaw, the wisp of stubble marring the surface of his gaunt cheeks. He was as tall as ever—some things, a body couldn't hide. But his coat hung loosely from his frame, and his sandy hair, once so neatly trimmed as to nearly be flush against his scalp, brushed the lower edge of his neck. Did they lack barbers in Moraig?

Or was this part of his disguise, a diabolically clever way of hiding in plain sight?

Channing was studying her, too, but the inspection felt clinical, imparting none of the wolfish appreciation offered by either her earlier traveling companion or the driver. He wore the same dispassionate look he had given her across his father's study that cold November day, when she had tearfully related all she had seen—and some she had not—to the local Summersby magistrate.

When he spoke, it was with a flat baritone that made Julianne blink in surprise. "Are you injured in some manner I cannot see beyond the state of your coiffure, miss?"

She shook her head, even as her hand flew instinctively to tuck an unruly curl behind one ear. "I . . . no . . . I mean, I struck my head. On the coach door."

He leaned in for a closer look. "There is no visible blood." He peered at her as if she was a specimen for dissection, rather than the woman who had once accused him of murder.

Julianne fought a building impatience. How could he be so . . . *impersonal*? Day or night, this man had occupied a central place in her thoughts for eleven long months. She wanted to scream at him. Shake him to awareness. Make him look at her as more than just a patient.

Instead, she asked, "Do you not remember me at all?"

His eyes continued their impersonal march across her various and sundry parts before settling back on her face. "Of course," he said, his voice not changing inflection in the slightest. "You always did have a flair for a dramatic entrance, Miss Baxter."

Julianne's heart skidded sideways in her chest. However impassive the acknowledgement, he knew who she was. And yet, he hadn't bolted.

She wasn't quite sure what to make of it.

Apparently satisfied she wasn't on the verge of pitching over in the street, Channing turned and made his way toward the injured animal. She watched as he shrugged—quite *un*-diabolically—out of his coat, one blurry shoulder after the other.

"He's unconscious but breathing," Channing called out. "But he's lost a good deal of blood. The leg will probably need to come off."

She watched as he placed his coat over the still body and then he was returning to proper focus with the animal cradled in his arms. "I'll need to take him to my clinic and see what can be done in surgery." The clinical intensity with which he had earlier regarded her dropped away, and for the first time his eyes flashed in challenge. "You might as well come along with me, Miss Baxter. That is, if you trust me."

"I . . ." She hesitated, feeling the stares of a few curious Moraig residents on her, even though she couldn't precisely see them. All she could see at this moment was this man towering over her, his arms full of beast and coat, a smear of blood wrapped around one wrist.

There had been blood on him the last time she had seen him, too. A copious amount of it, vivid scarlet turned to rust. She remembered it now, how he had stood in his father's study as if hewn from granite, covered in his brother's blood.

That, more than anything else, cemented her decision, sane or not.

"I will come with you." She lifted her skirts, not even caring that she was probably exposing a good bit of ankle to those gawking Moraig townspeople. Perhaps, if she were lucky, that bit of stocking might distract them from her hair, and discourage any speculation regarding why she was conversing—without a proper chaperone—with a man charged with murder.

"It's a half mile walk." Channing's gaze roved downward and settled on the exposed heel of one of her boots. "Try not to twist something en route, Miss Baxter. Because I assure you, I'd rather carry the dog."

JULIANNE. BLOODY. BAXTER.

She was here. In Moraig. About as far as a body could go in Britain and not plunge into the Atlantic. Which was really where he'd like to toss her, those tottering heels and fetching red curls be damned.

As they walked, Patrick fumed. He had spent the last eleven months in this small, sleepy town, cloaked in anonymity and immersed in hard work. Not hiding, exactly—after all, he had not taken an assumed name, or booked transport to America, or done any of the predictable things a hunted man might be tempted to do. But neither had he offered an explanation for his sudden appearance to anyone nor confessed his circumstances, even to his closest friends.

He refused to wonder, at least in the near term, how this woman had learned where he was, and why she was here now—unchaperoned, by the looks of things. And he further refused to wonder why the sight of her pert nose and probing green eyes—both of which she famously used to pry into others' business—simultaneously felt like a punch to his solar plexus and a breath of crisp autumn air.

Patrick knew there were those in England who still

bayed like hounds on the trail of a fox, demanding his blood and their own idea of justice. He assumed Miss Baxter was one of them given the nature of their last meeting. His father's last letter had suggested opinion was slowly but surely shifting in his favor, and that when he returned he was likely to see a reduced charge of manslaughter instead of murder. But the last correspondence he had received from his father had been a month or more ago, and unless today's letter carried some vital new information, it was not yet safe for Patrick to return.

And now he had just been discovered by the one woman who wouldn't know how to keep a secret were her tongue cut out.

Strangely enough, though he was certainly irritated, he did not feel panicked. There was some relief in having the decision so firmly taken out of his hands. He was tired of skirting the demands of his moral compass, no matter that doing so had made logical sense once upon a time. He missed his family, and the fresh, rolling hills of Yorkshire. The leaves had probably started to turn, his favorite time of year to spend in the country. He missed the stables where he spent most of his time.

Missed his brother, although there was no help for that.

Miss Baxter's discovery of his whereabouts was unfortunate, but it was not going to send the noose over his neck in the next five minutes. He had time enough to concentrate on saving the life of the mail coach's latest victim.

He'd sort out what to do about *her* later.

With the unconscious dog still in his arms, Patrick kicked open the door to his derelict house-turned-clinic. He hadn't needed to kick the door, of course. The latch didn't catch properly, just one of a hundred things that needed fixing about the tumbledown place where he laid his head and stitched up the odd farm animal. He could bump it open with his hip, and frequently did when his arms were full. But the extreme physical reaction and the satisfying thud of his boot against the wood improved his mood.

Better still, it made the woman trailing beside him jump like a bird flushed from the heather, and *that* made him glad, for no other reason than it gave him a brief upper hand in this situation bound for nowhere good.

As he stepped inside the clinic, a ball of yellow fur came hurtling down the steps and wrapped itself around Patrick's legs. Excited barking filled the air.

"Down, Gemmy." He skirted the exuberant and slightly off-balance antics of his pet, the very first animal he had treated upon arriving in Moraig. "Sit," he told the dog.

Gemmy stood.

His tail beat a furious rhythm in the air, and his pink tongue lolled happily. Miss Baxter removed her gloves, then crouched to rub the terrier's ears. "Who is this ill-behaved beast?"

"The mail coach's first victim," Patrick said dryly.

The dog's eyes all but closed on a satisfied groan as Miss Baxter's bare fingers worked some kind of female magic on him. Patrick stared in perplexed irritation. Gemmy had always struck him as a loyal dog, a *man's* dog. He liked to scratch himself exuberantly with his one remaining hind leg, and lick the area where his bollocks had been. He generally stayed on Patrick's heel unless there was a chicken or rabbit in close proximity.

But now this "man's" dog flung himself down worshipfully and presented the decidedly unmannish Miss Baxter with three limbs aloft and a belly to rub, which she proceeded to do with a familiarity that surprised him.

Though she bordered on slatternly this moment, with her hair falling down and her dress wrinkled beyond repair, Miss Baxter had always seemed a fussy sort of person to Patrick's eye, one more concerned about the cut of her clothes and the curl of her hair than any reasonable person ought to be. To see her remove her gloves to pet not just a dog, but a three-legged mongrel, struck him as slightly absurd.

"How many mail coach victims have there been?" she asked, her voice tight.

"Four since the New Year. Mr. Jeffers is always running late, and the townspeople refuse to put their dogs on a lead. 'Tis bound to result in the odd collision."

"I see you make a hobby out of lopping off their limbs."

The reminder sent Patrick cursing under his breath. He had almost forgotten the bundle he carried, so disarming was the sight of Miss Baxter—well, any woman, really—crouching in the foyer of his bachelor's quarters. But he *wanted* to save this dog, the same way he had saved Gemmy. His conscience had never let him leave an animal to fate, even when it seemed fate had it out for them both. And that meant he needed to move fast now.

He strode down the narrow hallway that led to the kitchen. A plaintive bleating came from the part of the house that had once served as the front parlor, but though it was almost time for the orphaned lamb's bottle, he ignored it for the moment. He settled the newest patient down on the kitchen table and carefully unwrapped his coat from the injured dog's body. Another jacket, ruined. This business was sending him to the poorhouse, sure enough.

Miss Baxter's outrageously tall heels clicked on the weathered floor boards behind him. "Do you live here all alone?"

He heard her sniff at his silence. Knew what her nose was processing, even if she didn't. *Eau du sheep*, musty corners, and weeks of muddy boots had left an indelible scent in the old house. *There was a bit of sweet hay mixed in there*, he thought defensively. Not that Miss Julianne Baxter would appreciate a thing like hay.

"Honestly, you are the son of an earl. You could afford a domestic servant or two."

Patrick didn't answer. No sense telling her he refused

to accept a single sovereign from his father while he languished in this self-imposed exile. No doubt Miss Baxter had never turned down a farthing in her sweet, pampered life.

He forced his gaze to remain on the mess of the dog's leg instead of pulling to her, as it wanted to. He still couldn't believe she had followed him to his clinic, tripping along beside him through the streets of Moraig and entering his *house,* for Christ's sake. It was a foolish risk for a woman to take, particularly after the terrible crime she herself had accused him of.

But he couldn't very well leave her standing in the street. Miss Baxter was many things—exasperating, conniving, lying—but restrained was not one of them. It would have taken all of thirty seconds for her to start poking about the afternoon crowd at the Blue Gander public house, asking questions, spilling secrets. No one in Moraig knew of these most recent circumstances of his past, not even his best friends.

And until he knew what his future might hold, he preferred to keep it that way.

A lid clanged loudly somewhere behind him, and irritation yanked at the edges of his temper. "Do you even cook in here at all?" she mused. "These pans appear unused."

Christ, would she not shut up?

"The kettle works," he growled in response. In fact, he kept it heated and at the ready, but his answer seemed to do little to deflect her prying. Patrick could hear her continue to poke around behind him, lifting things, setting them down. He swallowed his frustration over the feminine invasion and kept his eyes trained toward his newest patient.

The dog he had carried from Main Street was still unconscious, which concerned him. He'd given it a fairly thorough examination in the street, and while there was no obvious damage he could see other than the mangled limb, the animal's sluggish return to wakefulness suggested it might have sustained an injury to its head in addition to its leg. However, the continued state of unconsciousness also presented Patrick with an opportunity. If he moved quickly, he might be able to take off the crushed leg without the animal waking.

But quickly was a bit of a stretch, given that he had no assistant to help him.

He gave into the urge to look dubiously at Miss Baxter, who had moved on to the side counter and was running an elegant finger over his clean, washed tools. No, she would be no help. Quite the opposite. James MacKenzie, his friend and former roommate, had once helped Patrick with these more challenging procedures, but the man was probably sitting down to supper in his new house across town, wallowing in what appeared to be a healthy dose of marital bliss.

There was no one here but the infinitely nosey Miss Baxter.

"I thought you were taking the dog to surgery." She held up a long-handled implement with a vice clamp on the end. She raised it for a closer examination, squinting at it like a seventy-year-old woman who had lost her quizzing glass. She turned it left and then right, her lips pursed in study. "This is your kitchen," she continued. "Surely you don't see patients in *here*."

Patrick considered telling her he used the thing to castrate calves. Decided better of it.

After all, she might decide to use it on him.

Instead, he reached for the surgical instruments he kept in the nearby cupboard, right next to his meager tin of tea leaves and the shaker of salt. "One table's as good as another. I am not a particular man."

"Clearly." She laid the emasculator down on the far end of the table and came closer. Her eyes widened as she saw what was in his hand. "What is *that* for?"

Patrick set down a wickedly sharp knife on the table and enjoyed the quick blanching of Miss Baxter's already milky white skin. "Not for eating." The instruments of his trade tended to be crude and oversized, given that he used them on both cows and kittens alike. Next came the bone saw, a monstrous, well-oiled thing with teeth the size of a man's fingernail. He heard Miss Baxter's harsh indrawn breath as he placed it, too, beside the unconscious dog.

For the first time since he laid eyes on her, he was tempted to smile. She believed him a killer, after all. He might even be—he wasn't completely sure of himself, or the tragic events that had destroyed his family and re-shaped his future into a frail, furtive thing.

And that meant the next few minutes should prove entertaining, if nothing else.

*Next month, don't miss these exciting
new love stories only from
Avon Books*

When the Marquess Met His Match by Laura Lee Guhrke
Matchmaker Lady Belinda Featherstone's job is to guide
American heiresses to matrimony, and away from rogues
like Nicholas, Marquess of Trubridge. But the frustratingly
charming man needs a wealthy bride, and he hires Belinda
to help. Yet one taste of her lips leads his scheme awry and
his heart to Belinda.

Sins of a Wicked Princess by Anna Randol
Ian Maddox, aka The Wraith, is happy to leave his life as a
spy—as soon as he discovers who's been trying to kill his
friends. All clues lead him to the bedroom of an exiled
princess. Yet Princess Juliana isn't the simpering royal he
expects, and this irresistible beauty agrees to give him the
information he seeks . . . for a price.

The Wicked Wallflower by Maya Rodale
Lady Emma Avery has made a terrible mistake announcing
her faux engagement. But when the Duke of Ashbrooke
plays along, Emma realizes this alluring rogue is far more
tempting than she thought. Now, with a temporary
betrothal and a much more permanent attraction between
them, nothing will suffice but to prove there's nothing so
satisfying as two perfect strangers . . . being perfectly
scandalous together.

REL 1013

Visit www.AuthorTracker.com for exclusive
information on your favorite HarperCollins authors.

Available wherever books are sold or please call 1-800-331-3761 to order.

More romance from
USA Today bestselling author

Eloisa James

The Duke Is Mine
978-0-06-202128-1
Olivia Lytton's fate and desire will hinge upon a man and
a mattress in this all-new tale of "The Princess and the Pea."

When Beauty Tamed the Beast
978-0-06-202127-4
Stern and gruff, powerful and breathtaking,
the Earl of Marchant is well worth taming . . .

A Kiss at Midnight
978-0-06-162684-5
Kate has no interest in marriage or princes
or fairy tales . . . but she never dreamed
there would be magic in one kiss.

A Duke of Her Own
978-0-06-162683-8
Should a noble rogue choose an acceptable bride . . .
or pursue true love to possible ruin?

Visit www.AuthorTracker.com for exclusive
information on your favorite HarperCollins authors.

Available wherever books are sold or please call 1-800-331-3761 to order.

EJ1 0512

#1 *NEW YORK TIMES*
AND *USA TODAY* BESTSELLER

JULIA QUINN

TEN THINGS I LOVE ABOUT YOU

978-0-06-149189-4

If the elderly Earl of Newbury dies without an heir, his detested nephew Sebastian inherits everything. Newbury decides that Annabel Winslow is the answer to his problems. But the thought of marrying the earl makes Annabel's skin crawl, even though the union would save her family from ruin. Perhaps the earl's machinations will leave him out in the cold and spur a love match instead?

JUST LIKE HEAVEN

978-0-06-149190-0

Marcus Holroyd has promised his best friend, David Smythe-Smith, that he'll look out for David's sister, Honoria. Not an easy task when Honoria sets off for Cambridge determined to marry by the end of the season. When her advances are spurned can Marcus swoop in and steal her heart?

A NIGHT LIKE THIS

978-0-06-207290-0

Daniel Smythe-Smith vows to pursue the mysterious young governess Anne Wynter, even if that means spending his days with a ten-year-old who thinks she's a unicorn. And after years of dodging unwanted advances, the oh-so-dashing Earl of Winstead is the first man to truly tempt Anne.

Visit www.AuthorTracker.com for exclusive information on your favorite HarperCollins authors.

JQ3 0113

Available wherever books are sold or please call 1-800-331-3761 to order.

Don't miss these passionate novels by
#1 *New York Times* bestselling author

STEPHANIE LAURENS

Viscount Breckenridge to the Rescue

978-0-06-206860-6

Determined to hunt down her very own hero, Heather
Cynster steps out of her safe world and boldly attends
a racy soiree. But her promising hunt is ruined by the
supremely interfering Viscount Breckenridge, who
whisks her out of scandal—and into danger.

In Pursuit of Eliza Cynster

978-0-06-206861-3

Brazenly kidnapped from her sister's engagement ball,
Eliza Cynster is spirited north to Edinburgh. Determined
to escape, she seizes upon the first unlikely champion
who happens along—Jeremy Carling, who will not
abandon a damsel in distress.

The Capture of the Earl of Glencrae

978-0-06-206862-0

Angelica Cynster is certain she'll recognize her fated
husband at first sight. And when her eyes meet those of the
Earl of Glencrae across a candlelit ballroom, she knows
that he's the one. But her heart is soon pounding for an
entirely different reason—when her hero abducts her!

Visit www.AuthorTracker.com for exclusive
information on your favorite HarperCollins authors.
Available wherever books are sold or please call 1-800-331-3761 to order.

LAU5 1012

At Avon Books, we know your passion for romance—once you finish one of our novels, you find yourself wanting more.

May we tempt you with . . .

- **Excerpts** from our upcoming releases.

- Entertaining **extras**, including authors' personal photo albums and book lists.

- Behind-the-scenes **scoop** on your favorite characters and series.

- **Sweepstakes** for the chance to win free books, romantic getaways, and other fun prizes.

- Writing **tips** from our authors and editors.

- **Blog** with our authors and find out why they love to write romance.

- **Exclusive content** that's not contained within the pages of our novels.

Join us at
www.avonbooks.com

AVON
An Imprint of HarperCollins*Publishers*
www.avonromance.com

Available wherever books are sold or please call 1-800-331-3761 to order.

FTH 1111

*G*ive in to your Impulses!

These unforgettable stories only take a second to buy and give you hours of reading pleasure!

Go to *www.AvonImpulse.com* and see what we have to offer.

Available wherever e-books are sold.

AVONIMPULSE

IMP 0811